# BAD BLOOD

C R DEMPSEY

CRMPD MEDIA LIMITED

# CONTENTS

For Mena and Maya

# CHAPTER ONE

# ENCROACHMENT

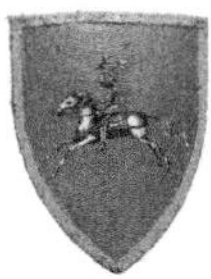

Corradovar village lay before the strangers, neatly tucked into a gap between the luscious forests and the lake whose waves gently lapped upon the shore. The villagers had laid out fields of barley at every available opening as a protective barrier against starvation. Cows roamed freely and grazed on the delicious grass with a profusion of young calves to support the healthy herd. Pigs poked around the periphery of the village and searched the nooks and crannies of the palisade and the gnarled and knotted roots of the trees on the shore of the lake for any morsels of food they could find. The village had thrived under several years of peace. However, the scars of raiding scratched the surface of the prosperous facade, as testified further up the lake shore by the blackened soil of burnt crops. The lead stranger smiled. He had his leverage.

Out in the fields a boy called Eunan Maguire was roaming with his Irish wolfhound, Artair. A striking lad of muscular build, Eunan energetically threw a stick for his dog and when Artair returned it he showed how well he had been named by the boy's father, for he was like a bear compared to the thirteen-year-old. The dog's grey coat appeared matted, for he loved nothing more than swimming in the multitude of lakes around the village or lying in the mud outside Eunan's house along the shore. Eunan could never work out his dog's obsession with mud, and when he indulged Artair with a mud bath, his father would reward him with a good clip around the ear. But Eunan was fast gaining on Artair's athleticism as he chased his dog through the fields and low hills at the perimeter of his village.

Now Artair froze, forgetting about his stick, and through his exposed teeth came a blood-curdling growl. Eunan ducked behind his dog. Between the tufts of fur on Artair's back as the dog's spine shook to his guttural growl, Eunan saw the cart and the two strangers who had come from the direction of the Pale stand up on the driver's seat and observe his village. He stooped behind a tree to spy on them and saw the sun glint off something metallic hanging from one man's belt. Eunan took to his heels and ran all the way back to the village screaming, "The English are coming! The English are coming!" at the top of his voice.

He ran through the centre of the village to his father, who was warming himself by a fire at the lakeside beside his house. His father was making jokes with men from the village who sat with him before they had their evening dip in the lake to clean off the dust and mud from working in the fields all day. The boy stopped and stood in silence as his dog bounded onwards, for his father looked jovial and at peace. He was here to ruin his father's day again. But his father could not miss the flash of his son's red hair or his giant dog bounding through the village, even if he could ignore him screaming his head off.

"What do you want, boy? Save us from your infernal racket!"

"Father, father! Strangers are here! Englishmen with a cart full of grain! I think they are armed."

His father scowled and repaid the boy's diligence with a clip round the ear.

"Go see where they are and be quick about it, boy!" he replied. "I suggest the rest of you come with me and see these visitors off!"

The two men and their cart entered the outskirts of the village and smirked at the fear their appearance brought out on the faces of the locals. After clearing a path for the strangers, the villagers gave directions to the shoreline and the chieftain's house. The men of the village came out from behind the stone and thatch buildings and surrounded the cart. They signalled for the men to get down. They escorted the Englishmen into Eunan's father's presence and stayed in case they had invited in assassins. The strangers bowed.

"My name is Peter Squire, originally of Leicester," said the larger of the two men, "and this is my friend, John Brodie of Liverpool, but we now live pleasantly in the Pale. We bring you greetings from Queen Elizabeth and her Lord Deputy in Dublin and a cart full of goods and grains from Dublin port." He was paunchy, a little weather-beaten, with a tan from sitting exposed on his cart in the summer sun. Eunan's father stood forward.

"I am Cathal O'Keenan Maguire," he said, his face as friendly as granite. "I am the chieftain of this village and the surrounding countryside. Sit, eat, and drink, but you'll find no business here. It is harvest time, and I am expecting the men from the Maguire to collect their dues any day now. If they catch you here, it'll mean your death. Your deaths will mean my lands full of Galloglass until I can fill the Maguire's pockets with enough reassurance of coin that I am loyal. If that fails, I'll have to send him the first male born of the finest men in the village to persuade him of my loyalty. As time is short, excuse my bluntness, but why are you here, and what have you got to offer me?"

"The protection of the Crown and an army far more powerful than all the Gaelic lords can put together!" replied Peter Squire.

"As much as I wish the world outside the boundaries of my village would not come and bother me, I know it will never happen," replied Cathal. "Now no disrespect to your Queen, your Lord Deputy or whoever. The Maguire is my kin, and it is to him I pledge my loyalty. If you want to play politics, go play it with him."

Peter Squire smiled and pointed to the large log seats that created a circle for the men to sit around the fire.

"May I?"

"If you must," said Cathal. He rubbed the back of his neck with such aggression it turned red. But Cathal sat also, so as not to appear rude.

"We come to offer you that peaceful life you seek, free of all the inter-clan warfare," said Peter. "We come with the offer of lands and titles supported by the

Crown. Your son can inherit your title and your lands. You can pay a nominal rent to the Crown and owe no loyalty, duty or warriors to a chieftain who imprisons your children and forces them to fight to extend their power. You can have the protection of Connor Roe Maguire and live a life of peace."

Cathal swayed from side to side, as if the battle in his brain had unconsciously manifested itself in his body movements.

"I want peace," said Cathal, "but fear it will not come in the way you suggest. You want to side with one Maguire against another. I will be the pips squeezed and squashed on the floor when the winner grips his prize. Connor Roe Maguire has offered me better terms for my loyalty, and he is the lord of the closer branch of the Maguire clan. But as soon as I make a move against Cúchonnacht, my rival for control of the village, Michael O'Flanagan, will be straight to the Maguire to usurp me!"

Peter ignored his protests, for they were all the same from village to village.

"There will be no prize and no squeezing when the Crown gets its way. There will be no clan wars, no retributions. You will all be landed gentry, not interfering with one another, everyone minding their own business, bringing their produce to a central market and getting predictable, consistent prices, all under the protection of the Crown. You want to be on the right side of this war, which is coming whether you look over the top of your hill or not."

Peter contemplated the reaction on Cathal's face, which was a scowl of confusion.

"The Crown is weak in this part of the country." Cathal stuck his hands out as if they were weighing scales for the pros and cons of the argument. "Cúchonnacht Maguire keeps the peace through his political skill while the old lords of Ulster slog it out for supremacy. That is why we have peace, not because of the Crown. As I have said before, sort out what you want with Cúchonnacht and don't drag my villagers and me into it."

Peter sat forward, for he realised the time to make his point was growing short.

"The Crown is coming to assert herself on her lands of Ireland once more. Look at the O'Reillys to the south. Have they not been quiet since they surrendered their lands back to the Queen and were regranted them with English titles? Hasn't the raiding stopped? Surely it is best to be on the winning side?"

"I'll be long dead before your Queen does any winning," said Cathal, growing tired of the same regurgitated arguments. Peter saw he had to take another tack.

"I'm sorry you have so little faith in the Crown. However, we have brought you a gift of wheat seed as a declaration of goodwill from the Queen. You have no wheat, and this is merely the first down payment from your mutually beneficial relationship with the Crown."

"And how does the Crown assert herself in Fermanagh exactly?" said Cathal as he turned and signalled to his men.

"Through Connor Roe Maguire and your support for him." Peter smiled to assure him.

"I cannot support Connor Roe now. He is weak, and Cúchonnacht Maguire is strong and supported by the O'Neill clan. Now leave before you get me in trouble, and Cúchonnacht replaces me with a more pliant chieftain." At Cathal's gesture his men surrounded their guests.

"Thank you for hearing us out and please have the grain seed as a gift from the Crown, as a reward for being a loyal subject," said Peter. He rapidly looked around to ensure he was still safe before making a last plea to Cathal. But Cathal cut him off.

"Leave the grain and come back when Cúchonnacht is old and frail, which I fear will not be too long." Cathal pointed towards the Pale and bowed his head so as not to look upon his guests anymore.

"So we have your support if Connor Roe was ever to put himself forward to become the Maguire?"

"If those circumstances were ever to arise, then Connor Roe would be my favoured candidate." Cathal walked towards the Englishmen to force them to leave.

"Then we bid you farewell."

Cathal gave a sarcastic smile and instructed his men to unload the wheat seed, and the strangers departed with an empty cart.

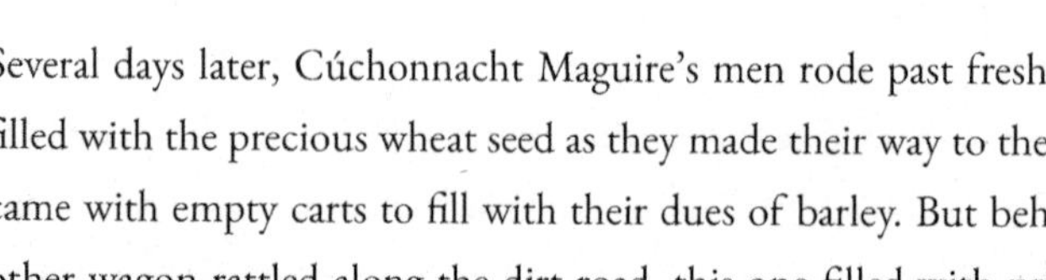

Several days later, Cúchonnacht Maguire's men rode past freshly hoed fields filled with the precious wheat seed as they made their way to the village. They came with empty carts to fill with their dues of barley. But behind them another wagon rattled along the dirt road, this one filled with prisoners. They were greeted with less distrust than was reserved for the Englishmen, for most strangers brought trouble with them these days. The men stopped their carts in the centre of the village and sent for Cathal O'Keenan Maguire. Cathal's men went to the stores to fetch the sacks of barley they had set aside from the harvest. Cathal conjured an air of congeniality within himself, despite his feelings, as he strode down to meet the men. They greeted him with the grinning faces of ambitious youth – the worst kind for a job like this.

"Not travelling via boat this summer?" said Cathal. He pointed to the lake to emphasise his point and flashed a smile to create a good first impression.

"Not everyone has the fortune to live by a lake," said the young Galloglass constable. "Some chieftains are paying with cattle, and we have to drive them overland. A much longer and arduous trip for me this year." He was a young man barely in his twenties who stood wide-legged with his hands on his hips for he thought it would convey authority. Cathal's smile did not falter, for he wished to end this encounter with the least aggravation in the shortest period.

"I trust all is in order and you have received twenty per cent of our crop as agreed?" said Cathal. He waved his arms towards the two full carts to show their abundance. The young man was having none of it and was determined to show who was in charge.

"I have looked in your stores, and I will take your word, for what it's worth, that you have paid in full," he replied.

"What do you mean 'for what it's worth'? You are addressing a Maguire chieftain, not some mercenary lackey you can throw a couple of coins at for his obedience!" Cathal's patience had quickly evaporated, for even though the crop had been poor for several years in a row, the Maguire had not lessened his demands in accordance. The young man smirked and swaggered over to Cathal to assert himself.

"You, sir, are addressing Donal MacCabe, the recently promoted Galloglass constable and enforcer for Cúchonnacht Maguire in these parts. Let me assure you, I know who I am addressing. While we collect dues, we are also searching for disloyal chieftains, ones who take a fancy to the English coin, seed or presents of Connor Roe's cattle.

"We noticed on our way in you had planted a new crop, straight after harvesting the other one. Now I said to my men, I can't remember you planting so many crops when I was here six months ago, or a year ago! How did dear Cathal come into such good fortune to plant a second crop? Was it all the protection the MacCabes gave him to save him from being raided by the O'Reillys? Well, yes, and that is partly why the Maguire gets his twenty per cent, thank you very much. But if Cathal O'Keenan Maguire is doing so well, surely he should contribute more? Since I have recently been promoted, surely I should try to impress the Maguire and increase his yield from this area, and we'll all get rich together? Wouldn't that be nice? But the Maguire wouldn't like me taxing loyal subjects too much, so I thought twenty per cent was just fine for everyone. That is until I discovered this!"

Donal clicked his fingers, and his men threw Peter Squire and John Brodie off the back of the prisoners' cart and onto the ground. Donal's men kicked out the Englishmen's knees and made them kneel before Donal and Cathal. They looked almost apologetic as they raised their eyes towards Cathal.

"These two confessed to giving you the Queen's wheat," said Donal. The judgement of Donal's index finger hovered above the prisoners' heads. Donal then returned his attentions to Cathal enjoying the feeling of power of holding the chieftain, his village and these vagabond English merchants all to ransom. "Now we like to know where everybody stands. It keeps everything nice and simple. These people support the clan and the Maguire. These people should piss off back to the Pale and the English where they belong." Donal moved his hands to indicate where boxes should be placed on different carts. But the judgemental index finger returned and circled the two Englishmen kneeling before him. "Now, these two, where do they belong? I'd say in the middle of a dark wood with their throats slit by robbers trying to steal their wheat seed." He turned once more to Cathal. "But you? I don't know where you stand. Do you support the Maguire? Will you sell him out if the price is right? But in your favour, you have an abundance of crops, more than enough for you and your villagers. The Maguire needs loyal servants in this area and to protect his interests from Connor Roe and his English masters. So it may be in everyone's interests that the Maguire looks upon you favourably, exercises a bit of forgiveness, and takes you back into the fold. The best way for you to show loyalty and to repay the Maguire's generous offer is to extend coign and livery to a troop of Maguire Galloglass and have them live here with you. What do you say to that?"

Cathal went pale.

"No!" said Cathal. "I mean, we have only had one good crop and are surely too far away from the county borders for the Maguire to base any Galloglass here! The O'Reilly raids have died down! We would be more than willing to make a greater contribution to the Maguire if that should meet his needs?" He panicked and pointed at the stores as an invitation for Donal to take more barley if he wished. Donal gave Cathal an evil grin, for now he knew his weakness, what he was really afraid of.

"Here is a perfectly fine place for my master's Galloglass," he said, relishing Cathal's discomfort. "Please do all you need to make them feel welcome. Maybe they could replace the children that your disloyalty made us take? Nevertheless, they will be with you in due course."

"Take whatever crops you wish," begged Cathal. "I'm a loyal subject to the Maguire. I'm a loyal subject!"

Donal laughed as he ordered his men to throw the Englishmen back on the cart so they could meet their destiny in a wood in the O'Reilly lands.

Cathal gasped for breath as he felt his control slipping away, and his disgruntled villagers filed back to their homes.

## CHAPTER TWO

# BIRDSONG

The cows mooed, the hens squawked, and the goats bleated. Feathers flew, hooves carved frustrated canyons on the mud floor and the smell of fresh animal excretion wafted through the poorly ventilated room as anxiety took possession of the farm animals. Amongst the swirl of people, prayers and animal faeces sat Artair, and he raised his throat to the roof and howled as if to crown it all off. Eunan sat cross-legged beside him, his hands over his ears, his eyes squeezed shut with only the tiniest of openings to let the tears roll down.

"Clear the room of those animals and the boy!" roared his father. The pitch of his voice cut through the tense atmosphere in the room.

Eunan opened his eyes and looked on at his father as he gripped his screaming mother's hand. Cathal's face contorted with anguish and tears. The occasional unoccupied hand of those helping rested on his back to soothe him. A single candle illuminated the room from its position beside his mother's bed. His mother's screams filled the cavern as the furniture, ornaments, and candle smoke absorbed them and echoed them back in an endless loop. He wanted to help, but he was brushed aside by adults rushing around, for he was in the way, as usual.

His mother had seemed unusually bright and cheerful during the pregnancy, and both she and his father cradled the womb as if within it lay the path to happiness. But once it had come to the actual act of giving birth, nothing seemed to go right.

He wondered why they wanted another child because, for all of his thirteen years, it never seemed like they wanted him. His father beat him and his mother would blame him for all her ills every time he went near her. He baulked when watching his mother in agony, for every expression of pain penetrated the thick wall surrounding his heart, but his father made him stay to 'see what you put your mother through'. His childhood had been a patchwork of pain sewed together with intermittent periods of pleasantness, mainly when his parents left him to do what he wanted. But not now, for his mother's suffering suffused his very sinews. The birth hours dragged, and her screams got worse. Father and the physician were both worried that the birth had been going on for too long. Eunan would much rather have taken out his frustration by throwing his axes at the wooden target at the back of his house, but his father insisted he shared his mother's bounty of pain. Her generosity was endless. Eunan squeezed his eyes shut and covered his ears, but the ground beneath his soggy bottom would not let him escape where he was.

"Come here, you," and a pair of hands came from behind Eunan and a pair of powerful arms lifted him up and placed him on the seating logs outside beside the fire with the view of the lake. A long canine tongue left a loving trail of saliva on his face. Eunan felt the wind and his nostrils could at last relax. He opened his eyes to see they had banished him outside with the farm animals. His father's men hemmed in his animals so they could not take this opportunity to escape.

A hand came from behind and played havoc with Eunan's hair.

"Why don't you play with your axes, for your mother and father will be some time yet," came a warm voice. Eunan looked up and one of his neighbours gave him a kindly smile. "Come on, Artair," Eunan called to his compliant dog. He decided the suggestion of some target practice was a good one.

The axes thudded with monotonous repetition, not that anyone noticed. Those adults that were kind enough to speak to him said that one day he would become a great warrior and fight in many battles far away from here. But whenever he called his father to see him throw his axes, he was told that he was only good at it because of his bad blood and that his parents wished they had a better son, one who was not polluted like him.

Eunan kept throwing his axes until he heard one last howl, and the screaming stopped. He ran inside. His father was crying, covered in blood, holding the new baby. But only his father howled. Cathal saw his son looking expectantly at him. Cathal balanced his dead daughter in the nook of his elbow and showed his son the back of his hand.

"You're cursed," he hissed. "Look at my beautiful daughter. Barely out of the womb and unable to take a breath!" He held the baby forward so that Eunan could see her. A tiny blue baby, with eyes that would never open, a neck that would never grow the strength to support the head, and lungs that would never take in air to cry for her mother's help. But Eunan's lungs could fill with air. He could scream for help. He did, but once again, it fell on deaf ears.

Cathal sank to his knees, wrapped up in his pain.

"She is dead! Yet you live!" Neighbourly hands came from behind to rest on Eunan's shoulders, but they could provide no comfort.

Eunan burst into tears and ran over to his mother to seek solace. But she lay on the bench, her head turned as if she were asleep. The physician battled to stem the flow of blood from between her legs.

"Get out of my way, boy! I have to stop your mother from dying!" he roared as he brushed Eunan aside.

The tears became a stream upon which solace floated away. Some women from the village came in and tried to help the physician. A benevolent neighbour by the name of Mary stood between Eunan and his parents and took him by the hand and led him outside.

"I know your parents can be mean, but one day you will realise why and hopefully forgive them," she said. Her face radiated a kindness he never saw on the faces of his parents.

"I know why," Eunan said. "It's because of my bad blood. They tell me all the time. I wish I could cut my arm open and watch all the bad blood flow away into the lake. Then my parents would love me." He tearfully looked up at his neighbour, hoping to elicit at most an answer to his theory, or at the very least some sympathy.

"Don't say such dreadful things," said Mary. "You're just a boy. Stay a boy for as long as you can. If you ever need any help, just come around to my house." She gave him some sprinkles of the sympathy he so desired. But it was all too much. Eunan sat on the ground and found more tears. But they could disturb even his tears as he heard a commotion and saw the sunken faces of the women of the village emerge from his house.

"The baby is dead. Something went dreadfully wrong. I don't think the mother will ever walk again. That boy has brought a curse on their house," said one. "Such a curse as we'll never be rid of you for the Galloglass have you protected." They turned from Eunan as if he was a little demon. Mary stood in front of Eunan to protect him from the barbs of the mourning women. "Don't be stupid. He's just a lad. It's not his fault what happened. And shush, he'll hear you." Mary turned around, but Eunan was gone. Evidently, he had heard her. Mary panicked. "We must find him! We must find the chieftain's son before the Galloglass come back! If they find him gone, surely they will kill us all?"

The terror of imagining the Galloglass who stayed in the village at the time of the boy's birth coming back to find Eunan missing gripped the village.

"What? The boy is gone!" "Organise a search party!" "We must find him! We must find the boy!" came the cries of the villagers.

They immediately organised search parties and began their quest in the surrounding woods.

Eunan ran for the lakeside to hide amongst the reeds. Artair could feel his young master's mood and bounded ahead, as if he knew where to go. Each tread of his lumbering paws scattered animals and birds alike and they squawked and howled to warn each other this beast was coming. Eunan cursed his dog and his lanky features, for it made them easy to follow. But the villagers were far behind. Artair stood above a particular clump of reeds and looked for his master's approval. A pat on the head and a 'good boy' meant he got it. Artair was by now covered in mud, and Eunan stroked his hand along the sides of his dog to assemble the mud on and between his fingers. He combed his hair with his freshly muddied fingers and boy and dog were alike with their spikes of mud. Eunan smiled, and Artair barked his approval. Eunan pulled out a plank of wood from one set of bushes and held it over a little pond of water until he found some solid ground on the island in the middle to rest it upon. Once it was secured, the boy and dog crossed onto the little reed island and drew in the drawbridge.

They went into the centre of the island where the reeds had already been hollowed out. Eunan produced a blanket from a bag he'd brought and laid it across some rocks and reeds he had arranged into a form of crude seating. They both lay back listening to the birdsong and waiting for the local fauna to forget they had just seen a bear of a dog and a boy come by. This was Eunan's refuge, where he could take up his drawbridge and hide behind his wall of reeds and forget about the world and its worries. But it couldn't last. He knew he would eventually have to heed the villagers' calls in order not to give up his hiding place.

The villagers marched Eunan back to the village after they had found him wandering in the woods. His father stood waiting for him at his house. Cathal had somewhat recovered from his previous outburst, but his blotchy face and tearful eyes left a telling trace. But now his primary emotion was anger. Anger at the boy. But one slap around the head was not enough to dissipate all he felt.

"Go see your mother," said Cathal. "She is awake now. We'll deal with your running away later."

Eunan bowed his head to avert his father's stare. He entered the house, each leg stiff with trepidation as he forced it forward. Shadows and darkness bathed the house except for the solitary candle that illuminated his mother's bed. A moo and a flash of light showed the faces of the animals that had the same idea as he, to flee, but they too had been forced to re-enter. The blankets of the bed moved awkwardly as beneath them thrashed exhausted limbs.

"Eunan, is that you?" came a timid voice in the darkness.

"Yes, Mother," he said. His nervousness now brought him to a halt.

"Do you want to see your sister?" she asked.

"I already have," he replied. "Father showed me."

"That was an order, not an invitation. Come and stand beside me."

Eunan stood rigid in the centre of the room.

"Come here, boy," she ordered.

His mother sat up on the bed, propped up on her pillows. Eunan stood beside her and peered over the edge of the bed. His mother grabbed his ear and yanked his head down.

"Look at your sister. Look at what you've done."

She held out her arm and nestled by her breast was the blue baby who neither breathed nor moved. Eunan cried again.

"Why do you hold her still, Mother? Why not give her to Father?"

"Do you want to know why I say you have bad blood?" she demanded. She moved her face closer to his, and Eunan grew afraid of the mania in her expression.

"I have been curious since you go on about it so much, but fear I don't want to know the answer."

His mother ignored him but he could tell from her face that she was wrestling with herself in her mind.

"Many hundreds of years ago the Vikings came from the sea and sailed down the Erne and arrived in the lower lough. They destroyed all the monasteries, killed all the monks, and stole everything of value. Those animals then sailed further down the Erne to the upper lake and did the same again. They stole the valuables and burnt the fertility from the land. They will be remembered forever as a blight on this land."

She thrust her face forward and gritted her teeth.

"Your father stole into my womb and ripped out all that was good and left me you. Just like the Vikings sailed down the Erne and destroyed our churches and lands, you sailed out of my womb." She released his ear.

Eunan ran for the door.

"That is why you're my little Viking, my boy of the bad blood, tainting all you touch!" she yelled after him.

Eunan ran straight past his father, Artair, and all the villagers and up into the woods.

Eunan ran through the woods his head filled with the tales told to all Maguire children of how the Vikings rampaged through Fermanagh and tried to destroy the essence of the Maguires themselves by burning all the monasteries founded by their patron saint Colmcille and desecrating all the churches they came across. It wounded him deep in his soul that his mother could associate him with these, the darkest foundation myths of the Maguires. It was as if she had intentionally set out to hurt him. But he was determined to be rid of this bad blood so his mother would love him and take him back.

Eunan sat on a stump deep in the woods and slashed himself on the arm with his knife. He had heard that physicians thought there were different types of blood, both good and bad and that you could tell them apart. Eunan watched the blood trickle slowly from the wounds, looking to see if he could identify different colours or if there was any other way of distinguishing the 'good' blood from the 'bad' blood. He grew frustrated with the lack of flow for all his blood looked the same. He sucked his blood out and spat it on the ground for he thought the bad blood must be hiding under his skin and if he sucked enough it would come out.

Someone heard his angry mutterings, and a twig snapped behind the boy. He turned, and a giant stood before him, his beard a blaze of red, in chain mail and a metal helmet, with a giant axe that reached as far as the man's shoulder and had an enormous curved blade the size of his face. Eunan trembled. Was this the Galloglass he'd dreamed would come and save him?

"What are you doing, boy? You'll hurt yourself!" said the Galloglass. His voice exuded authority, which only encouraged Eunan to think this man was his saviour. But first, he must confess his sins.

"I just killed a baby, and I'm trying to get rid of this bad blood!"

The warrior put down his axe, sat beside the boy, and took his arm. He squeezed the cut closed with a tenderness the boy seldom felt.

"How did a boy like you kill this baby? I don't believe it. Is someone playing a cruel joke on you? If they are, they'll have me to answer to!"

The Galloglass smiled at him, and Eunan's eyes brightened.

"Will you protect me?" Eunan asked. He looked wide-eyed at the warrior and thought there was not a man in the village that could stand up to him, not even his father.

"I can show you how to protect yourself," said the Galloglass. "How to be a great warrior if you like? But first, wrap this cloth around your arm to stop all that bleeding."

Eunan nodded and smiled, and hope came back into his veins. He took the cloth, wound it around his wounds and showed it to the Galloglass, who nodded his approval.

"What's that on your belt?" asked the warrior.

"It's my axe. I throw it. Do you want to see?" said Eunan.

"Show me, boy!"

"See that branch?" Eunan pointed to a tree twenty yards away.

"Yes?"

"Watch me snap it!"

Eunan threw his axe, and it whizzed through the air. But it only grazed the branch. Eunan frowned.

"Don't be angry, boy. That was good for someone your age."

Eunan flopped down on the ground. He looked up at the soldier again.

"Can I come with you?"

"You're far too young for where I am going," said the Galloglass.

The boy's disappointment made the soldier smile.

"Show me where you live."

"Do I have to go home?"

"Your parents will miss you," the soldier said.

"They won't!"

"Come on!" the warrior said, picking Eunan up by the arm. They went over to retrieve the throwing axe and the Galloglass made Eunan point the way home.

Eunan trudged towards the edge of the forest. He did not want to go home but felt he had no choice, and to cry like a baby would undo all the good work he had done to impress the soldier. But he felt he needed to know more about this man's life before he returned to his unhappy one.

"Are you Galloglass?"

"I am. How did you know?" The soldier smiled down at him.

"I can tell by your axe. Can I be a powerful warrior like you someday?"

"Yes, but you have to train every day!"

They came to the edge of the woods and ran into one of the search parties. One villager grabbed the boy and shielded him from the warrior.

"We have nothing to give you for the boy. We are poor, and you have no use for him," said the villager. They huddled together as if that afforded them some protection.

The Galloglass pointed his axe at the villagers.

"Why is this boy running around the forest trying to hurt himself?" he boomed. He pointed his axe at the woman trying to hide Eunan behind her skirt. "Are you his mother?"

"No. The boy's mother is sick," replied the woman.

"The boy still needs looking after. If I find the boy in the forest again, or see any more self-inflicted injuries, I will do more than point my axe at you!" The Galloglass hefted the shaft of his axe in his hands to ensure they got his message.

"Be away with you and don't threaten us!" said the woman. "The village warriors will be here soon! Go before they find you!"

"Mark my words and look after the boy!" the Galloglass said as he disappeared into the woods.

The villagers huddled around the boy and turned for home when they were sure the Galloglass was gone.

"Do you think he sent him?" asked one.

"Maybe. Let's just bring the boy home," said the woman.

Back at Eunan's home, the villagers told the tale of the Galloglass finding the boy. Upon the mention of Galloglass in the forest, Cathal was civil to the boy, though his world was collapsing around him and he sought to vent his frustrations elsewhere. He left the boy alone while casting glances into the woods to ensure he was not being watched. Eunan was left to reunite with his dog and they returned to their castle in the reeds to listen to the birdsong.

Fiona O'Keenan Maguire seldom left her bed after the stillbirth, for a pit of illness and depression came to settle in her head. Her dark moods led her to banish Eunan from the house, and she forbade him from visiting her. Eunan took up lodgings in the outhouse, and Artair happily joined him there. There he stayed and did his chores and practised with his axes, and kin and villager alike left him be.

The physician regularly attended Fiona because she was the chieftain's wife, but he could do little to help her except assess what was wrong and attempt to ease her mind from worry. He assigned her prayers and many potions, none of which he thought would do her any good. Because of her complications during childbirth, she would never walk again. The local carpenter made her a barrow within which she could sit. Cushions and blankets from her neighbours made it comfortable. Her husband would sometimes wheel her into the garden, and Eunan would peer at her through the neighbour's window. Her face was a storm of anger, and Eunan still did not go home, for no invitation was extended. Eunan was pleased, for Mary the neighbour was kind and fed him, and they left him in peace to throw his axes. He vowed to run away and become a Galloglass. That hope helped him persevere.

# CHAPTER THREE

# DONAL OF THE FIVE HOSTAGES

Several months passed, and no Galloglass appeared in the village either to raid or take up residence through coign and livery, much to the relief of Cathal and the villagers. Harvest time came again and this time they considered themselves blessed, for it was a bountiful oasis after several years of hardship. They gathered the crops, filled the stores, and planted the seed for the next season. Then they danced and celebrated and were thankful for their good fortune. But while all manner of beasts gathered to live off the harvest – the villagers chased rats from the stores and crows from the freshly hoed fields – the biggest monsters had yet to make themselves known.

One morning, the call came.

"Boats on the lake! Boats on the lake!"

Boats on the lake were a common sight since they were the primary mode of transport in Fermanagh, and you could get almost anywhere you wanted in the county by taking to the Erne river and navigating the two lakes. But everyone knew what the call meant.

The village went into a frenzy. Villagers emptied the store and hid the grain where they could. There was no time to transport it to their best hiding places on the islands of the lake. They hid their valuables and their children. But such treatment was not for Eunan. No, his father invited him back into the house and dressed him in his best clothes. Cathal was even pleasant to him.

"Boats to shore! Boats to shore!"

Cathal went down to the shoreline and covered his eyes from the sun. Out on the lake were three large riverboats of the Maguire. Harvest time meant the Maguire collected his share of the grain to store it in his Crannógs in the northern part of Upper Lough Erne. These man-made fortified islands were almost impossible to capture or rob, which meant the Maguire could hide out on the islands of the lakes of Erne indefinitely.

From behind the large boats came smaller boats filled with soldiers and tribute collectors, which rowed towards Cathal and the other villages on the southwest side of the lake. Cathal saw no point in hiding, for if he hid, the Maguire's men would take whatever they wanted. So he sat and waited as three boats rowed ever nearer.

Once the boats reached the shallow waters, Cathal's men grabbed the ropes cast from the vessels and moored them to the shore. Donal MacCabe leapt from the lead boat and strode ashore, straight to Cathal.

"Hello, Cathal," he said. "I hope the harvest went well. The Maguire needs the help of all his loyal chieftains, and I assume you will prove yourself loyal?" He gave Cathal the youthful smirk of a man who had recently gained a lot of power and was keen to show it off. Cathal ignored him, for he knew there was little point in bruising Donal's shallow ego and provoking him.

"Come this way and see what I can contribute to the Maguire!" he said, pointing towards the stores.

The villages had their own, much smaller, Crannógs in which they stored their grain, separate from the islands they used as hiding places. Two swordsmen guarded the only entrance to the largest Crannóg via a footbridge. Donal counted the sacks as the villagers brought them out from the store and stockpiled them on the shore for the Maguire. When Cathal informed him that what was in front of him was his share, he sent two of his men to count what bags remained in the Crannógs to tally the harvest yield.

After a while, the men came back and whispered in Donal's ear. Donal laughed to himself.

"The harvest's down this year, isn't it?" he said. "Now, I can only judge your honesty by what I can count, and you have given me twenty per cent of that. Previously, we've found grain you've hidden, so I hope you've done a better job of hiding it this year. But I'm afraid I have some bad news for you. The Maguire has had to pay the coign and livery of the English soldiers imposed upon Fermanagh soil. We passed the cost on to you. That means the tribute is now thirty per cent."

Donal grinned and his Galloglass stood erect and watched for any signs of trouble. The veins in Cathal's neck bulged as he calculated the impact of this new rate.

"What! I can't afford that! My people will starve!" said Cathal.

Donal remained perfectly calm, for he knew he had more than enough armed men to impose his will.

"No, they won't," Donal said. "They'll just have to eat all the grain you've hidden from us. I'd be careful now, between you and me, and don't get the blame for the supplementary tribute, for it was treacherous chieftains like you that undermined the Maguire and led to the English being on our lands."

"I am a perfectly loyal chieftain to the Maguire! How dare you insinuate I am anything but!" said Cathal.

Donal walked over and put his arm on the shoulder of the red-faced Cathal.

"It's a long fall from your high horse," he said. "I've been coming here for years, and I know you. That's why we need to sort out who's who and who should be the chieftain in particular districts, for things are always happening to chieftains and then someone more Maguire-friendly takes over.

"The Maguire needs you to swear loyalty to the clan. We've been hearing rumours that you have received emissaries from Connor Roe and also the English, yet again. The Maguire needs to know that you are with him."

"Do I not pay the Maguire his dues at every harvest, send my men to fight for him when he calls? Are these not true proofs of my loyalty to him? Why is it strange that I should have contact with the most powerful Maguire in my region? Is that not the clan hierarchy? Why don't you ask Connor Roe about his contacts with the English? Whatever the Maguire does about it, when he comes to call, I will answer, as I always do."

Cathal stopped and looked at Donal, hoping that if his words could not convince him, then maybe his facial expressions would.

"We are glad to hear you state your loyalty so forcefully," said Donal. "However, the Maguire hears you have a son close to coming of age. The Maguire would like to invite him to enjoy an education only the Maguire can provide."

Cathal had been expecting this. The two things that Donal could do to ensure loyalty were to impose Galloglass upon them or to take hostages. Hostages, given their experiences, were the least bad option. But he would not give in easily.

"Thank you for your offer, but my son needs to grow up protecting his people. There's many a raider out there today, and we need all the men of fighting age we can get."

"The Maguire would view it as disrespectful for such a generous offer to be refused!" said Donal.

Cathal's resistance finally broke.

"Please don't take my boy," he protested.

Donal laughed.

"The Maguire will take a boy and return a man. In fact, he will take several boys and return several men. Gather the sons of the prominent men of the village and deliver them to us by sunset. Then we will return to the Maguire with your loyalty pledge."

Cathal saw it was useless to protest. He looked around at the faces of his villagers and they put their heads down and would not look at him. They did not like it but would put up little resistance.

"I will see you at the centre of the village at sunset," Cathal said.

"Good," replied Donal. "Think of it as the first step to proving you are a loyal servant. I trust you will order your men to stand aside while we take our additional ten per cent?"

It was Cathal's turn to look at the ground.

"I am a loyal servant of the Maguire."

Donal MacCabe grinned and savoured his victory by looking at the crowd of villagers and making sure they saw his smile and Cathal's bowed head. His ego boosted and his authority assured, he ordered his men to enter the stores.

Cathal ensured Eunan remained within his sight for the rest of the day, resorting to paying attention and listening to him if so required. He took Eunan by the hand at the appointed time and led him to the centre of the village. Eunan was happy to go with his father and was puzzled why he had lavished so much attention on him. Cathal promised Eunan that he would meet some warriors who would give him some training. This delighted Eunan, especially because he supposed his father would spend some time with him to help him train as he did with the other boys of the village. The light turned to shadow, and grim-faced men stood in the village circle with their first-born young sons in front of them. They lay their hands on their sons' shoulders to show they would not be easily parted. They glared at Cathal when he arrived with his smiling boy.

"What have you told him?" asked one. But Cathal ignored him. He thought that if he took this opportunity to assert his authority then Donal would gleefully accept his chance to humiliate him.

"I thought you'd be the one smiling when you got rid of him!" said another. Cathal glared at the mass of faces but could not identify who was making the comments.

"If you give him to Donal and his Galloglass surely the others will take it out on the village for you abandoning your pledge to look after the boy?" said one red-faced man who wrapped his arms around his crying boy.

"How can they complain or take it out on the village if I send the boy to Enniskillen to get an education with the house of the Maguire and become a little lord?" said Cathal. "We all win then."

Ten Galloglass stood in the centre circle of the village. Their hands were pressed to their axe shafts and they ensured they had easy access to their boats moored on the shore. Holding Eunan's hand, Cathal crossed the circle to where Donal MacCabe still had not tired of his grin.

"How many of our children does the Maguire wish to take?" Cathal said.

"Enough to ensure your loyalty," said Donal. "This is not a negotiation. We will take as many children as we deem necessary. They will be well taken care of in Enniskillen. I'm sure you've schooled them in the duties of noble boys towards their clan?"

Cathal shook his head.

"They're just that, still boys," he said. "How many do you want?"

Donal paused, studied the faces of the villagers, returned to Cathal's and then pondered on the confusion in Eunan's eyes. He squeezed his features together as if he was exaggerating the amount of thought he was putting into his decision. Donal was clearly enjoying this.

"Five, including yours," he said eventually.

"Here, take him and be off with you," replied Cathal.

Cathal let go of Eunan's hand, turned and walked back towards the villagers. The other fathers knelt and hugged their boys goodbye and praised them for their bravery, while Eunan looked at the line of Galloglass beside Donal and cried when he realised his father had tricked him.

"Cathal?" called Donal across the circle.

Cathal sighed, stood and looked to the heavens, turned, and walked back across the circle again.

"Take him back," said Donal. "We want your boy, not some impostor." Donal picked up Eunan's arm and held out his limp hand to his father.

"He is my boy!" Cathal fumed, and he stormed over the last couple of steps.

The Galloglass raised their axes to defend their master. Eunan cried, Donal smiled.

"We came for the chieftain's son, and we are not leaving without him," said Donal.

"He is there, standing in front of you!" said Cathal. He thrust his arms out towards the boy in the most forceful rejection without getting physical.

"You would have us believe a chieftain would give up his son without so much as a tear or a goodbye and walk away from him?" said Donal.

Cathal's face stiffened. He had to keep his cool to get through this. "We said our goodbyes in the house," he said.

"This boy is an impostor," said Donal. "How can a chieftain's son close to fighting age cry so much? Hand over the real boy, and we'll not mention this deception to the Maguire."

"He is the real boy!" said Cathal.

Donal grabbed Eunan by the arm and held him in front of him.

"He doesn't look like you. We don't want any bastards!" said Donal.

"He is born of my wife, resembles his disabled mother, and is my son!" said Cathal. "What more do you want of me?"

"Why did you give him up so easily?" said Donal. "No father I have seen has given his boy up so easily as you."

"He is brave and doesn't want his father to embarrass him," said Cathal.

"So he does that himself by bawling his eyes out crying? No, hand over the real boy, or we'll return and take him."

Cathal threw his arms up in despair.

"Enough of this nonsense," he said. "Take your prisoners and go. I will discuss this with the Maguire the next time I am in Enniskillen."

Donal laughed and his smirk grew wider the more he got under Cathal's skin.

"Is the real boy a prisoner of Connor Roe?" Donal said.

"Take the boy and leave!" Cathal said.

The Galloglass leader stared at Cathal, and Cathal turned his back and walked off.

"Leave the impostor, take the rest. Let's go," said Donal.

The Galloglass walked across the circle and took the first four boys and walked towards the road. The other fathers pointed at Eunan and shouted, "Take the boy! Take the boy!" They turned to Cathal and demanded that he make them take the boy. Cathal ran and grabbed the boy's hand, and they caught up with Donal MacCabe.

"Take the boy. He's mine. I wish to pledge my loyalty to the Maguire. Take him as a sign of my loyalty. All the other fathers can vouch that he's mine."

Donal stopped and looked at the other fathers, who had also come after them.

"The boy is his?" he said.

"He may not seem it, but he is the boy's father." said one.

"Take him," said Donal, pointing at Eunan. "But I would pray, Cathal, that when the boy turns of age he does not come back and repay you for this night."

Eunan looked back at his father but could only make out the back of his head. He had finally done it, Eunan thought. He had finally rid himself of his monster of a son. The bad blood seared through Eunan's veins.

## CHAPTER FOUR

# ROUNDING THE EDGES ON THE EGO OF A CHIEFTAIN'S SON

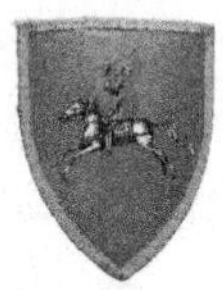

Donal ordered his men to circle around the hostages in case any of the fathers changed their minds and attempted a rescue. But Eunan knew Donal should not have bothered. His father would not be making any attempt to retrieve him. His father had finally got rid of him. He could feel the bad blood within him and thought that he may as well give in. If his father thought he was so bad, he may as well live up to it. He willingly lined up behind the other boys to get on the boat.

The boys tripped over themselves as they were bundled into the boats waiting for them by the shoreline. The Galloglass were still loading the grain onto the other vessels, but Donal MacCabe could not wait for them to finish. They had to leave now. He could come back for more grain when he was less exposed.

The darkness melted land and lake together, the only spots of light being the torches of the guards. Eunan elbowed his way to the front of the boat, and the other four boys had to contest the seats in the middle. The boys were given blankets to wrap themselves in and gruffly told to be quiet. Of all his fellow hostages, Eunan knew Senan the best. He was a skinny lad with black hair and inquisitive nature and lived just across the way from him in the village. He would play with Eunan sometimes, when his parents allowed, but would often feed

Artair scraps, as he did not have his own dog. They could not talk, but Eunan gave him a knowing nod, as if to say he would look out for him if he would do the same for him. Senan nodded back, for he was also in need of a friend or ally.

The craft set off with the only noise, the gentle ripple of the lake being split apart on the bow. The boys looked in the direction they were going and the moon showed the shimmering path to Enniskillen. Despite what had happened that evening or knowing what the future held, the boys developed a small sense of excitement for most of their swordplay and stories revolved around Enniskillen and now they were finally going there. They rowed for a considerable time until they saw the lights of the Crannógs at the lower end of the lake bouncing on the gentle waves that lapped around the boat.

There was a set of four Crannógs controlled by the Maguire himself in the lower reaches of the lake, each of varying size. The boat made for the largest of these, which was about one hundred yards from the shore. They moored on the pier on the north side of the Crannóg.

"Everybody off," said the Galloglass guard. The boys were only too willing to obey.

A wicker wall protected the man-made island and on it were several large buildings, all used as store rooms, and several smaller ones, used as barracks for the Maguire's soldiers. There were several more small piers where other boats of different sizes landed and dispatched their cargoes of smaller livestock and grain. The Maguire did not build these islands. They had been there for as long as anyone could remember; hundreds, maybe thousands, of years old. The Maguire merely adapted them for his purposes.

"This must be where the Maguire stores his tribute before it gets transported up to Enniskillen," said Senan. "My father told me about this."

"Where are all the cattle?" said Eunan. "I thought the Maguire liked to get paid in cattle?"

"They go overland," said Senan. "More dangerous, but you'd never fit the cattle on the boats."

"Enough talking and follow me," said a guard.

Eunan and the others were led to one of the smaller houses where they were fed a thin gruel, given straw to sleep on and blankets to wrap themselves in. The five settled in as best they could, cold and hungry. As they shivered, other groups of boys arrived later in the night and found Eunan and his friends had taken all the blankets.

The night grew chilly and as Eunan and his comrades slept, the other boys armed themselves with sticks and stones. They descended upon Senan, unravelled him from his blanket, and beat him when he tried to resist. Senan's yelps awoke comrade and guard alike. Eunan leapt up and punched the nearest boy full in the chin. Then he grabbed an end of Senan's ex-blanket and tugged as hard as he could. The other boys attacked him and forced him to let go. Eunan fell to the ground, and the hand that broke his fall felt some stones. Eunan picked these up, and his arm remembered the hours of practice with the throwing axes. By the time the guards came in and broke up the fight, Eunan had recovered the blanket, and the faces of his assailants were a mess of blood and bruises. Eunan's prize was that they informed Donal MacCabe of his fighting skills, and he kept all the blankets.

Nobody got much sleep that night, since the air of distrust had only grown as the night got colder. Senan and the other boys huddled behind Eunan. When dawn broke, the guards came and bundled them onto another boat destined for Enniskillen. This was a larger riverboat, and it could take the boys and a sizeable cargo of grain. There were few Galloglass on the vessel but there were several cargo boats in convoy and several smaller boats full of soldiers escorting them.

The boat ride was relatively pleasant, for it was much more reassuring to travel during the day to somewhere you knew you were going to. Most of the time, Eunan just lay back in the boat and enjoyed the view as the guards left the boys alone. To ease the boredom, he also took pleasure in pissing over the side of the vessel when he knew the boys from the previous night were downwind and could do nothing about it. The guards just laughed as long as he did not piss on them.

By nightfall, they could see the lights of Enniskillen and the boys crowded to the front of the boat to get the best view.

Enniskillen Castle was the seat of the Maguire. The Maguires had chosen an almost perfect defensive position upon which to build the castle. It was built on an island, surrounded by the River Erne, which acted as a defensive barrier to keep out all but the most determined of enemies. The castle had gigantic walls and a singular bridge that protruded like a tongue to lap up any visitors and swallow them inside. A sister island held the castle island protectively to her breast, which contained most of the bustling town. Mooring posts and jetties spiked into the river at any available gigantic walls and the River Erne was flush with small boats either fishing or carrying produce up or down the river from other parts of Fermanagh, to be sold at the busy markets of Enniskillen.

The boat moored in the town of Enniskillen, and the cargo was unloaded. The guards escorted the boys through the town, over the drawbridge, and into the castle. Most of the boys were in awe, for they had never left their villages and only heard of such citadels and the Maguire in stories or games.

The guards lined up the boys in the castle's courtyard. They held a roll call based on the notes Donal MacCabe's men made. Rank in the clan hierarchy parted boys from their village fraternity. Rank also meant privilege and the important boys joined families that made up the inner Maguire clan or associated families. Eunan was one of those more important boys, as he was the son of a chieftain.

Donal told the boys they were here for several years and promised them an excellent education. The MacCabes would teach them fighting skills if they showed loyalty to the Maguire, and the sons of chieftains could become the Maguire's favoured heir for their clans. Eunan liked the sound of that, but was mainly glad he was a chieftain's son, for he did not have to clean up the boats like the lesser boys. Eunan had impressed Donal MacCabe with his fighting skills in the Crannógs, so they gave him to Desmond MacCabe, an old Galloglass warrior who had faithfully served the Maguire clan throughout his career.

Eunan waited to be claimed by his new family in an enclosure guarded by Galloglass. Desmond MacCabe sent his servant to collect him. The servant made himself known to the Galloglass and claimed Eunan. He introduced himself as Arthur and asked Eunan to refer to him by that name. Eunan stayed with the Galloglass while Arthur fetched the horses. Arthur was nervous, for Eunan was a strong young man who could easily overpower him. Eunan assured him he would not ride away and escape and that he was looking forward to meeting his new master, of whom Donal MacCabe had said many good things. Arthur eyed Eunan suspiciously but reverted to loyalty to his master. They rode out of the castle together. Arthur was tall and skinny and quivered like a frightened rabbit, yet Eunan considered the proposition of following him far more exciting than going home.

They rode for a couple of hours through forest and field until they arrived at a large house planted amongst a grove of trees on the banks of Lower Lough Erne. It reminded Eunan of home: the rolling fields, the lake dotted with small islands, the fields of barley. He cried for the reminder of home and the emotions of the past couple of days finally got to him.

"Please don't do that when the master comes," said Arthur. "He doesn't tolerate any crying. You'll find yourself a stable boy, and that would be very demeaning for the son of a chieftain."

Eunan nodded and dried his eyes. He straightened his clothes and wiped his face, for he wanted to look impressive.

Arthur inspected Eunan, and upon being satisfied he was presentable, opened the door of the house.

"Master, I have returned with the boy from Enniskillen. He is eager to meet you." Arthur announced to an empty room.

Eunan was anxious, but not in the manner Arthur meant. Eunan heard some noise from upstairs. Then came a roar.

"Bring him to the kitchen. I will meet him there."

Arthur turned to Eunan.

"The master is coming."

Eunan did not reply.

Arthur brought Eunan to the kitchen and invited him to sit on the bench. Eunan sat and waited while fidgeting with his hands.

"Don't do that either. The master doesn't like it!"

"He sounds just like my father," muttered Eunan.

"Don't do—"

"I know. He doesn't like that either," said Eunan.

The kitchen shook with the pounding of the stairs. A large hand hooked around the door, and a round body bounded into the kitchen and sat itself down. Eunan's new master was a once-muscular man whose body had succumbed to the good life, like a retired bear with an endless pot of honey. He sat and grinned. But at Arthur.

"Arthur, is it time to eat?"

"Soon, master."

Desmond MacCabe eyed the boy.

"Is this him? He looks a bit miserable to me. It is going to be such a chore if he is going to be like that all the time."

Arthur turned and looked up from his kitchen chores.

"He's had a long journey, master," he said. "The conditions would not be of the manner you are used to."

Desmond rubbed his brow.

"I hope he hasn't come here with expectations in the sky of being a petty lord! What can you do, boy?"

"Nothing," said Eunan.

"Pardon? Speak up, boy!" said Desmond.

"What do you mean 'what can I do'?"

"Tend the horses, cook, fight? Read, write? Whatever young boys are supposed to do these days?"

Eunan pondered his answer and thought of what he considered his host would think most useful.

"I can help around the house," said Eunan. "I used to help my mother!"

Desmond crossed his arms and sighed.

"Arthur, I think this piece of babysitting is going to be rather tedious," he said. "Give him my weapons to clean and show him the stables. What a way to earn the pennies of pension from the Maguire!"

Arthur produced a bowl of stew, gave it to his master, and Eunan was forgotten, both in mind and stew distribution. Eunan sat and watched Desmond shovel food into his face, but said nothing for fear of insulting his host.

Arthur led the hungry and disappointed Eunan out of the house and to the shore of the lake. He directed him to sit on a couple of tree stumps that looked like the perfect place to look out over the lake and ponder on the mysteries of the world. Eunan sat down. He looked across the water, and every lap of the waves whispered to him of home. Dark clouds blurred the reflections on the lake. White horses energised the waves. Meanwhile, Arthur had fetched an eclectic collection of weapons.

"He likes to see his face in the blade when you're finished," he said. "Oh, and if you want to gain favour with him, stand up and present the weapons as if you were a warrior saluting his lord."

Arthur left Eunan sitting amongst a pile of dirty weapons. He sat alone by the lake. Anti-climax hung heavy on his shoulders. Time passed slowly, and Arthur did not come back, so he cleaned the weapons.

Several polished weapons later, Eunan looked around for he was bored. The oranges and purples glistening on the shimmering surface of the lake made his eyes moist again. Desmond emerged from the house and strolled over and sat on the free tree stump. It was the first time Eunan noticed his limp, which led Eunan to wonder how he got it. There were two piles of weapons, those loosely acquainted with Eunan's cleaning cloths, and those that were not. Desmond picked one from the smaller collection and inspected it. The curl of his lip told Eunan that Desmond was not impressed.

"Is this supposed to be clean?" he asked.

"Yes, lord," said Eunan.

"I don't know if this is laziness, inexperience, or both. Either way, it won't do." Desmond dropped the sword.

The weapon clanged as it clashed with the other supposedly clean weapons, and Eunan's heart dropped with it. Desmond got up and turned towards the house.

"Arthur."

Arthur came running out of the house.

"What is it, master?"

"Get the boy to clean out the stables. He's terrible at cleaning weapons."

"Yes, master. Come here, boy."

Eunan obeyed, and Arthur led him to the stables.

"I tried to tell you. I tried to give you a chance. Now you are a stable boy and will have to do well at this to dig yourself out of the repercussions after your performance of the previous chore!"

Arthur brought him inside the stables, and Eunan baulked at the smell.

"That's your first job," said Arthur, using his hand for a fan. "We haven't had a stable boy in a while. Get to know the horses, so when the master comes down to take them out, they'll be well behaved. Then he may let you clean his weapons again!"

The veins in Eunan's neck bulged.

"I am a chieftain's son!" he said. "My father is a great man in the Maguire court!"

"Don't speak like that in front of the master," said Arthur. "You wouldn't be here if your father were such a great man. Be quiet, follow my advice, and all will be well. The shovel is over there, and there is plenty of water in the lake. I will return before sundown to inspect your work. I would advise you to deal with the smell first, or else it will be difficult for you to sleep out here."

"What! I should sleep in the house like a chieftain's son and not be out in the yard like a dog."

But he was protesting to Arthur's back.

"You will find it more comfortable if you first deal with the smell," said Arthur over his shoulder. "I would get on with it as you have until sundown." He went back to the house and closed the front door to signal to Eunan he would not be allowed back in until his chores were done.

Eunan picked up the shovel once he realised Arthur meant what he said, that he was sleeping out here. All the stables had been cleaned out by the time Arthur returned. Eunan had created a pile of manure, downwind from them.

"Half a job well done," was the limit of Arthur's praise.

Eunan's knuckles whitened as he made a fist.

"Half a job?!"

"You've got to spread the manure evenly over the fields," said Arthur, "not shove it into a pile. But we can leave that until tomorrow. Here is your dinner." He handed Eunan a hunk of bread. "You can have a proper meal when your chores are done, by order of Desmond."

Eunan cursed Arthur after he left and thought of even more vicious curses for Desmond. He sat in the stable and stared at the house until he realised they were serious about not letting him in. Eunan prepared his bed but had to take straw from the horses, for there was nothing else for him to use. He lay his head down and felt the bad blood surge through his body. Surely he deserved this. Was this the culmination of his parent's revenge upon him? That he ended up a friendless stable boy in the middle of nowhere, good for nothing but shovelling horse manure? He settled down for an awful night's sleep.

# CHAPTER FIVE

# "WITH BRUSH AND SHOVEL, I DUB THEE SIR HORSE BOY"

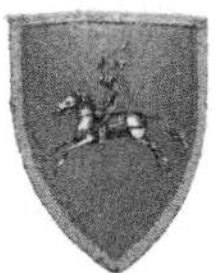

Eunan spent the next couple of weeks cleaning the stables, distributing the manure across the fields, and waiting for Desmond to treat him like a chieftain's son. Desmond ignored him, and Eunan kept shovelling. Eunan's anger rebounded off the walls of his manure prison, producing an endless stream of curses and tantrums, and making it hard for him to sleep, no matter how exhausted he was. Finally, after asking every day for two weeks, Arthur invited Eunan back into the house.

Eunan forgave the mess of the house, for the stables had considerably lowered his standards. But the fire warming his bones immediately lifted his mood and his anger dissipated somewhat. Desmond stomped down the stairs and with each step Eunan's resentment rose once again.

Arthur had learned long ago to be punctual with dinner and he went to the stove and ladled out three bowls of broth. Desmond got the biggest bowl and Eunan the smallest.

"You're a better shit-shoveller than weapons cleaner," said Desmond. He shoved another spoonful of broth into his mouth. Jest danced upon his face and he took his freshly cleaned spoon and pointed it at one of Eunan's shoulders and then the other. "With brush and shovel, I dub thee, Sir Horse Boy."

Eunan exploded from his chair.

"Horse Boy? Horse Boy! I am the son of a chieftain! Yet you tie me to your stables to tend to your horses. I should be treated with the respect I deserve!"

Desmond just laughed.

"Boy, you are. They would split your head in two on the battlefield by now, with a temper like that. You have to earn respect, and shovelling shit only deserves a modicum. You can come and stay in the house when you earn it and are more useful to me."

"When will that be? What do I have to do?" said Eunan.

"You will find out when you are ready," said Desmond. "Anyway, I called you in, for I need to go to Enniskillen to consult with the Maguire. Instead of leaving you here, I thought you could come with me. Then we can see if this 'chieftain's son' has any uses."

"I would like that." Eunan calmed down, sat down, and ate his broth.

"Good. We will set forth after this meal. But first, a surprise inspection of the stables."

They strode down to the stables, making subtle accommodations for Desmond's limp. Eunan was nervous, for he wanted the inspection and prospective trip to lead to better things, like being a resident in the house, getting better chores, and going home. No. Eunan cut that thought off at the knees. Even life with Desmond and living in a stable was better than that.

Desmond donned a serious air for his inspection. He patted the horses and looked for signs of mistreatment. Eunan was lucky he had fed the horses and cleaned the sheds just before he was called to the house, so the horses were content and had little time to make a mess.

"You are getting better, boy," said Desmond. "You always need to look after the horses, for you have no better friend in a fight."

Eunan nodded and absorbed his praise without exchanging it for emotion. Desmond turned to him.

"My usual horse, please, and gather the weapons. There are still bandits in this county, despite my best efforts."

Arthur had instructed Eunan thoroughly about Desmond's likes and dislikes about horses and weapons. Eunan had memorised his instructions, for sometimes there was little to do between horse defecations.

Desmond looked rather pleased with Eunan as he mounted his horse and tied his scabbarded sword around his waist. Arthur fetched his own horse and allocated to Eunan a far less impressive mount than either of the others. Then they set off for Enniskillen.

Eunan enjoyed the wind on his face, being out in the fields and the forest once more and especially being on the way to Enniskillen with a mission. He hid his new-found excitement from Desmond, whose horse trotted a few yards ahead. Arthur took no notice of either of them, but kept watch at the rear for bandits.

Desmond slowed down before they got very far and allowed Eunan to catch him up. Eunan smiled at him and was glad he looked like he wanted to make conversation. If he befriended him, there was less chance of him remaining a horse boy.

"Do you know who I am, boy?" Desmond said.

Eunan shivered and looked him up and down. He contemplated his answer, for he could not yet read Desmond and did not want to get sent home for insulting him.

"I assume you mean in the past, for I know what you do now," he said.

"I can still muster days with shades of my past glories," said Desmond. He shook his cocked head at such insinuations that his best days were behind him. Eunan thought a guess would more than likely lead to insult, so a new strategy was required.

"No, I don't know who you are, but I can smell a tale or two from someone with such a prestigious standing in Enniskillen."

Desmond smiled. "Good answer," he said. He pointed at Eunan. "I knew you'd be all right once you settled in."

Desmond looked at Eunan to see if he was ready for his revelation. He decided he was, for he would find out for himself soon enough.

"I am one of the Maguire's key advisors on military and political matters," said Desmond.

Eunan looked somewhat confused. How could this old, fat man with a limp have such knowledge of military matters and other such complicated worldly things? But Desmond could read his reactions like a book.

"I know I may not look it now, but I used to be the head of the MacCabe clan, the main Galloglass family of the Maguires. That is until I got wounded and could no longer fight."

Eunan looked behind at Arthur for reassurance, and Arthur nodded with such enthusiasm that he believed him. Excitement swelled in Eunan's chest as he recognised his opportunity.

"Can you teach me to be a Galloglass?" his mouth asked, and his eyes begged.

"I can train you if you show yourself worthy of my time," said Desmond. "Then you can do with your skills as you wish. Become a Galloglass, remain a chieftain's son, fight for the Maguire, follow your father. All choices."

Eunan only heard Galloglass and ignored the wisdom.

"I would like that. May we start training when we return?"

But Desmond wished to cap this new-found well of enthusiasm.

"Let's see how we get on together on our trip first, shall we?" said Desmond. He rode ahead once more, leaving Eunan to dream of being a Galloglass and riding all over Fermanagh to slay the enemies of the Maguire. Then he would return home in triumph to claim his father's position of chieftain from him.

They made considerable progress on their journey before Desmond wished to converse again and slowed his horse down.

"So why do you want to become a Galloglass?" he said. "Why not become a chieftain like your father, or is being a Galloglass part of the plan to become a chieftain?"

Eunan was not expecting this question and did not have the guile to deflect it.

"I want to get as far away from my father and his village as possible," he said.

"I see," said Desmond. "There are chieftains, and then there are chieftains. You're here because the Maguire considers your father to be disloyal. Too quick to turn his head for the English shilling. Every Maguire has a duty to his clan, to the clan leader and to the Gaelic ways of life. But some clan leaders need to take the boys of wayward chieftains as hostages to remind them where their loyalties should lie, all for the good of the clan, of course!"

The prick of the needle penetrated Eunan's skin.

"I know where my loyalties lie. I want to be part of the Maguire Galloglass and rid these lands of all that are disloyal!"

"How much do you know about the Galloglass?" said Desmond, probing further.

"They are heroic warriors from the isles of Scotland that came to Ireland many centuries ago," said Eunan, his face lighting up at his dreamy tale. "They found themselves in the employment of kings, clan chiefs and chieftains and they fight for them and ensure the freedom of the people."

Desmond roared with laughter.

"I should employ you as my balladeer and get you to write some ditties about my exploits! It won't take long for those illusions to be shattered, boy, given that the north is in an almost perpetual state of war. You'll soon change your mind once you experience actual war. I'm going to Enniskillen because there is a power struggle in the O'Neill clan, and, just as your village is subservient to the Maguire, the Maguire is subservient to the O'Neill. That is, once we are sure which O'Neill it is we are subservient to. Then there is the question of the English garrison in Enniskillen. When these issues seek their resolution in blood, then you will see who the Galloglass are."

"But you led the Galloglass?!" said Eunan.

"So I should know, shouldn't I?" said Desmond. "Anyway, I have no intention of shattering all your illusions in one afternoon. I still want you to do some work and not mope around with an air of despondency. Just watch and learn and receive the education worthy of a chieftain's son."

They arrived at the bridge to Enniskillen town, beyond which lay the castle. Desmond led him through the busy town with its market stalls and bustling crowds and straight to the castle. They passed back through the gate which Eunan had previously followed Arthur through to start his big adventure. The guard came and greeted Desmond by name, impressing Eunan. He was now more sure of himself, for he believed Desmond was who he said he was and was not trying to show off or lie to him about his past. He looked around at the imposing stone walls which protected a large central tower, which was the home of the Maguire. All very impressive to a boy who had seldom travelled beyond the upper lough or the rim of hills around his village.

The courtyard was full of important men dismounting their horses and greeting their clansmen, for there had been a general summoning of the Maguire nobility. Most had brought the hostages they hosted on behalf of the Maguire to show that they were being well looked after, and the Maguire had nothing to fear. Eunan tied the horses in the stables and went to find the boys from his village. They warmly embraced him, even those who he had previously not been friends with. The boys told him they had been well treated and exchanged many tales, but the dynamic had changed. They now looked to him for protection.

They soon found themselves in the fields surrounding the town, wielding weapons, and training with other boys, who had also become reluctant guests of the Maguire. Eunan was delighted since Donal MacCabe himself was giving the lessons and he excelled under Donal's tutelage. Arthur stayed on the periphery of the fields and kept a close eye on Eunan, for he knew his master would summon him once he was needed.

The heady days whizzed by until Eunan had spent a week in Enniskillen, mainly undertaking military training with the other boys and sleeping under the stars. He did not see Desmond even once. But all good things had to end, and Arthur came to fetch him.

"Come now, it is time to go home," said Arthur. He stood on the side of the training field, like an impatient parent wishing to go home.

"But I don't want to go back to my father, anything rather than that," said Eunan. He played the petulant child, retreating further into the field to make himself harder to retrieve.

"Lucky for you that's not the home I meant," said Arthur. "Hurry along now. Desmond is waiting for us in the castle."

Arthur didn't recognise Eunan as he ran towards him sporting such a broad smile.

"Can I continue with my training when we return home?" Eunan said.

"If you have earned yourself enough of the master's time, you can," said Arthur. "Now come on."

They rode to the castle to wait for Desmond, who soon emerged. The ashen-faced master called for his horse and rode ahead of them after the most cursory of pleasantries. Desmond was silent most of the way home, and Arthur told Eunan to hang back. The boy had never seen Desmond look so troubled. In fact, he was so distracted, he even allowed Eunan to sleep in the house.

The next day Eunan was up early and exploring along the lakeside, counting the islands and imagining all the treasures the Maguire could have hidden among them. Some men arrived to wake Desmond and Arthur. Eunan could hear them talking in the distance and realised they were young men from the village. Indeed, they looked only a couple of years older than him. Then he realised why they were there.

"If he's going to train them, then he can train me!" and he rushed over to join the group before Desmond could separate him. Too late!

"Eunan!" said Desmond. "Stand over there. These boys are going to be horse boys, and I need to train them so. It's no role for you. Arthur will give you some jobs to do!"

Desmond waved at him to stand aside. Eunan refused to move and let his wooden sword drop to the ground in order to argue.

"You promised me training, so when is my training to begin?" said Eunan.

"This is no time to debate!" said Desmond. He was determined not to give in to the insolent boy. But Eunan's face got redder and redder as angry words tumbled out of his mouth. Desmond threw his hands in the air in despair, for he knew Eunan would just argue on until he got his own way. It was just not worth fighting about. "Oh, just get in there!" Desmond said.

Eunan's training began, to his delight. He relished every swing of the axe, each parry against his foe, all the swordplay, and every moment of target practice with the bow. He excelled over the other boys, for he seemed to have a natural skill in fighting. He also stood apart from them, for he was a chieftain's son, and they were merely common boys from the local village. But they all felt war was coming, and the army would need every man and boy it could get.

Desmond admired Eunan's aptitude for fighting and because of this, Eunan and Desmond soon became firm friends, and Desmond placed much reliance upon him. They would walk together every evening by the lake shore and Eunan would request stories from Desmond's seemingly endless stock of tales. However, as time wore on, Desmond spent more time in the house with his papers that a steady stream of messengers brought from Enniskillen.

Desmond returned to Enniskillen several more times and left with the escort the Maguire sent him, leaving Eunan and Arthur behind. He told Eunan that he did not want to burden him with the Maguire's problems and that he should enjoy what little remained of his youth. Each time Desmond would return several days later in a black mood and take to sitting by the lake on his own, saying he himself wished to clear his mind of the issues and not talk about them. But Eunan thought Enniskillen was where his destiny lay and was determined to offer his services to Desmond and to make himself known to the Maguire.

## CHAPTER SIX

# FIRE AND SHADOW

Eunan enjoyed living with Desmond and Arthur far more than he did living with his parents. Desmond was nothing like the surly, grumpy goat he first met when Desmond came down to the kitchen after his prize grass. That is not that Desmond did not possess any of the traits he displayed on that first day. He could be lazy, but Eunan could break any resistance to Desmond not wanting to do something or help him by constant badgering until Desmond gave in, which was normally quickly. He was moody, especially in the morning, but Eunan learned to read his face and he copied Arthur when he would either ignore Desmond or counter his unsociable behaviour with some wit. There was that special face, where both the snarl and the horns of Desmond the goat appeared especially pointy, the face and brain in tetchy unison when both Arthur and Eunan would steer well clear until he had at least eaten and even then they would approach with caution. But today would be different.

This morning was disturbed by riders coming from Enniskillen and pounding their fists on the door and demanding to see Desmond. Arthur knew he could not refuse and went to wake his master. Eunan slept near the door so when he was woken by the sound of hooves he hid in the house so he could listen in to the conversations. He could not make out much except that the English, the O'Neills and the O'Donnells were all pressuring the Maguire to do what they wanted them to do. The Maguire seemed to be pressuring Desmond into giving him advice on the right thing to do and who to side with. It had all become substantially more serious since the Maguire had forced the English garrison off his lands. Desmond stumbled to the door and cursed at the men. They told him the Maguire needed a quick decision on the papers they gave him and they would leave some soldiers to protect Desmond as he decided. Desmond took the papers and wished them a pleasant trip back to Enniskillen and then retreated to his room, only appearing for meals.

Eunan was concerned for his friend but followed Arthur's advice to leave him alone.

"We have more pressing issues to be concerned about," he said. He signalled to Eunan to follow him and they both snuck out of the house and to the stables. "We must stop the soldiers from leaving," said Arthur as he selected two horses. "I fear he is in more danger than he lets on. He thinks he is a young champion and can beat anyone with a sword or an axe, but we both know he is a fat old man."

Eunan sniggered as he mounted his horse.

They rode swiftly and soon caught up with the soldiers, who had not broken out of a slow trot. Arthur rode up to the captain.

"Forgive my master, for he is a fool. We would like to take you up on your offer of protection."

The Galloglass constable raised his hand to bring his men to a stop.

"Does your master know you are here?" he said, as he smirked at Arthur.

"You can be the guardian angel he never sees," said Arthur. Eunan nodded in agreement behind him.

"Desmond is a powerful man, despite his humble abode," said the captain. "I wouldn't want to get in trouble for disobeying his orders."

"Would posting a couple of men nearby so they could monitor the house be disobeying his orders? Surely the Maguire would be disappointed if you left nobody to guard his key advisor?"

The constable scowled, as he knew he could not wriggle out of Arthur's trap.

"See that hill over there?" The constable pointed to a hill about half a mile from Desmond's house. "I'll leave three men beneath that hill, and you can fetch or signal to them if you need their help."

"The boy and I are grateful the Maguire employs such a wise constable." Arthur bowed his head.

"Ride back to your master, and I'll check back with you in a week."

Several days passed, and Desmond's mood got no better. His refusal to explain what was wrong proved frustrating to both Eunan and Arthur. They left him alone and sought their own pleasures rather than loitering on the periphery of his misery. Eunan would travel every day to the local village to train with the boys there. He had appointed himself Desmond's bodyguard and had taken one of Desmond's prize axes and hidden it beside his bed.

Then one day, as he was exchanging practice swings with his friends, he noticed strangers enter the village. Such was the distraction of these armed men being offered hospitality by the villagers that he lost his concentration and received a blow to the side of the head for his troubles. His friends gathered around him and brought him to one of their parent's houses where his head was treated with a wet cloth.

As Eunan came to his senses, he remembered the men who had captured his attention. He turned to the woman who nursed his wound.

"Where are the men that came today?" he said.

She smiled down at him.

"Shh now, don't trouble your injured head on them," she said. "We have many a Galloglass wander up from down south looking for employment, forced up by the English, who make their masters abandon them. We give them bread and ale so they won't steal from us and send them on their way. Some want directions to the Maguire, but most head north to the O'Neills or the O'Donnells, whoever is hiring at the time."

"Where did they go?" said Eunan.

"To the O'Donnells," she said. "Now don't you be thinking of following them. You have your work cut out for you looking after your master."

Eunan nodded, and he smiled gratefully at the woman for all her kindness.

"My boy will bring you home," she said. "Now let that be a lesson to you not to get distracted when you have a staff in your hand."

"Yes, ma'am," said Eunan, and he lay back to enjoy being attended to.

They escorted Eunan home that evening and he received a scolding from Arthur for allowing himself to be injured when he had so much more ability than that. He retired to his bed to dream of the woman attending to him and pretending that she was his mother instead of his actual mother. It was no good. He could feel the bad blood pulsing through his veins. The memories of his mother were the volcano that pumped the bad blood around his body, leaving in its wake his black heart. He did not deserve his mother's love for scraping out her womb and leaving her broken, like the Viking raider she always accused him of being. He felt for his axe. A boy with a black heart like him could always find solace in an axe, the way to express to the world the bad blood in him. He drifted slowly to sleep all his bad thoughts and dreams succumbing to his injury and other exhaustion of the day.

He slipped from darkened room to darkened dreams until he heard a noise coming from the front door. His head hurt and in his dazed state, he was unsure if he was awake or in a dream. He picked up his axe and tested its weight in his hand. He hid behind the door.

"Where is he?" came a voice from the kitchens.

"We don't need him," came another voice. "We just need his papers the Maguire sent to him." There followed a confused shuffling of feet and a sudden crash as Desmond's dirty dishes hit the floor.

"I thought you knew where everything was?" said the first voice.

A flaming torch appeared in the room, casting everything in fire and shadow. Eunan sprung from behind the door and propelled his axe downwards with all his strength. He caught a hand. Its owner shrieked. The hand hit the table, and the axe lodged itself in it. The arm fell away spraying blood in every direction. The fire torch hit the ground and illuminated two bearded men in capes.

"Run!" said the uninjured man. The injured man stuffed his bleeding stump in his left armpit in the vain hope of stopping the bleeding. They bundled towards the door as Eunan struggled to free his axe from the table. The room caught fire. First, the table went up and then the various clothes and other combustible materials followed. The flames illuminated Arthur's panicked face.

"Eunan! Eunan! Are you all right?" he said.

Eunan let go of the shaft of the axe.

"I'll live," he said. "Where's Desmond?"

"I'm over here!" Desmond's voice sounded distant and was punctuated by coughs resulting from smoke inhalation. The flames were spreading fast, and the room was almost overwhelmed by smoke and flame. Then Eunan glimpsed Desmond trapped on the other side of the room by the flames, holding up his arms to shield himself. Eunan knew he had to save him, and it was now or never. He gripped the shaft of the axe and pulled it free. Then, taking hold of the table, he flipped it over, creating a bridge over the flames. He knocked the legs off the table with a couple of swift blows and then held out the blade to Desmond.

"Grab on, and I'll drag you across," he said. Desmond instinctively grabbed beneath the blade, and Eunan hauled him over, then bundled him out the door. Desmond screamed, for the bottom of his shirt was on fire. Arthur dosed him with a bucket of water he had fetched to fight the flames. Desmond collapsed to the ground, exhausted. Eunan went to help Arthur put out the fire, but it was too late. By the time the guards the Maguire had sent had arrived, the house was irretrievably ablaze.

## CHAPTER SEVEN

# POKING THE FIRE STOKES THE STORIES

Desmond lay on the ground unconscious, and Arthur knelt beside him and lifted the tattered remains of his tunic. He recoiled at the extent of the burns on Desmond's midriff.

"He needs to be brought to the islands at once," Arthur said. "You," he said to the guard standing nearest to him. "Go to Enniskillen at once and tell the Maguire there has been an attempt on Desmond's life. Bring bodyguards and arrange for Desmond to be brought to the islands to recuperate." Arthur turned his attention to the other guards. "We need to bring him to the village nearby, but I need your vigilance, for Desmond is not safe until more Galloglass arrive." Arthur turned to Eunan. "You know the villagers. Bring a cart to transport Desmond and find out who the local healer is, and make sure they are free to look after Desmond. I will stay here and attend to him." They all nodded acceptance of their instructions, and Eunan and the guard set off on their missions.

Eunan returned several hours later with a cart and several adults from the village who appeared to be trustworthy. They loaded the barely conscious Desmond onto the cart and set off for the village. The woman who had previously nursed Eunan's head injury was also the local healer, so Desmond took up residence in her house.

The next day, Desmond was feeling considerably better and could sit up and receive visitors. He requested to see Eunan alone, and Arthur went to fetch him. Eunan entered the modest house made up of a single room with space for the occupant's two cows and several chickens who made their homes on some hay spread on the floor in one corner. The room smelt of smoke and cow faeces, but Desmond looked content sitting beside the fire. Eunan gazed upon him.

"Desmond, I am so glad you appear well," he said, shaky with relief.

Desmond gave a weak smile. "Looks can deceive," he said. "I could show you my wounds, but Máiréad has done such a fine job of tending me and bandaging me up, it would be a shame to undo her work. The Maguire should employ her to look after his wounded men. She would be a fine addition to his physicians. But before you get overexcited, look at the awkward way I sit in front of the fire. I cannot expose my wounds to the additional heat, for the wound burns again as if it had unfinished business."

Eunan smiled at the memory of the tender care she gave to him. "I am familiar with her work," he said, pointing to the lump on his head. "We are planning to move you to the islands where you can recuperate. I have sent a messenger to the Maguire to send men to protect you."

The visit of his young apprentice heartened Desmond. "Come sit beside me," he said and patted the other end of the bench he was perched upon by the fire. Eunan leapt at the invitation and beamed at Desmond from the other end of the bench.

"I'm glad you can still smile after all we've been through," said Desmond. "The politics of the north seem determined to wrench you from your youth."

"The sooner you consider me a boy no more, the better," said Eunan. He sat up ramrod straight as if to enforce his earnestness.

"No one makes the most of their youth and I fear yours is already gone," said Desmond.

"That was not what I was looking for, but I accept it all the same," said Eunan. "Now, who were those men that tried to kill us the other night? You owe me an explanation for that, at least."

Desmond laughed. "For a man you think of as a grumpy old goat, someone I had to convince you the Maguire held in such esteem, I have so many enemies I could not name their master for fear of a grave error. Let me just say that despite appearances, Fermanagh is the most stable of the northern clans. The O'Neills and the O'Donnells are both fighting succession wars. The various factions in each clan lay claim to the overlordship of Fermanagh. The Maguire is old and has not long to live. Those that think they can succeed the Maguire seek outside help to enhance their bid for the title, including going to the English. Any of them would like to see the Maguire's key advisor dead, for it would destabilise the clan and potentially bring forward the battle for succession."

"And who do you hope will be the new Maguire?"

"I wish long life and happiness to the current one, for there is no candidate that is a patch on him for his wisdom and political cunning. Half the rest would deliver us into the hands of the English and most of what is left would bring us down in the internal wars of the O'Neills or the O'Donnells. But who would I support? For all his hotheadedness and other faults, the Maguire's son Hugh is the most likely to keep the Maguires independent while we wait for a leader to emerge that is equal to Cúchonnacht. You never know, responsibility may mature young Hugh and he could develop into a fine leader, though he would still not be his father."

Eunan's head dropped at father/son comparisons.

"Do not despair, young man," said Desmond, leaning over to stroke Eunan's cheek. "Like it or not, we all get compared to our fathers and we do most of the comparing ourselves. Soon you will be a man, and you can put your youthful insecurities behind you."

Eunan sighed, and Desmond saw that his display of affection had not worked. It was time for a change of tack.

"Do you want to know why I do what I do? And before you get confused, I mean acting as the Maguire's advisor."

Eunan paused and thought better of the answers that immediately came into his head. "Please tell me."

"Now would appear to be as good a time as any," said Desmond. "I once had a son, a lot like you. In fact, I think you'd be of a similar age if he were still here."

"Where is he?" said Eunan, his face a picture of confusion and concern.

"I had a wife as well, bless her. She was such a beauty when she was young. I thought I was the king of the world when she agreed to marry me. I thought our happiness would never end."

Desmond became almost tearful as he stared into the fire.

"She bore me three children. The eldest was my son, and he had two little sisters. Adorable little angels they were."

"You keep saying were," said Eunan with growing concern.

"You think the head of the Galloglass is a powerful man, don't you?"

"Yes."

"Well, I felt totally helpless when they took my family away from me," said Desmond. He stared at the flames and his mind followed the smoke until it dissipated on the ceiling and the remains straddled along until it reached the corners of the room and became an odour. It was Eunan's turn to advance towards him, and Eunan placed his hand gently on Desmond's shoulder.

"What happened?"

"I was head of the MacCabes until barely a year ago, when I could take it no more, the death of my family," said Desmond. "I had given up active service in the field several years earlier. My injuries, though not life threatening, had accumulated to such a degree that I could no longer fight to an adequate standard. It was deemed I posed a threat to my men for if I fell in battle, it could cause them to lose. So I retired to Enniskillen to concentrate on advising the Maguire and training new Galloglass. My retreat from active duty left a vacuum that my underlings were eager to fill. The factionalism in the clan was getting worse and Cúchonnacht, in his wisdom, thought it was better that the

MacCabes reflected the composition of the clan, to act as a catalyst to bring the clan back together rather than become his personal bodyguard.

"This brought in the disparate factions in the clan and many of the old-school MacCabes who had been previously ejected from the Maguire's Galloglass as they had sided with the claim of Connor Roe Maguire from the senior branch of the Maguire clan. This led the once united MacCabes to become fractured along factional lines like the rest of the clan. Violence erupted when Turlough O'Neill came down with his men to enforce his claim over the loyalty of Fermanagh and the raiders struck around the outskirts of Enniskillen. They slew my whole family as I was in Enniskillen castle negotiating with Turlough's men."

Desmond's head bowed, and the ground beneath his eyes bore his tears. He sniffled and wiped his nose.

"I know I was betrayed! I know it but cannot prove it!" His face went red, spittle flew, and he shook until he twisted his burn in such a way that he had to sit and recuperate.

Eunan put his hand on Desmond's shoulder to reassure him.

"If you place your faith in me and give me the skills," said Eunan, "I will get you your revenge."

Desmond looked deep into his eyes, and Eunan did not flinch.

"I believe you, boy," said Desmond. "Arthur will teach you to read and write, and I will teach you the skills to be a warrior. And if you listen, I'll put wisdom in your head. I will bring you to court and you can go places I cannot, for everyone will consider you a foolish boy. We shall find out who killed my family and get my revenge. Then you must return home to your parents and reconcile with your past."

Eunan flinched and tried to pull away.

"The bravest thing you can do, boy," said Desmond, "is to face the fears in your own head. By the time I have finished, you'll be ready. Now go get some sleep for I feel reinvigorated and can feel a new plan coming on. Call in on me as soon as you wake."

Eunan got up and smiled, for he was reinvigorated as well.

# CHAPTER EIGHT

# "DEVILS FLY WITHIN THEM VEINS"

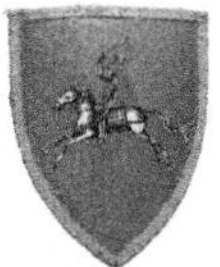

Eunan returned to the house where Desmond was staying as soon as he rose the next day. The Galloglass guards had come from Enniskillen and surrounded the house. After Desmond's story last night, he did not know whether he could trust these men, for he could not tell what faction they supported. He nodded as he tried to pass them by.

"Who are you, boy?" said a Galloglass standing directly in Eunan's way.

"Let the boy in," said Desmond from inside the house. "He is my assistant, and you are preventing him from assisting me."

The guard noted the cheeky grin Eunan gave him as he walked in.

Desmond was in bed with the healer attending to his wounds and Arthur was seated nearby, looking anxious.

"Arthur," said Desmond. "I have appointed Eunan as my assistant in matters of the Maguire court. You are to take it upon yourself to teach the boy to read and write sufficiently so he may be of use to me in his new role."

Eunan beamed, and the incredulity almost fell off Arthur's face.

"How am I supposed to teach the boy matters that take years rather than weeks in something the boy has shown little aptitude for?" said Arthur.

"Just as I have found a way to bear the pain of these burns, you'll find a way to teach the boy," said Desmond. "Just as once I dreaded the moment you would step into the kitchen, now it is the highlight of my day. We'll make him a chieftain in the court of the Maguire yet."

Arthur shook his head and went outside to curse. Eunan went over and sat beside Desmond.

"He'll come round," said Desmond. "He just needs a little time."

He smiled at Eunan, who smiled back.

"It'll be a couple of weeks until I am well," he said. "I will ask the captain of the guards to train you and follow up with Arthur." Desmond leaned over to whisper in Eunan's ear. "Fortify yourself. There are some grim times ahead. Enjoy these couple of weeks."

It was several weeks until Desmond could physically comply with the many summonses the Maguire had sent for him. He wrote to the Maguire, and each time told him he was incapacitated and that he should send him detailed updates and he would advise as best he could based on them. After a week, Desmond could sit up at the table in the healer's house and read the letters sent by the Maguire's secretary. Eunan would attend to him as long as he agreed not to disturb Desmond as he worked. Eunan stayed in the shadows and made sure Desmond's letters were organised, his cup was full, and was on hand to deal with any ad hoc requests. Desmond proved to be quite the awkward and grumpy goat to work for, but once Eunan got used to his habits, he was easy to read.

But as the weeks wore on, Desmond seemed to fall more and more into despair. He refused to discuss why with Eunan, telling him it was not the secretary's place to question the master. In the meantime, Desmond would get up and every day leave the house under escort and walk around the perimeter of the village. Gradually he managed to complete the course without a pained expression on his face, and he got faster and faster. One day, he called Eunan in to see him.

"Prepare my papers and my quill," he said. He turned around from his seat to face Eunan. "It is time I returned to Enniskillen, for the Maguire urgently needs my face-to-face advice."

Eunan frowned.

"Why now?" he said. "If the Maguire has made do with your advice through your correspondence until now, why do you have to return when you are still poorly?"

Desmond's face tensed, and he stroked his chin to use up his agitated energy.

"We had a conversation some weeks ago about a story I seldom tell," said Desmond. "It is in their memories that I not only seek revenge against the perpetrators but also seek the pre-eminence of the Maguire and the end to all of this factionalism."

Desmond reached down to the table and picked up some of his recent letters.

"What they suggest in here may be viewed by some as pragmatism in a weak position, but if Cúchonnacht agrees, then he may well be the last Maguire and my family's death will have been for nothing."

"And if you go to Enniskillen, will it change the Maguire's mind?" asked Eunan.

"Not even I am so arrogant to think that. Let us continue your lessons. Now, this is one of those situations where I need to use my guile. What unites the Maguires, the north, and most of Ireland together?"

Eunan looked up and to the side as if searching for the answer.

"I don't know. Cows?"

"Not a bad guess, but we'd need to round up all the cows in Ulster to assemble enough for the Maguire to bribe his way out of his predicament. The answer is religion, or more precisely, the Catholic church. Therefore, prepare yourself, for we are off to the islands to seek our answer."

They set forth the next day in a small boat with two bodyguards to Devenish Island. Eunan was excited for Devenish Island featured in many a story of a Maguire boy. It was the main sanctuary of the Maguire in Lower Lough Erne, the traditional burial ground for the Maguire and the main monastery of the chain of churches spread all over the islands of the lough. Eunan sat up in the boat's bow so he could get the best view.

The island was rimmed with a thick blanket of reeds which acted as a protective impenetrable perimeter for any boat. Two hills protruded from the island base, one covered in forest and one crowned by a lookout tower constructed by the monks who lived there. The reeds were cut away, and a jetty jutted out into the lake, inviting visitors in. Galloglass stood on the quay to ensure that any visitors seeking to land on the island were friendly. Indeed, they were the friendly ones when Eunan's boat pulled up alongside, for they knew Desmond by name and greeted him warmly.

"I'm here to see the archbishop," said Desmond to the lead Galloglass.

The Galloglass frowned.

"Only you, the rest, stay here," he said.

"Agreed, but please show them your best hospitality," said Desmond.

The Galloglass nodded. "This way."

Eunan idled away for a couple of hours waiting for Desmond, watching the monks at work in the fields of the island or observing the birds in the reeds and on the lake. He felt a little homesick for the first time since he left. Sure, he spent many a night wishing his dog Artair was with him and dreamed of returning to the village with the sole purpose of kidnapping his dog. Those dreams would normally be ruined by his father, the ogre, or his mother screaming at him about his bad blood. But observing the birds made him feel nostalgic for the times he used to hide in his reed fort with Artair and listen to the birdsong.

Eventually, Desmond returned with a monk.

"Come on, we must depart, for we must make it to the island of the Seer." Desmond signalled for everyone to board the boat.

Eunan's mouth slackened at the announcement of the destination. Desmond slapped him on the shoulder.

"Don't look so shocked. The Vikings have been evicted from the island long ago. It just still bears the name. We are going to see a Catholic priest who can physically see evil and lives on the island to battle the spirits of the pagan Viking past. I think he is the key to resolving our problems."

Eunan was not so sure. His bad blood itched in his arm.

They rowed for many hours, for the island was at the far end of the Lower Lough. By the time the monk pointed out the island, the sun was setting, and the Galloglass exerted the last of their energies to get the boat to the shore before darkness fully set in. They had to row around the island before they could find a gap between the reeds which led into a mini cove which was large enough to land upon. The Galloglass helped Desmond off the boat and onto the shore.

"Set up camp and light a fire," said Desmond. "Then see what you can find to eat." Desmond looked at his companions and could not see a cook amongst them. "Oh, Arthur, where are you now? You can work magic with rat, rabbit, or fish."

"Are we going to seek the priest?" said Eunan.

"It is not a large island, so come with me and the monk will show us the way," said Desmond. "I urgently need to be in Enniskillen, so we should be gone by sunrise."

"He lives in a small hut on the other side of the island," said the monk. "The woods may be dense, but the island is small. I will lead the way, for he is blind and will know me by my sound and smell. He does not get many visitors here and seldom leaves the island except to visit Devenish Island on holy days."

Desmond nodded. "We'll follow you, for we don't want to frighten the poor man. He may be more receptive to our proposal if it comes from you."

They lit some fire torches and set off into the woods.

"Be careful with your torch, Eunan," said Desmond. "Much like Ireland, this island is like a tinderbox. There's so much dead wood lying around."

Eunan took heed and held his fire torch straight up in the air.

They came upon an old stone hut whose stones must have been brought to the island, for Eunan had not noticed any exposed rock from where the stone could have been mined. A lone light flickered within the hut.

"Father Aibhistín," called the monk towards the door of the house. "It is Brother Ross from Devenish Island. I have some men with me who need your unique spiritual skills."

Banging and clattering came from the house as Father Aibhistín found his bearings. The door creaked open and a mass of white hair emerged.

"My curse is indeed unique and I pray each night in my selfish torment that it be removed from me in reward for my service to God and placed upon the shoulders of an enemy of both mine and his. Yet, within my soul, it remains, and I have been assigned the task of channelling it to do good. I hope it is in the completion of this task that these men are here to assist me?"

"They serve the Maguire, who protects you and these holy islands. They do God's work. Will you see them?"

Father Aibhistín paused and looked upwards as if receiving instructions from a higher power. He nodded and out from behind the door came a guide stick. He emerged from his hut and Eunan saw his matted white hair and beard and an old monk's habit that was torn and covered in mud. What Eunan could see of his face was a windswept red and his eyes were glowing white balls.

"Do you need me to cut your hair and get you some new clothes, Father Aibhistín?" said the monk.

The priest exploded, and his arms gesticulated in the air as if caught in a storm of evil. The night air was filled with electric energy.

"I have no time for such vanities. I have demons to fight. The devil comes to me every night with such temptations, but every night I cast him back to hell."

The veins in his neck bulged as his face went red as if he truly were holding back the demons at the gates of hell.

Desmond was both taken aback and impressed by this display but hesitated; if he showed him his documents, there was every chance the priest may have a heart attack. But Desmond decided that if this was the daily torment the priest went through, he might be better off dead.

"Father, may I be so rude as to interrupt you?" said Desmond. He paused and waited expectantly.

"Who are these outsiders you have brought to my island?" the priest said to the monk. "I am not a performing dog for their amusement. You know I cannot walk amongst men not dedicated to the faith, for all I see is their evil, and their evil seeps into me."

"You know I would not do this lightly, Father, but there is a grave threat to the islands. The heretics grow stronger by the day and foolish men cast in their lot with them and seek to benefit from our beloved lands falling to them."

The priest pushed his face into that of the monk until the monk could see the liquid coating on the priest's bulbous, white eyes.

"I am merely the instrument of the hand of God. If he so wishes, he will see that I help these men, even though it may cast me into a pit of sin."

The monk stepped back and appeared to shrink into himself.

"Then may they show you their documents?" the monk said.

"Have them laid out so I may see them," the priest said.

Desmond clicked his fingers at Eunan, and Eunan scurried past the priest to pick up a small rickety table which he stood between Desmond and the priest. Desmond then took the documents out of his satchel and placed them on the table. The priest loomed over the table, his long white hair hanging over the sides. His eyes bulged as if the words said something to him that no one else could see.

"He's not really reading that, is he?" said Eunan in a hushed voice.

"Shut up!" said Desmond.

They all waited on tenterhooks for the priest's reaction to the papers. The priest bent his head into his inner elbow and began to vibrate. The vibrations became more and more violent until he exploded in a sea of flailing arms and a rain of spittle.

"Lies! I see the demons dance upon the words as their lies are woven into them. Cast these papers into the fire, for all they bring is despair. Not one word will remain intact on these pages that will not be possessed by the devil and his little demons."

Desmond smiled to himself.

"He's way better than I thought," he said, turning to Eunan. It was only then that he noticed Eunan was rigid as a post and white as a sheet.

Desmond tapped the monk on the shoulder.

"I think we should end the demonstration here and Eunan should collect the papers," he said.

The monk nodded, and Desmond snapped his fingers at Eunan again.

Eunan crept over towards the table, fire torch in hand, so that he would not disturb the priest, who seemed now to be experiencing convulsions that followed on from his vision of evil. Eunan picked up the papers, delicately pinching the corners with two fingers so as not to alert the priest to his presence.

"YOU!" said the priest. He threw an accusatory finger at Eunan and as Eunan followed the finger up the arm, the white eyes strained to get out of their sockets. Eunan flew backwards and fell to the ground and his fire torch hurtled into a dead dry bush, which immediately caught fire.

"Devils fly within them veins," the priest said, his nostrils flaring and his own veins popping from his neck. "I can see them crawl around your face. They climb out of a black hole in your heart and rummage around your brain, causing their mischief and taking hold of your mind. You have bad blood, boy. You have bad blood."

Desmond threw himself between the boy and the priest.

"Why not let the brother take you back into the house for a drink and I'll take care of the boy and the fire?" Desmond said to the priest as he smiled and held out his arms to calm him down.

"The demons have come for me, the demons have come for me," said the priest, as he became more and more agitated. "The boy has come with the demons in his veins and they have brought the fires of hell with him."

The monk came from behind the priest and put his arm around his waist to reassure him and bring him back to his hut. The priest did not see who was behind him and turned and elbowed the monk in the nose. Blood streamed down the monk's face. The priest panicked and tried to run away.

"Get him," Desmond ordered his Galloglass. They ran towards the priest, but the fires had spread fast and they were all encircled. The priest's house caught fire. The priest threw his arms to heaven.

"Have you finally come to take me, Lord?" he cried to the skies. "If you are here to do that, take me now, take me now!"

One of the Galloglass dived for him and knocked him to the ground.

"Show him some respect," hollered Desmond at him. Desmond saw that Eunan was cowering in the bushes and thrust out his hand to pull him out. The flames raged as they climbed the trees, and the little group were now trapped. The smoke was overwhelming, and they all coughed and spluttered. Desmond waved to his men to gather by the shore. The reeds made a thick, almost impenetrable wall between the land and the sea. Desmond called out into the blackness of the night sky on the lake for his men on the other side of the island to come and rescue them. The monk came down to the shore holding his still bleeding nose in his habit. Suddenly, the priest broke free and tried to run back into the forest. The monk went after him. He grabbed the priest by the elbow.

"Come, we need to leave the island before we all get burned alive," he said.

"You brought the demons here!" said the priest. "Leave me be to live in peace."

He shoved the monk and ran down towards the shore. The monk fell backwards, tripped over a branch and fell to the ground. The sleeve of his habit caught fire. He leapt off the ground, screaming. His habit went up quicker than the dead dry trees. He became a pillar of flames running around the small circle that was still spared the flames screaming like a banshee. The Galloglass who were left at the campsite had taken to the lake to find their commander after they heard him call for them. They saw the pillar of fire and immediately rowed towards it. They soon ran into the reeds. Eunan and one of the Galloglass began hacking at the reeds from their side and the men in the boat cut from theirs. The other Galloglass held the priest while Desmond tried to corner the monk and force him to jump into the lake to put out the flames. But the flames quickly overwhelmed the monk, and he fell to his knees, then to the ground, where he ceased to move. Desmond turned away and bit his lip.

The men in the boat created a wedge in the remaining reeds and held the ends of their oars out to help those on the island onto the boat. Eunan found himself at the back of the boat, terrified at having been forced to sit beside the wailing priest. No matter how fast they rowed, the burning island loomed in the distance.

## CHAPTER NINE

# CAGING THE FERRET

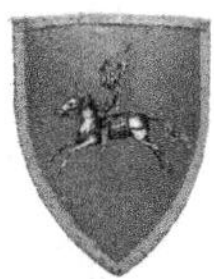

Desmond immediately regretted taking the priest from his island, for he proved to be the most feral of ferrets he could have captured. He almost capsized the boat several times such was his wriggling, shouting and general hysterics. Desmond and Eunan had to take over the rowing, for the two Galloglass had to hold down and subdue the priest. He became so unmanageable that they could not complete the trip to Enniskillen. They stopped off at Devenish Island at the dawn of the next day. They left Eunan to guard the boat as they dragged the priest onto the island and Desmond went in search of a safe house for him. Eunan waited until midday before gaining sight of Desmond again. His belly began to gurgle, for he had been faithful to Desmond and had not abandoned his post to go in search of food.

Desmond walked down the hill with his shoulders hunched, as if he was carrying the weight of the world upon them.

"Get the boat ready," he ordered Eunan, "for we need to set off at once."

Eunan frowned. "Are we going to bring the priest?"

"He is in no fit state to travel," said Desmond. "The holy men of the island will calm him down and my two Galloglass will make sure he does not run away. Things are too urgent in Enniskillen to wait. I will come for him when the time is right."

Eunan nodded and went to prepare the boat.

They pulled up at a quay below the castle. Galloglass patrolled the quays, and several came to greet Desmond and help him out of the boat. But where there was once a welcoming hand extended, there was a suspicious one, and where once there was a warm welcome, there were now only questions. Sighs and slumped shoulders escorted Desmond to the castle gates and his former comrades wished him good luck in the viper pit they were escorting him to. Eunan followed in Desmond's footsteps, not wishing to interrupt the men's conversations and hoping he could overhear. But he could not follow what they were discussing, for the news tumbled out of the men's mouths as fast as they could tell it. What he could discern was that they told Desmond they had a plethora of enemies and the clan was so divided that the only people they would end up fighting would be themselves. Desmond nodded along and listened intently. They reached the gates, and Eunan stood behind Desmond as they waited for them to open.

The gate seemed more intimidating now, as if the apprehension of the men waiting for it to open had given it some kind of evil spirited possession. The gate creaked open, and a well-dressed middle-aged man with a neatly shaped beard, well-maintained hair, a wiry body and otherwise pleasant features stood there with open arms and the most insincere smile Eunan had ever witnessed.

"Welcome back, Desmond," he said. "I thought you had retired to the islands? It seems such a shame that you had to bother yourself to come all the way here."

Desmond walked straight past and did not look the man in the face.

"Hello, Donnacha," he said from the side of his mouth. "You really shouldn't have bothered to come and greet me. I know the way."

Donnacha skipped in front of Desmond so that he could not ignore him.

"On the contrary, I could not miss the opportunity to enlighten the misinformed. The Maguire is old and frail enough without having you add to his confusion."

"I have no intention of confusing the Maguire," said Desmond. "Quite the opposite, in fact. I am here to ensure the Maguire makes an informed choice over the most important decision for the clan in generations. Now get out of my way."

"I am here to help you. I wouldn't want you to make a fool of yourself and anger the Maguire and lose your pension on the islands. But if you don't want my help, then so be it."

Donnacha raised his hands in reluctant acceptance and skipped off ahead and up the tower that was the main body of the castle.

"Who was that?" said Eunan.

"You'll soon see," said Desmond.

They entered the tower and climbed the narrow circular stairs to the great hall. The two Galloglass guarding the door nodded to Desmond.

"The session has not started, Lord," said one. "The Maguire will be down soon to begin the next one."

"How is the Maguire doing?" Desmond said.

The guard shook his head. "He'll be the better for your advice, but I fear his days may be numbered."

Desmond placed his hand on the man's shoulder. "Thank you for your honesty. I hope you'll heed the call if the Maguire needs you?"

"I will, Lord. Even if it leads to both his and my demise."

Desmond nodded his appreciation and went through the door. He trudged reluctantly towards his place at the table of the Maguire. However, the awe of the great hall absorbed Eunan's attention. Huge tapestries adorned the walls, depicting the great myths and battles of the Maguire clan. The battle standards, the flags and emblems of the Maguire and the different septs that comprised the clan Maguire gave the impression of their greatness and long history without even a nod to their status in the real world. The stories and tales of those who inherited their legacy who wanted to impress those that did not, perpetuated the exaltation. Such emblems were bittersweet for the youthful Eunan. The men of his village would gather fireside and tell tales of old times. The exploits of the Maguire. Glorious battles. Saint Colmcille. However, Eunan would be on the periphery, for his father made him look after his mother, and he could only overhear. He longed to show them how worthy he was of their respect, and if he was as successful as the Maguires of old were on their tapestries, he could have his own tapestries and then those who once despised him would tell tapestry tales about him too.

Desmond clicked his fingers at him and he snapped to. The Maguire's servants had brought Desmond some books and paper that Desmond had requested, and it was Eunan's job to organise them. Desmond shook his head at the boy's dreamy admiration for his surroundings. The great hall created no such illusions for Desmond. He had been in many a great hall up and down the land and found nothing great about them. Their size, construction or how they were adorned may or may not have been more impressive than that of the Maguire's, but they were all brought low by the words and deeds of the men who occupied these halls and put themselves forward as being so grand, so wise, so benevolent while being really no such thing. These were the halls for clever words, setting legal traps and concealing one's intentions. Desmond expected a masterclass today.

The room filled with the important men of the Maguire clan. The faces of the men reflected their resigned and sombre mood as they shuffled in and stuck to the walls. Desmond was standing near the door and a mixture of landed gentry and hardened warriors alike embraced Desmond warmly as they entered. Eunan gave a shy smile to all those who acknowledged him as Desmond's servant, and he was proud to be in service to such a well-respected man. The men of the Maguire then spread throughout the room and whispered rumours to each other as they waited for the Maguire. Finally, Cúchonnacht and Hugh Maguire entered the room, and their faces fuelled the flames of an already tense atmosphere. They took the two seats at the head of the table and whispered between themselves whilst their advisors stood behind them and looked at the ground.

Cúchonnacht was old and frail; his long white hair and beard showed his wisdom but his bony hands and sunken eyes betrayed an illness. However, his mind was as sharp as ever. The reverence that surrounded him rivalled that of the tapestries, for just as the colour and stitching of the thread in the tapestries gave form and meaning to the scenes they portrayed, he was the stitching that held the Maguire clan together. The greatest Maguire in living memory kept the Maguires relevant in an ever-turbulent world, no matter who tried to invade and control them. However, there was an underlying apprehension in the air that soon Cúchonnacht and the tapestries would be as one in reflecting the past and the greatness of the Maguires squandered by youth, and the illusion of the tapestries would be broken.

Hugh Maguire was several years older than Eunan, but was being groomed by his father to be his replacement. He was handsome with his ink-black hair and youthful beard. He had obviously honed his physique on the training ground. His restless energy did little to hide his ambition to lead. Kind words said about Hugh Maguire were that he was a warrior, had a considerable level of skill, and showed good aptitude on the battlefield. However, many of the nobles had a different assessment of the aspiring leader. Hugh Maguire lacked his father's diplomatic skills, was arrogant and held the belief that the Maguires could win their way out of the bind they found themselves in if only they could show enough aggression. They thought he spent far too much time on the training ground and far too little with them, the Maguire nobility, learning the art of politics. They thought his recklessness was likely to extinguish the Maguire flame in pursuit of glory, when defeat was the only certainty. The youth of Eunan yearned for glory and recognition and did not want his ambitions doused by frightened old men, so he reserved his judgement no matter what Desmond said.

Cúchonnacht also had a younger son, named after himself, who was around Eunan's age. He was more thoughtful and circumspect than his brother, for they did not expect him to lead. His father was aware of his son Hugh's deficiencies and he had ensured that the two brothers were close and that his youngest son could support his brother. Therefore, Cúchonnacht the younger also occupied the shadows alongside Eunan and learned his court skills by assisting the head of the Maguire court, Donnacha O'Cassidy Maguire.

The various factions previously mentioned by Desmond were not discernible to the inexperienced eyes of Eunan. But everyone noticed the absence of the most obvious dissenter, Connor Roe Maguire. Another sphere of influence gravitated around Edmund Magauran; a senior member of the clergy, friend of the Maguire, and the primary Maguire contact with the Spanish throne from his contacts built during his training in the religious colleges of Spain. He stood in the opposite corner of the room, attended by a secretary.

The Maguire arrived to silence, and beneath the silence, tension grew. Desmond fiddled with his belt to burn off his nervous energy in anticipation of an awkward meeting. Eunan stood at the edge of the room in the shadows, waiting if Desmond needed him.

Cúchonnacht lifted himself out of his seat with straining sinews and an intake of breath. A sea of eager faces looked to him.

"Fellow Maguires, I have nothing but grim news for you, and I don't know where to start. We are under grave threat. But this time it is not the war of the O'Neills, but the English!"

The room went quiet, for Fermanagh had been awash with rumours, and refugees had taken to wandering into its forests, often leading to violence. Many a roaming band of Galloglass had heard of the growing tension and entered Fermanagh to offer their services to find the coffers of the Maguire empty.

"The MacMahons of Monaghan and O'Hanlons of Orior have both been shired. They renounced tanistry for hereditary titles because of the pressures exerted by the Crown."

There were only low-level murmurs in the hall, for most already knew.

"Does the O'Neill know of this?" said one chieftain.

"MacMahon and O'Hanlon owed their allegiance to Hugh O'Neill, and O'Neill has brought his protests to the Irish Council and the English Privy Council. He is demanding compensation and the reinstatement of his traditional rights. However, now the English demand the same from us. They have a treaty of surrender and regrant for us, the price of which is very expensive indeed."

"Let them present us with a treaty," said one of the lesser chieftains. "We'll pay them off and they will be gone and we can carry on as before."

"I'm glad you view the diminishment and impoverishment of the Maguire clan as being nothing. The Crown means to divide up the clans into their rival parties, thereby destroying the clan structure and their strength. Thus, nothing truly does become nothing.

"Hugh O'Neill's fight in the Irish Council and the English Privy Council is like attaching a giant leech to clan Maguire. To get anything done, you need to bribe everyone with cattle and coin, and they do not come cheap. Everything Hugh O'Neill achieves comes at a price to us. We also have to pay Turlough Luineach while he plays the opposite game and tries to win favour with the English as the block to Hugh O'Neill becoming the master of Ulster.

"But the English are more serious about Monaghan than they were last year with us. The MacMahons would not accept a sheriff, so Bagenal, the English lieutenant of Tyrone, invaded and imposed one upon them. That, my fellow Maguires, is the fate that awaits us."

The room was silent.

"Where is Connor Roe? Why is he not here?" said one chieftain.

"I may be old and frail, but I can still hold the Maguires together. My best Galloglass are upon his lands, ensuring his loyalty and guarding the borders against incursions from the MacMahons."

"This indeed is tragic news," said another chieftain.

"Tragic though it may be, it is not the worst of my news."

Desmond bowed his head, for he knew what was coming.

"The English have kidnapped Hugh Roe O'Donnell, the obvious successor for the O'Donnell clan!"

There were audible groans around the hall.

"The O'Donnells are now preparing for another war of succession. The Maguire will stay neutral, as before, while the O'Donnells and the O'Neills fight it out!"

"Have we ever been in such a precarious position?" said one chieftain. "Our allies disintegrate before our eyes, and the English surround us and destroy our brethren one by one.!"

"The Maguires are still here. We still have our lands, and we can fight," said Cúchonnacht. "Therefore, we have been in worse positions. We need to stick together and bide our time."

"Half the O'Donnells have sided with Turlough and half with Hugh O'Neill, all to gain the upper hand." said another.

"Bide our time for what?" sai a third chieftain. "We are going to get swallowed up by someone. We may as well pick a side and join the fight."

"That is only an excellent strategy if you can pick the winner," said Desmond. "Otherwise, we'll just be one casualty on the roadside the winner steps over."

The room broke into factions where most picked one of the O'Neill septs, and others sided with the O'Donnells. They argued furiously while the Maguire sat and caught his breath. The arguing soon got too much for him, and he rose again to rebuke his followers.

"We will remain united, or you will suffer my Galloglass. Now get out, all of you!"

Cúchonnacht collapsed into his chair, the meeting having visibly drained him.

The MacCabe Galloglass moved in and cleared the room. Desmond lingered in the shadows until it was safe to approach Cúchonnacht.

"I fear the worst. I feel we may perish soon," said Desmond.

"Indeed, destiny will have us die, but the Maguire must live on through my son Hugh," said Cúchonnacht. "A little rash and quick-tempered he may be, but he is an outstanding warrior and can lead. If Connor Roe becomes the Maguire, then we are doomed."

"If we are to be doomed, would it not be better to surrender now and spare the lives of our people?" said Desmond.

"There is some hope. The Pope has made Edmund Magauran, a good friend of the Maguires, archbishop of Armagh," replied Cúchonnacht. "That gives us better standing with the King of Spain, a man of the true faith. Edmund can persuade him of the righteousness of our cause, and the King will send aid."

"I hope you are right, Lord," said Desmond. "I hope you are right! But we need to unite the clan in the same direction if we are to fight. Let us discuss the surrender and regrant bill tomorrow in the court and bring the actual document they are asking you to sign. Send word to everyone who attended today to return. I will unite them all against the agreement and then the Maguires will stand together again."

"I hope you are correct," said Cúchonnacht. "I will pray this evening that everyone else accepts your wise council."

Desmond bowed and clicked his fingers at Eunan to follow him as he hurried towards the exit. He expected some difficulties in getting the priest to Enniskillen Castle.

## CHAPTER TEN

# READING, WRITING AND THE DEVILS THAT DANCE ABOVE THEM

Desmond hurried to the great hall early the next day, barking orders at all that would take them. Eunan looked slightly fresher, but that was because his youth had a better capacity to absorb such stresses and he recovered quicker. The guest they brought had proved so troublesome they have to put him in the cells beneath the castle so his shouting and cursing could be passed off as that of an insane prisoner. They had had little sleep, for they had to resort to kidnapping in order to get the priest safely into the castle before the light of day. Desmond hoped all he had been told about the priest would be true and that when the time came for him to go to the great hall, he would prove to be too distracted by the proposed treaty to tell the Maguire how Desmond had treated him.

Eunan laid out the books and papers the way he thought Desmond liked them, but the grumpy goat seemed exceptionally agitated today as he changed the order of the books or opened one and closed another with seemingly the sole purpose of showing Eunan he was wrong. The room filled and there were fewer warm greetings for Desmond than the day before, for the new factional divisions had been given time to stew and ferment. A fissure appeared within the room as it split down the middle between those who supported the O'Neills and those who supported the O'Donnells. There were varying levels of loyalty and loathing for the English, ranging from those who wanted the surrender and regrant deal and saw it as progress, to those who wanted to tear down the tapestries, fly them as a flag and die on the last square foot of land the Maguires could declare their own. Desmond would have naturally gravitated towards the O'Donnells, but with the kidnapping of Red Hugh O'Donnell and the senility of his father, he knew their troubles were just beginning. He saw Donnacha had been whispering in the ears of those who leaned towards the O'Neill and also Connor Roe Maguire, the most eligible male from the senior branch who appeared rarely in Enniskillen. He was also using Cúchonnacht Óg to whisper in the ear of his brother, Hugh.

The Maguire entered and sat with his son Hugh at the top table. Donnacha approached them and leaned in to whisper to them. The Maguire stood and cleared his throat to get everyone's attention.

"I have called you here today for a very serious matter, that of the English offer of a treaty of surrender and regrant where I am supposed to give up my title of 'the Maguire'. While I am loath to do this, I feel I must make my clansmen aware of the offer and the potential road ahead."

The door opened and several MacCabe Galloglass entered the room. Their constable went and whispered in the Maguire's ear. The Maguire's face went ashen. He summoned both Desmond and Donnacha to come and speak with him. They bent down so he could whisper in their ears.

"Eoghan McToole O'Gallagher has arrived," said the Maguire. "He claims that Inion Dubh sent him on behalf of Turlough O'Neill. O'Gallagher has turned up with a contingent of mercenaries. He says that he will not interfere with what decision we make regarding surrender and regrant, but that he will assert Turlough O'Neill's rights."

Donnacha bit his lip.

"So how do you want to proceed, Lord?" he asked. "I am in the middle of negotiations with Hugh O'Neill, but if they learn of these discussions, they may not be best pleased."

Desmond leaned forward. "Leave it to me, Lord," he said. "My plan will both unite the Maguires and rid us of surrender and regrant. Once the Maguires are united, the O'Neills and O'Donnells will come to offer us treaties and not look at us as a source of tribute."

Donnacha shook his head and smiled.

"The floor is yours, old man," he said. "My negotiations with Hugh O'Neill will take time, so if you can delay this sufficiently to buy me some time, I'll take my hat off to you."

Desmond scowled at Donnacha, but looked to the Maguire for approval. The Maguire raised his bony hand in agreement. "I think we have nothing to lose. As long as O'Gallagher keeps his mercenaries on a leash, there'll be no bloodshed this day."

Desmond nodded and went back to his papers and Donnacha returned to his. Desmond saw a window nearby that looked out onto the courtyard. When the Maguire spoke, he edged towards the window to see O'Gallagher and his men arguing with the MacCabes guarding the tower door. It was getting heated, and Desmond considered alerting the Maguire to the fracas outside. However, among the mercenaries, he saw a face from the past. Desmond squinted to make sure it was who he thought he saw. But he would recognise that face anywhere. It was Seamus MacSheehy, the notorious Galloglass mercenary.

"I haven't seen you since the Netherlands," Desmond said to himself. But Eunan came and nudged him because the Maguire was looking at his back.

"May I continue?" said the Maguire.

"Sorry, Lord," and the crimson-cheeked Desmond bowed in apology.

"Now, as I was saying," said the Maguire, "we must discuss the terms we are presented with for surrender and regrant."

Desmond grabbed Eunan by the shoulder. "Fetch the priest," he said. "We need him up here now."

Eunan froze. "But he is like a wild animal. How am I to get him up here by myself?"

Desmond looked around and behind him were two MacCabe Galloglass. Desmond clicked his fingers at them and pointed to Eunan. "They'll help you," said Desmond. "Now hurry."

Eunan struggled to force the priest up the stairs as he was swearing hellfire and damnation at all who pushed him or passively passed him by. The priest's shouts certainly gained the attention of O'Gallagher, who he passed as the MacCabes barred the entry of the O'Donnell's men.

"What are you doing to that priest?" O'Gallagher shouted up the stairs after Eunan. "Unhand that priest or by the hand of God, we'll assault this door to free him."

"The priest is here to assist the Maguire," Eunan shouted back, for he did not want to be involved in a melee at the door, especially on account of this priest. "He is blighted by visions. We are helping him."

With one almighty shove, Eunan got him past the bend in the stairs and out of sight of O'Gallagher and his men, who continued their arguments at the door. Eunan got the priest to the door of the great hall and realised that timing was everything with the priest's entrance. If he had been uncontrollable on the stair, he dreaded to think what he would be like in a room crowded with the nobility of the Maguire.

"Hide him in the stairwell whilst I listen in to the conversation," Eunan told his MacCabe assistants. He nodded to the guards at the door, who recognised him and let him pass. Eunan put his ear to the door but could not make out what was being said because of the bulk of the door. He nodded once more to the guards and held the door ajar so he could listen. He saw Desmond was addressing the room, so he pushed his way forward through the crowd to make himself known to Desmond. Desmond looked down and signalled to him but carried on talking. Eunan went out to fetch the priest.

"We are given this treaty to sign," said Desmond, his face and words aflame, "that will mean the end of the Maguire and all the Maguires stand for. This treaty robs us of our titles, our wealth, and our heritage. You say that we cannot stand up to the Crown, but by the grace of God I say we can. I have been to the islands, and I have brought back Father Aibhistín, who has been given special visions by God that can see in what spirit a document has been written and what its future effect could be. For those who are sceptical, I shall place the treaty here in front of the Maguire and I now call upon Father Aibhistín to give us his verdict."

Desmond signalled to the doorway for the guards to let Eunan and the priest in. The door creaked open on a vision of Eunan in mid-wrestle with the priest as he struggled to get him to face the door. The priest pushed Eunan to the ground before he detected he had an audience. The priest froze and strained his white bulbous eyes to absorb any light they could. But all he saw was smoke, a red clouded roof and streaks of lightning. The thunder reverberated around his head.

"What pit of hell have you brought me to, boy?" he hissed at Eunan. "I can see those demons trying to rip through your veins, for they have conquered your heart and destroyed my island."

The priest could not see, but every neck in the room craned to see the priest in the doorway. Father Aibhistín straightened up.

"Whoever has summoned me," he said, "it is now time for me to face you. Boy, since you brought me here, it is now time to complete your devil's work. I cast my soul into the dark abyss and pray for God's protection."

Eunan cowered on the floor and eyed the stairs to see if he could make his escape. His father's beatings and his mother's abuse never seemed so tender. Desmond made his way to the front of the crowd, scowled at the crouched Eunan, and signalled to him to take the priest's arm and lead him into the hall. Eunan tried to crawl away, but the Galloglass at the top of the stairs responded to Desmond's signalling and blocked the way. He turned to see a wall of eyes pressing upon him. He reluctantly took the priest's arm.

"Your demons try to poke through your arms and possess my soul. But they will never succeed," he hissed.

Eunan shook in every limb but tried to steady himself.

"The Maguire needs your help," he whispered. "Help him help the priests on the islands, if nothing else."

"I care nothing for the kingdoms of men, for as men grow with power, their soul rots from within. Only the coming of the Lord is what mere mortals should concern themselves with."

"Step this way, Father," Eunan invited him. "Take my arm and help to rid the world of a little of its evil."

The priest stared down at the boy, his bulbous eyes almost popping out of his face.

"Only if you promise me, boy, that you will go to the islands to be healed of your bad blood?" he said.

Eunan saw something out of the corner of his eye. It was Desmond nodding so vigorously, Eunan thought his head might fall off.

"I will, Father," promised Eunan. "Now follow my lead."

Eunan stepped forward but was pulled back by the priest's refusal to move. "Come on now, Father," said Eunan. "Remember my promise?"

The priest took a step forward and the wall of prying eyes in the doorway parted until the way was clear to the table of the Maguire. Desmond darted in front of them and placed the pages of the surrender and regrant treaty on the table in front of the Maguire and gestured to Eunan to lead the priest to it. Desmond stepped back to the front of the onlookers. Eunan led the priest forward one step at a time. The cleric's head lolled from side to side as if he was trapped in some demonic vision and not passing through the lines of Maguire nobility who had been transformed at the sight of the priest into so many confused, frightened boys.

Desmond stepped forward and lifted the treaty off the table to show the priest.

"Father, please use your blessings from God to review this treaty we have been offered and give us your opinion."

Desmond bowed and reversed so he would not get in the way and interfere with the priest's visions. Eunan led the priest by the arm until he hovered over the treaty. Catching sight of those bulbous eyes, both Cúchonnacht and his son scraped their chairs back on the floor so they could be out of range of the priest. Eunan tapped the treaty with his finger to get the priest's focus and attention. The priest looked downwards. The men in the room held their collective breaths. The priest looked down, and he was drawn into the document. He rested his hands on either side of the document and his eyes strained as he absorbed his visions. He reeled backwards and hid his head in the crease of his elbow. Desmond crept forward from the front of the crowd.

"Do you want me to read it to you?" Desmond asked. But the priest did not hear him. He was caught amidst his swirling visions.

"Devils dance above them words," the priest exclaimed, "no matter if you read or write them. These treaties are so full of lies, devils lie between the lines. Whoever would sign this would surely be the last Maguire."

Desmond bounded to the centre of the room vacated by the priest and threw his hands in the air to capture everyone's attention.

"See what the priest says?" Desmond said. "The priest has spoken. His vision from God has told him whoever signs this is the last Maguire. Who here can vote for their own demise?"

Desmond's face and outstretched arms called on anyone out there who had the nerve to rebut him to come forward. He stared down all eyes that looked at him except one pair.

"I could go to the islands and get any priest to agree with anything I wanted them to," said Donnacha, who pointed towards Lower Lough Erne. "Listening to this priest will not bring forward the death of the last Maguire. It will bring forward our occupation and assimilation by the English. This treaty is the chance to cement down the successions for your family and to leave behind a life of constant feuds and raiding. But this priest will unknowingly place the yoke upon your shoulders." Donnacha's accusing finger had set itself firmly on the priest.

The priest turned, loomed over Donnacha, grabbed his face, and stared straight into his eyes. "The devil dances upon your tongue and does his jig upon your words. He lives inside your head, nestled amongst all the lies."

Donnacha shook him off but reeled as if the priest's insight had wrenched out his very soul. He melted back into the crowd.

"We cannot sign such a treaty if a man of God says it is a pack of lies," said one of the Maguire chieftains in the front row of the crowd. Desmond's eyes lit up, for his plan was working.

"See," and he stood out in front of everyone and pointed to the man. "He is right. How can we go against the word of God?"

Pandemonium broke out in the hall as the crowd dissolved into passionate factions arguing amongst themselves.

In amongst all the chaos, Desmond sought Eunan to return the priest to the cells as his mission had been completed. But through the swirling chaos of his mind's eye, the priest could pick out the bad blood crawling through Eunan's veins and the trail of pimples the demons would leave through Eunan's arms, and he was not afraid to call it out.

"The demon boy comes for me. Are your devils boiling with fury because I exposed them to the world?"

Desmond came from behind the priest and shoved him towards the door. The priest lost his balance and fell to the ground.

Hugh Maguire sprang from his seat, his eyes ablaze with youthful zeal. "The holy father has spoken. Let us cast this treaty into the fire and free ourselves from the oppressors that wish to enslave us." He raised his axe in the air, his blood vessels bulging in his neck. "For the Maguire."

His father's head dropped into his hands as his son led the youth of the room to confront the O'Donnells at the foot of the tower. Desmond bundled the priest into a room to hide out until it was safe to smuggle him back to the dungeon below.

# CHAPTER ELEVEN

# THE BOUNDARIES OF VISION

The Maguires sat in silence with their advisors around the table in their great hall debating whether they should see sense and surrender. Guards stood at the doors and around the walls as Turlough O'Neill's men and their O'Donnell allies sat outside the castle. Cúchonnacht appeared frailer now, but Desmond still sat beside him even though his fall in standing within the clan had been Icarus-like and he had yet to hit the ground. But Cúchonnacht still turned to him to ask him for advice, if not because his recent advice was poor, but because Desmond had always served him well through thick and thin.

"Where is your priest?" Cúchonnacht said. His voice had become but a timid whisper.

"He became the priest of the clan when your son declared him the spiritual advisor for it. Therefore, he is no longer mine," Desmond said. His stomach rumbled, for little could dissuade his appetite, not even the next round of criticism, even though it was much justified. With the enemy at the gates, all Desmond felt he had to lose was his hunger pangs.

Hugh's face contorted, and he picked up the knife before him that was supposed to be a dinner utensil and waved it in Desmond's direction.

"Are you criticising the future Maguire and the spiritual leader of his people?"

Desmond looked to the ceiling, for there was the only place he could find reason, as the world had tipped into madness.

"I wouldn't dream of it, lord. But you had better remind our besiegers outside how useful you could be to them if you are to avoid the rope."

Cúchonnacht placed his hand on his son's arm, and Hugh sat down.

"Is the priest coming to join us?" Cúchonnacht said.

Desmond turned to the door and clicked his fingers. "Eunan, fetch the priest and make sure he is presentable as he is here to eat." He then turned to the Maguire.

"He will be here soon, lord. Let us hope his predictions are a little more sanguine as we sit down to enjoy our meal."

Donnacha sat at the end of the table and fidgeted, crossing and recrossing his legs as he waited for his opportunity to speak. Finally, he could wait no more. He rose and pressed his hands onto the table.

"Lord, I have some plans I have been hatching in order to free the clan of its present predicament. May we please discuss them in private, preferably not in the presence of the priest?"

The long absent smirk returned to Desmond's face.

"Even if you sell us out to the English, they'd have to get past Turlough's men, never mind the priest, to get to us. We'd all be long dead before you could pocket your thirty pieces of silver."

Donnacha glared at Desmond.

"At least we'd be out from under the yoke of the ravings of a madman."

The fury possessed Hugh Maguire once more, and he rose again to threaten with his dinner knife. "The priest comes to us with the visions of God and encourages us to fight. Is your plan to turn lions into lambs?"

Donnacha stood erect and drew a breath. "It is so that we have lands to roam in that I concern myself," he said, "no matter what animal in your analogy you chose."

Hugh sat down slowly with a sneer. "Words are important. You've got to pick the right animal."

Desmond turned his head towards the stairs. "Speaking of animals, I have little control over the priest, but it is better that we distract him with some food rather than he come in and face an empty table and his imagination run wild. May I suggest we serve dinner first, Lord, so he may sit down and join us?"

It was the Maguire's turn to click his fingers for his servants to ready the meal.

Eunan crept into the corridor of the dungeon below to seek the priest. They had offered the priest his choice of lodgings in the castle but he stayed in the dungeon, for that is where he felt safest from the demons, and to a certain extent the thick damp walls protected him from his visions. Eunan nodded to the guards at the door, who looked at each other in a silent signal. They felt sorry for Eunan for having to go through this again. Eunan could hear the mumbling of the rosary from the other side of the door. He pushed the door as quietly as he could, but nothing got past the priest.

"So they sent the devil boy to fetch me," he said without moving from the spot where he knelt in prayer. "First, you burn down my island, then you make me into a soothsaying toy for an earthly king eager to postpone his demise. I don't need a vision to see that one day you will bring me to my death. Is it today, perhaps?"

Eunan stood there shaking, and fought back the tears. Nothing on this earth he had met so far had terrified him as much as the priest.

"Why do you torment me so?" Eunan said. "I am just obeying my instructions."

The priest lifted himself up off his knees. "Ah, the excuse for many a heinous crime throughout the ages." The priest turned to the boy. "It is the bad blood in your veins that drives you here. Before you lead me to my death, promise me you'll go to the islands and seek a cure?"

Eunan's chin quivered as he spoke. "I will seek a cure, Father, but I am here to bring you to eat with the Maguire himself."

The priest gave a deep, throaty laugh.

"The master wishes to tug on the chain of his caged monkey, hoping for some tricks. Nothing can stop a minnow from getting eaten when the big fish takes over the pond. He should console himself in the lies of his stories about how great his ancestors were when they were no more bound in servitude than he was. He can revel in how great his civilisation is, based as it is on a continual fight to be the top beast and stealing your neighbours' cattle. This is what your Galloglass glory really is, what all his tapestries mean. Soon his house of lies will burn with him and his sons in it."

Eunan turned towards the door.

"If you are going to be this disagreeable, I may as well make an excuse for you and suffer the consequence."

"You will not suffer on my behalf, but on your own. If the master wants his monkey so he can pull his chain and wait for the tricks, then he should be careful what he wishes for. Lead the way, boy, and don't look back."

The priest walked willingly into the room, much to the relief of everyone sat waiting for him. There were no histrionics or visions and Eunan ran ahead of him to pull his seat out for him with the energy of hoping he could run back to the stairwell without being subject to the priest's taunts. The priest sat and stared ahead as if his visions were mild and not unpleasant.

"I trust you are getting along well in your cell?" Cúchonnacht said. "Is there anything you need to make your stay more comfortable?"

"And through that comfort lies the path for the devil. You don't realise what I did for you out on that island, keeping the devil at bay. If my knees did not hurt as I knelt to pray, the devil would have had you long ago."

Cúchonnacht hesitated and looked at those seated around him. Most looked away, for they were at a loss as to what advice to give. The priest stared at him.

"I thank you for your efforts," said Cúchonnacht, who nodded his head to the priest. "Both for those efforts we can see in the material world and those we can't in the spiritual."

The priest continued to stare.

"You have possession of wise words and the skill to weave them in a pattern to persuade men to do your will," said the priest. "All this will die with you. You'll not be the last Maguire, but the last the people will look up to."

Hugh Maguire leapt from his seat. "You talk in riddles, priest. There is no point in passing off wisdom if no one understands what you say."

"Sit down, boy," said Cúchonnacht. "The priest is a guest in our house, even if you find some of his words disagreeable." He looked over and he could see his son turn another shade of red. "Let us sit and eat together and see if we can find a solution to the world's woes as we break bread."

Desmond saw the bait cast into the water and the priest was about to make his bite. He thrust his hand into his pocket and picked out a coin and flicked it in the air. The priest recoiled at the sight of the coin, and Desmond picked it up from where it landed with a satisfied smile. The priest could be controlled, after all. The table was silent as they waited for their food whilst the priest lolled around in his chair, trapped in some personal vision. In the meantime, Donnacha called one of his assistants and handed him a piece of paper.

The meals the Maguire's servants brought in were modest by their usual standard. Their brief siege had deprived them of venison and reduced them to eating pig. The pig's heads were placed in the centre of the table, and they were accompanied by assorted meat pies. The servants presented the priest with a much simpler meal of rabbit, some vegetables, a hunk of bread, and some berries. The serving boy placed the plate in front of the priest and Desmond signalled to him to get out of range in case the priest took a dislike to it. The priest lowered his head to contemplate what they had placed in front of him. Desmond leaned over and smiled.

"It's all as plain as you'd get on your island," he said. "Nothing to distract you from fighting devils or paying attention to the Lord."

The priest followed the voice. "I sustain myself to carry out the Lord's work and to fight against purveyors of lies, like you."

Desmond withdrew to his seat, for this was as well as he could have expected the priest to behave given he was in company and company that practised politics. "Well," said Desmond. "I hope you enjoy your meal, anyway."

The others at the table sliced up the pies and chewed on their bread. The priest looked a little lost as his head lolled from side to side. "Here, Father." Eunan came up from behind and placed the knife and fork in the priest's hands. "Eat the food the Lord has provided."

"I will only thank the heavenly Lord, for it is through his goodness the earth provides."

Eunan smiled. "You thank whoever you wish, as long as you enjoy your meal." Eunan placed his hands on top of the priest's and guided him towards the plate. Once the priest could navigate where his food was, Eunan withdrew.

The priest cut some of the rabbit and took some vegetables and placed them in his mouth and chewed. Everyone felt a sense of relief and talked more freely amongst themselves. The priest made gagging sounds and everyone ignored him, for they all thought it was the inevitable vision for the rabbit proving too decadent in either the sauce where it lay in its deceased state or over burrowing when it was alive. The priest grabbed for his neck whilst his hands and face went pale and no one moved. They all stared, waiting for the priest to jump up and accuse them of being agents of the devil. The priest fell off his stool, grabbing his neck and slapped the ground to help him breathe. Eunan rushed over. "I think this is real." He knelt down beside the priest as he writhed, gasping for air. A white foam dribbled down the side of his mouth. The slapping ceased, his jaw loosened, his face went red. He did not move. Desmond knelt down beside him, and he touched the priest's hand and face, checking for signs of life. Everyone by now made a circle and stared down at the priest.

"I think he's dead," said Desmond as he looked around to see everyone's face in a frozen sweep of denial. Everyone, that was, except Donnacha, who remained seated at the table finishing his food. Now everyone looked accusingly at Donnacha.

"He can't have been that holy," he said as he threw down his napkin, "if he couldn't see the poison. Surely that is evil? A little devil would love to do a jig upon that."

Donnacha stood up from his seat and walked over to the Maguire. "Now Desmond's political parody is over, may I suggest, lord, that we discuss serious business?"

The Maguire rose and fell back into his seat, his lower jaw yet to be united with his upper since the priest had died.

"Lord, my sources tell me the English have crossed the border commanded by the Lord Deputy himself and they mean to force you to sign the surrender and regrant treaty if you will not do so willingly. May I suggest that we firstly let Turlough O'Neill's men in and let the sight of the English drive them away rather than anything we have done to upset them? Then you should sign the English treaty, for I fear that if you don't, they will make an example out of you for the other northern lords. But fear not, lord, the plan I present to you is not one of submission but one to buy you time. I have sounded out Hugh O'Neill, and he will allow his daughter to marry your son. Once we have worked our way through our immediate problems, there is light ahead."

Desmond rose from beside the priest, his face alight, his veins bulging.

"He was a good man, that priest, and you murdered him." Desmond's accusatory finger poked into Donnacha's chest. Donnacha looked unmoved.

"Oh really? Was it my plan to manipulate the man and his fire and brimstone speeches and use him for your own gain until you found you could not control him? Was it an extension of your plot to blame his death upon me? Was it not you who everyone witnessed select his food and your servant boy who made him eat? It is not my place to say, it is up to the judgement of the Maguire to untangle this knot. But step aside, for your plan is a clear failure, and it is up to the Maguire's trusted advisors to clean up your mess."

The Maguire nodded to Donnacha. “Make good on your plan and leave me here with Desmond.”

Desmond looked at the face of the Maguire and saw him shake his head. He knew he was finished.

# CHAPTER TWELVE

# A SMILE, A TOAST, A SALUTE

Eunan's eyes were like saucers. He was a poor country boy who seldom saw over the small hills surrounding his village or further than the lake that lapped upon the village shore. Now he found himself in Enniskillen a couple of steps behind his master Desmond at the most prestigious wedding the Maguires had thrown in at least a decade. Desmond was quieter with his eyes towards the ground, his head buzzing as all the latest politics and the permutations ricocheted around inside it.

The Maguire had spared no expense in arranging the most lavish wedding he could for his son to the daughter of Hugh O'Neill. He may have lost half his cattle herd as payment in the surrender and regrant settlement and been in dispute about the full payment since two hundred of the seven hundred cattle agreed upon went missing, but he saw this wedding as the best way to escape his woes. No more could he settle for trying to play the O'Neills, the O'Donnells, and the English against each other. He had to pick a side and Hugh O'Neill appeared to be the rising power. As for Desmond, his failure with the priest and the subsequent signing of the treaty of surrender and regrant hung heavy on his shoulders. He trembled at the thought that in the past couple of years his reward for years of faithful service was to lose both his family and his status. But Donnacha had arranged this marriage, and he was the principal advisor now.

Eunan and Desmond walked through the carnival that had assembled to celebrate the wedding as the Maguire had announced his son's marriage far and wide. They picked their way through the various carts and tents of the entertainers, poets and bards that had flocked from all over the north to congregate in Enniskillen. The carts created a temporary small town beside Enniskillen itself, and anyone who wished to enter the castle had to pass through it.

"Hurry, Eunan. Come on," Desmond said as he shuffled through the crowd. The boy was stopping at every stall, staring at every performer and conversing with every tradesperson that wished him to stick his hand in his pocket, though they would end up disappointed for all there was at the bottom of Eunan's pockets were his own fingers protruding through the holes.

Desmond caught sight of the gates of the castle.

"Come on, boy, we are nearly—." He looked behind him, but the boy was gone.

Eunan had been dawdling behind Desmond, looking at a particular stall that had caught his eye. A voice came from behind a cartwheel. "I know your mother."

Eunan looked around to locate the voice, partly to assure himself it was not in his head. A chaffed and dirty index finger came from behind the wheel and enticed him to follow it. Eunan turned to see where Desmond was, but could only see his back disappearing into the crowd. A gang of hands reached out from behind the wheel and dragged him in.

Eunan tumbled to the ground and saw he was surrounded by agitated men with their faces hidden under hoods.

"Is this him?" said the owner of the dirty index finger. The man emitted a peculiar growl and Eunan could not work out whether it was supposed to intimidate him, or his companions, or to cover up the man's own nerves. An old woman emerged from behind another wheel in a tattered monk's habit, her white hair flowing wildly behind her, and with rosary beads wrapped so tightly around her hands her knuckles were white. She bent over Eunan as the men held him down.

"I can see the bad blood in his veins. He is clearly marked."

"That'll be the mother then," said Index Finger, determined to attribute blame. "This is for my old master," and he threw the first in what became an avalanche of fists and kicks.

Desmond bit into his leg of lamb. Sure, they cooked it well with the meat falling off the bone. He washed it down with the finest imported wine from Spain, a gift from whoever was the dominant O'Donnell. He stared over at Donnacha at the top table with the Maguire, the groom, the great Hugh O'Neill himself, and various dignitaries from the various factions of the O'Donnells. O'Neill had taken up residence in Enniskillen at the invitation of Cúchonnacht. O'Neill was keen to cement the new alliance with the Maguires, and the local lords came and paid homage and pledged allegiance. Every time he greeted someone new, Donnacha was skulking in the background. If circumstances had been different, it could have been him.

He received a hefty slap on the back. He looked up and saw it was the grinning face of some new Galloglass recruited from Lisnaskea. "Where's your priest friend?" he said. His voice was full of the melody of laughter. "I heard he's not coming because he didn't survive the last feast you brought him to?"

Desmond sprang from his chair and went for his dagger. The Galloglass only laughed again. "Easy there, old man. I don't want you to get a heart attack or anything like that."

Desmond pointed his dagger. "Don't you insult an advisor to the Maguire like that or I'll have you thrown out of the MacCabes so quick you won't know what hit you!"

"Sit down, ghost of Galloglass past!" said the man. "It must be handy having the Maguire for a friend to get you off being in front of the Brehon for murder."

"Take that back or I'll stick this in your chest." Desmond waved his knife, but it was hard to tell if he was red-faced due to anger or his exertions. Someone took his arm.

"Easy there, Seamus." It was Donnacha. "We all know what happened, but the Maguire's absolution won't convince everyone. I'll get the constables to have a word with the boys, and they'll leave you alone."

"But they did not absolve me!" However, the noise in the hall drowned out his protests as the Galloglass, still laughing, returned to his seat. Desmond sat down again too, but he had lost his appetite.

Someone slapped him on the arm.

"Desmond?" said one of the MacCabe guards.

"What?" Desmond grunted, for he did not want his melancholy disturbed.

"There's some kid at the gate who claims he's your servant. He looks pretty roughed up so we didn't let him in."

Desmond threw his leg of lamb into his bowl. He rose after being deprived of his only source of enjoyment.

"My boy did indeed go missing, but I would be surprised if he was in the state you claim, for he can handle himself."

"This way," said the guard. "You can identify him yourself."

Desmond walked out to the gate through the drunken revellers and the bards who entertained them. Then he set eyes upon Eunan.

"Hells bells, I would not have recognised you if the guard hadn't told me it was you."

Eunan curled the side of his lip, for he knew he was in a state. He could only see his torn shirt and bruises on his body and arms but he felt the black eye and lump on his head.

"I'm still owed a couple of favours around here," said Desmond. "So I'll get you a change of clothes, and in the meantime, you can invent a story where the other fella got it a lot worse than you."

Eunan bit his lip and yelped when it reminded him where it was split.

Desmond and Eunan were back in the hall within the hour, once Eunan had been sufficiently patched up to be seen in respectable company.

They found the main meal was still in full swing, so they sat at a table to the side of the great hall.

"Sit and eat," Desmond said. "You may not get as good a meal for a while yet."

Eunan wondered at such a morose statement and if Desmond knew something he did not. Still, the lavish feast soon captured his attention and filled his belly.

Eunan knew few people at the feast for the hall was full of dignitaries and invited guests, but those he knew were from the Maguire family's inner circle. Even Connor Roe was in attendance, apparently at the insistence of O'Neill, who said there was enough division in the north already and he wished to be allied with a united clan. Those from the clan who were less important enjoyed the feast sitting at tables in the courtyard. But as Eunan ate, Desmond seemed to have lost his appetite and was staring across the room. He cracked his knuckles, a habit Eunan had not witnessed before, and when the anger swelled in his face and erupted with Desmond stabbing the table with his knife, Eunan had to interject.

"What is the matter, master?"

Desmond ground his teeth, and as he stroked his beard, Eunan could feel his spine twitch with the abrasion. Eunan reached out and placed his arm around his master's shoulders.

"Is there anything I can do to help, master?"

Desmond wrenched his knife out of the table and pointed at a group of Galloglass eating and drinking as they sat at a table across the hall.

"Yes, there is. You can come of age and kill that man over there. Remember his name, Aonghas O'Braoin."

Eunan followed the tip of the blade to a boisterous old Galloglass with tied-back red hair and a fiery beard. He looked like a man you would not want to take on if you could avoid it based on his size alone, but Eunan had opened the door to confrontation with his offer.

"Why would you wish to kill one of your master's constables?" Eunan said.

"I may not know it conclusively with enough evidence to put to the Maguire, but I know in my heart that even if he did not do it with his own hand, he is responsible for the death of my family. His men spread rumours I was responsible for the death of the priest and they came and ridiculed me."

Eunan shuddered, for he had never seen his master so. But if this was the price of gratitude, then he must pay it.

"Master, I will deliver his head to you as repayment for all you have done for me."

Desmond could not take his eyes off the man's back. "That certainly would be a gift well received. And while you're at it, kill the young henchman to his right, Cúmhaí Devine. He ridiculed your master and you must avenge my honour."

Eunan gulped, for the men Desmond pointed at were far more numerous and accomplished than he. But he saw something he had never seen before. Desmond's hand shook with anger.

Desmond received a tap on the shoulder.

"The Maguire wants to see you in his private room."

Desmond shuddered, for he did not know what the Maguire wanted, for he now turned to Donnacha for his advice.

Desmond entered the room rather sheepishly, having practised excuses for every scenario he could envisage. That was every scenario save for the one he found himself in: the marital negotiations between the Maguires and the O'Neills. On one side sat Cúchonnacht, Donnacha, and an elated Hugh Maguire recently invigorated with power. On the other were Hugh O'Neill and Cormac MacBaron, while Edmund Magauran, the Archbishop of Armagh, stood by to mediate. Red-faced and trying to conceal his nerves, Desmond took the seat the

Galloglass guard offered him and edged back towards the wall to what he hoped was temporary anonymity whilst he got his bearings.

The Maguire delegation looked shifty, eager to get on with the discussion, whilst Hugh O'Neill looked to the lands beyond the window as if he wanted to be somewhere else. Cúchonnacht knew the O'Neill had the whip hand and picked himself up out of his seat to join him by the window, hoping that the kindling of friendship might get him a favourable hearing from the rising Gaelic power in the north.

"That way is towards the lake," the Maguire said, placing a guiding finger in the window frame. "It is the sanctuary of the Maguires in times of war, and beyond that lies the O'Donnells. I am glad you are here, for one day all this turbulence will settle and I hope that the O'Neills and Maguires will remain allies just as they have done down the ages."

The O'Neill did not flinch, for he was a dab hand at the politics of the Gaelic lords.

"There is a long struggle ahead, Cúchonnacht," he said. "Age is turning against me as it is against you, but it isn't a time for old men. The vibrancy and foolhardiness of youth are what is needed to carry the fight to the English. We over-think," and he pressed his index finger into his right temple.

Cúchonnacht's eyebrows drew together. "I know my time is nearly up. But it is my duty as the Maguire to his clan to steer them on a path that they will both survive and prosper on. We have many enemies and fewer guns, pikes, axes and swords than them. Why should I commit the fate of my people to you, to perish with you on the fields of Tyrone and have them suffer the wrath of the victor?"

"Our fates are intertwined whether we like it or not," said the O'Neill. He turned to Cúchonnacht and crossed his middle finger over his index finger.

"We are fighting for no less than the survival of our Gaelic culture and the one true church. The English are coming for you and are likely to string you and all your family up so they can make Connor Roe the Maguire, and he will be the last to hold that title. If we lose this war, both our clans will be scattered and divided at the behest of the English. Do you think I offer you a choice?

It's simple. Live and fight for your freedom, or watch from the side while your future generations – as they toil as English tenant farmers – wonder why you didn't fight for them!"

Cúchonnacht turned away from the window.

"I know the graveness of the situation that you have so admirably painted with your words, and the Maguires will fight to the last for our freedom. However, my main gripe is with the English. I have no desire to fall to the sword of Turlough Luineach or the MacShanes if they win and take revenge on your allies!"

Hugh O'Neill turned to face Cúchonnacht.

"You will only know the victor when it is too late! I have stood up for the northern lords in both the Irish and Privy Councils. I have solidified the houses of O'Neill and O'Donnell with the marriage of my daughter to Red Hugh O'Donnell, the favoured successor to the O'Donnell clan. God help him in that English jail. I have spent more money than you would believe in trying to bribe the boy's way to freedom. Now I offer the same alliance to the Maguires. What has Turlough or the MacShanes done to unite the north except retell tales from the past and hope that you see their glory reflected there?"

Hugh Maguire came across the room with his hands outstretched to show that his impending marriage would resolve any lingering doubts between the two clans.

"He is right, Father. If there is any hope, it is with him!"

Cúchonnacht turned and snapped at his insolent son. "Just as much as it is my duty as the Maguire to protect the clan, it is also my duty as your father to stop you from getting your head blown off!"

"I'd rather my head was blown off and lying in a ditch than rot in an English prison!"

"At least you'd still be alive!"

"Which brings me back to my first point, Father," said Hugh Maguire. "What we, what the Maguires, what the north need are headstrong young men who can lead their clans into battle. I remember the stories of your bravery under Shane

O'Neill, a headstrong young man just like your son. Now I think it is time for your son to take over!"

Cúchonnacht and Hugh O'Neill looked at each other until Cúchonnacht broke the silence.

"When you truly are the O'Neill, and you have united with the O'Donnells and the lords of the north, we will gladly follow you with my son as the Maguire!"

The room was silent. Hugh Maguire beamed from ear to ear, but Hugh O'Neill was silent.

"I trust your word, Cúchonnacht, and your pledge is good enough for me," said Hugh O'Neill finally. He raised his mug. "Do you see the fine wine contained within? That is the best wine you can get, all the way from Spain to lubricate our alliance. It is also given to you on the day of the sealing of our alliance through holy matrimony. My spies tell me a huge Spanish fleet has set sail to invade England and to inspire all the good Catholics of the land to throw the yoke off of the heretical Queen. With the support of the fleet and army of the most powerful kingdom known to man, how can we lose?" The wide-eyed cheer on the face of Hugh O'Neill searched the room for detractors. He could find none. He raised his mug to the sky. "To the Maguire and the rebels of the north!"

"The Maguire and the rebels of the north!" The room echoed back, mugs lofted on high.

"Let's get this wedding done!" cried Donnacha, and he made another salute.

The room returned to the celebration, and Hugh O'Neill turned to Cúchonnacht and Hugh Maguire.

"I know you can't openly support me, but I'll take my future son-in-law under my wing and ensure he's a fine soldier and leader for when the war comes. There's no point for anyone if he has to learn when it's too late!" He patted Cúchonnacht on the back. "You know it makes sense!"

Cúchonnacht smiled, the smile of a man whom destiny had left behind. Hugh Maguire followed his future father-in-law to discuss his prospects. Donnacha grinned at Desmond, for he knew Desmond's days in Enniskillen were over. But Cúchonnacht came and patted Desmond on the back. "I may well have a mission for you yet," he whispered in his ear. "But try not to get yourself killed first by waving a dagger around my hall. I will ensure you are given respect." A red-faced Desmond absorbed his new diminished position.

# CHAPTER THIRTEEN

# FISHING FOR SOULS

Over the following months after the wedding, Hugh Maguire, with the assistance of Hugh O'Neill, gradually took over the running of the army of the Maguire and the secret hiring of Scottish mercenaries. He progressively side-lined his father with the help and influence of Donnacha. They kept all of this secret from the other lords of Ulster for fear of reprisals from Turlough Luineach.

The lords of Ulster listened to the news of the ongoing saga of the Spanish Armada first with elation and then with a dreadful disappointment. News came that Spanish ships had been seen off the coast of Scotland and would make their way past Ireland. Defeat in battle, and terrible storms off the shores of England and Scotland had decimated the fleet. The Irish lords heard rumours that the remaining ships were full of soldiers and modern weapons such as guns and pikes and were eager to retrieve as many men and materials as possible should the storms continue and the opportunity arise. The lords posted men along the shores of northern Ireland to look for ships that may have run aground.

The lands of the Maguires were landlocked, but Hugh Maguire did not want to miss out on any potential weapons bounty or Spanish soldiers he could get his hands on. He could not turn north for the O'Neills, and the O'Donnells were being pressured by the English to show their loyalty by executing or handing over any Spanish sailors that came ashore and handing over any weapons. Hugh Maguire turned west to the O'Rourkes, the Sligo O'Connors and the Burkes of Mayo, for he was trying to forge alliances with lesser clans so he would not be so reliant on the O'Neills and O'Donnells. These clans were in a similar position, fighting for survival against the steady encroachment of the English. Hugh Maguire sent Donnacha to negotiate, and all the clans readily agreed to co-operate.

But all this passed Eunan and Desmond by like two dead reeds floating on the lake as Desmond settled into his retirement. They would get up late, train first, then maybe indulge in some fishing, or rowing out onto the lake to visit various islands, followed by dinner prepared by Arthur. If Eunan was lucky, tales from Desmond's past would top the day off, which Eunan had to guess if they were tall or true.

Under Desmond's care, Eunan was growing into a sturdy young man, with a muscular build and a shock of red hair. His skill with axe and sword preceded him, and he was a devout follower of Hugh Maguire. He looked nothing like his father, a fact he revelled in, telling Desmond whenever the subject came up. Desmond still trained the local boys, mainly because Eunan wanted him to, but with much less enthusiasm than before. Desmond said he should aim higher and that he would learn nothing by constantly beating the same boys.

But the Maguire was not finished with him yet, for a messenger came to encroach on a relaxed summer morning. Desmond growled as he snatched the message from the boy's hand. The message was digested and spat out with a curse. "What does he want?"

Eunan's brows knitted. "Does it not say?"

Desmond's jowls wobbled as he shook his head.

"No, it's just a cryptic message saying how urgently he needs me. Maybe he realises what a snake Donnacha is!"

Eunan's eyes brightened as he thought Desmond may contemplate a return to Enniskillen. "I will gather your things and prepare the boat!" he said. But before Desmond could object, he was gone.

They were soon in the boat with Eunan straining every sinew to return as he rowed and Desmond stared at the reeds on the river bank as he fixated on his previous downfall.

The jetty by Enniskillen Castle was welcoming, and they were directed first to the castle and then to the private room of the Maguire. When they entered, only Hugh Maguire and Donnacha O'Cassidy Maguire were waiting for them.

"Welcome, my old friend!" Hugh Maguire embraced Desmond as he stepped into the room.

Desmond's suspicion suppressed the thought of reciprocating any warmth. But he noticed the confidence in Hugh's eyes; he appeared to have grown up and the mantle of the Maguire, or more accurately the Maguire-in-waiting, sat easier on his shoulders.

"We have a mission for you that fits your unique expertise," said Hugh Maguire. He smiled warmly at Desmond, hoping it would thaw any lingering animosity. It did not.

"What expertise is that? I've been enjoying fishing on the lake because that's all I thought you wanted from me."

Hugh extended his hand towards a chair. "Please sit so we may talk more comfortably. You served overseas as a mercenary, did you not?"

"And got paid good money for it, and then from your father. But you know all this. Why are you asking?"

"Because we have a special mission for you if you wish to do a great service for the Maguires."

"I have continuously given great service and my health and youth to the Maguires, so why stop now that I am old and crippled?" said Desmond. His words were accepting, but a pinched face and soured expression told another story.

"Good. Donnacha will tell you all about it!"

Desmond and Eunan rode in front of a band of MacCabe Galloglass on the way to the lands of the O'Rourkes, a clan just down the road and the pecking order from the Maguires. One-time rivals, now useful allies.

Desmond had served with many of the older generations of O'Rourkes, both in Ireland and on the continent, as a mercenary for the Spanish army. He had gained a knowledge of the Spanish language and their weapons and tactics in his days in the Netherlands. The mission the Maguire gave Desmond was clear. He needed him to train the MacCabes in the new fighting techniques from the continent and recruit some Spanish officers to assist him.

Hugh Maguire warned Desmond that the Lord Deputy of Ireland knew the Spanish fleet was coming. The Lord Deputy had decreed that severe punishment would be bestowed on any lord found harbouring Spanish fugitives. English troops were dispatched from Dublin to enforce the decree. But Desmond knew that any mission Donnacha had volunteered him for would be dangerous for his personal welfare.

Upon his arrival at the village where they met their guides, Desmond found himself amongst old friends, and they exchanged stories from the past and updated themselves on their failing health and expanding broods of children and grandchildren. Once the niceties were dispensed with and business began, the guides led them to a sympathetic village in Sligo O'Connor territory, and Desmond and Eunan took up lodgings in a village on top of a cliff overlooking Sligo bay.

"You'd better make yourself comfortable, boy," said Desmond. "The way the remains of the Armada are circling Scotland, the O'Neills and the O'Donnells will get the first pick of the carcasses, and we'll get the dregs as per usual. The more Spanish and weapons we can save, the better the chances the Spanish king will send an army to help us!"

All Desmond's insightfulness brought to Eunan's face was a frown.

"With the destruction of the Armada, surely King Philip will suffer the same fate?" replied Eunan.

Desmond sat on a stool as Eunan continued to unpack their satchels.

"King Philip is the richest, most powerful king in the world. He has a power way beyond what the northern lords or you and I could ever dream. Even I have respect for him. He is a devout Catholic and hates the heretic Queen with almost as much passion. I'm surprised we've had to make so much effort to persuade him to invade!"

"So, what do we do while we wait?" said Eunan.

"Make allies of the O'Rourkes and the O'Connors and train their men so they can fight alongside the Maguire. This is what you have to do when you are a chieftain." Desmond put his hand on Eunan's shoulder to make him realise there were lessons to be learned from this excursion. But Eunan was too tired for lessons and continued with his tasks.

They spent the next couple of weeks in the village waiting for the Armada to arrive. News came of great storms off the islands of Scotland and rumours that the remains of the fleet had been sunk. Despondency set in, but Hugh Maguire told them to stay where they were, for there were still some stragglers limping back to Spain.

They remained in the village until one morning they heard a shout.

"Ship ahoy! Ship ahoy!"

Eunan ran to the top of the cliff, and Desmond hobbled after him.

"Master, look yonder! We prayed, and God has provided!"

Desmond reached Eunan, leaned over to catch his breath, then looked out into the bay. On the jagged rocks was a Spanish galleon, jack-knifed in two. Out of its belly spewed men, ropes, barrels, and shattered wood. The men washed ashore, and the locals wasted no time in going down to rob them, killing anyone who resisted.

"And what he giveth with one hand, he taketh away with the other! Summon the O'Rourkes!" ordered Desmond. "We must stop this slaughter before they kill all the useful ones!"

Eunan ran as fast as he could while Desmond made his way down to the beach with the MacCabe Galloglass at his back. The O'Rourke warriors drove off the locals, and they gathered all the boxes and barrels that had washed up on the beach in one place. Desmond took command.

"Gather any weapons or supplies together and don't touch them until I inspect them. Don't kill any more Spanish! Gather the survivors together so I may speak to them. This is very important. The O'Rourke will deal with any disobedience."

The men of the O'Rourke grunted their obedience. They gathered together the injured and dishevelled Spanish sailors, along with their equipment, then dutifully rowed out to the bay and fished out what men and equipment they could.

Desmond stood and stared as he took in all the destruction on the beach and in the bay.

"What's the matter?" said Eunan.

But all Desmond could do was stand there, remove his helmet, comb his fingers through his hair, and stare. An energy suddenly possessed him, and he rushed over to speak to the Spanish survivors.

"Who's your leader? Can any of you speak English?"

They all looked away.

"I'm a friend, the best hope you have of getting off this beach alive! Now, can any of you speak English?"

A man of indiscernible rank got up, his uniform having disintegrated into rags.

"I can. I can speak for the crew. The ship's captain is dead, and many of the surviving crew are ill. I am Captain Arlo Ruiz."

Desmond waved him over and then walked with him out of earshot of the O'Rourkes. They sat down, and Desmond took some bread out of his bag and offered it to Arlo. He wolfed it down. After a quick burp, he looked ready to talk.

"What was your ship carrying, may I ask?" said Desmond.

"Soldiers, weapons and bibles for the English infidels," said Arlo. He lowered his head; hours before he had stood astride on a great ship, but now he was reduced to begging for his life and bread from a savage.

"So if you didn't shoot them, convert them?!"

"Why do you speak of the Lord so?" Arlo said.

"I am an old man who has seen many battles, including serving with the Spanish army of the Netherlands. I have seen many more deaths than conversions. The barrel of a gun does not win many hearts and minds!"

"You served with the mercenaries?" Arlo said.

"I spent many of my best years earning the Spanish King's coin, drinking his wine, fornicating with the local prostitutes, and all I had to do for him was kill who he told me to. A bargain at half the price. Are there any more ships with you?"

Arlo looked to the ground.

"We got blown off course in a storm in the middle of the ocean two days ago. We saw some ships wrecked off the coast to the north of here. There may be some ships behind us, but for now, we are alone."

"Are there any more galleons out there, or just smaller pataches?"

"The other ships have survived your horrific weather much better than our cursed ship. Only the minnows and the weak perish on your rocks."

Desmond put his hand on Arlo's shoulder.

"Try to redeem yourself and earn your life, little minnow. There are a lot of greedy war chieftains to satisfy, and yours is the only shipwreck with any guns. Are you a captain in the navy or infantry?"

Arlo's head dropped, and his shoulders stooped.

"Most of the survivors, including myself, are land infantry."

"Ah, you wriggle off the dinner plate, little minnow. You are most welcome here, Arlo," said Desmond as he slapped him on the back. "We have plenty of work for you to do here until we can arrange a safe passage home. Now I must see what my men have salvaged. You return to yours, and we'll arrange accommodation for you all!"

Desmond got up and walked over to inspect the haul of treasure that had spewed forth from the ship. Arlo followed him over after he had consulted with his comrades regarding their welfare. When the shipwreck had been picked clean, they assembled one hundred and forty working guns and over two hundred pikes.

"That's a decent haul for a single galleon," said Desmond. He turned to Arlo. "Can you train us how to use these?"

"I could, but the guns aren't very reliable. You could learn to use them in a couple of weeks, but you wouldn't know how many guns would survive the training."

"You do the training and let me worry about that," said Desmond. "Now let's load all of this up and bring it to the village and make it look like we were never here. The English will soon hear of this shipwreck!"

The one hundred survivors of the shipwreck were brought to the village, fed and re-clothed. Eoghan O'Rourke arrived, having been sent by his father to supervise splitting the spoils with the Maguires.

Desmond walked around with Arlo and spoke to the survivors individually and established their rank and skill levels. With this task completed, Desmond dismissed Arlo and went into a house with Eoghan. The chieftain's hut in the O'Connor village was a sombre place to be. Desmond and Eoghan were worried. They had gained a limited amount of weapons, a hundred new mouths to feed, and the English army was coming for them.

"It is time for us to leave," said Desmond. "It's only a wee galleon, poor pickings for all our labours. Why don't I take the survivors and their baggage back to Fermanagh for safekeeping? Your messengers have said that the English are bearing down hard to get here!"

Eoghan's face flushed red. "The O'Rourkes are not taking all the risks and none of the rewards."

"And those rewards will get you hung before you can use them. They are better off in Maguire country and out of the reach of English sheriffs. Once the heat has died down, the Maguire will share the rewards with you."

Eoghan circled the room and returned to the table.

"My father will kill me for this. Take the most skilled and the better weapons back to Fermanagh. Give me a promise that you will split the spoils evenly and a token to give to my father, and I will make sure the English do not pursue you."

Desmond nodded.

"Then I will keep my side of the bargain," said Eoghan, "and may God curse you if you do not keep yours."

There were no horses for Arlo and the other Spanish soldiers, as the spare horses had been attached to the carts to transport the newly acquired weapons. So they began their forced march to the River Erne. They had nothing but rags on their backs, and any decent pairs of boots had been stolen. The men were at their wits' end so Arlo came to speak to Desmond as they could stand the wind and rain of the bogs of Ireland no more. Desmond tried to ignore Arlo as the Spaniard trotted to keep up with Desmond's horse.

"What will happen to my comrades? Your chieftains have made so many approaches to my King looking for help, and here we are now. I assume you are going to treat his subjects well?"

Desmond stared straight ahead, for he could make no promises.

"We must split you up to ensure your safety from the English. Then we can smuggle you back in groups to Spain. You need to be patient as we wait for the heat to die down."

Arlo saw he would get nowhere with Desmond, and he would just have to wait. He went back to his men and lied to them about what Desmond had said. They smiled all the way to the River Erne, the cold and rain now less of a burden.

The next day, the English arrived in the O'Rourkes' village looking for survivors from the shipwreck. They were greeted by the bodies of the O'Rourkes' Spanish sailors swinging from the trees. Eoghan came out to plead for the villagers' lives and was rewarded with a bag of coins and a bitter taste in his mouth.

Once they arrived at the River Erne, the Maguires assembled several boats to transport them up the river. They dropped most of the Spanish off at various islands in Lower Lough Erne so they could go into hiding. They brought Arlo to Enniskillen to meet Hugh Maguire so that Hugh could assess Arlo's usefulness. Hugh Maguire insisted Desmond stay with Arlo and help him train the Maguire Galloglass. They gave Desmond and Eunan lodgings in the tower, and the additional responsibility of ensuring Arlo was content and did not try to escape. They had to convince him he was not a prisoner.

As for the training, unfortunately, the Maguires suffered from a severe lack of guns; those they had retrieved from the shipwreck had suffered water damage, as Arlo had predicted, and therefore jammed or otherwise broke quickly. The Maguire metalsmiths could not replicate nor repair the guns. Guns were otherwise hard to get hold of since the English restricted the distribution of firearms to their forces only, and Hugh O'Neill controlled most illegal gun importing by northern lords with Scottish connections. The pikes could be more easily replicated and the Maguire's craftsmen set about producing as many as possible.

Arlo was very uneasy about his new situation, irrespective that the Maguire had tried to make him feel as comfortable as possible. However, Desmond dismissed any inquiries into the fate of his comrades or how he was supposed to get home.

Arlo did, however, cooperate fully in training the men and kept his frustrations with the quality of the soldiers to himself until he was alone with Desmond. Desmond reassured him they had plenty of warriors at the same level as Eunan, but they needed the attention to expedite their learning. Desmond warned Arlo that if he failed to produce outstanding warriors, he would be diminished in the eyes of the Maguire to his old 'minnow' status and thrown back into the sea.

Hugh Maguire, under the influence of Cúchonnacht, tried to keep his support for Hugh O'Neill as quiet as possible in order not to offend any of the other northern lords, as Hugh O'Neill had not yet decisively established his supremacy. Hugh Maguire concerned himself with gaining the support of the chieftains of the Maguire clan for the inevitable election of a new Maguire, as Connor Roe had already started canvassing in the south of the county.

# CHAPTER FOURTEEN

# LAMENTATIONS

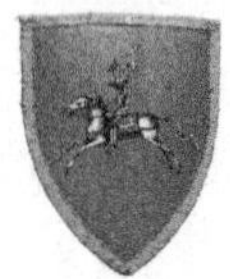

A year later, the clouds hung low in the sky, a swirling mass of grey sagging like a dark underbelly before pouring forth onto the world. The clouds melted into the low hills of the landscape, as the entire region seemed to have taken to mourning. No banners flew from Enniskillen Castle and the courtyard and surrounding town were full of soldiers, soldiers from all over Fermanagh no matter to who they pledged allegiance. There were Scottish mercenaries hired by Hugh Maguire, and there were O'Donnells who supported Donnell O'Donnell, the pre-eminent O'Donnell who had struck an alliance with Hugh. Even Connor Roe Maguire had come from Lisnaskea to pay his respects. They all filled the castle courtyard for the funeral procession of Cúchonnacht Maguire.

The needles penetrated the cloth for the tapestry dedicated to Cúchonnacht as the people wailed for their dead leader. For even when there had been famine, even when they had been invaded by the lords of the north, both of which were common, and when they had sheriffs and treaties imposed by the English, he had always remained steady and wise. He was to be enshrined in a picture not of battles like his famous ancestors but with the lough behind him, the tower of Devenish Island rising behind his right shoulder. He would stand on a rock with the cross carved upon it, addressing his people with cows behind them in the fields to show those onlookers in the future he presided over a time of relative plenty. His death appeared to be the end of an era and a harbinger of bad times to come.

Desmond and Eunan waited in the courtyard with the great of the clan, for they would be the first to follow the procession when the body was brought forth from the castle. The crowd swayed like the waves in the sea, such was the crush in the overfilled courtyard. But it was more than overcrowding that was causing ripples.

"Vote for Connor Roe to be the next Maguire. He is from the senior house and has both the support of Hugh O'Neill and the English. A vote for Hugh is a vote for your own demise."

Desmond turned volcanic red and wadded into the crowd to find the culprit. "He is not even in his grave!" he shouted. "Have some respect!"

A young man's face, which could far better take the various shades of red, appeared between two onlookers' shoulders. "He is the worst Maguire we ever had. Too senile to see what is the future."

Desmond pushed his way through the crowd to confront the man. "How would you know?" he shouted. "You were not even born to see the previous Maguire. Hurl one more insult at Cúchonnacht and I'll cut out your tongue."

"I may be young," the man said, "but all I've witnessed is Cúchonnacht the capitulator."

A firm, welted hand on the shoulder prevented Desmond from throwing a punch at the man. "Easy there, Desmond." Desmond turned to see it was a Galloglass constable he knew well. "Cúchonnacht wouldn't want to see you fighting on a day like this."

Desmond shook his shoulder free and dusted down his tunic. "As long as you do your job today," he said to the Galloglass, "and see there is no politicking or disrespecting the old Maguire, then I can mourn in peace."

"I'll do what I can," said the constable, "but Hugh Maguire is a law onto himself."

A group of Galloglass came out of the main tower in full ceremonial dress as the crowd parted. They lined the path from the door to the gate of the castle. The Archbishop of Armagh came next, surrounded by the most prominent priests of the county. The archbishop held aloft a wooden cross and cast his prayers towards the sky. All the priests bowed their heads and cast their prayers to the ground with rosary beads wrapped around their knuckles and mumbled prayers in Latin. A cry rose from the crowd as a thump came from the tower door. Hugh Maguire and the head of the Galloglass struggled to get the casket through the door, such was the throng of the crowd at the sight of Cúchonnacht's casket. Galloglass came from the gate to hold the people back.

Hugh manoeuvred the edge of the casket around the door of the tower, for the door was positioned to aid the defence of the tower rather than to facilitate grand funerals. Once they had navigated the turn, Cúchonnacht was again raised high upon the pallbearers' shoulders. However, the emotions of the day reverberated on the walls of the castle and back into the crowd. A wail was heard, and the crowd swelled and moved as one so the people of Fermanagh could place their hands on the casket of their dead leader. The crush halted the casket in the middle of the courtyard and the casket stood as if it were an island in a sea of hands while being gently peppered with flowers from the mournful crowd. More Galloglass came from the tower and formed a wedge to cut through the crowd to free the casket so it could continue its journey from the castle to the river quays.

A cry came from the middle of the courtyard. The press of people proved too much for the pallbearers, and the edge of the casket crashed to the ground. A wave of hands fell upon the coffin as his subjects tried to connect with their dead leader one last time. Hugh tried to pick up his corner of the casket once more, only to be overwhelmed by the weight of the crowd, who also tried to place their hands upon him so they could bless him and pray that he could be half the leader his father was. The Galloglass forced the crowd back not only to restart the funeral procession but also to protect his likely successor from assassination.

Eunan and Desmond were caught in the crush, and Eunan could see Desmond was struggling. "Grab my hand," he cried as he reached across the face of a man trying to lay his hands on the casket to get to Desmond. The man bit down hard on Eunan's arm. Eunan howled with pain. Desmond was having difficulty breathing now, having various elbows and pommels of swords poking into his ribs. The crowd swayed back and forth, and he had lost his footing twice now. Eunan responded by elbowing the man in the face, and his nose exploded on the backs and necks of all those in front of him. The ensuing scuffle allowed Eunan to pull Desmond by the arm into the small space his violence had created. "We should leave," he said. "They don't have a spare coffin for you today."

Eunan looked beyond them at how they should escape. The crowd swelled past them, and Eunan had to elbow his way to the gate. "Open the gate now!" he cried at the guards on the gate tower. "We are all going to get crushed in here."

The guard disappeared momentarily. "We closed the gates to stop the crowd on the other side getting in," he said back.

"We need to clear the people out or the funeral won't happen and someone will get crushed here," Eunan said. The guard disappeared again.

"The crowd push with equal ferocity on the other side," said the guard upon his return.

"Just get someone in charge to open the gate and clear the way," Eunan said. "We're dying down here."

The guard disappeared again, and Eunan resumed his quest to force his way to the gate. The crush had not subsided, for the only place for the people to go was on top of the walls, and they were quickly filled. They got to the gate, but they were still closed. Eunan banged his fists on the door, and the surrounding people joined him. Eunan took the initiative and struggled to lift the door bar off the gate. "Help me lift it off if you want to live," he said to those around him who were also banging on the door. They lifted the door bar and opened the gate, only to face the clamour of another crowd. They shoved Eunan in the back and to the side. The Galloglass had, at last, arrived to clear the way.

Desmond was a little worse for wear, so Eunan brought him through the crowd outside the castle and to a hill where they could get a good view of the rest of the procession. Once the Galloglass had come out in sufficient force, they lined the route from the castle gate to the quayside. The casket was paraded slowly to the quay, to the sounds of mourning subjects and a steady shower of flowers. They set the casket on a specially constructed platform. Dignitaries and noblemen of the clan had formed a line behind the casket along its route, and when it was laid on its platform, they came to pay their final respects.

Desmond sat on the hill to rest, for the crush of the crowd had been too much for his ageing body. His mind grappled with the fact that his great and much-admired friend Cúchonnacht had finally passed away, and the entire future of Fermanagh and of the Maguire clan had been thrown into jeopardy. But his first concern was for his apprentice, Eunan. He took the recently arrived package Arthur had given him and placed it behind his thigh, out of sight from Eunan.

"Come sit beside me, boy," Desmond said. Eunan looked down at him and set aside his game of naming as many dignitaries as he could who were paying their respects, and sat beside his mentor.

"I know I'm a grumpy old man and can be hard to put up with at the best of times. But I think we've formed a bond and become friends, having overcome the obstacles of my, your, and our, personalities."

"I agree." Eunan laughed.

"I thought you might. I have a present for you." Desmond turned and reached behind himself, and his hands returned with a large, heavy leather satchel.

Eunan's eyes lit up as he placed the package on his lap and heard the dull thump of leather-wrapped metal.

"Well, open it then!"

Eunan untied the leather straps and unfurled the leather bag. Inside four small pockets were handcrafted throwing axes, decorated with beautiful Celtic designs surrounding the symbol of the Maguire.

"Did you get these made for me?" said Eunan, eyes wide and tearful.

"They are specially weighted to make them fly better. When you throw them at someone's head, please try to retrieve them. I went to a lot of trouble to get them made.

"Now you have come of age, a heavy burden will weigh upon your shoulders. Now that Cúchonnacht is dead, the future of Fermanagh and the Maguire clan has been thrown into doubt. Fight for Hugh to become the Maguire to ensure the survival of the clan. It is time for you to go home and ensure your father backs Hugh Maguire, raise some soldiers and fight. The time for old men is over and our time together, unfortunately, is done."

"But I don't want to leave!" said Eunan as he fought back the tears.

"Don't be like that now! Be tough! You have a lot of hardship in front of you if you live long enough. It is time for me to leave, as they have invited me to go with the family to Devenish Island for the burial. After that, I will be in Enniskillen no more."

"Where are you going?"

"To the islands. It is safer there. I fear there will be a civil war between Hugh and Connor Roe, or worse, we will fall to the English! You must go home and do your duty. Stop Connor Roe, save the Maguire. Arthur has left you a fine steed in a farmhouse nearby to bring you home. You are a warrior now. You can beat anyone, be they English, Irish or Galloglass. Goodbye, but if you ever need my help, come to look for me on the islands."

Desmond lifted himself and walked down the hill. Eunan fought back the tears as he remained on the hill with Arthur. He felt like an abandoned little boy once more.

# CHAPTER FIFTEEN

# RETURN OF THE PRODIGAL SON

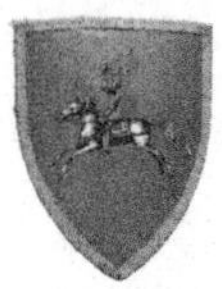

Eunan was not expecting much, so he got nothing. Not the sun nor wind on his back, the chirping of the spring birds nor firm ground for his horse underfoot greeted his journey. The callous day of his return was frosty, as if even nature was telling Eunan not to return. He rode his horse into the village, which was untroubled by his presence, and received no warm embrace from family, friend or neighbour.

His weary head spun, and the bad blood crawled in his veins, so he found an abandoned house on the outskirts he could rest in. It was better than going home. He had outgrown the outhouse.

The village looked different, backward compared to cosmopolitan Enniskillen, as if the years had not been kind to it in his absence. Or maybe the village was showing its displeasure at Eunan's return. The burned fields and houses told that the raiding had returned, but the scars did not reveal the perpetrators.

"Hey! Who goes there?" came a voice from the shadows.

Someone had discovered him. The sounds of his horse gave him away. He threw caution to the wind and stuck his chin out.

"Eunan O'Keenan Maguire has returned!" He threw his arms wide to catch any embrace that came forth for him.

"I would've stayed away if I were you!" said the voice. "Who wants you here?"

Eunan's shoulders slumped as any hope or expectation washed away. The shadow emerged. It was his uncle Fergus. Eunan never knew why Fergus disliked him so much, but with his newfound experience, he put it down to family rivalry.

"No matter your opinion, Uncle, I have returned," said Eunan. "Is there somewhere I can shelter, as I don't want to disturb my parents?"

His uncle turned his back and walked back to his house.

"I wouldn't disturb your parents at all. I can give you my outhouse. The pigs might still like you, and you'd do no better with your father. I'll feed you, then show you the road. It will be all the O'Keenan Maguire hospitality you'll get!"

Eunan skipped after his uncle and tried to catch up with him.

"Well, thank you, Uncle, for this evening's hospitality nonetheless. We shall judge tomorrow morning when its light shines upon us."

His uncle growled, for his words had bounced off Eunan's ears.

"This way."

His uncle led him to his house and pointed towards the outhouse.

"Everyone would forgive you if you left before morning!" his uncle said, leaving him. "I wouldn't even disturb your parents by telling them you were ever here."

Eunan looked in the doorway and saw some fresh hay, probably the best he could have hoped for.

"Thank you again, Uncle. I will see you again when the sun shines."

Fearing his message still needed to get through, his uncle decided upon a more direct approach.

"Heed my warning! Things have become a lot worse around here. Food has become scarcer now that the MacMahons have been driven from their lands in Monaghan by the Queen's sheriff. Many of them have come here to Fermanagh. The people are in no mood to be reminded by the likes of you of Galloglass and coign and livery. Trouble follows you here, as it has always done. Do us all a favour and be gone at first light. I don't want to see you again."

Eunan hid his rejection deeply.

"As I said before, Uncle, thanks for the hospitality nonetheless."

Eunan awoke and felt for his throwing axes. Today was a day he thought he would be glad of them. They were still beside him. His bad blood boiled as he lay on the straw to remind him he was home. He tried to plan what he would say to his father, but he got up when words failed him. He tried to think positive thoughts, for he would need something to power him through the day. Memories of his dog Artair filled his mind and his chest ached with how much he missed him. It was all the motivation he needed. He dusted himself off and walked into the morning sunshine outside. Nature's beauty had not diminished in his absence, but it all felt hollow to Eunan. He could not wait to leave, to get back to Enniskillen and this time take his dog with him. But he was here to do his duty.

He left the village and went up a nearby hill to Senan Leonard Maguire's house. Eunan had heard he had gone home before him.

Upon seeing Eunan, Senan ran out and warmly embraced him.

"Why did you ever come back?" Senan asked. "You were far better off in Enniskillen!"

"I came back to do my duty for Hugh Maguire. I expect you to do the same. Cúchonnacht is dead, and Hugh needs us. Are you ready?"

Senan's face dropped a little, for he had not heard the calamitous news.

"Well, yes. But the village is more of a nest of vipers than the court in Enniskillen."

Eunan felt for his axes, for they might well be needed.

"Are all the boys here?"

"Yes, they're all back and waiting."

"Well, there's no time like the present." Eunan strode down the hill towards the village until he turned and realised he had left Senan behind.

"Are you sure?" said the still static Senan.

"Is anyone? Come on, then!" cried Eunan.

They entered the village as it bloomed into life as the sun raised its head over Fermanagh's low rolling hills. Everyone rushed around to prepare for the planting season, fetch food for their families, ready themselves to go to the market, or engage in other chores. No one seemed to recognise or pay much attention to Eunan. He knew where his father would be and made his way there cautiously. His mind was alight with doubts and his bad blood reminded him of what a disappointment he had been. The urge to see Artair drove him on. He sent Senan to get the Enniskillen boys.

His father sat fireside, lakeside. It was just as Eunan remembered him, deep in conversation with some of the important men of the village. He had aged considerably; the lines in his face were more pronounced, his belly more rounded, his hair nearly white and his beard not far behind. He looked jaded, but could still muster the energy to impose his will on the dissenting voices from the village. Eunan only recognised a few of the surrounding men. There was no sign of Michael O'Flanagan Maguire, who was his father's rival when he left for Enniskillen, or anyone of Michael's ilk.

Eunan stepped forward and stood on the other side of the fire and held his hands out as he had done to greet his uncle.

"Hello, Father, I have returned!" he announced.

Cathal lifted his eyes with his scowl scurrying after.

"You should have stayed in Enniskillen. You'd have a far better life there."

It was the kindest thing Eunan remembered his father saying.

"Come here, boy, and let me bring you to your dog and mother. That can quell any nostalgic urges you may have. Then you can leave and go off and lead another life."

Cathal strode across to Eunan, hooked him by the arm, and walked towards the house. Eunan shook him off and stopped to confront him.

"Father, I am here on a mission. Cúchonnacht is dead. I am here to gain a pledge of loyalty from you to Hugh Maguire and to raise soldiers in his name."

Cathal shook his head and laughed.

"If you did that, you'd probably be dead and me along with you before you got to the road to Enniskillen. This is a frontier village. It is almost too much for me to stop the rival factions from killing each other. As soon as war breaks, this will be the front line."

"The very survival of the Maguires is at stake," Eunan said.

"My very survival is at stake daily," his father replied. "Cúchonnacht was never a good friend to us. His Galloglass always took too much, stole some of the Maguire's share, and then blamed me. The next time the Galloglass came, they would ask for more, and so on and so forth. Hugh Maguire is cut from the same cloth, except he wants to start a suicidal war with the English. At best it will be back-breaking taxes, at worst we all get wiped out.

"Connor Roe is just across the lake and has powerful English allies. If I side with Hugh Maguire, the destruction of the village is my reward for the outbreak of hostilities. If I side with Connor Roe, Hugh will concentrate his attack on the other side of the lake and will be sick of war by the time he turns on us, and will readily accept our surrender. Therefore, while the two leading contenders for the Maguire slog it out, we survive."

It was Eunan's turn to shake his head.

"Father, there comes a time to fight and not be a coward. Don't stand in my way when I declare the village for Hugh Maguire."

Cathal grabbed Eunan by the forearm.

"Eunan, go live your life somewhere else and don't sacrifice it for somewhere you've always hated and which has always hated you. Now come see your mother, say your goodbyes and then leave."

They turned the corner and Eunan saw "Artair!" The dog leapt from his bed beside the door of the house and jumped on Eunan with such power he knocked him over. He slobbered all over his returned master. Eunan wrestled his dog off himself.

"Oh Artair, I have missed you so." Eunan ruffled the top of the dog's head and greased his own hair with the residue as he used to do in his childhood. His father hooked him around the arm again.

"That's the pleasant reunion over and done with. Now for your mother."

Cathal invited him into the house. His mother was there, sitting in her barrow, her broken spindly legs on either side of the wheel. There lay before Eunan, a bitter grey old woman. His bad blood pumped guilt into every crevice of his body. She still remembered her son.

"What are you doing here? I thought we'd got rid of you for good."

She stared at him stonily, her bitterness magnified by the fact she had to look at him, for she could barely turn her head because of her multiple afflictions. Eunan shrank beneath her gaze, feeling like a little boy once more. He summoned the sparse courage he had remaining to tell her directly what he had become in the hope she would be proud of him.

"No, Mother. I have been to the big town and have returned older and wiser. It is now time we all fight for the glory of the Maguires."

"You just don't get it, do you!? I don't want to explain. Your father may have protected you from the truth, but if you do this, he may not anymore. Go before you destroy everything."

Eunan fought back the tears. His soul was crushed.

"I don't know why you both hate me, but I'll leave now and won't be back!" Eunan ran out of the house.

"Good. Leave this place and don't return. Good riddance!" his father yelled after him.

Eunan ran, his heart broken in two. Not even the pebbles would collide for him when he kicked them. Artair bounded after him and nuzzled beneath his hand. It was too much for Eunan. He knelt and cupped his dog's face in his hands.

"I need to do something, and I want you to be safe. You need to stay here, but I will return for you later. Now go home and wait for me." The dog just stared at him with his huge brown eyes, begging to come with him. "No, you can't. Now go." Eunan smacked him on the back and Artair sloped back to his bed and watched his master walk away.

Eunan walked towards the centre of the village, trying to suppress the emotional eruptions in his soul, only to be disturbed by some jovial voices. He looked up. Senan had gathered the other boys who had been to Enniskillen. They all smiled at Eunan and showed him their hidden weapons. "We are here now."

Eunan felt a bitterness solidify in his heart. He was partially reinvigorated. He stood up stiffly to his full height.

"My father is a coward!" he said. He scrunched his fist until his knuckles were white. "He still sides with Connor Roe. It is time to stand up for Hugh Maguire against all his enemies. Let's take this village for Hugh Maguire!" He lifted his axe aloft.

"Let's take this village for Hugh Maguire!" the boys chanted back.

They laughed and made merry as they walked. However, as they walked, the men of the village hurried past them.

"Cathal Maguire is about to speak. Raiders are coming!"

"Quick, let's hide until we see who they declare for!" said Eunan.

He grabbed Senan and dragged him behind a house.

"I will go into the crowd and see what my father says. You hide with the boys and jump out at the right time."

"How will I know—"

"You will know."

Eunan left to hide amongst the houses nearest the centre circle.

# CHAPTER SIXTEEN

# THE FIRST USE OF AN AXE

An eerie sun illuminated the fog floating on the lake. Gossip flowed through the village that Cathal O'Keenan Maguire had something important to say. The men came from the fields or across the lake to gather in the village. Women and children forced their way to the front eager to listen to their chieftain.

Cathal marched from his house surrounded by some burly men, most of whom Eunan recognised. Michael O'Flanagan Maguire stood at the edge of the circle with several men, half of whom Eunan did not remember. Eunan reckoned they were displaced MacMahons from Monaghan or renegade O'Reillys from down south, fleeing surrender and regrant. The volatility of the crowd ebbed and flowed. Cathal and his scrum of men forced their way into the centre of the circle, and his men carved out space from which Cathal could address the crowd.

Senan and the other Enniskillen boys hid on the outskirts of the circle. However, they had a sudden bout of nerves.

"If we're going to do this, I need a drink," said one. "Old man O'Keenan Maguire isn't known for his short speeches!"

The other boys nodded in agreement, and they went off to find some ale.

Eunan crouched behind some baskets at the side of a house. He made sure he was within axe-throwing distance of his father. He concealed his hand from prying eyes as he reached for his belt for his weapons. The final villagers arrived at the circle just as Cathal began speaking.

"Villagers, you may have heard that Cúchonnacht is dead and the succession of the Maguire has begun! We have always tried to steer clear of inter-clan warfare, but some young usurpers have come into our midst to declare the village for Hugh Maguire—"

Michael O'Flanagan Maguire and his men forced their way through the crowd.

"This village will not change who we support in clan Maguire—"

Eunan reached into his leather pouch and carefully selected his most trusted axe from Desmond's gift set. The blade was beautifully polished, the haft as smooth as silk, and she flew as straight as an arrow. Any error would be the fault of the thrower. He trusted this axe with his life to swiftly end the lives of others. The axe quivered in his hand as he contemplated his next move.

"—while I'm still alive!" continued Cathal.

Eunan kissed the face of the axe.

"Fly straight and true!" he whispered to her.

Eunan stood on a block of wood he had found to give him sufficient height to get the axe over the crowd. He flung the axe and crouched down again behind the basket. A tear fell from his eye.

Michael O'Flanagan Maguire stuck his hand beneath his coat and pulled out his axe. As he leapt towards Cathal Maguire, axe flailing, Cathal Maguire froze – and was covered in the spray of blood, brains and bone as the head of Michael O'Flanagan Maguire disintegrated beneath the beautifully polished blade of Eunan's axe. Michael fell onto Cathal's feet, staining his clothes with blood. Michael's supporters fled. Cathal's men ran towards him to see if he was all right. Eunan looked over the basket and saw the huddled crowd and the shrieks of mourning. He could not see his friends leaping to seize the moment, so he went to look for them.

Moments later, a man came running through the village, panting with exertion.

"They're coming! They're coming!" he cried to whomever he came across.

Nobody stayed to ask who. Eunan put down his axes and looked south. In seconds, a group of horsemen appeared and rode straight for the centre circle of the village, making for Cathal. Cathal had no time to pull his weapon, nor the axe from Michael O'Flanagan's head.

Cathal stood in the circle. A handful of his supporters stood behind him. An English mercenary, who they recognised as a former sheriff called Captain Willis, pulled up his horse before them and spat on the ground. His horsemen gathered behind him.

"Are you a Mac or an Oe?" he said.

Cathal spread his arms to protect his supporters and puffed out his chest to hide his fear.

"Maguires are neither Macs nor Oes!"

The captain sneered through his rotten teeth.

"Who's your dead friend? Are you Irish having a bit of a tiff? Can't decide which Maguire to support?"

"State your business or leave! My men will be here soon!" said Cathal as he stepped forward to confront the intruder.

"You and your couple of friends are audacious, thinking we will not shoot you where you stand," said the captain. "We're here on behalf of the Queen and her supporter, Connor Roe. Who's that you've just killed?"

"I've killed no one!" said Cathal.

"Oh, the brave liar. You stand before me covered in blood with a man with an axe in his head at your feet. I presume you're Cathal Maguire?"

"The very same."

Cathal's face twitched as he saw behind the captain that his foot soldiers had caught up and entered the village.

"Now we always had you down as a Connor Roe man. Is that correct?" said the captain.

Cathal edged back to protect his men.

"I've always supported Connor Roe in any clan dealings where I was required to choose."

"Very good. Now, how did this man come to die?"

Before Cathal could reply, a chant was heard, coming from the village.

"We're going to take this town for Hugh Maguire! Hail, Hugh Maguire!"

Eunan's friends had found their courage in alcohol.

"So that's how he died?" said Captain Willis.

"No! No! No! You've got it all wrong! I'm a loyal supporter of Connor Roe! Come on, look at the blood! It's all over me because he died beside me! Someone threw the axe, probably to defend me from him!"

The shouts for Hugh Maguire grew ever closer and louder. A glint on the axe caught the eye of the English captain. He turned to one of his foot soldiers who had gathered behind him.

"Bring me that axe and be quick about it!"

The man ran over and pulled the axe from Michael's head.

"It's got the symbol of the Maguire on the axe, sir. Looks a pretty fancy axe to me."

"Show me."

The captain looked at the symbol on the axe and grinned at Cathal.

"Oh, you think you're so clever trying to deceive me?"

The captain drew his gun and shot Cathal in the chest. Cathal flew backwards, his chest disintegrating into a mass of burnt flesh and lead.

Eunan almost threw up in his hiding place.

Captain Willis rode into the centre of the circle and threw the axe to the ground in disgust. His entourage of ten Irish horsemen stood behind him while he unrolled his papers.

"By order of the Queen, we represent the sheriff of Monaghan. We are here to take all cattle we believe stolen from the sheriff for use by Her Majesty's army for how they see fit. The Maguire also owes the Queen money, and we're here to collect. We will crush any resistance with brute force." The captain turned to address his men. "Fetch the cattle and kill anyone who resists. Also, go find who's singing that stupid song about Hugh Maguire and kill them."

Eunan hid until the raiders had vacated the circle. He trembled in his hiding place. His father's death had not yet sunk in. All he could think about was Desmond and the prize axes he had given him. He peered out of his hiding place and snuck across the centre circle.

The axe glinted in the morning sun. Michael O'Flanagan Maguire lay beside it. The anger of his righteous rebellion would be frozen in his face until it rotted in the mass grave he would be buried in and became worm food. His father lay a couple of yards away. Eunan's eyes lingered upon him. He lay there in heroic death, having stood up for the village. Why had he never been his hero and stood up for him? Cathal's arm twitched! Eunan scrambled over and lifted his father's head. Cathal still breathed! He fixed his gaze on his son.

"I tried to love you, but just couldn't. Looking at you brought me shame, guilt, and back to shame. Others could have, but not me. I failed you as a father, but you can be a better man than me. Forgive her. Forgive your mother and go save her."

"Father!" Eunan choked. But Cathal's head lolled to the side, and he was gone. Eunan held his father's bloody head to his chest and cried. But he saw more soldiers coming and placed his father's head gently on the ground. He looked at his father one last time then picked up his axe and ran to warn his friends.

In the meantime, several boatloads of Galloglass had rowed across the lake to the village. They drew their swords and axes, leapt into the shallow water, and waded ashore. They ran and grabbed the nearest woman they could.

"Where's the boy?"

"What boy?!"

"Don't make me kill you!"

"Oh. Oh! He hasn't lived here for years!"

"Where's Cathal Maguire?"

"In the village square. That way!"

The Galloglass threw her aside and marched towards the village square.

At the same time, Senan and his friends were marching down the street towards the circle, laughing and chanting as they went. Ale had provided them with a backbone. They dismissed the villagers fleeing from the circle as 'cowards' and sang the praises of Eunan O'Keenan Maguire and how he should lead the village instead of his treacherous father.

Suddenly the English soldiers were in front of them, blocking their way. The boys looked at each other and then at the English soldiers.

"This is it!" said Senan. "Come on, boys! Charge for Hugh Maguire!"

"HUGH MAGUIRE!" came the boys' chant as they raised their swords and pitchforks and charged. Eunan spotted his friends from a distance and broke into a run. The English soldiers lifted their muskets and, in a puff of smoke, where once Eunan's friends stood there now lay a tangle of bodies, their lives draining into the soil.

Eunan jerked to a halt and bit his lip. A line of blood rolled down his chin. His hands formed fists, and his nails dug into the palms of his hands so hard they also drew blood. He cursed himself for his cowardice in the face of his friends' bravery. But what now? His father was dead. His friends were killed, and the place was crawling with English soldiers. He grabbed a battle-axe from a fallen village soldier. What to do next? Save his mother! Eunan ran towards his father's house. But between himself and the house were English soldiers ransacking the village. He saw the doorway and out leapt Artair to defend his home. His teeth sank into the cheek of the nearest soldier and he and the dog howled together, one in the joy of victory, the other in the pain of defeat. But Artair received the butt of a musket to the head and leapt back yelping. The soldiers released their lead into him, and Eunan's childhood friend howled no more.

"ARTAIR!" Eunan's vision became blinded by tears and his head clouded in pain. He raised his axe and charged at the soldiers. A hand hooked his elbow from behind. He raised his axe to release himself from the grip, but it was his uncle Fergus.

"Don't be a fool all your life! Get on your horse and tell Hugh Maguire. It'll do your mother no good to have a dead son and a dead husband on the same day. Go! I'll take care of her. Return swiftly!"

Eunan tried to shake his uncle off, but his grip was solid. Eunan's tears abated, and he saw the soldiers turn towards him and reload their muskets. He bade his uncle farewell. He changed direction and ran towards the lake shore, knowing he could find a horse there. The sheriff and his men were going berserk by now, running down villagers and shooting them in the back. Those villagers who could were running towards the sanctuary of the woods. None of them got there. Eunan made his way around the backs of the houses, trying to make as little noise as possible.

Suddenly one of his neighbours ran in front of him from between two houses. She tripped on an overturned basket and fell to the ground. Behind her came the bulk of a horse belonging to the sheriff's men. With a tug of the reins, the horse's hooves came down upon the woman. Eunan was incensed. With a flash of his axe blade, the horse was felled. But the battle-axe was trapped under the body. Eunan grabbed one of his throwing axes, and the sheriff's man staggered up from under his horse's saddle and drew his gun. Eunan hesitated. What if he missed? The man's finger hit the trigger. From behind the man, an axe fell and swiped his arm straight off.

"I told you to run!" cried Eunan's uncle as he stood over the man to finish him.

Eunan ran. He turned when he heard a gunshot and saw his uncle fall as another of the sheriff's men shot him from behind. He ran down to the shoreline and sure enough, near his father's house were some horses tied to a post. Eunan noticed the Galloglass making their way towards the village square but was too busy freeing the horse to see whose side they were on. He jumped on top of the horse and dug his heels into his horse's sides, fighting back tears.

He rode through the centre of the village, for that was the most direct way. He thought of Desmond and what he would do. He rode through to the centre circle. At the sight of his father's body, he pulled his horse up.

"I am sorry, Father, for this day I have failed you."

"What are you doing, you Mac scum!" came a voice.

Eunan instinctively reached for his belt and turned and threw the axe towards the sound of the voice. It was the first time he had killed a man up close. He retrieved his axe, remounted his horse, and fled.

# CHAPTER SEVENTEEN

# BANDITS IN THE WOODS

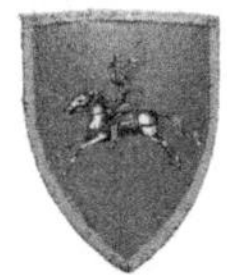

Eunan rode as far away from his village as possible until he and his horse were exhausted. He stopped, dismounted, and gave her a rest, while he could not resist the urge to look back through the low, rolling hills. He did not turn into a pillar of salt, but a pillar of guilt and regret cemented together by mourning. A plume of smoke dissolved into the sky. Then, to the right, he saw another plume of smoke, and to the right of that again, another. He did not know what had happened in his village, but the burden of being their last hope lay heavy upon his shoulders. All he knew was he must ride to Enniskillen and get the Maguire. He had to put all the pain and death he witnessed aside. His village, the remains of his family, were relying upon him.

It was a day's ride, and there were many stragglers along the route searching out the sanctuary of Enniskillen or venturing further north to seek the protection of the O'Donnells. They were mainly women and children with some lightly armed men who would be no match for the English soldiers. Eunan did not stop for anyone. He kept on riding, only pausing to rest and water his horse.

The road eventually went through a forest. The horse slowed to a trot, for the path was stony, and the last thing Eunan needed was a lame horse. Eunan rounded a corner, and before him, a felled tree blocked his path. A man, bare-headed but dressed in the chain mail of a Galloglass, stood in his way with his axe drawn across his shoulder, ready to strike.

"Where did you get that axe, boy?" he said, gesturing towards the battle-axe Eunan had slung behind his back.

Eunan reached for one of the throwing axes on his belt.

"I wouldn't do that if I were you," said a voice.

Eunan looked around, and three archers had their arrows pointed at his head.

"Throw your axe to the ground and get off your horse slowly," the voice said.

Eunan obeyed, realising he had encountered a travelling band of lightly armed soldiers known as Kern. Once he was off the horse with his hands raised, the men removed the back axe from its holster and his belt laden with throwing axes.

"I need them, keep them safe," Eunan said. He did not feel afraid, for all his senses had been dulled, but his heart sank at the thought of being parted from his axes, his only connection to Desmond and the only person he knew he had left.

"Oh, we will," said the man with a smirk as he shoved Eunan in the back to get him moving.

"I have little money, but you can have it," said Eunan. "I'm a local lad, and someone will miss me. If you give me back my possessions and let me on my way, we'll say no more about this."

But all his pleadings got him was another shove in the back.

"Quiet, lad! There's someone we'd like you to meet."

The men brought him to a campsite in a little clearing some distance from the road. There were more men there, all in various states of dress and battle readiness. They had the chain mail, helmets and axes of the Galloglass, but they appeared to have fallen on hard times. Beyond the men was another camp with women and children. There were some animals there, the odd cow, but both human and animal looked skinny and not well kept. The men brought Eunan to the tent of their constable, the leader of their Galloglass sept.

Eunan stood in front of the constable, doing his best not to appear afraid. The constable was older than the rest, dressed in his chain mail with his worn, grey beard. He seemed to be jaded, as if kindness had abandoned his soul many years before.

"So what have we got here then?" the constable said.

"We found him wandering in the woods," one captor said.

"I wasn't wandering, I was—"

"You were what? Are you an English spy?" said the constable.

Eunan spat on the ground.

"If you are the sheriff's men, just kill me now just like you killed my family. For as sure as night becomes day, I will have my revenge upon you and slit your throats as you sleep."

The constable laughed.

"Calm down, lad, we're not the sheriff's men, but if all your family is dead, you're of little use to us. There's no ransom money for orphans. Give us a reason not to kill you."

Eunan was too emotionally and physically exhausted to be afraid.

"You don't look like bandits," said Eunan. "You wear the battle dress of Galloglass."

"Who's to say we're not bandits, and we just killed the Galloglass and stole their armour?"

"Bandits couldn't do that. What clan are you? Who are your masters?"

"We have no masters, and you talk a lot like an English spy. I'll ask you one last time, why should we not rip out your tongue and roast your body over our fire?"

"You are here because you think war is coming?"

"War always seeks the Galloglass out. Death or glory, or if we're lucky, we get paid before we have to make that choice."

"I can get you permanent employment with the Maguire."

"And who are you to have such a brag?"

"I am Eunan, the son of Cathal O'Keenan Maguire."

The constable flinched.

"Never heard of him! Anyone ever heard of him? You told us your family was dead, so I assume you're lying. Take out his tongue."

The men grabbed Eunan.

"No, no! Wait! I am the son of Cathal Maguire. If you come to our village, he will pay you. We need protection from the English sheriff. Hugh Maguire is his cousin. War is coming, and there is plenty of land to pillage and steal."

The constable did not flinch.

"Why should I believe you? How can a man you previously said was dead pay me?"

"Have you got a better offer? If you did, you wouldn't be hiding in the forests."

"We're not hiding."

"Well, you're certainly not gainfully employed."

The leader considered Eunan's offer.

"We'll go to your village, and if we don't get paid, we'll kill you instead. How does that sound?"

Eunan nodded. At least he knew the village terrain better than these bandits. If it came to it, he had a reasonable chance of escape.

"My ears will ring with your gratitude when you are handsomely employed. Are you going to release me now, your talisman of good fortune?"

"You talk yourself up so much I don't know which I'd prefer: to kill you now slowly or to take all the riches you say you have on offer, then discover you are a liar and then spend even longer killing you. Release him. State your name again for the record, boy? I need to know so I can get all your promises written down for my amusement. Get the priest. Get the priest. I have a contract to make! Bard! Bard! Strum a song that laments me as a hero, one here to free this green, fair land from your oppressive English overlords while I strike a bargain with this young man so that he may win his freedom." He turned his attention again to Eunan. "Sit, sit by the fire, and let us make this contract."

Eunan made himself comfortable. His energy suddenly drained from him as if it were tension alone that kept him standing. Someone gave him some food and ale. He nodded his head in appreciation before tucking into his meal, for he was famished. The constable sat beside him.

"Priest, priest, come and sit down. We have a bargain to make. Now it is between Eunan Maguire, if I remember correctly?"

"You do."

"And me Seamus MacSheehy."

Eunan pondered. "I've heard of you."

"Good. My reputation precedes me. Then you know I am expensive!"

Eunan smiled. The priest scribbled.

"Now, how many heads of cattle does your village have?" said Seamus.

"About twenty."

"So your plan for your village is to swap oppression by the English for famine? How do I know your father, if he would be so kind as to leave his grave, will keep such a bargain?"

"How many warriors do you have?"

"I have to pay each of my men a cow. They're risking their lives, you know."

"The Maguire will pay you handsomely for protecting his subjects."

"Are we back to ripping out your tongue so soon? You go back and forth from your dead father to the most powerful man in the land you claim is your relative to cover any potential debts. Have you so little to bargain with?"

Eunan steadied his gaze on Seamus.

"If my father cannot pay you, the Maguire will. He is an honourable man. I have connections with him and his favoured advisor."

"Which one of these men is the honourable one? I have buried so many of my kinsmen fighting for 'honourable men'. Look at me now. You say I am in the forest waiting for gainful employment. I am here because of non-payment by so-called 'honourable men'. All my wealth is my men. If I throw their lives away fighting for 'honourable men' with nothing to show for it, their wives and children starve. It looks like all we have to exchange with each other is whose group of siblings die of starvation. And there we are, back to ripping out your tongue again."

Eunan blurted out the first thing that came into his mind.

"If my father doesn't pay you, I will go into your service."

"But you would already be in my service. I would be entertained by watching you getting your tongue ripped out."

"I would provide you with far better service as a warrior."

"So, I suppose you can start entertaining me now. If you can beat one of my warriors in single combat, I will take you up on your offer. Finn, would you do the honours please?"

A young warrior, slightly older but smaller than Eunan, stepped forward. He had a glint in his sky-blue eyes that showed he would enjoy this, and he had more at stake in this fight than was apparent.

"Try not to kill him," said Seamus. "I'm talking to him, not you, Eunan."

Eunan smiled. The man was a similar size to many he had taken on and beaten before. "What are the weapons?"

Seamus threw out his arms and cast his voice.

"Axes, of course. We are Galloglass."

Another of the Galloglass stepped forward and offered each of them an axe.

"Can I have my own?" Eunan asked.

Seamus nodded his approval.

"Fight!"

The Galloglass formed a circle around the combatants and cheered Finn on. Finn circled Eunan, trying to corner him, jabbing with his axe. Finn unleashed a semi-circular swing. Eunan dodged out of the way.

"Try to leave him in one piece, Finn. We may get a couple of cows for him yet," said Seamus.

Finn jabbed some more and his comrades stepped back to form a funnel Finn could trap Eunan in. Finn swung his axe from right to left. Eunan worked out the balance of Finn's body and kicked him in the supporting knee and hit him in the cheek with the butt of his axe handle. Finn went down like a sack of potatoes. He pleaded for mercy with Eunan's axe blade on his neck. The circle of comrades parted, and Seamus stepped in.

"You've done this before. As much as I hate to see my men beaten, spare him, for I only have twenty. Finn can be a scout until he earns his place back."

Eunan smirked. "I won, so why don't I become the Galloglass, and he the horse boy?"

"You're so sure of yourself! I'll tell you what. We'll take you as an apprentice Galloglass, and Finn can be an apprentice Galloglass horse boy."

Finn's face was a mask of fury, but he could do nothing, for he was still beneath the axe blade.

"However, Finn gets the opportunity to challenge you once a month. If he wins, he becomes a Galloglass again."

Eunan raised his blade and shook Seamus's hand to seal the bargain.

"And what happens to him?" said Finn. He had by now got to his feet, in a thunderous mood of embarrassment and fury.

"That depends on how many cattle and how much land he can get for us. Now, firstly Father Padraig will finish writing our agreement, then let us all get some sleep, for tomorrow we head for Eunan's village."

# CHAPTER EIGHTEEN

# IN THE EMBERS

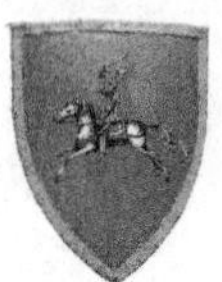

The next day, fifteen Galloglass set out for Eunan's village with five left behind to guard the women and children. They rode two by two with Eunan and Seamus at the front, with Finn demoted to scout. Finn rode ahead and returned to point to the numerous plumes of smoke on the horizon before them.

"It looks like the sheriff has been busy," said Seamus to Eunan. Eunan bowed his head and dug his heels into his horse's side.

They met various stragglers along the road who told tales of the English pillaging and destruction. Eunan became even more downhearted.

"I've seen this all before, the same old pattern," said Seamus.

"How so?" said Eunan.

"We are veterans of the Desmond rebellions in the 1570s and 1580s. Put down by the usual band of English, their mercenaries and Irish traitors like the O'Neills. We fought for the Desmonds. We were the pride of his Galloglass. Only to be defeated with help from Irish traitors. I'll never forget that, and neither should you. A friend is a friend as long as you have enough cows and land to pay him."

"You must know the O'Neills are the power around here," Eunan said. "Only the O'Donnells can challenge them. But you've come to the right place if you are looking to get hired for war. It never ends, but it's hard to remember who's on whose side."

"Well, we heard about the MacMahons getting cleared out of Monaghan," said Seamus, "and we reckoned the Maguires were next."

This only added to Eunan's sense of despair.

"Why fight for a losing cause? Everyone else you have fought for has lost."

"The English have always been our sworn enemies, back to our Scottish forefathers. Some have succumbed to the English shilling, but we've always remained faithful to the Galloglass code."

"Albeit for whichever Irish lord paid the most."

"Don't get too cheeky, lad. Your father still has to come up with the cattle you promised us. We were on a retainer with the Desmonds, their best men. Technically mercenaries, but name me a soldier who isn't?!"

"Me."

Seamus laughed.

"It's great you can keep your sense of humour with the bleak days ahead! Your village should come up soon, shouldn't it?"

Eunan just looked at him.

"It's just beyond the next hill, beside the lake."

They rounded the hill, and the devastation of the village hit them straight in the face. The houses were smouldering ruins, dead people and animals littered the ground, and all the boats were taken or destroyed.

"Not a cow in sight," sighed Seamus, but he was silent when he saw the reaction on Eunan's face. He wasn't quite that cold-hearted; not when he still hoped to be paid. Eunan leapt from his horse and ran into the village. He went straight to his mother's house. Seamus called Finn over to him.

"I have indulged you before," Seamus said, "but now is the time you can earn the honour of being a Galloglass despite all you have done in the past."

Finn gave him an evil grin.

"You want me to kill him?" He fondled the pommel of his sword.

Seamus grabbed him by the scruff of the neck. "No, I want you to befriend him. I want you to be loyal to him. I want him to be the man you never could be. He must never know who you are or what lies in the past. The only thing that is dead is the past. If you succeed, I will make you a Galloglass."

"And if I fail?"

"Then you had better make sure that both Eunan and I are dead. Now be off with you."

The burnt embers of Eunan's former home lay at his feet. He searched through the rubble and the charred remains surrounding it. He found what he assumed to be his uncle's blackened body and the horse of the mercenary he had taken down. He searched around the back of his house and found the wooden stump he used to chop wood. There was no sign of his mother. He found carbonised wood that resembled her chair. A piece of her blanket. But not a body. Nor could he find the body of his dog. He ran to the centre of the village to find his father's corpse.

The once proud village circle where they used to have meetings was full of bodies, some intact and some burned. He could not identify his father's body amongst the charred remains. Finn caught up with Eunan and offered to help him look. Eventually, they found someone who was still alive. It was Padraig O'Dwyer Maguire, a man who had lived on the outskirts of the village. He often used to combine with Eunan's father and uncle to trade with other villages or make the weekly or monthly trade trip to Enniskillen, depending on the season. Padraig raised his head and croaked for water.

"Where are my mother and father?" said Eunan.

"The well, look down the well..." And with that, Padraig was gone.

Eunan laid his head gently on the ground.

"Goodbye, my sweet friend," he said. He took one last look at the village before running off to the well with Finn.

The well was outside the village, beside the forest. The hut beside the well was still intact. There were no outward signs of violence. Eunan and Finn crept towards the well, wary of who might lurk at the edge of the forest. Finn kept watch as Eunan looked down the well. It was deep and dark and sucked Eunan down into an emotional swirl. Finn picked up some stones.

"Here, throw these down and listen for the splash of water."

Eunan's hand shook as he took the stones. No splash met the falling stone.

"I think the old man was right," said Finn.

Eunan broke down and cried until his bitter tears seeped into the ground.

"Come on, we've got to go."

Finn walked away. But all Eunan could think of was the years of pain and heartache he had put his parents through in his life, and when they needed him the most, he was not there to defend them.

Finn ran back and grabbed him by the arm.

"Come on, let's go! The English will be here soon with their lackeys. Come on!"

They returned to the entrance to the village where Seamus and the other Galloglass were waiting for them.

"Poor pickings here today, boy!" said Seamus, and Eunan ignored him. "So, how are we going to get paid? I haven't seen any cows today. As handy as you are with an axe, it isn't going to feed my men. So what is your suggestion before we start to live off the land?"

Eunan bit his lip. Then he remembered something his father told him, the cause of all his strife.

"The new Maguire is getting inaugurated near Lisnaskea. If we leave now, we may make it there on time. All his chiefs and allies should be there. If we are going to get gainfully employed anywhere, it will be there. But we need to set off now."

"That's music to my ears. Shall we depart?"

# CHAPTER NINETEEN

# STICKS AND STONES TO PROP UP AN EGO

Eunan and the MacSheehy Galloglass set off for Lisnaskea and the traditional inauguration site of the Maguires. Neither wind nor rain nor bog underfoot could slow them down, for Seamus smelt money. Eunan, as the provider of the opportunities for wealth, could never wander out of Seamus's sight. A plot had hatched in Seamus's mind, an inauguration born and a contract signed. Eunan was now the O'Keenan Maguire, whether he liked it or not.

The pressure of being the O'Keenan Maguire weighed heavily on Eunan's shoulders. An O'Keenan Maguire with no O'Keenan Maguires. His new mentor may have an answer, or at least provide some solace.

"What will I tell the future Maguire about who I am?" Eunan said. "I have no battle honours to brag about, no people who follow and look up to me, no cattle to feed my people. I am nothing, nothing but saddle-sore."

Seamus shook his head.

"In that, you are wrong. One thing that buys you respect, especially when war is in the air, is muscle. You have us, your Galloglass. There will be chieftains at Lisnaskea with fields full of cows, villages full of people, but they will have no Galloglass, and the Maguire will turn his nose up at them. But when you show up there, you will have your name and your Galloglass, and nobody will care about cattle or peasants. They'll be too busy thinking about the war and what they can gain, or how long they will stay alive for, or who might want to kill them."

Eunan was perplexed.

"How come you know so much?"

"I have served many, many chieftains, good and bad, lofty lords and low-born landowners, and seen much death and many, many wars."

Seamus smiled at Eunan, and Eunan gazed out to the road ahead and tried to picture his destiny, be it good or bad: a lofty lord, or dead in a ditch. But Eunan's bout of nerves would not end. Seamus was tired of the boy's melancholy, as he knew the boy would have to act big to gain the respect of the upper echelons of the Maguires. They passed through a forest, and at a suitable knoll, Seamus leapt from his horse and ordered the column to stop.

"Go stand up on that rock, boy."

Seamus searched around for a suitable stick and a smooth stone. The Galloglass got down from their horses and gathered beneath the rock. Seamus climbed up behind Eunan.

"Take these." Seamus placed the stick in one hand and the rock in the other.

"On this rock, I now anoint you... Oh, I need some water."

Finn threw up his water container. Seamus opened it and threw the contents at Eunan.

"I now anoint you the O'Keenan Maguire." He gestured to his Galloglass.

"Hurray."

"Damn it," said Seamus. "It's not as if I haven't seen this done a hundred times." Seamus reached down and took off his shoe. He placed it upon Eunan's head. "Always remember, no matter what, you are always under someone else." There was a bigger cheer for that than before.

"As per our previously signed contract," Seamus continued, "you agree to pay us for our support, and you delegate all decision-making, military or otherwise, to me. In turn, you become the O'Keenan Maguire."

"But I have no people to lead," said Eunan.

"What do you call them?" Seamus pointed down to the Galloglass, who laughed below. "Don't insult your followers as your first act of becoming chieftain. Oh yes, I forgot something."

Seamus grabbed Eunan by the shoulders and spun him around.

"Don't forget who you are. Don't forget who you are."

Eunan was so dizzy he fell to the ground.

"Don't lose your rock. Put it in your pocket. That is the lucky rock of the O'Keenan Maguire."

The Galloglass laughed, and Seamus climbed down and got back on his horse.

"In your own time, chieftain. We've got the Maguire's inauguration to go to."

They travelled for two days, over bogs, through forests and, if they were lucky, roads in the right direction, until they came to the Enniskillen / Lisnaskea road. They were slowed down mainly by the lack of discipline of the Galloglass, who slipped off to steal food or cause mischief at the first sign of temptation. Seamus did not stop them, for he knew his men were hungry and needed to be at their best for what was ahead.

They followed Eunan since he knew the path well. His father had brought him to Lisnaskea occasionally in his youth when gatherings of the Maguires were called, or sometimes to the regional markets. Eunan had wanted to take a boat across the lake. However, Seamus had insisted on travelling overland as he considered they needed to bring all of their equipment to look impressive for the upper echelons of clan Maguire, and also to protect themselves if they got attacked.

There were many war parties on the road to Lisnaskea who eyed each other nervously, for they could not tell who was in the pay of the Crown or which Maguire. All chiefs and warriors were battle-ready, fearing an ambush – especially those loyal to Hugh Maguire.

Eventually, Eunan and his band of warriors had the market town of Lisnaskea in their sights, and Seamus stopped his men in the forest so that they could clean and refresh themselves to look their best before parading into town. However, Eunan wondered whether such efforts were worthwhile, as the town was probably already full of soldiers and mercenaries and nobody would pay them much attention. Seamus ignored him as he most often did if he did not need him, and ordered his men to ride into town two-by-two, led by himself and Eunan.

The backdrop of Castle Skea, the home of Connor Roe Maguire, dwarfed Lisnaskea town, the traditional home of the Lisnaskea Maguires. The Lisnaskea Maguires were from the traditional senior branch of the family, and the Enniskillen Maguires were the junior branch. While Connor Roe nestled comfortably in the pocket of the English, the fact that outside Lisnaskea was the traditional inauguration ground of the Maguire meant that the inauguration had to happen there. If the Maguire were not inaugurated there, the inevitable challenges to the new Maguire's legitimacy would follow, so it was worth the risk of holding the ceremony there.

The town was full of makeshift alehouses and market stalls run by opportunistic local farmers trying to cash in on the influx of visitors keen to show their generosity and wealth. Once Seamus saw all the alehouses, he rode at the back of his entourage to keep their attention on the task at hand, while also inflating the importance of Eunan O'Keenan Maguire.

Connor Roe Maguire's Galloglass stopped them when they approached the castle. Seamus and his men had reached the point beyond which only the Maguire clan chiefs, their important guests, and select bodyguards could go. Seamus recognised the Galloglass were MacCabes, the traditional elite troops of the Maguires. The Lisnaskea Maguires employed a specific branch of the MacCabe family, and the MacCabes had been granted lands in the region for their services. They invited the MacSheehy Galloglass to camp on the outskirts of the town, while Eunan was allowed to take Seamus as his bodyguard when he returned to enter the castle.

Villages of tents surrounded Lisnaskea, a small cluster for each of the Maguire nobility and their followers and soldiers. The cluster size depended on the person's importance. The most significant clusters were those of dignitaries invited from other clans. It was a time to make alliances both in the county Maguire and the counties beyond. Eunan and his entourage of Galloglass pitched their tents at the edge of the southern tent village. The Galloglass were left behind under strict instructions to behave themselves. Temptation lay not too far away. The favourite for the title of the Maguire had brought a herd of cattle and set them to graze nearby in anticipation of the alliances he had to pay for, and the debts he had to pay off, to fulfil his ambition, not to mention the abundance of alehouses.

The centre of the village had been cleared of citizens and surrounded by a ring of MacCabe Galloglass with their beautiful chain mail and polished hooked axes – evidence that they worked for the regional power. Everyone who entered the inner circle was disarmed and allowed only one unarmed bodyguard.

The MacCabes and the MacSheehys had a long-running feud. So long-running that no one could remember how it started. They rarely stopped and paused to remember before swords were drawn. They had been, like all Scottish houses of Galloglass, on different sides in the many conflicts of Ireland, but also sometimes on the same side.

Eunan and Seamus approached the guards.

"Only Maguire kin with voting rights or invited dignitaries are allowed past here," said the guard. "There's no bearing arms. State who you are and declare your intentions!"

Eunan stepped forward and removed his throwing axes from his belt.

"Eunan O'Keenan Maguire, son of the deceased Cathal O'Keenan Maguire of the Knockinny Maguires. Claiming voting rights for the O'Keenan Maguire sept." He stated it with such confidence even Seamus believed him.

"Go to that house over there and see the priest." The Galloglass pointed to a large hut. He stepped in front of Seamus and looked him squarely in the eye.

"And who may you be?"

Seamus embraced the merest sniff of a fight.

"I'm the chief's bodyguard, and where he goes, I go."

Another MacCabe came and stood between them.

"Not with that, you're not. Leave the sword here, and you can collect it when you leave."

Seamus spitefully undid his sword and his belt with scabbard attached fell to the ground.

"I think I know you," said the first Galloglass.

"That's 'cos I'm pretty, just like all the proper Scottish Galloglass!"

The other Galloglass stood between them again.

"Follow your master, and we'll try not to piss on your sword."

"That sword is as good for scooping oysters as it is for chopping the balls off gutless, so-called Galloglass. Remember that before you put your cocks anywhere near my sword."

The Galloglass ignored him.

"Follow your master there and hold your tongue, or else he'll be looking for a new bodyguard!"

After a swift rude gesture, Seamus caught up with Eunan.

"You've got to stand up to these pretend warriors or they get too cocky. And if they get too cocky, their master will ask for compensation when he finds two corpses!"

Eunan ignored him.

"I'm worried, Seamus. What if they find out I'm a fraud and all the villagers are dead, and that it was my fault?"

"As I have told you before, it's a war. You have twenty Galloglass, and that's worth a lot."

"But how do I pay you?"

"Don't worry about that. You get me in, and I'll get plenty of payment enough."

They entered the hut, and a priest sat before them, bent over some papers with a quill. A guard had run ahead and pre-announced Eunan's arrival. The priest raised his head.

Eunan nodded in greeting. "Eunan O'Keenan Maguire is here to claim his rights."

The priest consulted his ledger.

"What brings you here?" said the priest. "I heard that Cathal O'Keenan Maguire was dead. How can you claim his rights?"

"He is. I am his son, and I inherited his title," said Eunan.

"Was elected into his title!" said Seamus. "My men and I all voted for him."

The priest ignored Seamus.

"My condolences to you. I hope your father has a swift journey to heaven."

The priest looked down and examined his papers.

"So you are lucky enough to have been elected into your title just before another war. Long may you enjoy the fruits of your father's labour. But now it is time to defend your clan. What can you contribute to the efforts of the Maguire?"

"I bring twenty Galloglass."

"The harvests over by the Cladagh River must be good, for my records have your lands as being bogs and forest and sparsely populated, and you don't look like a man of means," said the priest.

"He is a great warrior, a master of the axe and the best cattle rustler I've ever known," said Seamus. "Hugh Maguire himself would be proud to have such a warrior ride with him."

Eunan signalled to him to be quiet. Seamus didn't take it well.

"He also volunteers to help the Maguire consolidate his power, if you know what I mean. If the Maguire doesn't get voted in unanimously."

The priest glanced at Seamus.

"I have noted your request and will pass it on. There is a great need for a person of your skills."

Seamus smiled at Eunan's scowl.

"The feast will begin at sundown, and the voting will be after that. Your fellow chiefs are in the great hall, should you wish to converse with them before voting commences. I suggest you speak to Hugh Maguire and court his favour. You should be able to obtain much gainful employment."

"I think we will, won't we, Eunan?" said Seamus. "Where's this hall you speak of, and when is the ale served?"

"The guards will show you, and you will have as much ale as you desire. However, I would keep your wits about you and watch your backs."

"This gets better and better. Ale, a fight, and plenty of profit. Good luck, priest. I'm sure you will be very busy crossing off the names of the dead from your book while we bear arms to protect you!"

"Look after yourself, Eunan," said the priest, ignoring Seamus again.

The guards pointed them toward the castle and the great hall, but the destination was obvious.

The MacCabe Galloglass lined the streets on the way to the great hall. Interlopers approached from both sides of the street and engaged in probing conversation to find the person of influence and an indication of which way they were likely to vote.

"And who may you be?" said a nobleman dressed in a red cape to Eunan.

"Who are you?" grunted Seamus as he stood in front of his master.

"Please, I am addressing the lord."

The nobleman turned to Eunan. Eunan immediately recognised him but said nothing for fear of being outed as an impostor. Donnacha did not recognise him for he had grown several inches in height since they had seen each other over a year before, and the weeks on the road had provided Eunan with a scraggly beard, unbecoming of the Maguire court.

"I am a representative of Hugh Maguire. You may have heard of his exploits fighting the English?"

Eunan hesitated, for he feared being recognised and ejected from the proceedings for being an impostor.

"I have."

"Well, he wants your vote, wants you to join him and also to know what you can bring to the fight. What part of the family are you from?"

"O'Keenan Maguire, and I've got twenty Galloglass."

"Oh, really? Wait, do I recognise you? You seem familiar." Donnacha put his arm around Eunan's shoulder.

Seamus saw Eunan's lip tremble and his opportunity slipping away.

"Really?" said Seamus, who parted the two men. "And his Galloglass needs something to do to get paid. Who around here do we need to talk to so I can strike a bargain?"

"You can talk to me. Once you have voted for Hugh Maguire, we can talk about serving the Maguire's cause."

"My own cause is a bit more pressing. Now, how about you make us an offer before we look around and talk to the other candidates?"

"The Maguire will have created a few enemies along the way to getting elected. But he will still need their support for the upcoming war. He will need some loyal, trustworthy men to visit some of his clan for him."

"For a fixed rate, we can negotiate, but we would also require additional compensation dependent on what level of persuasion we need to employ and what expenses we incur both in coin and men. If you consider these points and pose a reasonable offer, we may have a deal."

"As long as your master votes for Hugh Maguire, there will be plenty of work for men with your special talents. Come and ask for me, Donnacha O'Cassidy Maguire."

Seamus slapped Eunan on both shoulders.

"Do you hear that? You have sorted us out already. All you have to do is vote for Hugh Maguire. My men and I get paid, you get trained as a Galloglass, and we get to kill Hugh Maguire's enemies for fun. You can even throw your little axes at them."

"How do I know I want to vote for Hugh Maguire? Should I not talk to the other candidates first?"

Seamus gave him a friendly pat on the face.

"One of the things I like about you is your sense of humour! You wouldn't want to stand between your Galloglass and a good payday, would you?"

Seamus turned to Hugh Maguire's emissary.

"What's your name again so we can meet up afterwards?"

"Donnacha O'Cassidy Maguire. Don't worry. I will come and find you after the vote."

Donnacha was about to leave but looked at Eunan again and tilted his head. He stood with his finger in the air and Eunan's name on the tip of his tongue.

"I remember now, you were – ."

But Seamus put his arm around Donnacha's shoulders and edged him away.

"Oh look, there's lord so and so. I heard he was going to vote for the other fella."

Donnacha looked, and when his head was turned, Seamus and Eunan disappeared into the crowd.

Eunan let out a sigh of relief. "I'm glad he didn't recognise me."

"I'm insulted he didn't recognise me," said Seamus. He remembered his previous dealings with the Maguire court and thought his reputation extended more than it did.

Eunan and Seamus reached the entrance to the castle. Its rounded towers, which loomed overhead, impressed Eunan. Seamus, by force of habit, made a note of how many arrows were trained on them from the towers and castle walls and how they could make their escape if need be. Two Galloglass standing in the entrance parted their axes, and they entered. Eunan was surprised Seamus did not insult them.

"They're the good ones. They guard the lord. I may have a big mouth, but I'm not stupid."

The courtyard was patrolled by soldiers and filled with the gossiping nobility of the Maguire. It was not long before they were all invited to join Connor Roe and the other influential guests in the main hall. Seamus hooked Eunan by the elbow, for he did not want to lose him in the crowd.

They made their way into the great hall, but both Seamus and Eunan had been in greater. A throng of people created a din harsh on the ears of a country boy from a small village. Seamus and Eunan slipped down the sides of the room until they could find a suitable observation point. Seamus watched the men and Eunan stood back and observed the walls of the hall.

The colourful war banners of the various septs of the Maguire clan hung in swags from the ceilings. It was impressive, but nothing like Enniskillen. Three long tables parallel to each other dominated the hall and an overarching raised head table at the top overlooked the others.

Hugh Maguire stood at the top table and puffed his chest out to make himself look important. Eunan remembered him as an arrogant boy. Though everyone made mistakes when they were boys, it looked like Hugh had not learned from his. But at least he had made an effort for today's vote, looking every inch the future Maguire; richly dressed but still a warrior, his arrogant smile deployed to charm votes from lesser chieftains whose peoples were squeezed between himself and Connor Roe.

Eunan's eyes fell on Connor Roe, the man who had played the devil in the background for most of his life. The man he held responsible for his father's death. Connor Roe had undoubtedly made an effort, decked out in the most elegant imported clothes from England. Eunan could smell his pitch from where he stood: prosperity, and the English coin. It worked on some, for there was a queue of chieftains waiting to speak to him.

Seamus did his own assessment of the candidates for the Maguire, nodded to Eunan, and they tried to make their way through the crowd to the top table. They were accosted en route.

"Hey, where are you from? I haven't seen you before," said a well-dressed man who stood in their way.

"Unless you've got a good offer, get out of our way. We're voting for Hugh Maguire," said Seamus.

"The Lisnaskea Maguires can offer you cattle."

"How many?" said Seamus, grabbing Eunan and stopping to listen.

"How many warriors do you have?"

"Twenty Galloglass."

"Forty cattle."

"I can steal them off you when Hugh Maguire kills off his enemies. Get out of my way!"

"Eighty cattle."

"Eighty cattle is good for one vote," said Eunan. "That would replace the lost village herd."

"It's an insult. I could steal eighty cattle in a day and still come back and fight for the Maguire the next. Enjoy being hunted down when you lose." Seamus cut the conversation off.

He pushed past the Lisnaskea Maguires, going to where he considered the real power to be.

Hugh Maguire showed his bejewelled wife off to the room, never forgetting to remind anyone within earshot that she was Hugh O'Neill's daughter and that he had her father's full support in any endeavour he would undertake if he became the Maguire. Hugh Maguire then stood beside emissaries of Hugh O'Neill and Donnell O'Donnell. His puffed-up pride and less-than-subtle hints said he had the support of the O'Donnells and the O'Neills, and he dished out enough promises of land and cattle to win the election by a landslide. The finest young men of Fermanagh swarmed around Hugh Maguire, as he seemed to be the rising star and possessed an aura of a man destined for greatness. Connor Roe Maguire did not have a chance.

The northern clergy also gathered around Hugh Maguire, and they let it be known to anyone who would listen that he was the favoured candidate of both the Pope and the King of Spain. The sound of Spanish came from men lurking in the shadows of the hall, from men who looked Irish in their dress and appearance but had the etiquette of a faraway and more sophisticated land. Fresh Scottish accents were also to be heard. No such interest surrounded Connor Roe Maguire, but the stench of English money had its attractions for some.

Seamus walked towards Hugh Maguire, but two Galloglass stepped forward and barred his way. Seamus spoke over the edges of their blades.

"I'm pleased to make your acquaintance, lord. I have here my master, Eunan O'Keenan Maguire, a fresh victim of the English. He lost his family and village to the English sheriff and is here with his twenty Galloglass, which he has paid for with the last of his village's cattle, to plead his allegiance to you to help you rid Maguire Country of the English pestilence! He would love to meet you."

The two Galloglass looked over their shoulders for their master's reaction.

With his ego fanned and recognising a familiar name, Hugh Maguire waved them through. He was young, ambitious, and impatient. Hugh also liked dramatic gestures and to appear benevolent. He itched to get this election over with so he could get back on his horse and fight again. But he could always do with more warriors.

A red-faced Eunan froze, so he gripped his lucky stone in his pocket and approached. Seamus prodded Eunan, and Eunan bent his knee and his head.

"Eunan O'Keenan Maguire and his Galloglass at your service, lord."

"Please rise, I am not the Maguire yet!" Hugh said. "Eunan! It is so good to see you again! I hope you enjoyed your time in Enniskillen?"

Seamus beamed like he had found his pot of gold.

"Indeed, I did! Is Desmond with you?" said Eunan.

"Alas, he is retired. He has not been seen in Enniskillen for many a moon. But now the Maguires need warriors. I assume you can ride a horse with the skill of a warrior?"

"As good as any man in my village," said Eunan as he rose and found himself taller than Hugh Maguire, even though Hugh stood on an elevated platform.

"You should come and ride with the Maguire noblemen. The Maguire horsemen are the envy of all the north, as well you know!"

Seamus could feel the Maguire's coin slipping into his pocket but did not wish to lose his money maker.

"He has twenty MacSheehy Galloglass, all veterans of the Munster wars, who silently vanquished the Earl of Desmond's disloyal kinsmen and are expert cattle rustlers. Not to mention his lordship's skills with throwing axes. He's an accomplished assassin."

Hugh Maguire's eyebrow stretched northwards. He slapped Eunan on the shoulder.

"There's always a great demand for men of your skills. Come and see me tomorrow after the sun goes down. I will have plenty of work for you before this day is done."

"We will, sir, we will." Seamus grinned from ear to ear.

He grabbed Eunan by the elbow, and they bowed as Hugh Maguire went to speak to his next kinsman. Seamus and Eunan slipped back into the crowd.

A few moments later, Connor Roe Maguire's chief steward slammed his staff into the floor.

"Gentlemen, please take your seats and let the feasting begin!"

Both Maguire candidates sat up on the top table, along with the representatives from the O'Donnells, O'Neills, the clergy, and other dignitaries from other minor clans. Stewards showed Eunan his allotted seat. He had a good view of the top table, while Seamus stood in the wings and watched his master.

The stewards served food, and Eunan was treated to endless meat, bread, and wine, while Seamus watched from the side and tried to guess who he would be asked to kill when Hugh got elected. Seamus noted the boy had difficulty fitting in, for Eunan still felt unworthy. He was quieter than the rowdy old chiefs who ate as if it were their last meal. The hall became rowdier and rowdier as the bards came out and the ale was drunk. The inevitable songs of heroes, battles, and glory began. There were endless salutes to the various Maguire heroes of the past, and how the chosen Maguire would emulate and better them. Eunan felt the effects of the ale, and his tongue became looser. Seamus thought he might have to intervene until the steward slammed his staff on the ground again.

"Gentlemen, the time has come to elect the new Maguire! Please take your seats!"

The singing stopped, and the drunken chiefs slowly returned to their allotted places. The steward stood before the three benches.

"Clansmen of the Maguire! This is a momentous evening where we elect the new Maguire. We face a grave threat to our existence, for we only have to look across the border at what happened to the MacMahons. Our fate could be the same as theirs!"

"It is not the time for grandstanding. We must see things in perspective!" shouted Connor Roe Maguire as he rose from his seat.

"You will each get your turn," said the steward. "We have for you two candidates, both from different branches of the family and both with very differing views on which direction the clan should go. And of course, for you all, many gifts as they share the wealth of the Maguire clan."

The roar of the chieftains almost lifted the roof off the castle.

"So first, we have Connor Roe Maguire, to whose generosity and the generosity of the Lisnaskea Maguires we are indebted to this evening."

The chieftains again roared their appreciation. As Connor Roe Maguire rose to speak, Seamus signalled to Eunan to come and talk with him.

Connor Roe Maguire gave a speech stating the MacMahons had brought their fall upon themselves and how cattle rustling had decreased since the MacMahons were displaced.

"He's in the pocket of the English," said Seamus. "Watch who votes for him and how many soldiers they have, as they're probably our first jobs for Hugh Maguire."

The hall rang out with the roars of appreciation of the chieftains to the promises of the lavish gifts Connor Roe Maguire would give them on his confirmation as the Maguire. Connor Roe constantly affirmed that he was the representative of the senior branch of the clan and that he would bring peace. They all sat down, and Hugh Maguire rose.

"Now must I tell you the tales of my dearly departed father, Cúchonnacht Maguire, who brought peace to Fermanagh? Peace with the O'Neills, peace with the O'Donnells—"

"And sold us out to the English," said a heckler.

Hugh Maguire froze and then recovered his composure.

"My father also secured peace with the English. He had a simple choice. Become subject to the Crown or be removed by the Crown. But how does this tarnish the greatness of the Maguires? Did the O'Neills and the O'Donnells not submit to the English Crown on similar terms forty years ago? And where are they now? They sit amongst us as the lords of Ulster, sovereign in their own lands, leading the resistance against the Crown! Does this deal diminish them? I say no, and if you say differently, look at the evidence you see before you today.

"As much as it pains me to say it, the forces of England were too strong for us at the time. The lords of Ulster were divided. But who brought them together? Who gave them time to gather their strength? Who got back Fermanagh for the Maguires in perpetuity? My father, Cúchonnacht Maguire."

There was a vast roar from the hall.

"But now it is different. We have allies. Some are here with us tonight from the great clans of the O'Neills and the O'Donnells. Some remain in the shadows but will come to our aid should the need arise. But we, the great clan Maguire, will throw off the oppressive yoke of the English and rise once again!"

The chieftains roared and banged their goblets on the table.

"Do I need to recite the stories of how I have vanquished our enemies and brought glory to our clan, or should I just serve ale and let the bards sing you the songs?"

There was an immense roar from the chieftains.

"The generosity of the Enniskillen Maguires is equally legendary, but as yet, not put to a tune."

"Hurray!"

"But it is not my exploits or my generosity that I am here to win you over with tonight, even though they would help—"

"Hurray!"

"It is with these," said Hugh Maguire with a flourish as he stepped back. The main doors of the hall were flung open and in marched a hundred Redshanks, Scottish mercenaries armed with muskets, a gift from the O'Donnells to their preferred candidate. The Redshanks lined the walls of the hall.

"And I also brought these." Hugh Maguire's men carried in large wooden crates and placed them on the platform upon which the top table rested. Hugh Maguire picked up an axe and smashed a box open. He pulled out a musket.

"I have enough muskets to arm ourselves and defeat any of our rivals, and any force the English may throw against us!"

The hall erupted in cheers.

"Now, who wants to vote against me?"

The chieftains mobbed Hugh Maguire. Connor Roe Maguire slipped away in the commotion.

# CHAPTER TWENTY

# UNDER THE SHOE

Bodies of the Maguire chieftains littered the hall. After searching for several minutes, Seamus found Eunan beneath a bench in a pool of ale, food, and vomit. Seamus had been the guest at many a feast where usually he was one of the more enthusiastic participants, but the previous evening he was not allowed to join in. He realised this was Eunan's first feast. It was now daylight, and the preparations for the inauguration had begun. Both Hugh Maguire's Redshanks and Connor Roe Maguire's Galloglass had assembled in the courtyard of the castle to escort the dignitaries to the traditional Maguire inauguration mound, Sciath Ghabhra. Seamus needed to invest in a bucket of cold water and fresh clothes to ensure the Maguires would accept his master. The bucket of cold water was applied much to his master's consternation.

"What the hell are you doing?" said Eunan as he spat water from his mouth.

"Get up and get dressed," said Seamus. "You've got work to do."

The hall was being cleaned and cleared while Eunan got changed.

"I feel like I've been beaten over the head with a hammer! What happened last night?"

"You set yourself on the path to becoming a Maguire, and now you've got to complete the task."

"Did Hugh Maguire get elected?"

"You really can't remember, can you?"

Seamus led Eunan out into the courtyard and stood him near the Hugh Maguire Redshanks for safekeeping. Eunan was one of the first of the dignitaries to arrive and not the most dishevelled. After what seemed an age of standing, Seamus had to prop Eunan up.

"Here, drink this." He gave Eunan a flask of liquid.

It seemed to do the trick, as Eunan was almost immediately revived.

"Here, give me that! I may need it if walking to the inauguration is necessary."

Eunan put the flask in his pocket and liberally drank from it whenever he felt he was fading.

"Watch how much you drink! We want you to remember today! It's the day we start working for the Maguire!"

Hugh Maguire finally arrived, surrounded by his Galloglass, the most important clergy in Fermanagh, the O'Neills and O'Donnells, and the closest of his supporters. No one, armed or unarmed, could get near him. Standing aside from him, surrounded by MacSweeney Galloglass, was Donnell O'Donnell, currently the leading power in Tirconnell.

"The big boys are here!" Seamus rubbed his rough hands in glee.

Hugh Maguire's aides accounted for all the nobles, and the short procession to Sciath Ghabhra began.

Cheering crowds met the procession as they left the protection of the castle walls. The crowds chanted Hugh Maguire's name and hailed him as the new Maguire. Eunan and Seamus were near the back of the procession, and Seamus had them nestled in amongst the Redshanks, for no one would be foolhardy enough to attack the Scottish mercenaries.

The procession left the town behind and walked towards the sacred mound they could see before them. The Redshank peeled off and created a defensive circle around the hill to protect the dignitaries from ambush. Dignitaries then surrounded the mound and only Hugh Maguire and his right-hand men, Donnell O'Donnell, and the clergy climbed to the summit. Seamus was allowed to stand beside Eunan and watch the ceremony. Eunan needed Seamus, for the ceremony was long, and he was still unsteady on his feet.

As the procession approached the mound they saw a shoe had been left on the stone ceremonial seat of the Maguire. The procession halted, for Hugh Maguire lost his nerve. "Connor Roe has left that for me as a trap. It is the shoe of the O'Neill, and to disregard it would be a grave insult." Donnell O'Donnell came to investigate why the procession had halted. Donnacha pointed to the shoe on the mound.

"I am the only master here today," said Donnell. "The only shoe you are going under is mine." He picked up the shoe and flung it away. "All right, let's get on with it."

The priests draped Hugh Maguire in the ceremonial robes of the Maguire. He stood before the stone chair of state that protruded from the mound. The Brehon stood before him as the officiator of the law and read the Brehon laws applicable to the Maguire and what was expected of him. Hugh Maguire recited the oath of the Maguire, and the clergy blessed the ceremony. Donnell O'Donnell then presented Hugh with the long white rod of sovereignty. Hugh bowed in reverence, acknowledging the O'Donnell power to nominate the Maguire, as Donnell held his shoe over Hugh's head. Hugh Maguire presented himself to his clansmen while his attendants recited his lineage to the first-remembered Maguires. Donnell O'Donnell then spun Hugh three times to the left and three times to the right, to survey the lands of the Maguire, while Hugh repeated the Latin chanted by the clergy. The priest gave his blessing and pointed towards the stone seat carved from a large rock. The bards and harpists played a celebratory song, and the crowd roared as Hugh sat down.

They invited the lesser chieftains onto the mound to file past their new leader. Eunan was towards the back of the line. Seamus stood back and watched the ceremony. Eunan was now feeling physically better but had become overwhelmed with nerves, being a country boy in such illustrious company. He reached Hugh Maguire. Eunan took his hand and kissed it and said, "The

Maguire." He nodded in subservience to Donnell O'Donnell, who stood beside Hugh Maguire.

Eunan took his place with the other chieftains.

Hugh Maguire rose from his chair, and the crowd hailed him as "The Maguire."

They all paraded back to the castle to continue the feast.

Eunan sobered up and took his place on the benches once more. The formality of the event had loosened somewhat, and Seamus could sit beside Eunan. Seamus found himself much more comfortable in the present company than Eunan, and he was soon mouthing along with all the Maguire war songs, even though he had not heard most of them before.

On his way back from the latrines in the yard, Seamus saw Hugh Maguire arguing in the corridor with Connor Roe Maguire and Connor Roe swiftly exited again. Seamus was curious and went to see what was going on. He walked straight into Donnacha O'Cassidy Maguire.

"It is time to make our bargain," said Donnacha.

"Well, my master has an empty village and empty fields, which is nothing when compared to my empty purse."

"Nothing fills a field like a Maguire cattle raid. I foresee your master's fortunes changing soon."

"Just as I see your master's fortunes changing, too. However, every good chieftain needs a united clan. I believe I can be that unifying force."

"The Maguire can be very generous in his gratitude to those who help him. First, we feast, then we raid, while throughout it all, noting those that waiver. Stick by me tonight while your master gets to know his clan better."

"Lead the way, my lord!"

Seamus and Donnacha left to spend their evening in the shadows.

The next day, Eunan awoke to find himself in his tent with Seamus shouting at him through the flap.

"Get up, you lazy eejit! We've got work to do!"

Eunan crawled out of the tent in his soiled shirt to find that Seamus and all twenty Galloglass were fully armed and armoured with horses at the ready.

"I wouldn't advise you to go like that. A little cow might stick her little horn in you, and you'd be no good to nobody." Seamus and the Galloglass laughed.

Eunan crawled back into his tent and got ready for battle as quickly as he could.

"And don't forget to pack all your little axes. We may find you someone to throw them at."

Eunan climbed back out and stood before the Galloglass. Finn ran forward and helped to adjust his chain mail.

"At least you look a little respectable now in front of the Galloglass," said Seamus. "Come on, we haven't finished yet. Time to collect the first payment for your vote."

They marched around Lisnaskea, and there they were met by the other chieftains and their men, but with a few notable exceptions.

Hugh Maguire rode to the front. "Come on, men! It is time to fill the coffers of the Maguires with plunder from the English!"

He pointed forward, and everyone cheered.

It did not take long for Eunan to realise that they were heading to the new plantation of Monaghan and the old MacMahon lands. Sir Ross MacMahon had died, and now Monaghan was breaking down into a war of succession. The English were attempting to break up the county, but Brian MacHugh Óg had established himself as the MacMahon, as per the Irish custom. Hugh Maguire was keen to support him by diminishing his rivals. Eunan saw the delight on Seamus's face as, at last, he was about to see some action. Eunan was nervous, for now he had to prove himself in battle with all the Maguire clan.

"Send the Kern forward," ordered Hugh Maguire. The lightly armed troops led the way into Monaghan.

The Maguire had a definitive route once he got to Monaghan, and the cattle were plentiful and the opposition sparse. But Seamus had another plan. Some of the east Fermanagh chiefs had sided with Connor Roe Maguire but still went on the cattle raid under the assumption that Hugh Maguire wanted to heal the rift. He did, but not in the way they thought.

Donnacha O'Cassidy Maguire directed the raiding parties and sent Seamus out with Shane Óg Maguire, one of Connor Roe Maguire's key allies. They arrived in a wood on a hill above a village. Fifty cattle grazed the land before them, with a few villagers in attendance.

"Lead the way, lord. I am but a mercenary and servant."

Shane Óg sneered at him as his horsemen gathered at the top of the hill. Seamus and his men lined up behind them.

"Lord?"

"What do you want, Galloglass?"

"Prepare to meet thy maker!"

The Galloglass swung their axes into men and horses indiscriminately and whatever the blades penetrated fell. The Galloglass finished off the bodyguards and left a wounded Shane Óg to grasp the remaining half of his right leg and crawl away.

"Politics isn't good for your health," said Seamus, and he lopped Shane Óg's head clean off.

Seamus kicked the head into a bag and slung it over his back.

"If you want paying, you always need to keep a receipt," he said to a shocked Eunan.

They returned to the main force of the Maguire after rustling some more cattle along the way. Seamus explained to the chieftains that Shane Óg had gone off by himself after a herd of cattle he had been spying on and did not return. Seamus said his first duty was to mind his young master and not Shane Óg. The Maguire gave his blessing to the story and would hear no more grumblings.

The Maguire sent out more raiding parties, and he paired Eunan and Seamus with Art O'Byrne MacMahon. It was not long before the head of Art O'Byrne

MacMahon found itself in Seamus's bag. Before the raid was out, Seamus had three bags full of heads, two of the newly settled English farmers of Monaghan, and one of the enemies of Hugh Maguire.

After several days of raiding, the Maguire considered it a suitable success and gave the order to return to Castle Skea and distribute the loot. The whole party was in a jubilant mood with few casualties, but with a few notable absences who were assumed to have defected to the English. Connor Roe Maguire had stayed with the party, but that was considered to have been under duress. They reached Castle Skea, where a hastily assembled court convened in the courtyard. The Maguire took his seat, surrounded by his Redshank. The stolen cattle awaited distribution according to the instruction of the Maguire.

The entire event became a celebration of the cattle raid and everything and everyone that was robbed, murdered, or both, for the glory of Hugh Maguire. Eunan's turn came, and Seamus handed him one of the sacks. They dragged their booty across the yard, a trail of blood marking their route. Seamus upturned his bag first. The heads bounced off the ground and settled in a bloody, muddy pool. Seamus rolled the foreheads with his foot and gave a running commentary about why he had removed a particular head.

"—and this one is a local English farmer from whom we liberated one hundred cattle. No, it's not him. Where is he? Sorry, lord. Eunan, can you empty your bag?"

The mound of heads grew.

"Ah, there he is," and Seamus kicked the head like a ball towards the Maguire.

Hugh Maguire smiled as the head came to a stop before him.

"Donnacha. Give this man the one hundred cattle he liberated and also the gratitude of the Maguire. I believe I will see you later before you go?"

"At your earliest convenience, my lord," said Seamus as he bowed.

Eunan looked at Seamus, copied his bow, and hurried back to their place amongst the chieftains.

"Can we go home now?" said Eunan.

"We have not finished our business, yet the village will be more prosperous than ever when we return, and this is from only one raid!"

The assembly broke up, and Eunan and Seamus went to collect their cattle from the stolen herd. Seamus directed his men to take the cattle to their encampment outside Lisnaskea.

"Eunan, come on, I have arranged for us to meet Donnacha. Pick up your bags and let's go."

Eunan dragged the bag after Seamus as if he was the lord.

Donnacha and Hugh Maguire met them in the twilight outside the castle walls. Seamus took the bag from Eunan's hand, walked up to the Maguire and dumped the heads at his feet. One head bounced off Hugh's shin.

"Here are your enemies, lord. If there are any hesitation marks on the neck, they were the work of the boy," Seamus said with a gleam in his eye. "We offer our further services to enable you to consolidate your power." He bowed.

"That is excellent work," said the Maguire. "How fortunate am I to find such skilled Galloglass with a shortage of work and empty pockets. If you can fill your sacks with the heads of my enemies, I can fill your pockets with their money, and your fields with their cows. Are you ready for more work?"

"My axe is sharp and clean and eager to hack your enemies out of Fermanagh and beyond."

"I thank you both for your service from the bottom of my heart. Help yourself to a further one hundred cows with my permission. Return to your lands, and I will call for you when I am ready. I need good warriors like the both of you."

"Thank you," said Eunan as they backed away. Donnacha handed some papers to Seamus, and Seamus and Eunan left to collect their additional reward.

As they left the castle grounds, the Maguire picked his hostages to ensure the loyalty of the lesser clansmen. Eunan and Seamus were exempt.

They joined up with the MacSheehy Galloglass, and Seamus dispatched two of his horse boys to ride ahead and collect their families and bring them to Eunan's village. After several days' ride, slowed by having to herd the cattle, they arrived back in Eunan's village. It was still deserted, except for the Galloglass families waiting amongst the ashes of the old village for the warriors to return. Once these were back, they put the cattle to pasture and set about rebuilding the village.

# CHAPTER TWENTY-ONE

# MAKE A PLEDGE

Seamus got up the next day and summoned his men to the centre circle of the village. He stood and surveyed the ruins and the surrounding lands and devised a plan.

"Bury the dead, start building shelters and a stockade, and a few boats while you're at it," said Seamus. "We're always going to be a frontier town."

"But that will take forever. Surely we must go and fight!?" said Eunan.

Seamus saw the impatience of youth and did his best to quell it.

"We did a good job back there. They will come looking for us when the time is right. In the meantime, you are the O'Keenan Maguire, so we need to get you something to be a chieftain of."

They spent several months working hard, planting crops, building houses, and constructing the stockade. Eunan proved himself invaluable at exploring the nearby islands on the lake so they could provide shelter and provisions for the villagers in times of danger. They even attracted some new residents as word of a village of Galloglass spread across the region. Seamus put these new residents to work and also trained new soldiers.

In the meantime, Eunan continued his Galloglass training and made good progress. Seamus thought it would be about a year, with more actual combat experience, before Eunan could be called a Galloglass. Eunan continued to hone his skills at both making and throwing axes.

But eventually, he had to return to his house and be alone. In the shadows of the night as he slept the ghosts of his parents would come back to haunt him and his bad blood would boil. He would end up sitting in the middle of the night where his father used to sit with the men of the village debating and putting the wrongs of their little world to rights, hemmed in by the rolling hills and the lake. He remembered his father's dying words, 'be a better man than me'. As the moon struck the ripples on the lake, he swore he would be, but only if Seamus got out of his way.

However, he became increasingly sidelined in running the village. Seamus had told him that a great war was coming and he needed to perfect his skills as a warrior instead of doing 'peasant work' like sowing crops or resolving the petty gripes of the villagers. Why would he need to do such things, since he would be off fighting for the Maguire? Seamus said that he would take care of that as he had much experience of running his Galloglass units. The only time Eunan was needed, it seemed, was when someone with the name Maguire was required to meet some dignitaries or attend some event. On these occasions, Seamus had Eunan on a tight leash.

It was quiet until the spring of 1590 when a rider came with a message from Donnacha O'Cassidy Maguire. He handed it to Seamus. Seamus went straight to Eunan where he was out in the fields with Finn, practising throwing his axes in continuation of their ongoing uneasy rivalry.

"Eunan!" Seamus called.

"One moment, please!" The throwing axe scraped the top of the distant shield target and fell to the ground behind it.

"He would have lived and is now charging towards you with his sword to slice you in two. You may have to send your horse boy out to throw his javelins at him to slow him down," said Seamus, pointing to Finn.

"You distracted me!"

Seamus laughed.

"There are many distractions on the battlefield. For one, your friends and neighbours dying because you didn't kill your opponent!"

"Well, we're not on the battlefield now, and I've plenty of time left for training."

"No, you don't. We have more missions for the Maguire."

"What do we have to do now? Isn't Fermanagh at peace?"

"He still has enemies, I still have holes in my pockets, and you are no nearer to being a contender for the Maguire. So no, for hired assassins, there is no such thing as peace."

"Who is our next target?"

"I don't know. We'll find out when we get there. But we have to leave now. The Maguire has summoned us to meet him in Enniskillen in two days."

After a hard ride, Eunan and Seamus approached Enniskillen. They stopped to admire the view. In the fields before them, they saw the MacCabe Galloglass both in training and training others. Galloglass taught young farm boys how to fight with spears, axes, and swords. In other fields, squares of pikemen grappled with their pikes and learned to fight in formation to varying levels of proficiency, while a select few fired muskets and men on horseback learned tricks.

"They are preparing for war," said Seamus. "They don't train in secret anymore, so they expect it to start soon."

"And a new type of war," said Eunan. "Look how the Galloglass fight."

"War is easy firing at a shadow in the distance. What skill and cunning is there from squeezing a trigger? You learn nothing until you smash a man's head open with an axe and feel the blood spatter on your face. They may have their weapons designed to fight from afar, but there is always a place for a warrior like me, and you someday, on the battlefield."

They saluted the men training as they rode past and the men saluted back. Seamus recognised the language spoken by some instructors as Spanish. Some men from the Armada still survived. Eunan and Seamus crossed onto the larger island and then to the bridge before the castle. Their letter, signed by Donnacha O'Cassidy Maguire, got them straight through to the main castle and an audience with the Maguire. Hugh Maguire was waiting for them.

"Welcome. Come in, my friends. You have had a long journey."

"Thank you, lord," said Eunan. "We are here to serve."

"And the Maguire is grateful for your service. I presume my previous gratitude has been to your satisfaction? I hear your lands prosper again by the lakes?"

"Your generosity has reaped a wonderful harvest for us, lord."

"What troubles our Prince of Fermanagh?" said Seamus.

"I trust you have seen the men training outside?"

"Your men train with the weapons of modernity, but you still call for the Galloglass?"

"I always have a place for men with your unique skills. But I also need men to make up my armies. How many warriors have you gathered as you consolidated your territories?"

"We now have forty Galloglass, all nearly fully trained," said Seamus.

"Any horse?" asked the Maguire.

"None, I'm sad to say," Eunan said. "What nobility there was did not survive the last English raid, and the axe is more my weapon, so I have dedicated myself to the Galloglass."

"Forty Galloglass is a good number for your territory. I have faith you have trained them well. Now I have a problem with some of the O'Rourkes to the west. I put out a similar call to them, for them to state how many warriors they can declare. I got no response, and some alarming rumours came back to me.

"There have been outbreaks of violence between Sir Brian O'Rourke of West Breifne and the Governor of Connacht for the past couple of years as part of the general resistance to English rule in the province. However, Sir Brian has finally been defeated and has fled for Scotland, and Bingham and his men have occupied his land and are preparing to settle it with English farmers. Sir Brian's son, Brian Óg, has fled to Fermanagh, and I have offered him your services to help persuade some of the O'Rourke chieftains on the borders of Fermanagh to declare for us. One such chieftain is Shea Óg O'Rourke, and if we can convince him, I think others will follow.

"So meet with Brian Óg, solicit a respectable pledge of warriors from Shea Óg O'Rourke, or if not, find someone else in his clan who can pledge the warriors, taking, of course, your fee for your troubles. Donnacha will supply you with some men, for I wish to see your ability to command. We'll need some commanders in the days and years to come."

Seamus was dubious of the standard of men he would lead.

"The MacCabes and the MacSheehys don't exactly see eye to eye."

"War is a fickle business, and to be a chieftain requires flexibility regarding who is your enemy and who is your friend. You understand that, Eunan, don't you?" said Hugh Maguire, turning to address the master.

"Yes, lord."

Seamus was suitably humiliated and swore revenge beneath his breath.

"If you complete this mission," said the Maguire, "and yourselves and the MacCabes don't kill each other, and I get my pledge, I may consider you for a more important mission – one that, if you complete it, could solve your money issues forever."

"Consider the MacCabes to be closer to me than my brother," said Seamus. He was cheered by the talk of a handsome fee.

"Your dead brother?" said Donnacha, who had done his research.

"The pre-death closeness I felt for my brother. If I avenge the MacCabes half as well as I avenged my brother, they would be lucky to have such a friend as me."

Eunan, Seamus and the ten MacCabe Galloglass slowly rode up the narrow roads in the hilly, barren terrain. Their meeting with Brian Óg along the way had been brief, but he had at least given them a local scout to help them circumvent the worst of the bogs. Their journey was made doubly difficult by the lack of forest cover, which meant their party could be spotted some distance away. After a tricky trip, the party rode into the main village of Shea Óg. Seamus was not impressed.

"This is a bit shabby looking to me," he said.

"What do you expect in this land of hills and bogs?" said Eunan.

"I expect to get paid. My sword may judder as I withdraw it from Shea Óg in bitterness for his life being sacrificed for so little. No, I'll be more sadistic. I'll let you kill him. Let him feel the shame of being a poor chieftain by having a cheap, inexperienced assassin take his life."

Eunan glared at Seamus, who shrugged his shoulders. "I'd be insulted," said Seamus.

They reached the village, but Shea Óg's men had followed them in the bogs for miles. There was no protective wall, so they rode straight into the centre of the village where a hefty, greying warrior with one hand firmly on the haft of his axe stood.

"To what do I owe the pleasure of twelve armed soldiers riding into the centre of my village?" said Shea Óg.

"You owe the pleasure to your lord, the Maguire," said Seamus. "He protects your lands with the lives of his soldiers like us. While you may admire our weapons, we are here to count yours and see what you can pledge to the Maguire and his cause."

Seamus dismounted, fingering his scabbard and stood before Shea Óg. The chieftain eyed him suspiciously.

"Why didn't you say you were emissaries from the Maguire? Please, come in and join us." Shea Óg pointed towards his hut whose entrance was guarded by his three burly sons.

"Wait here," Seamus ordered the MacCabes. He signalled to Eunan, and they edged their way towards the hut.

"Please, leave your weapons there," said Shea Óg, pointing to the ground in front of his waiting sons.

Seamus stopped and felt for his scabbard again.

"If I kill you and all these Galloglass, how will my village ever repay the Maguire, if not with our lives, when he comes seeking compensation?"

Seamus shrugged his shoulders in response.

"Then why disarm us?" said Eunan.

"How can we enjoy our meal with swords pointing at each other?" said Shea Óg.

Seamus smiled as if he had been in this situation before. Eunan froze, for he had not, and did not know what to do, except follow Seamus's lead. They laid their weapons on the ground. When Shea Óg's sons made a move to retrieve them, the Maguire Galloglass went for their weapons. The sons backed off. The area around the arms became no man's land.

Both parties, now disarmed, entered the hut and sat down, followed by Shea Óg's sons. Shea Óg invited Seamus and Eunan to eat.

"After you, good lord," said Seamus. "I like to talk business on an empty stomach."

Shea Óg helped himself to the meat and bread and smiled at his guests. However, Eunan could only hold back, but not disguise, his hunger. Shea Óg reckoned Eunan was the softer of the two.

"All that riding must have made you hungry, boy."

"I'm a Maguire chief," said Eunan, determined to stamp his authority on the situation. Shea Óg laughed.

"They get younger all the time. What is the life expectancy of a Maguire chief these days?"

"About an hour," said Seamus.

Shea Óg's sons reached for their hidden weapons.

"Now then, boys, be careful who you point your little cocks at. Let the big boys have their chat before you try to tickle us to death. Shea Óg, how many men can you pledge to the Maguire?"

"Who says I want to pledge to the Maguire? Brian O'Rourke has fled, the English are on my doorstep, and the Maguire is next on their list."

Seamus laughed.

"Very well, either tell me how many men you want to pledge, or if not, how many cattle you have so I can get paid and be quick about it."

Shea Óg rose to his feet and pulled out a dagger.

"No one comes to my house and threatens me."

"Sit down, or you'll hurt yourself with that," said Seamus. "Now, how many men do you have to pledge?"

"Who says I want to pledge for the Maguire?"

"Look, pledge, just bloody pledge or hand over the knife and I'll get someone else to be the chieftain and to pledge."

Eunan ate on. He was nervous but did not want to let on, even though he was sure Shea Óg and his sons could smell the fear emanating from him.

"No one threatens me!" Shea Óg lunged at Seamus.

Seamus dodged the knife, grabbed Shea Óg's wrist, pulled a knife from the small of his back and skewered Shea Óg's hand to the table. Shea Óg's screams pierced the ears of all in the house but Shea Óg's sons froze.

Seamus turned to them, with not a pearl of sweat on his forehead.

"You gentlemen have a decision to make. You can sacrifice your lives to save a dead man, count how many men you can pledge, and the highest pledge becomes chief. What's it to be?"

No one moved. Eunan ate on.

"And the pledge is?"

One son made a run for the door.

"Eunan!"

Eunan whipped out a throwing knife he had concealed on his person. It whizzed through the air and struck the man in the back of the shoulder. He collapsed and tried to reach back and pull the knife out.

"Oh, for God's sake!" said Seamus. "Just kill him!"

Eunan pulled out another small knife from his boot and threw it. It grazed the man's arm.

"Can you not kill a man in one go?"

The other two sons looked at each other.

"Look, these two think they have a chance now! Even Shea Óg is tugging at his dagger! Just kill him!"

Eunan leapt from his seat and drowned in the screams of agony as he wrenched his knife from the man's shoulder. One son moved to help his father. Seamus picked up a knife from the table.

"Not if you want to live!"

Eunan incapacitated the son with a stab to the neck and his inexperience drenched him in blood for his troubles. Eunan stood above the dying man, the knife shaking in his hand.

"Your dinner is getting cold," said Seamus.

Eunan edged back to his seat, not taking his eyes off the man he had just stabbed, sat down and went through the motions of putting food in his mouth and gently chewing, all while covered in the man's blood. Shea Óg knew he would not survive.

"So now we know that none of us is unarmed. What is it to be, Shea? You either pledge, or whichever of your remaining sons who want to be chieftain pledges. Either way, I'm leaving with a pledge. You can also throw in some cattle for all the inconvenience you have put me through.!"

"I'll never pledge for the Maguire."

"You don't know when to give up, do you?"

Seamus pulled the knife from Shea Óg's hand. Shea Óg screamed and pulled his hand back to cradle it in his chest, as blood ran down his arm and onto his clothes.

"You forced me to do this, Shea!" Seamus got up and grabbed Shea Óg by the neck and dragged him towards a pot boiling over the fire. "Watch them!" Seamus ordered Eunan.

The two sons made a move for Seamus, but Eunan waved his knife at them and they froze.

"Last chance for a pledge!" Seamus said, dangling Shea's head over the pot.

"I'll never pledge!" cried Shea.

Seamus thrust Shea's head into the boiling water. The two sons screamed for their father.

"I'll pledge," said one son as tears streamed down his face.

Seamus let go, and Shea Óg dropped to the floor and held his hands above his face, trying not to touch it, so excruciating was the pain.

"You can serve me dinner now that business is over. I'm famished," said Seamus as he sat down at the table.

Seamus and Eunan rode into Enniskillen Castle with thirty cows and a pledge of ten horsemen and forty Kern from Shea Óg's son. The son had also given four young boys from his immediate family as hostages to ensure their ongoing loyalty.

Seamus's cruelty left Eunan with a bitter taste in his mouth. He had not joined the fight for the survival of the Maguire to intimidate some old chieftain stuck in the middle of a bog while taking his children to ensure his dubious loyalty. Was this how he had ended up in Enniskillen?

Seamus rode proudly at the head of the column, for he had gained himself the respect of the MacCabe Galloglass, as someone who could get things done. A man who knew, and could do, what was needed in times of crisis.

When they arrived, they were invited straight into the tower, given a change of clothes, and then went to meet the Maguire.

"Welcome, my friends. I hear we will have no more trouble with Shea Óg O'Rourke?"

Seamus laughed.

"He needed some persuading, but he paid us handsomely for our troubles."

"I will not ask, since the Maguire does not want to get his hands dirty," said Hugh. "Donnacha will arrange your fee but please remain available, for I may call upon you again soon."

Seamus smiled, and Eunan bowed. They went to find Donnacha to get paid.

# CHAPTER TWENTY-TWO

# SMUGGLERS

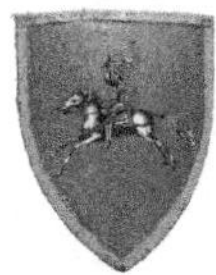

The once-great county of Tirconnell after years of decline had descended into chaos, and clan O'Donnell was involved in a chaotic war of succession that had first started in 1580. Hugh McManus O'Donnell, the reigning O'Donnell, had gone senile. Donnell O'Donnell, his son from his first marriage, had been declared sheriff by Lord Deputy Fitzwilliam and had the support of the Crown and Turlough Luineach O'Neill. Donnell O'Donnell had subjugated much of western Tirconnell, and after seeing off several rivals, was now challenging his father for the title of O'Donnell. Hugh McManus O'Donnell was protected by his wife, Finola MacDonald, better known as Ineen Dubh.

Ineen Dubh was from the powerful MacDonald clan of Scotland and had been a courtier in the Stuart court. Her mother had married Turlough Luineach O'Neill. Both marriages had been arranged to increase the power and influence of the MacDonald clan over all of northern Ireland and not just Antrim and Down. Both these women had powerful connections in Scotland and controlled the recruitment of Scottish mercenaries coming to Ireland. Ineen Dubh was determined to hold the title of O'Donnell for her son Red Hugh O'Donnell, who at the time was imprisoned in Dublin. However, Donnell O'Donnell was wary of Ineen Dubh and her methods of warfare. Her son's previous leading rival for the title of O'Donnell, Hugh O'Gallagher, who led the forces of Turlough Luineach to victory over Hugh O'Neill at the battle of Carricklea, had gone to her castle in Mongavlin and been murdered by her Scottish mercenary bodyguard.

Donnell O'Donnell called out to all his subservient chieftains in southern Tirconnell and surrounding districts to face Ineen Dubh, her mercenaries and the O'Donnells of north western Tirconnell. However, he was soundly beaten and killed at the battle of Doire Leathan in 1590. Ineen Dubh consolidated power in Tirconnell for both her husband and her imprisoned son without any new contender emerging.

Hugh Maguire kept to himself and continued his preparations for war, while demoralised by the defeat of his ally at Doire Leathan and eager to refill the ranks of the Galloglass he lost in the battle.

1591 was a relatively quiet year for Eunan and Seamus. They returned to their village all the richer for their exploits working for Hugh Maguire. They escorted home, with the help of the MacCabes, one hundred and fifty cattle, which they released into their meadows surrounding the village. The village now had a stockade, and the population had swelled to three hundred civilians. No one had survived the massacre from Cathal O'Keenan Maguire's time, so the core of the population were the families and men of the MacSheehy Galloglass. More stragglers had joined them: fleeing MacMahons, O'Rourkes and O'Reillys keen to escape the English and their new plantations, and displaced Maguires seeking sanctuary. Seamus and Eunan had around twenty Galloglass and twenty trainee Galloglass, which was a sizable force considering the population. They had plenty of boats and an island network that, in times of trouble, could sustain several thousand people for short periods of time. Their village had become a substantial hub in the region.

Seamus returned to his wife and settled down. He led the village, supervised its construction, and trained the men like any other Maguire chieftain. But Eunan would remind everyone that he was the O'Keenan Maguire, even though no O'Keenans were left. Whenever someone tried to contradict Eunan, Seamus and his Galloglass would interject and silence the dissent by whatever means were appropriate. The villagers wondered why Seamus favoured Eunan so, making him chieftain in name only, when in these times of war only might and muscle counted. But Eunan was a Maguire and as such held the key to Enniskillen, for without Eunan, Seamus was simply a wandering Galloglass.

Eunan and Seamus themselves came to a sort of understanding where Seamus would train Eunan and teach him how to train others as long as Eunan did not interfere in his business. Eunan was happy with such an arrangement as long as he progressed and the village prospered.

However, such domestic bliss would only be short-lived since a Galloglass of Seamus's skill was always in demand. In the cold of January 1592, they were once again summoned to Enniskillen.

Hugh Maguire had visibly aged, with the weight of the survival of the Maguires resting on his shoulders. Donnacha stood beside him, yet they both seemed brighter than the last time Seamus and Eunan had seen them, as if they had hatched a new plot.

"I need you to be discreet in escorting someone home!" said Hugh Maguire.

"Can you not keep your concubines in the castle?" said Seamus.

Hugh Maguire laughed.

"More discreet than that. I need you to bring Red Hugh O'Donnell home."

Seamus gave Eunan a stare that said, 'don't dare say yes until we fix a price!'

"Do we have to break him out of jail first?" said Seamus, not out of fear, but a desire to cost the job correctly.

"No, he managed that himself. He has many enemies, both Irish and English, who want him dead. Hence why I need my two best warriors, most capable of exercising discretion, to sneak him back to Tirconnell."

"This sounds like a dangerous job," said Eunan.

"It is, and you are also at Hugh O'Donnell's disposal, so make what arrangements you see fit. I foresee you both returning as prominent servants of the Maguire clan with suitable disposable wealth that would suit such a prestigious position."

"How suitable?" asked Seamus.

"You would be two of the wealthiest and most prominent men in southern Fermanagh!"

"And a good buffer for you, for your enemies would most likely come from the south!" said Seamus.

"I couldn't choose two better men to protect an exposed flank."

"So, when does this mission start?" asked Eunan.

"Be on your horses at midnight and set out towards Tirconnell. Your temporary master will make himself known. Now prepare yourselves, and tell no one of this arrangement."

They bowed and left the Maguire's room.

"Satisfied?" said Eunan.

"We could be the shortest reigning lords of southern Fermanagh in history, but we could not have struck a better bargain," said Seamus. "But getting to know Red Hugh will also gain us favour in Tirconnell, and where there is favour with a more powerful lord, lies opportunity!"

At the stroke of midnight, they set out from the town on horseback. They had left the castle earlier and entertained themselves in the town so as not to draw attention to themselves and the fact they may be leaving. The road was empty, for the countryside at that hour of the night was full of bandits. But Seamus was not afraid. He had spent the afternoon sharpening his weapons and had encouraged Eunan to do the same.

They rode for a little while, always wary of the few other road users. There was no sign of their guest. They continued on some more until the road became surrounded by woods. They turned a corner, to be surrounded by men.

"Out of my way or feel the wrath of my axe," said Seamus.

"The only wrath around here is mine," came a voice from the shadows.

"Show yourself!"

A dishevelled man on horseback emerged from the darkness.

"Put it down, that axe is mine!" he said.

Seamus and Eunan knew this was their man. Eunan smiled, for Red Hugh was not much older than he, yet he could feel his charisma even though Red Hugh had merely uttered two sentences. Even Seamus was impressed with his gravitas.

"Lead us as you desire," said Seamus as he bowed his head.

"Let us go to Tirconnell, but cross-country, for many of my enemies wish to prevent me from making it home."

He turned to his previous escort.

"Go, men of Maguire, and I thank you for your service. We must be discreet as we travel home this evening."

The Maguire men bade their farewell, but three of Red Hugh's companions remained; Turlough O'Hagan sent by Hugh O'Neill to escort Red Hugh home from Wicklow, where he hid after his escape, and two scouts sent by Ineen Dubh. The six men set off into the night on the journey to Tirconnell.

They rode for hours, silent but at a steady trot in the dark, following Red Hugh's two scouts. Eunan and Seamus rode either side of him with Turlough O'Hagan at the rear. It was a cold, windy night, and the wind seemed to pick up an additional chill when they could not avoid the thick bogs that dogged their route.

They eventually dismounted and stopped to rest. Eunan searched for wood.

"No fires!" ordered Red Hugh, for the paranoia of prison had not yet left him.

They did not sit down, as the ground was damp and cold. They paced and ate to satisfy their need for warmth and sustenance.

"We'll be at the castle in the morning," said one scout.

"Loyal O'Donnells," said Red Hugh in response to Seamus's inquisitive look.

"Loyalty is an expensive commodity these days," said Seamus.

"And most of the time it is only temporarily for sale," said Red Hugh.

Eunan noticed for the first time that Red Hugh had a limp.

"What troubles thy foot, lord? Do you need help to get back on your horse?"

"A souvenir from my time at Her Majesty's pleasure."

"We have heard the stories. What happened?"

"I fell for the cunning of the English in their desperation to keep my father under control. They pulled up their ship to dock and lured me and some of the O'Neill nobility on board. The promise of drink and women was too much for naïve youth. I was kidnapped and sailed to Dublin to spend my time in jail because of my weakness.

"For many a year, I sat chained in squalor, with my fellow Ulster nobles and rats for company. I escaped once and got as far as Wicklow, but the cold got poor Art O'Neill and would have got me as well except, in a stroke of fortune, I was recaptured. They cut off my toes, for they could not save them from the frostbite. They threw me back in jail, but some well-placed bribes by Hugh O'Neill provided for my second escape. Fiach MacHugh O'Byrne hid me in Wicklow until I could be smuggled north to Tyrone by the good grace of Hugh O'Neill. I spent several nights with him in Dungannon Castle plotting the expulsion of the English from our homelands. That leads me here, to you. On the verge of my bid to rescue the O'Donnell clan from servitude!"

"And a very commendable objective it is too!" said Seamus.

"Are you fit to travel?" said Eunan.

"Aye, I'm fine to travel and eager to get there. We should be in Ballyshannon Castle by morning, where we can rest and see what havoc the English have caused."

"How do you know the castle is still in loyal O'Donnell hands?"

"My mother has sent men from her bodyguard, the finest Redshanks in all of Ireland, to hold it for me. I am rested now, so help me onto my horse and let us depart and make haste."

They rode for the rest of the night, and just as Red Hugh had said, by dawn the castle was within sight. It loomed before them, covered in shadows in the morning light. A drizzle of rain made them feel even more uncomfortable after their long night ride.

"So what do we do now, lord?" said Eunan.

The grim smile he offered meant Red Hugh did not know, but he hoped for the best.

"Let us venture forth and see what the response is."

They rode up the road at a meandering pace, wary of ambush and wanting to keep out of archer range before the castle revealed itself as friend or foe. It was quiet until they reached the castle gate. Seamus got off his horse and rapped the butt of his axe on the timbers.

"Who goes there?"

"Red Hugh O'Donnell!"

The noise of scurrying feet was followed by the sound of the security chain being pulled up. When the gate opened, there stood Eoghan McToole O'Gallagher and his Galloglass constables. They looked for Hugh, and Hugh took the blanket off his head.

"Hugh," they cried, and they rushed to help him down from his horse. "You are injured?"

"I am fine. I am just grateful to be back in Tirconnell." He revelled in being able to grip his faithful clan members by the shoulders as he climbed off his horse.

Hugh took a few steps but could not escape his limp.

"Quick, quick, get the physician, get some hot water. Get him to the fire. Send riders to his parents. Tell them that Red Hugh has come home," said Eoghan.

"It is so good to see you," Hugh said, collapsing into Eoghan's arms.

Eunan and Seamus entered as honoured guests, and they were fed, bathed and rested before being brought before a refreshed Red Hugh.

Hugh's foot was now in bandages, and the colour had returned to his face. He still looked gaunt and had resisted the best efforts of his hosts to overfeed him, as he had to gradually recondition himself for being out of prison. Delighted faces surrounded him.

"Sit, my friends," he said to Eunan and Seamus upon their arrival.

"You look better, lord," said Eunan as he bowed.

"I feel better mainly for being home. But the news from Tirconnell is sobering. An English captain by the name of Willis has been made sheriff in Tirconnell. He has unleashed a reign of terror and theft upon the land. The house of O'Donnell is deeply divided. My father is old, but my mother and her Scottish mercenaries fight gallantly on. If only the O'Donnell men were as brave and crafty as her."

"I know this man, Willis," said Eunan. "He destroyed my village and killed my family. What will you do, Lord?"

Red Hugh bowed his head.

"We must rid the lands of the English by any means. It will be a long and bloody struggle with much pain and death of friend and foe alike. However, I need men of composure and stature to fight this war. Now, I also need men unknown to the English and less loyal O'Donnell brethren. The risks will be high, but the rewards are great. You both come highly recommended by Hugh Maguire. May I borrow you from him and have the loyalty of your axes?"

Seamus looked at Eunan, but Eunan's mouth had already opened.

"I pledge my axe both to you and Saint Colmcille," he said, bending his knee and offering his axe to Red Hugh.

A red-faced Seamus only had a second to react.

"My master speaks for me," he said as he bowed his head.

They were dismissed from Red Hugh's company and left the main hall. Seamus grabbed Eunan by the throat and pushed him up against the wall.

"What the hell was all that Saint Colmcille shit?"

"Let go... My throat... Let...go!"

Seamus released him.

"What was that for?" said Eunan as he regained his breath. "Saint Colmcille is the patron saint of the O'Donnells. Don't you know anything? Some priests predict Red Hugh is the chosen one to free us from the English. Pledging to Saint Colmcille will endear us to Red Hugh and get us an abundance of work."

"It's not the amount of work I take issue with, but I can safely predict that Saint Colmcille was not a good negotiator and exchanged his deeds for heavenly, not earthly goods. No matter for who or why I get my head chopped off, I'm not going to heaven, so there's no point in trying."

"Rest assured the work will come pouring in."

"Tell me your plan before you open your mouth the next time."

"You'll be the first to know."

Seamus slapped Eunan on the back, and they did their best to forgive each other, but they both failed.

# CHAPTER TWENTY-THREE

# HOMECOMING

Red Hugh sent messengers to all the O'Donnell clan chieftains loyal to his father across Tirconnell to announce his return. He promised to reward the chieftains for their continued loyalty and invited them to Ballyshannon Castle to pledge their allegiance to him. The pledge was open to anyone who could guarantee a minimum of four horsemen.

Tirconnell was still in chaos, for the defeat of his half-brother Donnell O'Donnell had left a power vacuum in the county which Lord Deputy Fitzwilliam had quickly, and profitably, filled with Captain Willis and two hundred English soldiers.

Captain Willis unleashed a reign of terror across the land. He first divided the lords of Tirconnell through bribery and the promise of land and power if they supported the Crown. He looted from those that refused his advances, and they were defenceless against him since there was no stout O'Donnell to protect them. The captain took hostages and ransomed them back to the chieftains. The primary resistance came from Ineen Dubh and her Scottish mercenaries. However, the lords of Tirconnell were trapped between the bribes of Willis and the strong-arm tactics of Ineen Dubh, so only those traditionally allied with Sir Hugh O'Donnell's branch of the family could initially be trusted.

The first to arrive at Ballyshannon Castle was Red Hugh's mother, Ineen Dubh, and her extended bodyguard of Redshanks. Upon her arrival at the gate, she was directed straight to the tower where Red Hugh waited, for he did not know what reception he would receive and his followers feared his assassination. They plotted and waited to see what other lords would pledge to Red Hugh.

They sent Eunan and Seamus to stay in a house in a small village within walking distance of Ballyshannon Castle. Eunan had nothing to do but reflect on how he had come this far. He felt an ache in his heart when he saw Red Hugh reunited with his mother, for he knew his mother never felt like that for him when she was alive. He thought of his father, and he blamed himself for his role in the events that led up to his father's death. It still grieved him deeply. He thought of Desmond, the nearest person he ever had to a real father, and wished he was by the lakeside with him. Eunan thought long and hard about his complicated relationship with Seamus and how Seamus had propelled him so far. He thought of Hugh Maguire, his scheming and his efforts to ensure the survival of the Maguire. Eunan thought of himself and his failings as a person, and his determination to do the right thing. He thought of Red Hugh and how the priests had told him he would deliver Ireland from the English. He could feel the bad blood in his body, but he was determined to do better now that Red Hugh employed him.

Several days later, Eunan joined the well-wishers at the main gates and witnessed the O'Donnell chieftains arrive. He stood beside the gate and ran his hands along the holes and scars of the walls that told him the castle had changed hands many times and the current occupants could only expect their stay to be temporary. In between the flashes of the colours of the O'Donnell war banners, Eunan saw Seamus. He went over to stand beside him. Seamus had befriended some of the local O'Gallagher Galloglass, who told them who everyone was.

"This sure beats Fermanagh, huh?" said Seamus, slapping Eunan on the back as he pointed towards the parade. Eunan acknowledged Seamus's new Galloglass friend. The Galloglass continued his commentary.

"Most of these are from southern or southwestern Tirconnell who either remained loyal to Hugh McManus O'Donnell or supported Red Hugh's half-brother, Donnell O'Donnell."

"So Ineen Dubh is the forgiving type?" said Seamus.

"A hard woman she may be, but she's also pragmatic. If she still doesn't trust someone, she can always put them on the front line. There's still plenty of fighting to be done, plenty of work for men like you."

"Men like me do the dirty work so that men like you don't have to," said Seamus. "As long as she's the forgiving type, I may have to pay her a visit."

Hugh McManus O'Donnell arrived separately from his wife, and he brought with him the war banners of the O'Donnells, held aloft by one hundred armed men.

"Is he still with it?" said Seamus.

"That's debatable," said the Galloglass, "but he still commands the general respect of the population of southern Tirconnell anyway. He can still raise a decent force in his name."

Seamus shrugged and shared some of his ale with the Galloglass to keep him talking. Seamus inspected the soldiers as they marched past, noting their quality, age, and armament.

"I don't see any guns or pikes. I thought Tirconnell was in a constant state of war?"

"It is, but we have also had English sheriffs dominating for years. They confiscate any guns or pikes they can find. The lords still have their Spanish trainers secretly hidden away, but if the sheriff found out about them, he would shoot them on sight."

Eoghan McToole O'Gallagher welcomed the dignitaries at the castle gates as they arrived. He saw Eunan and Seamus in the crowd and called them in to join them.

"Sorry, friend, I think this is us!" said Seamus, and he shook hands with the Galloglass. "See you on the battlefield!"

After they had weaved their way through the cheering crowd and past the O'Gallagher Galloglass, they were ushered into the main building. Entering the main hall, they saw an enormous feast laid before them to celebrate Red Hugh's freedom and the resurgence of the O'Donnell clan. Seamus's eyes glowed.

"Sure beats Fermanagh, huh?" he said again to Eunan, who refrained from reacting.

The battle banners of the O'Gallaghers and the O'Donnells adorned the walls. The displays were small in scale because this was one of the O'Donnell frontier castles, but it impressed Seamus and Eunan nonetheless. Red Hugh, his mother and father, sat at the top table with Eoghan McToole O'Gallagher, who acted as host, alongside several of the most noteworthy constables and captains. This time, they gave both Eunan and Seamus places on the long bench.

The mood in the hall was exultant, with endless toasts to the returned Red Hugh and cursing of his English captors. Red Hugh gave a rousing speech cheered to the rafters by all.

Eoghan McToole O'Gallagher carefully noted who was there, but more importantly, who was not.

Eunan let himself go at this feast, for he was a guest and the only expectation was for him to enjoy himself. He threw himself into it body and soul; it was such a relief to release the tensions of the previous hard weeks. He felt that, if only Red Hugh could become the O'Donnell, he would be the glue to hold the north together. He drank another ale and joined in the chorus of yet another song praising the exploits of Red Hugh.

Many a whisper was had in the ears of Red Hugh and Eoin McToole, as the lords of Tirconnell made known what they needed and what it would take for Red Hugh to be declared the O'Donnell. He listened and promised to act.

## CHAPTER TWENTY-FOUR

# CAPTAIN WILLIS

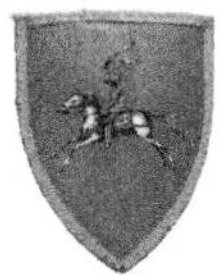

The next day, Eunan was awoken by a bucket of cold water.

"Wake up, sleepy head. It's time to earn your keep."

"What the... Oh, it's you."

"Nice way to greet me. You try to drink the place dry, while Uncle Seamus was getting to know all the important people at the feast to get us work and status."

"You're not my uncle," Eunan said, wiping his face.

"Try to cheer up before you meet Red Hugh. He can elevate us in the world."

Eunan dressed in the cleanest clothes he could find.

"I think Red Hugh would be more impressed by grass stains than vomit stains," said Seamus.

Eunan growled and changed clothes again.

They made their way to the great hall. Red Hugh awaited them with his mother, Ineen Dubh. Red Hugh was feeling better by the day and paced up and down the floor as he laid out his plans to Eunan and Seamus and how they fitted into them. Seamus tried to hide his smile as he thought of how much they could earn, while Eunan looked solemn and thought of how he could rid the lands of the English. This time they were offered lands in either Fermanagh or Tirconnell, whichever they chose, as long as they survived the mission. They did not have to be asked twice.

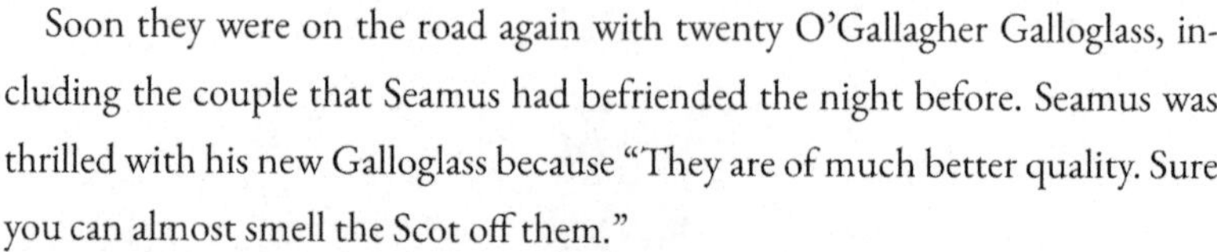

Soon they were on the road again with twenty O'Gallagher Galloglass, including the couple that Seamus had befriended the night before. Seamus was thrilled with his new Galloglass because "They are of much better quality. Sure you can almost smell the Scot off them."

Reports had reached Red Hugh that Captain Willis and his men had been raiding in south Donegal, and Red Hugh wanted to send some soldiers to deal with it who he could dismiss as 'rogue mercenaries' if it all went wrong.

Seamus narrowed down Captain Willis's location from reported sightings to a particular village and sent scouts ahead to check out the place and its surroundings. They returned and explained that Captain Willis was there with thirty men trying to expropriate cattle from the local chieftain. The chieftain did not have enough men to defend the village for most of them had abandoned him at the first sign of the English.

The village was in a lush little valley, surrounded on two sides by mountains. It was a valley the O'Gallagher Galloglass knew well from the long and bitter wars of succession, so their guidance was invaluable. Seamus could hear shots from the village. He placed half his force under Eunan's command and instructed them to circle around the village and hide on the road to Donegal town, which was the obvious escape route for the English. Eunan accepted the command but was visibly nervous, for there were many experienced Galloglass in the soldiers he commanded he thought could do the job better than him. But Seamus showed faith in him, alleviating some of his anxiety.

Seamus sent his men out to the nearby valleys to herd all the cattle they could find and bring them to him with instructions not to get spotted by the English. Once the herd was assembled, Seamus and his men lit torches and drove the cattle towards the village. The momentum of the herd became a stampede.

Seamus and his men drove the animals before them, and the cattle drove out villagers and Englishmen alike. The English soldiers ran out of the village and into Seamus's trap.

Eunan waited until the fleeing English soldiers were almost upon them and then let fly with his new throwing axes. His aim was true, and the sharp reinforced blade of the axe almost ripped the targeted English soldier's head in two. Eunan selected a new target, and the second axe was just as successful. Eunan and his men jumped out with their battle-axes and cut the English to pieces. Only the sheriff and a handful of men on horseback escaped.

Seamus and his men downed their fire torches, and the cattle disbursed into the fields. Seamus searched the village, found no one, and marched down the Donegal road. He found Eunan retrieving his axes.

"You could have left some for me."

"You looked busy playing with all the cows. Did we kill the sheriff?"

"Unfortunately, he got away. Once we have prepared, we will follow him straight to Donegal town. Fetch the horses," Seamus ordered one man.

They all mounted up, and after sending a messenger to Red Hugh to ask him to meet them with additional men in Donegal town, they set out in pursuit of Captain Willis.

The English had had a substantial head start, but local knowledge from the Galloglass cut their advantage considerably. Captain Willis only arrived in Donegal town an hour ahead of them. As they approached, they saw the Englishman had mobilised the rest of his men and was waiting for them.

"We need a bit of guile here," said Seamus to Eunan. "Hey, sergeant," he said to the senior Galloglass in their company. "Send more messengers to the local lords. Gather as many men as you can. We need to surround the town and then move in. You're in charge here now. Eunan, come with me. We've got a captain to kill."

Eunan and Seamus snuck into town in the dead of night. Captain Willis and his men had retreated to the Franciscan monastery and had sent messengers to Dublin to ask for reinforcements. Little did they know that O'Donnell's men had already intercepted them.

Captain Willis had his main force in the monastery rather than the castle because he wanted the locals to see that he was here to stay, and he was not afraid of them, hiding behind some castle walls. Besides, he had confiscated so many cattle and chattels, he needed more storage space. He had made no provision to defend the town. Eunan and Seamus were under strict orders to evict the English, killing as few of them as necessary to get them to leave without starting a war. Red Hugh did not feel strong enough yet for that.

Seamus looked around and saw random animals scurrying around the streets. That made up his mind.

"Eunan, get me some oil."

"What kind of oil?"

"Whatever you can get as long as it burns."

Red Hugh was well enough to get on a horse again, so when the messenger arrived, he set off for Donegal town with one hundred Galloglass and fifty horse. Other loyal lords had also responded to the call and warriors gathered outside Donegal town.

Seamus had spent his time well waiting for Eunan. He had found someone familiar with the monastery, knew of their old escape tunnel that ran beneath the streets and would readily accept money for a little danger. Eunan came back with a pot of oil.

"What are you going to do with that?" he said, pointing to the young pig Seamus had on a rope.

"Watch and learn. Now follow him there." A man came out from the shadows and led them to the tunnel.

As they walked through, the pig expressed its dissatisfaction with being held under Seamus's arm.

"Can you shut that thing up?" asked Eunan.

"The poor little fella is afraid of the dark. Leave him alone."

"They can't hear us. The door is sealed at the other end," said the guide.

They proceeded up the tunnel with the pig squealing most of the way, much to Eunan's annoyance.

"Sure, let him enjoy himself while he can," said Seamus.

They came to the doorway and Eunan greased the pig under Seamus's instruction. Seamus opened the door.

"Goodbye, little fella. Serve the O'Donnell well!" Seamus bent down and set the pig alight. The pig became a ball of flame. It ran through the monastery spreading fire and chaos wherever it went. The squeals tortured the ears of anybody within range. Eunan and Seamus remained hidden behind the door.

Red Hugh was now near the town. He saw the monastery was on fire and took that as the signal from Seamus. He rode into the town with the Galloglass following on foot. The other lords interpreted the fire in the same manner and moved in towards the town.

Captain Willis leapt out of his bed and ordered the evacuation of the monastery. His soldiers spilt out into the street and helped the citizens trying to put out the fire.

Seamus heard the chaos outside and deemed it time to make his move. The next English soldier running past the door had his shoulder blade smashed under Seamus's axe. Unfortunately, the man was dead before Seamus could question him.

"Get another one!" shouted Seamus.

Eunan grabbed the next soldier and shoved him down the tunnel. He held his axe blade to the man's throat.

"Where's Captain Willis?"

"Across the square."

"Where?"

"In the room beside the gate."

Eunan threw him aside and ran for the room. The English soldier reached for a knife in his belt and made after Eunan. One slice and the man's arm lay on the ground in a pool of blood. The next axe blow smashed his face.

"You're not supposed to leave them alive," said Seamus. "They come back and try to take revenge."

The pig ran across the yard, leaving a trail of flames. One of the English soldiers shot it to put it out of its misery. The English soldiers ran out of the gate to escape the fire. Unfortunately, Seamus did not know what Captain Willis looked like. Eunan did, but he had only seen him at a distance. They were looking for a captain's uniform, but the recently departed pig was so successful in his mission that the English soldiers ran around half-dressed in panic. The courtyard was filled with smoke, and whenever an English soldier came across them and realised they were intruders, the Irishmen had to kill him. But even as most of the English soldiers had evacuated to fight the flames, the smoke dissipated.

"Intruders!" came the shout, and Seamus and Eunan found themselves surrounded by English soldiers.

"Put down your axe," said Seamus to Eunan. Seamus turned to the soldiers. "We want to speak with Captain Willis."

"And who are you to be making demands of Captain Willis?" said a man who emerged from the crowd wearing only breeches and a shirt.

"The O'Donnell has sent us," said Eunan, raising his chin.

"Did he now? And which O'Donnell is that and what does he want with the Queen's servant?" said Captain Willis, squaring up to Eunan.

"Red Hugh wants to send you and your men back to England. You can leave the Irish traitors here, and we'll take care of them."

Seamus did not know what came over Eunan to make him so bold. Captain Willis pulled his knife from his belt and stuck the pointed blade into Eunan's chin until he drew blood.

"Now, you're a mouthy one, aren't you? It's a pity I don't have time to kill you properly. String them up! Hang them from the tree in the town for all to see!"

The soldiers marched them at sword-point out of the monastery gate. However, waiting for them outside were Red Hugh O'Donnell, fifty horse and a hundred Galloglass.

"Going somewhere, Captain Willis?" Red Hugh said.

The English soldiers dropped their weapons. Captain Willis stood in front of his men.

"I am here as a lawful servant of the Queen according to the agreement your father made with the Queen. These two renegades have set fire to my camp and killed an unknown number of my men. Let us pass and serve the Queen's justice upon them."

"I don't think you want any more justice doled out today. Release them and leave Donegal and leave all that you have stolen behind."

"I am a tax collector for the Queen. Any monies or chattels I have collected are not mine to give back."

"I would advise you to give them back, for I may not be able to hold the townsfolk back from you any longer."

"I'm sure you and the people of this town are aware of the punishment for murdering a servant of the Queen, carrying out the Queen's duties?"

"I am perfectly happy to discuss your antics in Tirconnell with the Queen at a future date, but now you and your men are leaving."

"Do you grant my men and I safe passage?"

"Yes, but only you and your men. All weapons, monies and chattels are to be left behind, or else I will leave you to the townsfolk and damn the consequences!"

Captain Willis pondered the offer. He turned and walked back to the monastery.

"Release the prisoners. Gather your things. We are moving out tonight."

The soldiers cut the ropes around Eunan and Seamus's wrists, and Red Hugh's men cheered. Red Hugh set his men to put out the fire in the monastery and escort Captain Willis to the county border.

## CHAPTER TWENTY-FIVE

# INAUGURATION OF THE O'DONNELL

There was widespread jubilation in Tirconnell with the expulsion of the sheriff, and the people declared Red Hugh their saviour. Red Hugh had quickly put out the fire in the monastery and sent messengers to the mountains to inform the Franciscan monks they could return. The people cheered, for they saw the restoration of the monks as a sign of their liberation. Ineen Dubh and Hugh McManus O'Donnell joined their son in Donegal Castle. The lords loyal to Red Hugh were called to a conference to discuss the unification of Tirconnell.

Eunan and Seamus busied themselves in helping to clean up the mess they had in large part created in the town while they waited for new instructions. At last, the news came about Red Hugh.

"Red Hugh is to be inaugurated as the new O'Donnell!" a messenger said as he ran through the town.

"I guess this means war," said Eunan.

"You're getting wiser in your old age," said Seamus.

Eunan smiled at such rare praise.

"Where are you going to ask for lands as your reward?"

"Don't get cocky. We've got to survive long enough to ask for our reward. We're not finished here yet."

Eunan's smile vanished. It was back to business as usual.

A Galloglass constable approached them.

"Red Hugh wants to see you."

Eunan glanced at Seamus to receive a knowing nod. They were escorted to the castle tower to be met by Red Hugh and Ineen Dubh. They bowed as they entered the room.

"You two have left me in an uncomfortable position," said Red Hugh.

"Surely not," said Seamus. "The man who banished the English sheriff and is favourite to be the O'Donnell looks to be in a pretty comfortable position to me."

Seamus saw the whites of Red Hugh's knuckles wrapped on the end of his armrest.

"You are lucky to be under the protection of one of my allies after a comment like that," said Red Hugh.

Seamus bowed low, for he knew he had overstepped the mark.

"I apologise, lord. You asked us to complete the mission of getting rid of the sheriff and here we are, ready to redistribute his ill-gotten gains with him beaten and gone. You took the credit for it to boot."

"You killed too many English soldiers. We can't afford a war."

Seamus swallowed hard before he spoke.

"What we achieved nobody could achieve before, through peace or violence. War with the English is inevitable, lord."

Ineen Dubh tried to placate her son.

"We have achieved so much. We need every capable warrior we can get. The road ahead is always going to be difficult."

"And littered with bodies," said Seamus.

"I would hold your tongue," said Ineen Dubh. "You are not that good a warrior as to say what he likes to the future O'Donnell. I am his mother and therefore can advise him so."

"Thank you for your patience, lord," said Seamus. "And you Ma'am." He bowed to show he would be silent.

"I know you are due payment for your previous exploits, but the house of O'Donnell still needs your help. My father is to step down as the O'Donnell, and I am to replace him."

"Congratulations, lord," said Eunan. "A very wise choice."

"Thank you. As you well know, there is never a better way to fall out with your family than to get declared chieftain. Some of my relatives and bondsmen need to be brought to heel, and some need to be replaced. Some of these relatives are very careful about their safety, and it would take a crafty outsider to get anywhere near them to persuade them by whatever means to step aside. I've promised you land and riches, but I cannot deliver these to you until I'm the undisputed O'Donnell. Therefore, I invite you to trust me to at least double your reward if you do me a service again."

"I think we may provide you with services for many years to come if there's no peace with the English," said Seamus.

"We'll get the English to accept my son and the peace," said Ineen Dubh. "It depends on what you will do for glory and money."

"I will double down on the money," said Seamus. "He'll take the glory." Seamus' finger pointed to the annoyance on Eunan's face.

"So be it," said Red Hugh. "We set off for Kilmacrennan tomorrow. But first, your anonymity is a great asset to me. If I remember from your stories, Eunan, you used to serve in the court of the Maguire?"

"I did, lord."

"I wish you to escort someone with a critical mission for me."

"Of course, lord."

Red Hugh looked to his servant in the doorway.

"Please invite him in."

A tall man in nondescript robes entered the room and took the hood from his head to reveal his face.

"Hello, Eunan. You have grown to be a man since the days of looking after Desmond."

Eunan did not recognise him at first. Many faces briefly passed through the court, and most had paid no attention to him. Then it came to him.

"Father Magauran!"

They both smiled and tipped back and forth on their toes ready to embrace but remained static, for they remembered they were in court.

"It's Archbishop Magauran, but I will forgive the inattentive memory of youth. It was a full-time job to look after Desmond. I'm on a mission to the King of Spain to fulfil what we discussed in Enniskillen for so long."

Eunan smiled and nodded.

"I need you to escort him under cover of darkness to his ship," said Red Hugh. "The letter he carries must reach the King of Spain. Then make haste back here to join us on the march to Kilmacrennan."

"The letter will arrive," said Eunan.

He went and shook the hand of Archbishop Magauran and invited him to leave the hall with his new escort. Seamus went to prepare for the mission while Eunan and the archbishop got reacquainted with Eunan and asked after Desmond.

They waited until darkness fell and brought the archbishop to a waiting ship hidden in Donegal Bay. Along the way, when Seamus had ridden ahead to scout the path, Eunan told Edmund the story of his childhood and how he was a prisoner in Enniskillen when they had met.

"That's a sad story that burdens the heart of a great warrior for Saint Colmcille. Here, take this piece of paper and on it is the name of a priest from the Franciscan monastery in the town. He can help you. It is your reward for helping me this night. But the Lord may call on you to fight for him again."

"Thank you, Father. I will be ready."

The next day, the messengers went to all the lords of Tirconnell and allies across Ulster. Red Hugh and the O'Gallagher Galloglass, Ineen Dubh and her

Redshanks and Seamus and Eunan set out on the trek across Tirconnell. They had but completed half their journey when Red Hugh received a messenger and immediately ordered the diversion of the party to Castle Doe, the main fortress of the MacSweeney Fannad, one of the leading Galloglass families in the county, on the north coast of Tirconnell.

"Why does Red Hugh have to go to Kilmacrennan?" said Eunan.

"If he were not properly inaugurated, his title of O'Donnell would always be in dispute," said Seamus. "I sense trouble ahead."

They marched for another two days in the rain and wind, through mountains, valleys, and forests. They marched to a granite castle jutting out into the sea, surrounded by cliffs on three sides. Tall, sturdy stone walls protected the tower and house of the MacSweeney. But the castle was too small to take the entirety of Red Hugh's entourage, so Eunan and Seamus had to camp outside with most of the soldiers. When Red Hugh arrived at the gates, Donnell MacSweeney welcomed him with open arms. Donnell took Red Hugh aside.

"There's trouble in the north, lord. Not all the lords are as enamoured as I am that you are going to be declared the O'Donnell. You'll have the allegiance of the MacSweeneys, but not much else."

Red Hugh embraced Donnell again.

"All I need is the MacSweeneys, and the O'Gallaghers, and all the rest will come to heel soon enough."

"Aye, lord. Let's eat and drink. We can spin our plots later."

They walked into the castle, each with their arm over the other's shoulder.

A feast was prepared for the lords, constables and captains in the relatively small castle buildings, but there was just wind, rain, bread and warm ale for their underlings. Seamus and Eunan had some difficulties acclimatising to their new-found status.

"If they're supposed to be the best Galloglass in all of Ireland, surely they'd build a bigger castle?" said Seamus. "If that's all his best men get, a rain-soaked oyster shell of a castle slap bang in the middle of nowhere, what are we going to get paid? I think he's not going to pay us until we're dead, or for simpletons like you, not going to pay us."

"Well, you led me all this way," said Eunan, "and there's no turning back, so we may as well make the most of it and try to live."

"You're getting more sensible by the day."

"And more soaked by the minute. Let's try to get in the castle."

They approached the group of MacSweeney Galloglass at the gate.

"No one gets in without the permission of the MacSweeney."

"We are bodyguards of Red Hugh."

"He has plenty of bodyguards in the castle."

"Can we come in?"

"No!" The firmness made Eunan take Seamus's arm.

"Come on. We'll just have to make do."

They waited outside for two rain-soaked days, watching messengers go to and from the castle.

"I don't know how the O'Donnells manage to fight wars if the weather is like this all the time," said Seamus.

"Ah, come on," replied Eunan. "It's not that different from Fermanagh."

"And I complain about it there, too."

"I suppose it's all sunny down in Munster?"

"Yes, but unfortunately currently occupied by English soldiers and settlers."

Red Hugh sent messengers to the other two branches of the MacSweeney clan and also the O'Boyles in central Tirconnell and waited for their response. Two days later, all three hundred of the MacSweeney Galloglass were united and assembled outside Castle Doe. Tadhg Óg O'Boyle arrived with one hundred warriors led by the breastplate of Saint Colmcille at the head of their column. Eunan took this as a sign that God chose Red Hugh to liberate the Irish, just as the priests had told him. A ray of hope spread around the camp. Then further behind in the O'Boyle column, Eunan saw a cart. The soldiers camped around the castle flocked towards the cart. At first, the O'Boyle men tried to hold them back, but Tadhg Óg waved to his men to stand down. The other soldiers brought the cart to a halt as they crowded around it to touch the stone.

Seamus and Eunan were standing back at the castle gates.

"What's going on?" asked Seamus of one of the MacSweeney Galloglass still guarding the gate.

"It's the Stone of Saint Colmcille."

"What did Saint Colmcille do with that?" said Seamus.

The Galloglass was almost insulted.

"He was born on it! An angel visited his mother and told her to give birth on a stone the angels raised from Gartan Lough. If you pray to it, you get the protection of Saint Colmcille, and it'll cure your ailments!"

Another Galloglass wandered up, rosy-cheeked from overindulgence.

"I heard it's a magic rock to give you the gift of chastity! Anyone who stands on it becomes sterile!"

"It's a pity your mother didn't stand on it," said Seamus.

"Hey!" said the insulted Galloglass, reaching for his axe.

"Did you drown your sense of humour in all the free ale?" Seamus said. "Put that away. I wouldn't want a poor English soldier to be deprived of the only kill of his military career."

The Galloglass guard laughed and shook Seamus's hand.

"I'm going to go over there," said Eunan.

"Get some good luck for me while you're at it," said Seamus. He ignored Eunan's scowl.

Eunan returned looking happy, having made his acquaintance with the rock. Seamus was seated exchanging jokes with the MacSweeney Galloglass when Eunan returned.

A messenger ran amongst the men camped around the castle.

"Attention! Attention! We leave for Kilmacrennan today! Be prepared! Be prepared!"

Seamus, the Galloglass, and Eunan ignored him and carried on talking.

"So why the big fuss about Saint Colmcille? Why pick a monk to be your mascot?" said Seamus.

"Saint Colmcille was a fighter," said Eunan.

"Is this one of those tales of Eunan the fat who slew twenty English by firing axes out of his arse?"

The Galloglass roared laughing.

"No, as I said, he is a fighter. Once, Saint Colmcille was called by a chieftain to slay Suileach, the many-eyed dreadful beast that terrorised the countryside. He set out with the local chieftain to find the beast. When it leapt out from his cave, the chieftain fled, leaving Saint Colmcille to face the beast alone."

Eunan leapt from his seat to act out the story.

"Colmcille fought the beast and managed to cut it in half. Head, tail," said Eunan, making rough measurements with his hands of the two imaginary parts of the beast.

"I get it," said Seamus, hoping it was the end of the story. "Is that it?"

"Then the tail came back to life! It wrapped itself around the saint while the head crept towards him! How could Colmcille survive!? He broke free and stabbed the beast in the head. With the beast now dead, Saint Colmcille was furious that the chieftain had abandoned him and went to kill him. The chieftain cowered before the saint, for he knew he could not beat him in single combat. He pleaded for the saint to wash the blade before slaying him, as he didn't want his blood mixed with that of the beast. Saint Colmcille went to a nearby stream and washed the blade, but as the blood entered the stream, the saint's anger dissipated and he spared the chieftain."

Eunan dramatically collapsed on the ground to signify his story was over.

"That's a 'firing axes out of your arse' story," Seamus said. "I bet Saint Colmcille was stuck in some dreary monastery copying the bible, dreaming of tall stories about his imaginary life he could tell eejits like you! But whatever gets your mob out on the battlefield, I suppose."

The Galloglass waved his finger in the air with a glint in his eye.

"I've got a better one," he said. "St. Colmcille told this prophecy. Saint Patrick gathered all the Irish people together, saints and sinners alike, and leads them to heaven. He sent a message ahead to tell Jesus of their imminent arrival. Jesus said to leave all the evil doers behind. But Saint Patrick said, 'What kind of host are you to turn people away?' Jesus and Saint Patrick exchanged messages until finally, Saint Patrick said that during Jesus's previous divine visitations he had given Saint Patrick the right to pass judgement on the Irish people. Jesus relented, and Saint Patrick and the Irish people march towards heaven..."

Eunan was on the edge of his seat, and Seamus was poking the fire waiting for a punchline.

"Then what happened?" said Eunan.

"They hear a bell."

"What!? The bells of heaven?"

"No, the lunch bell. It's time for Saint Colmcille's lunch!"

Seamus roared with laughter, and Eunan howled with disappointment.

"Attention! All men to prepare to march to Kilmacrennan!"

"Well, that's our lunchtime bell. See you on the battlefield, my friend." Seamus embraced the Galloglass goodbye.

At midday, the order came they were moving out. All the MacSweeney Galloglass lined up first and led the march to Kilmacrennan. It was more like an army marching to war than a celebratory inauguration procession. Word came that Niall Garbh O'Donnell had sent an army to oppose them, so everyone was on alert. A counter rumour said that Ineen Dubh had given Niall Garbh such a hefty bribe of cattle that if he was not the O'Donnell, at least now he was the richest man in Tirconnell. Another rumour was that Niall Garbh had gone to Dublin to seek help from the Crown to make him the O'Donnell. The opposition army never materialised.

They arrived at Kilmacrennan and set up camp outside the village. This time Eunan and Seamus were not exalted guests but ordinary soldiers with orders not to draw attention to themselves. The Galloglass created a ring of tents with Red Hugh and the other dignitaries in the centre. Seamus and Eunan waited for instructions on the periphery. The three northern lords, Niall Garbh, Hugh Dubh O'Donnell and Sean Óg O'Doherty, were conspicuous by their absence.

"It could have been worse. They could have shown up with their armies," said Seamus, and Eunan nodded in agreement.

The dignitaries went to the sacred grounds for the inauguration ceremony. Seamus and Eunan could see nothing, for the Redshank guards of Ineen Dubh surrounded the ceremony. Hugh McManus abdicated in favour of Red Hugh, and Red Hugh received his titles in the traditional manner. However, none of the lords of Tirconnell got to vote as they would have in a traditional ceremony. They had to stand by as Ineen Dubh orchestrated the event, so the title of O'Donnell passed peacefully.

Red Hugh solidified his new alliance with the lords of Tirconnell and Hugh O'Neill in the traditional manner with a raid. Hugh O'Neill was still fighting Turlough Luineach O'Neill, and Turlough's base of Strabane was in striking distance of Kilmacrennan. The armies of Tirconnell marched into Tyrone and laid waste to the lands of Turlough Luineach, stealing cattle and slaughtering any opposition. Eunan was awestruck, as he had only seen the much smaller, poorer quality Maguire army in action. Seamus was delighted for he saw his fortune in the destruction of north western Tyrone. The army of Tirconnell spent a week in Tyrone, for it was only a show of force and not a full-scale invasion. Red Hugh had yet to fully secure Tirconnell.

When the raid was over, most of the army marched south to Donegal Castle, which had been prepared for the inauguration feast, while the rest remained in the north, wary of retaliation.

"Thank God he chose a decent venue," said Seamus on the ride back.

"Try not to get us killed by disrespecting the O'Donnell," said Eunan.

Donegal town was festive and columns of nobles and soldiers streamed in to join the celebrations. Donegal Castle flung open its gates, and the revellers in the castle united with the common people celebrating in the streets. There was a tangible whiff in the air that Red Hugh was on the cusp of greatness, and they were all privileged to witness it. Various drunken salutes went around the town that God sent Red Hugh to liberate them from the English.

Seamus indulged himself with the local whores, all on the promise of payment from the riches he would receive when released from his bond with Red Hugh. Seamus hoped that the stories of his part in the glorious rise of Red Hugh would suffice as payment, since the women enjoyed them so much for he was not planning to hang around in Donegal town after he got paid. Eunan left Seamus to the whores; he was nervous as he had never done it before and felt guilty and afraid, remembering back to the teachings of his mother and the priest about fornication and sin.

When he heard Hugh Maguire had arrived for the festivities, Eunan went to fetch Seamus.

"He may get us released and paid," said Seamus as they set out to find him.

They arrived in the great hall at the special invitation of Red Hugh just as Hugh Maguire embraced him and declared to all listeners what an outstanding leader he would make.

Hugh Maguire took his seat below the main table as Red Hugh greeted the new entrant, Hugh O'Neill. Hugh Maguire joined them at the top table, and the chant of "all hail the three Hughs" reverberated around the walls. Anti-English chants swiftly followed, which Red Hugh did little to discourage.

Seamus made himself known to Hugh Maguire, and Hugh nodded in acknowledgement. About half an hour later, Hugh Maguire signalled to Seamus to step out of the hall. Seamus left Eunan to his ale. They met in the corridor.

"Lord, we need to be released from our bond to Red Hugh so we may return to Fermanagh."

"Fermanagh needs warriors like you. But alas, you have outdone yourselves! Red Hugh is very impressed with you and your unique skills. Once he consolidates his lands, he will be strong enough to release you. It'll not be long until you are back in Fermanagh, a rich man. Then I'll need you, for I fear the English plan, the absorption of our beloved county into the Pale."

"It is not for me, I plead. It's for the boy. He's a chieftain and needs to defend his people if he's to remain one!"

"The boy will be a great warrior for as long as he lives, and his tales will live long after. But it is for the greater good of Ulster that the O'Donnell and the O'Neill unite. Then we all have a chance. You do your best for the O'Donnell, and I'll do my best for the Maguires. Our paths will cross again soon enough. We must return to the celebrations, or we will be missed."

The Maguire turned to leave, but Seamus held out his hand as he had one last request.

"The boy must marry sometime and he has given much service to both you and the O'Donnell. Please keep him in mind if you become aware of any suitable young maidens."

"I was married at his age and have many alliances to strike," said the Maguire. "If I need a man of Eunan's status to do the clan a service, then I will call upon him."

"Thank you, lord," said Seamus. "That is all I ask."

They parted company and made their separate ways back to the party. Eunan smiled at Seamus when he returned and carried on the revelling. Seamus helped himself to ale and wine and thought up some more war stories to tell the local whores. He would be calling back to them again before the celebrations were over.

The celebrations continued for several days until the alcohol and most residents were exhausted. However, Red Hugh, with the passion and energy of youth, made his plans with Hughs O'Neill and Maguire, and his loyal lords.

# CHAPTER TWENTY-SIX

# THE MONASTERY

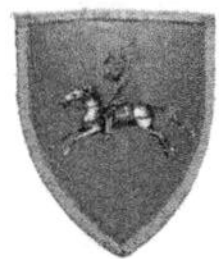

Red Hugh was obsessed with the O'Donnells' past glories and their place in the clan hierarchy of Ulster and Connacht. He was determined to return them to what he saw as their rightful place. That place was to be the most powerful clan in Ireland, including the O'Neills, and for himself to outdo the achievements of his ancestors. One of his first actions towards meeting his vast ambitions was to secretly supply men and weapons to the rebellious Lower MacWilliam Burkes in Mayo. Next, he wanted to turn his attention to reuniting Tirconnell.

However, Hugh O'Neill knew he had to get Red Hugh accepted by the Irish Council as the new O'Donnell before Red Hugh could unite Tirconnell. He smoothed the way for Red Hugh's appointment by a few strategically placed bribes, the largest to the Lord Deputy himself. Red Hugh was reluctant to go as his trust in the Council had been destroyed by his previous kidnapping and imprisonment. However, after much persuasion from Hugh O'Neill and Ineen Dubh, and the promise of safe passage from the agents of the Crown, Red Hugh went to meet the Lord Deputy in Dundalk. Hugh O'Neill escorted Red Hugh, and a deal was agreed. Red Hugh submitted to Lord Deputy Fitzwilliam, and the Lord Deputy accepted Red Hugh as the O'Donnell.

Meanwhile, Seamus and Eunan were left to their own devices as they waited in Donegal town. Seamus amused himself in the taverns and brothels where his credit was still good. Eunan went back to see the Franciscan friars, for he had been having nightmares. He could not rid himself of the dreams of his bad blood. He remembered Edmund Magauran gave him the name of a priest who may be able to help.

It had been several months since he had been at the monastery, but he could already see the changes. Gone was the debris once strewn everywhere, created in the wake of the screaming pig. The priests and locals had repainted the walls, and little visible scarring remained from the fires that burned when they drove out the English. He knocked on the door. A pair of eyes stared at him through the opened slit.

"Is Father Michael here?"

"Who's asking?"

"Eunan O'Keenan Maguire. Archbishop Edmund Magauran sent me."

The slit shut, and Eunan waited. After a few minutes, the door opened. A priest stood before him.

"Eunan!" Father Michael exclaimed. "I'm so glad you came. I heard of your exploits to save this monastery."

Eunan's heart lit up at such a warm welcome.

"I'm delighted the monastery looks so much better than when I saw it last, but I'm a troubled man, Father."

"Well, you've come to the right place," said the priest, inviting him in. "Seek solace in the Lord, my son. He is the one sanctuary on this cruel earth. Let us go to the chapel where it's quiet, then you can tell me all about it."

They passed by the monks that were still hard at work restoring the monastery after the damage done by the English.

"Even we priests get involved when war spills over into religion. The O'Donnell warriors do a fine job of defending the faith from the heathen English."

They arrived at the chapel, and Father Michael waved all the monks away so they could speak in private.

"Come and sit here, son, and tell me what's troubling you."

"Thank you, Father."

Eunan sat and tried to compose himself, but all he could do was shake and cry.

"Father! Father! Help me! I think I'm possessed!"

Father Michael raised his eyebrows.

"What makes you think that?"

"Everywhere I go, I'm in the shadow of death and destruction. With these axes, I fear that I have become their tool."

Eunan showed Father Michael his axes and dwelt on the glint of the blade in the sun.

"There are good wars and bad wars, son. It depends upon what you are fighting for."

"I try to fight for the righteous, Father, to free my people from tyranny, to give them a good life!"

"A man who fights for that is not possessed. You don't need a priest to tell you that."

"It only starts there, or should I say, it started in my youth." Eunan bowed his head. "My mother always said I had bad blood," he whispered.

The priest bent over to reply. "Everyone has bad blood. Why do you think they get sick?"

"I don't mean it like that, Father. I have bad blood like...like...like...I have some kind of evil that possesses me. Every time something bad happened that I was responsible for or could be held responsible for, my mother said it was the bad blood."

"And where did this bad blood come from?"

"I don't know, Father. My mother said I could be a Viking. Like one of those Vikings who destroyed Saint Colmcille's monastery on that Scottish island and undid some of his good works. Like the ones that used to raid and destroy Ireland. Their blood swam down through the ages and possessed me. That's why I created my axes, so that I could make amends for my bad blood. I can use my axes to defend Saint Colmcille and all he stood for. But my mother always said I had bad blood, and it has tormented me ever since."

"How does this 'bad blood' influence you?"

"Death and destruction follow me everywhere I go. The worst thing is, I'm good at mayhem and destruction. First Hugh Maguire, and then Red Hugh, took me into their service."

"I still don't know how this makes you a wicked man. Many in the church and Tirconnell believe Red Hugh is the chosen one. Chosen by God to liberate the Irish people and restore the one true faith. By doing the work of Red Hugh, you are doing the work of Saint Colmcille and God."

"I don't feel as if I am doing the work of Saint Colmcille. I feel I'm evil. How come people always die when I'm doing God's work? My little sister died in my mother's womb. They pulled my sister out in a pool of gloopy, sick, black blood. My mother said I was cursed, that my bad blood drowned my sister. My mother and father died, and I couldn't save them. I killed my father thinking I was doing the work of Hugh Maguire. Yet I survived. Then I met Seamus, who has been like a second father to me. But he's a vicious and cruel Galloglass, a perfect father for my bad blood. Was I drawn to him? Is he a devil? I want to be good. I want to repent and redeem myself by working for Saint Colmcille, but I can't. Until I rid myself of this bad blood, I will always be the tool of darkness."

"Rest easy, son. I may have the answer for you. Come back tomorrow morning, and I'll have a solution for you. Tomorrow is a good day on the all saints calendar."

"Thank you, Father, oh, thank you. I will return at first light."

Eunan could barely sleep that evening. There was no sign of Seamus. Eunan thought he must be telling tall tales to prostitutes again.

At first light, Eunan banged on the monastery door.

"Father Michael, Father Michael, I'm here as promised."

The door slit slid open, a pair of eyes regarded Eunan, and then the door opened.

"Father Michael is this way."

The priest brought Eunan into a room with a bed. Father Michael was seated on it, and a solemn monk stood at the edge of the bed. The monk stared forward as if in prayer.

"Come in, Eunan," said Father Michael, pointing towards the comfortable bed. "Lie down and rest, and we will help ease your pain."

"Are we going to pray?" said Eunan.

"We are here to help you physically and spiritually."

Eunan laid his axe to rest and then lay on the bed.

"Take off your trousers and your shirt."

Eunan raised his head in confusion.

"What kind of prayer is this?"

"Just do as I say. I said I would help."

Eunan obeyed and lay in his dirty undergarments. The nose of the priest twitched. "Get some new clothes when you get paid," said the priest.

Eunan was about to answer back, but Father Michael gestured to him to lie down. Eunan lay down and looked at the ceiling.

"This monk is a physician. He was taught in the finest houses of London and then returned home to help the people of Donegal. Your illness is a punishment for sin, but we do not know what sin nor who committed it. Therefore, let us pray."

Eunan closed his eyes and prayed to be better.

He felt a pain in his left arm, the searing cut of a blade.

"Keep your eyes shut."

He felt a pain in his stomach.

"Keep your eyes shut."

He felt a pain in his legs.

"Keep your eyes shut."

He felt a pain in his temple.

"Dear Lord, suck away this poor man's bad blood. Forgive whatever sin led to blighting this poor sinner with such an ailment. Make him an instrument of your plan on earth. Let him always be able to see what is the right thing to do for both you and those who carry out your will on earth."

Eunan felt a little ill and sat up. He looked at his body. He had open wounds and was covered in leeches.

"What are you doing?" he said.

"You said you have bad blood that afflicts you. With divine guidance, these leeches will suck the bad blood away. I am also praying for spiritual guidance for you, your soul, and me. This is what you wanted."

"What I wanted was to be free of this affliction. If this removes the curse, I'll do it."

Eunan calmed a little and lay down once more to rest.

"You must have faith. Faith cures all. Believe in the goodness of God, and you will be free."

"If I am to be free, attach more leeches. Suck it all away."

"You must be careful. Only a practitioner must apply the leeches to get the correct balance. Human error can undo Divine guidance."

Eunan lay down again, closed his eyes, and prayed as hard as he could. He imagined the suckers of the leeches crawling into his veins and hanging there until they attracted some of the bad blood that flowed through him. The leech consumed the blood and grew fat on its richness. Eunan felt himself grow weaker, but as he became weaker, he prayed harder. He prayed they would suck all the bad blood out of him and he would wake up restored, throw his axes away, and return to his village. All the villagers would be there, even his parents. His mother would have recovered and been able to walk. His mother and father were waiting at the village gate with open arms...

"Eunan! Eunan! Wake up!" the priest said, shaking him as hard as he could. Eunan awoke. He was covered in blood. The priest and the physician applied bandages to soak up the worst of it. Eunan raised himself onto his elbows. Even that was an effort.

"Is it gone? Is all the bad blood gone?"

Father Michael held up a bowl. Fat, bloated leeches rolled around in Eunan's blood soup, many times their previous size. Such evil repulsed him, and he gagged to remove the last of the bile from his throat.

"It disgusts me, but is it all gone?" he said as he pushed the bowl away.

"We shall see, son. Pray hard and return to me in a week when you feel normal again. If you still feel you are cursed or possessed, we can see about doing it again. But for now, go in peace, and remember, Red Hugh came to free us from the English. If you serve him, you serve the Lord."

Eunan struggled to sit up straight. The physician pointed to a chair and beside it a table with ale and bread. Father Michael went over and helped Eunan up and to walk over to the chair. Eunan threw himself onto it. The physician cleared up.

"How do you know all the bad blood is gone?" said Eunan.

"The body contains four fluids or humours, each relating to an element found on earth," said the physician. "Yellow bile is fire. Black bile is earth, air is blood, water is phlegm. These elements have to be in balance, or the body falls sick. I don't know which is out of balance, but if I were to guess, I would say earth, for your bad blood is likely to be black and the punishment for sins committed on earth. But we don't know, and we bless the leeches and let them do the Lord's work. If you are truly sorry, the Lord will forgive you and cure your ailments.

Eunan reached over with what little strength he had and grabbed the bowl of leeches. He peered down at them, swollen with blood, lolloping around in his dark blood, writhing around in his sin. He held the bowl closer to his face.

"I can see blackness in the blood."

"That's good," said the physician. "That's the bad elements we removed."

Eunan stared at the leeches, sucking in more blood in their greed for his sin. Eunan choked from the smell of the bowl. He threw his disgusting sin on the ground, and it shattered with pieces of the bowl, blood and leech flying everywhere.

"No!" said the physician as he tried to stop him. Eunan reached for his axe and bludgeoned every leech he could see until their insides melted into the floor. He only stopped when no more leeches were intact. He flopped back into his seat with a sigh, dropped his axe, and prayed.

"Those leeches were innocent," said the physician. "They only did the Lord's work and sucked away your sin. Yet you destroyed them!"

"You shouldn't have done that," said Father Michael. "You must compensate the physician! He brought his finest leeches to cure you!"

Eunan looked away and bit his tongue.

"I'm sorry. But they stank of greed and evilness. I had to destroy them like my curse tries to destroy me. Don't worry. Red Hugh owes me a lot of money for all the death and destruction I have brought on his behalf. I will reward you appropriately for your loss. When can we do it again?"

"I'm not sure I want to do it again with you," said the physician.

"Name your price, sir. It will be a long time until Red Hugh runs out of people for me to kill."

Father Michael looked at the physician.

"The monastery is much in need of repairs, and we always welcome contributions. We also welcome sinners and hope to set them on the path to redemption. If you come looking for help from us, you will always be welcome.

"However, you must use your strength and attributes to defend the faith and to do good. The first step would be to dedicate yourself to Saint Colmcille and Red Hugh. That will set you on the path to redemption.

"But now you must sleep, for the body needs to replenish itself after the exhausting process of the purging of evil."

"Thank you. May all my blessings be upon you." With that, Eunan was asleep.

# CHAPTER TWENTY-SEVEN

# HEART OF IRON

Eunan tried to keep his mind off his sins and put his efforts into his training and prayers as he waited a whole week before returning to the monastery. Father Michael and the physician were waiting for him. He showed up with the face of a beggar.

"Red Hugh has not paid me, so I have no money to give you, Father. But the treatment you gave me the other week was immensely helpful. I can do nothing but pursue it further."

Father Michael smiled and welcomed him in.

"You have something more valuable than money to give, which is your axe, your courage and your honour. When the time comes, I'm sure you'll pledge to Red Hugh and Saint Colmcille. That would be more than ample payment for us. Come this way and let us help you again."

Eunan returned to the campsite that evening. He hid his scars and tales of his visit to the monastery from Seamus. Seamus seemed preoccupied and did not notice that Eunan looked unwell, nor bother to enquire where he had been.

In the meantime, Red Hugh and Hugh O'Neill returned from Dundalk in triumph. They had another lavish celebration joined again by Hugh Maguire. The people of Donegal town celebrated the new government approved O'Donnell, while Hughs O'Donnell, O'Neill and Maguire cemented their new secret alliance.

The next day, Seamus and Eunan were confined by their hangovers to the wrecks of what were once tents. The camp outside Donegal town now resembled a battlefield with the bodies of the drunk strewn everywhere and the odd corpse stumbling around, looking for somewhere to piss. A messenger from Red Hugh picked his way through the mess and delivered a bucket of water and a piece of paper. Seamus, furious at being soaked, snatched the letter thrust in front of his face.

"Aw shit!"

Eunan roused himself upright and focused his gaze.

"What's wrong?"

"Hugh Maguire has left behind twenty rookie Galloglass for us to train," said Seamus.

"Is that it?"

"No, we must be up at Donegal Castle by noon."

"We'd better get a move on then!"

They arrived to see three hundred MacSweeney Galloglass lined up in columns ready to head south. Their rookie Maguire Galloglass stood behind them, paling in comparison. Seamus went and introduced himself to each one individually, while Eunan went to find out what was going on. Red Hugh arrived surrounded by Redshanks. He signalled to move out, and Seamus and Eunan found themselves at the rear.

"Where are we going?" asked Seamus.

"Belleek Castle," said Eunan as he paid more attention to inspecting their new Galloglass.

"Who's there?"

"Rebel O'Donnells."

Seamus sighed. "Do these clans ever tire of killing each other?"

When they left Donegal Town, Seamus noticed men in the surrounding countryside training to use the pike with mysterious men with Spanish accents.

"Look, Eunan. He's been swift to start the war preparations. An axe in the head is good enough for a rebel O'Donnell, so the modern fighting techniques must be for the English."

Eunan could only nod grimly in return.

Several days later, they arrived outside Belleek Castle. Hugh Maguire had joined them with some of his troops. Red Hugh rode up to the front gates and dismounted. He threw open his arms, daring the rebels to shoot him down.

"Why do you shut your gates before me? I am the O'Donnell. This is my land, and this is my castle!" he shouted at the walls.

"We have our orders from Hugh McHugh Dubh," came the reply.

"And if Hugh McHugh Dubh is a member of the O'Donnell clan, he takes orders from me! Open the gates or suffer the consequences!"

"We take our orders from Hugh McHugh Dubh!"

"So be it!" Red Hugh got back on his horse and rode back to his men.

"Surround the castle. Make sure no one gets in or out. We'll wait for them to surrender."

Later that evening, Hugh Maguire stole into Red Hugh's tent.

"I have connections in the castle, as some of their leaders know me because their lands are next to mine. Let me speak to them to see if I can hasten their surrender."

"Tell them I will make my final offer tomorrow. If they refuse, then I attack!" said Red Hugh. "If the Maguire can save the lives of loyal O'Donnells, the O'Donnell will be very grateful."

"I will do my best, and will be gone before you arrive in the morning."

With that, Hugh Maguire left.

The next day, Seamus, Eunan and their Galloglass found themselves in the fields surrounding the castle, herding all the cattle they could find. Red Hugh decided that if the castle defenders would not let him in, his men would strip the land of everything worth having.

Red Hugh rode up to the castle gates and dismounted.

"It is I, the O'Donnell, not Hugh McHugh Dubh O'Donnell but the actual, inaugurated O'Donnell, Red Hugh O'Donnell. As the O'Donnell, this is my castle and my lands. In my lands, you are my friends or my foes. If you open the gates, you're my friends, and I will return your property, less the costs of you inconveniencing me. If you do not open the gates, then you're my foes. I will take your property and kill you and any of your relatives I may come across on my journey to avenge myself upon Hugh Dubh. It is your choice. But make it quickly."

A voice came from behind the ramparts.

"We only take orders from Hugh McHugh Dubh O'Donnell!"

"So be it. But what do you think will happen now? I am out here with the MacSweeney Galloglass, the best soldiers in Tirconnell. Do you think Hugh McHugh will ride over the hill, beat the pride of Tirconnell and rescue you? Do you think the English will start a war to help you? Or do you think I will lay siege to you and either starve you out or assault the castle and put you all to the sword? Under how many of these choices do you think you'll live?"

The castle was silent.

"No? No opinion? Why don't you cease these games and put down your arms and surrender?"

Silence. Red Hugh extended his arms outwards.

"In my generosity and reluctance to spill my kin's blood, I will make one last offer. I will give a bag of gold to every man who helps us open the gate. But, also, to sweeten the deal, anyone who does not help will be decapitated, and we will throw your heads at Hugh McHugh Dubh's feet. My offer expires as soon as my horse takes a shit, and he hasn't been in a while."

At first, the castle was silent. Then the gates creaked open, and some soldiers walked out.

"Eoghan MacSweeney, you give out the gold. Seamus and Eunan, you deliver the axes," Red Hugh called out to the men standing behind him.

The soldiers slowly walked up to Eoghan MacSweeney. He gave them a nod, and they dropped their weapons. He handed them a bag of coins, and they burst out smiling and stood behind Hugh O'Donnell. The more reluctant soldiers looked out from over the ramparts, and their former comrades shook their bags of coin at them. The soldiers stopped coming out.

"There is more where that came from! Come out and pledge to me and receive your first payment before I send in my men to clear the place!"

The ordinary soldiers came out and gratefully received their coin bags.

But Red Hugh noticed the castle was not quite empty.

"Now, to the rest of you, there are no bags of coin. You missed out on that for your lack of trust in the O'Donnell. The rest of you are trading with your lives. With the number of men that came out, you don't have enough to defend the castle. I could come in and hunt you all down, but I would have to clean up afterwards, and I don't want to ruin my castle. So come out, lay down your weapons, and we will negotiate for your lives."

The castle was silent again, and Red Hugh was impatient. He signalled to Seamus, who readied the Galloglass to move in. With this last action, the defenders had had enough. The last of the common soldiers came out, put down their weapons, and surrendered.

One by one, the leaders of the rebels followed them out. They threw down their arms, fell to their knees, and pledged loyalty to the O'Donnell.

Red Hugh smiled.

"Some of your pledges I will take, for I believe them to be sincere. Some, I will not."

Red Hugh walked along the line. He stopped at the commander of the castle.

"Fian O'Donnell, always a thorn in my father's side. Ever the rebel, but stand for nothing. Seamus, please."

"But we made a deal with Hugh Maguire," said Fian.

"Be careful who you make a deal with."

With a swish of Seamus's axe, Fian's head rolled around in the mud, a perfect first-time cut, without a drop of blood on Red Hugh's trousers.

Red Hugh walked on.

"Ah, Hugh McHugh's cousin. I knew you'd not be far. I could smell the poison from here. Seamus?"

Another head rolled in the dirt.

Red Hugh continued his walk along the line of prisoners until sixteen headless bodies lay in the mud. Red Hugh turned to the remaining prisoners.

"I accept the pledge of loyalty from the rest of you, and you can join your comrades. But do not forget this day and tell those you meet who are disloyal to the O'Donnell what happened. Eoghan, give them each a bag of coin."

Red Hugh signalled to his Galloglass to follow him, and they secured the castle.

News of the massacre travelled far and wide. Lesser lords who had not been so eloquent in their pledges now fell over themselves to pledge themselves to the O'Donnell. Red Hugh moved north with his force and onto the lands of Niall Garbh O'Donnell. Without the possibility of government support, Niall Garbh quickly submitted without a fight and pledged his loyalty. Ineen Dubh arranged for Niall Garbh to marry Red Hugh's sister Nuala so that he would remain close to Red Hugh's side of the family.

There was only one remaining rebel, so Red Hugh travelled to the Inishowen peninsula and the lands of Sean Óg O'Doherty. This time, there was no instant capitulation. Red Hugh chased Sean Óg and his men around the peninsula with Sean Óg refused to engage.

Red Hugh was tired of the chase and burned Sean Óg's lands instead. Sean Óg soon agreed to meet. They met in one of Sean Óg's lord's houses, which were supposed to be neutral ground. Each man was only allowed to bring five escorts, be they bodyguards or advisors. Seamus and Eunan, as unknown quantities to the O'Dohertys, had the privilege of being selected for this job.

The two lords entered through separate entrances to the house. Everyone had to disarm before entering. Sean Óg's lord's men guarded the house and were the only ones allowed to bear arms. The two rival groups met in the drawing-room of the house.

"Welcome to the north, Red Hugh," said Sean Óg as he sat smugly in his seat.

"I am the O'Donnell to you and all men of Tirconnell. You have led me a merry dance in your refusal to acknowledge this. But this all must end, for we have much greater foes to fight than each other."

"At least we agree on something."

"So be a good man and surrender your forces and bend the knee, and we can find more things to agree about."

"I'll never bend the knee to you! You're an impostor! You should not be the O'Donnell!"

"I thought you might say that. Men, seize him."

Sean Óg's men bristled to defend themselves.

"I'm sorry, but your lord has let you down. Arm them!"

The lord's men handed Red Hugh's men weapons and Eunan his throwing axes. In a flash, two of Sean Óg's men were dead, with a flying axe in the forehead. The other three half-heartedly fought, then surrendered.

Red Hugh stood over Sean Óg, as Sean Óg sat with a sword to his throat.

"Sorry, but I can't be having my lords openly disobey me. Put him in chains and throw him in the cage."

Once Sean Óg was in the cage cart, and the lord paid, Red Hugh and his men marched back to Donegal Castle with their prize.

Red Hugh returned to Donegal Castle and threw Sean Óg O'Doherty into prison until he agreed to pledge to him as the O'Donnell. Tirconnell was now united.

# CHAPTER TWENTY-EIGHT

# PAYMENT IN KIND

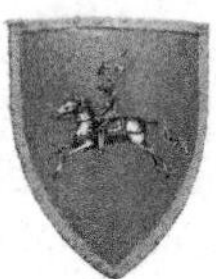

Eunan busied himself in their camp outside Donegal town training the new Maguire Galloglass. Several Spanish trainers, courtesy of Red Hugh, taught the men the art of fighting with pikes and fundamental gun skills. The Spanish trainers were devoted to the improvement of Red Hugh's armies, despite some holding resentment in their hearts because of the rumours that Ineen Dubh exchanged some of their comrades for Red Hugh while he was in prison, only for Lord Deputy Fitzwilliam to renege on the deal once he received the Spanish. But they would retreat to their tents at night and pray for the day their king would send a boat to retrieve them from their mission in this windswept, rainy godforsaken place.

Someone brought Eunan a message that he did not bother Seamus with, and he set off for the harbour. He arrived as an old friend stepped off a ship. Eunan ran and embraced him as the ship's cargo of weapons and gold was unloaded for distribution amongst the northern lords.

"The warmest welcomes to Tirconnell, Archbishop! What news from Spain?"

"So Red Hugh has sent you to greet me?" said Edmund Magauran. "I'm so lucky to be met with a friendly face. The news from Spain is good. So good that soon Red Hugh may publicly acknowledge me without fear of the Crown's priest hunters. The great King Philip promised to send troops, guns and gold by April, as long as the northern lords would come out in rebellion and support him. I must go to Red Hugh, tell him, and make preparations."

"I have my Maguire Galloglass with me to escort you."

"They will be needed for King Philip was most generous with his gifts to his new allies. But I forget my manners. What about you? Was Father Michael able to help with that which ails you?"

Eunan smiled.

"Father Michael was most useful to me and is continuing to help. I'm very grateful for your recommendation."

"You know the way to repay me is to pledge your axe to Red Hugh and Saint Colmcille and give your all in the upcoming fight against the heretics. King Philip will cleanse Ireland of these apostates and the country will be dedicated to Saint Patrick and Saint Colmcille once again."

"They have my axe and my heart, and when the time comes to pledge, I will pledge. But now is the time to make haste and tell your good news to Red Hugh. Your horse is there," said Eunan, pointing, "and your bounty from Spain will follow, escorted by my men. Mount up and let us go."

They rode as fast as they could, leaving the carts full of gifts to trudge along behind them. Once they got to the castle, Red Hugh was delighted with the archbishop's news. It breathed so much confidence in him he permitted a secret conference of the bishops of Ireland to be held in Tirconnell to discuss the impending Spanish invasion and the unification of Ireland. After the meeting, so optimistic were the bishops that the embers of rebellion would soon burst into flames that they wrote to the King of Spain that the lords of the north would support any Spanish invasion.

Eunan became Edmund's bodyguard when he was not training his men or in service to Red Hugh or visiting Father Michael. They became bonded together like brothers in the same cause.

Tirconnell was now united, and the only person in the northwest of Ireland who stood in the way of the secret northern alliance was Turlough Luineach O'Neill. Apart from cementing the new coalition, Red Hugh had his selfish reasons for attacking Turlough. It deprived his rivals in Tirconnell of potential Irish support, as he had choked off possible government help.

Red Hugh gathered his forces in the south and marched north to meet Tadhg Óg O'Boyle and also the rest of the MacSweeney Galloglass, and marched into the lands of Turlough Luineach. Seamus and Eunan found themselves amongst it all with their twenty raw Maguire Galloglass.

They made straight for Strabane, the capital of Turlough Luineach O'Neill. The horsemen of both sides skirmished outside the town, but Turlough Luineach made little effort to confront the main army. He retired in good order to Strabane Castle and sent messengers to Dublin, hoping that the Irish Council would force Red Hugh to retreat. Hugh O'Neill, in the meantime, left his lands and made his way to Strabane with his army.

Red Hugh camped outside Strabane town. Seamus and Eunan, along with the other leaders, were summoned back into Red Hugh's presence since they were outside Tirconnell and no longer had to remain inconspicuous. Red Hugh was nervous, for he felt exposed.

"We cannot stay out here for long. We have too many enemies back in Tirconnell and too few men to fight on two fronts. Hugh O'Neill is making his way here but does not have enough soldiers to finish off Turlough himself. Does anyone have a proposal they would like to share?"

"Withdraw," said one captain.

"Leave it to Hugh O'Neill," said another.

"Burn Strabane to the ground."

"What was that, Seamus?"

"You need to show him you're serious. Let him know you are here to end this. He is old. You are young. Burn the town down and wait for him to react. If he chooses to fight, Hugh O'Neill will be here before the fighting is over. It also shows your enemies back home you are serious. Burn it down."

"What about the English?"

"Make sure you steal enough cattle and money to pay them off. There is nothing they won't forgive for enough cattle and cash."

Red Hugh smiled, for he had adopted a decisive plan. "You heard the man. Steal everything and let it burn."

That night Strabane burned as Turlough Luineach O'Neill looked on from his castle and did nothing. Hugh O'Neill arrived, and the next day Turlough Luineach O'Neill sued for peace. The two Hughs persuaded Turlough Luineach to retire. Now Hugh O'Neill was the O'Neill, in all but name. Red Hugh returned to Donegal Castle, well paid for his troubles with Turlough Luineach's cattle. This time Seamus and Eunan were allowed into the castle, as Red Hugh was the undisputed master of Tirconnell.

Red Hugh, his nobles and soldiers, feasted long into the night. The entire castle was a mass of tables and benches and the floors, puddles of ale and lumps of discarded food. Amongst the most popular toasts of the evening, both sober and drunk, was declaring Red Hugh the O'Donnell the master of the north. Red Hugh beamed, for he knew he had succeeded.

The next day, the MacSweeneys started their preparations for war. Ineen Dubh sent another emissary to her Scottish allies to pay for more Redshanks for the forthcoming campaigns. She also asked for more guns and pikes so that Red Hugh could continue to modernise the army. Spanish voices rang in the fields around Donegal town and the castles of the MacSweeney Galloglass.

Seamus sat with Eunan by the fire in their camp and expressed his doubts.

"I didn't come here for war. I came to get paid so I could bugger off to some obscure part of this rain-drenched island and sow my oats. It's all getting real now. Where were they during the Desmond rebellion? Did they help? Yeah, O'Neill helped the English, that's what he did! The glory of war is for knuckleheads like you who are too young and naive to know any better. Who thinks splitting a man's head open with an axe for someone else's bidding makes them worthy of elevation and praise? Praise is hollow. You've got to live with yourself afterwards. Normally in some dive of a hut, while the order-giver lives in a fancy castle because of your murders."

Eunan frowned. "But what about freeing our lands from the English and other noble causes?"

"What do you know about freedom from the English? You live in a pretty little village beside a lake and never meet anyone unless you go to the market. The Maguire is like a benevolent God from afar who takes your crops and money and kidnaps your youth and, if you are especially unlucky, sends a few parasitic Galloglass to come and live with you and bleed you dry. All you would do is swap the Maguire for an English lord. You want to give your life up for some lord and the promise that your villagers will think you heroic for dying in a bog with an axe in your head? I'm old because I learned how to survive. I fear you won't make it as far, for all your yearnings to be a hero!"

"Nice speech, but I think we only get paid at the end, so you're here for the duration," Eunan tutted.

"We'll be so rich when we complete this job I'll be retiring. I'll get myself a lovely young wife and have loads of children when we return to Fermanagh. I'll hire you as my babysitter. You can mind them and tell them your heroic tales, like when you couldn't kill a chief and you forced me to boil him alive, or when your little axes would bounce off the armour of your enemies and I had to kill them for you, or when you could get it together, those many occasions when you axed warriors in the back of the head. Then you'll get loads of hero worship!"

"And I can tell them that their father was a big fat prostitute who wouldn't poison anyone to death unless the cattle already had his name branded on it?"

"My children will have a better life for it."

"I think your current wife will smack you round the head with a pot for that dream."

A messenger ran through the lines of men. Seamus cursed, for he was summoned again.

Seamus and Eunan walked into the main hall, where Red Hugh sat with his mother. Their jubilance radiated around the room.

"What has his lordship in such a glorious mood this morning?" said Seamus.

"Tirconnell and the clan have finally been reunited," said Red Hugh. "The English shall soon feel the wrath of the O'Donnells and the northern lords."

"Then our work here is done?" said Seamus.

"You may go home and rest until recalled for your services."

"Our axes are always available for your cause," said Eunan.

"Thank you, Eunan. Your dedication honours me. I have told Hugh Maguire that you would visit Enniskillen Castle to report to him on your way home. I believe it is on the way?"

"We shall make haste to Enniskillen Castle," said Eunan.

"Thank you, gentlemen, for your service to Tirconnell. I bid you farewell."

"There is just one more thing..."

"And what is that, Seamus?"

"We were given promises for our dedication and service?"

"Eoghan McToole will see to that on your way out. Thank you."

Seamus bowed and strode towards the door.

"Eunan, why do you stay?" said Red Hugh.

Eunan knelt on one knee, bowed his head, and held his axe aloft.

"I would like to dedicate my life, my axe to Saint Colmcille, yourself and your cause. I will raise a battle of Galloglass that I will call the Knights of Saint Colmcille, dedicated to freeing the land of the English, and the people of the false religion the English impose upon them. I fight for the Pope and the freedom of Ireland."

Red Hugh held his hand to his chest. "What a noble speech. I am truly honoured."

"I would also like to give one third of my reward back to you to help arm soldiers for the cause. The second third, to the Franciscan monks of Donegal. The last third will be for the welfare of my immediate clan!"

"You truly have become a mighty warrior. Eoghan, please ensure the reward is distributed as Eunan has said."

Eunan bowed again.

"Thank you, lord. We will meet again soon."

"Sooner than you think. Goodbye, Eunan."

Eunan left the hall. He felt elated, and the goodness seared through his body. He felt his mother would have been proud of what he just did. The leech treatment of Father Michael had freed his soul.

Eoghan McToole escorted Eunan and Seamus into the courtyard. Seamus could not bring himself to look at Eunan. Eoghan McToole waved them forward. They walked out of the castle, out of the town and into the fields.

"Let me show you your reward for your service to Tirconnell."

Eoghan McToole waved his arms with such grandeur Eunan's face lit up.

"So many cattle. That is surely enough to make the village the most prosperous south of the lake."

Seamus's reaction was more guttural.

"Two hundred fucking cattle for all that. Two hundred fucking cattle!"

Seamus grabbed Eunan and punched him full in the nose.

"You shut your fucking face the next time it comes to negotiations! You're an idiot! Knights of Saint Colmcille, my arse! How are the two of us supposed to get all these cattle home? You're an idiot!"

Eunan felt his nose. The bad blood seeped down his face, onto his lip, and back into his mouth. Eunan sat on the ground and thought of his father.

## CHAPTER TWENTY-NINE

# THE WEDDING ARRANGEMENTS

Seamus and Eunan rode through south Tirconnell with their twenty Maguire Galloglass, and herded the two hundred cattle towards home. Eunan rode upfront, eager to return to Fermanagh, while Seamus scouted the periphery, studying the countryside. With mountains, bogs and woods, it was treacherous country to be transporting your wealth across. He galloped down one particular hill to confer with Eunan. Eunan had not forgiven him for the punch in the face, while Seamus was fields away from forgiving Eunan for giving away most of their reward. However, Seamus was determined to protect what they had left.

"I think we're being followed," said Seamus.

"What makes you think that?"

"I have consistently seen men on horseback follow us since we left Donegal Castle."

"You continue to scout, and I'll alert the men," Eunan said, digging his heels into the side of the horse and riding back towards the herd.

A galleon loaded its hold in the northern Spanish port of Bilbao. Its cargo of guns, gunpowder, gold, bibles and a small retinue of soldiers was not that unusual for the time, but the passengers certainly were. A senior priest stood quayside at the bottom of the boarding plank and blessed the passengers as they came aboard. Irish priests from the Catholic colleges of Rome and Spain solemnly accepted the blessing and boarded the ship. Irish nobles, both banished or absconders, boarded, delighted to be going home, but also anxious about what fortune may bring them on their journey. Finally, the Spanish captain and the emissaries of the Spanish court climbed aboard with a small escort of Spanish troops. They were the scouts for the Spanish King's intervention. They pulled out of Bilbao port on a clear sunny day, full of the rebellious hopes of the exiles of Ireland.

Seamus and Eunan made slow progress through the valleys of south Tirconnell. Seamus tutted, and caught up with Eunan again.

"I'm telling you, we're being followed. There's more and more of them following us by the day," said Seamus as he apprehensively eyed the tops of the hills in the valley that lay before them. Eunan threw his hands in the air.

"Then what shall we do? The cattle won't move any faster."

"Send men forward to Enniskillen to the Maguire. With a bigger escort, we'll get these cattle home. He owes us for all the hassle we've been through," said Seamus.

Eunan turned away and ordered two of the men to go forth to Enniskillen to seek help.

The ship sailed along the coast of France. Archbishop O'Healy, the archbishop of Tuam, leaned over the side of the deck and stared at the French coast.

"How long since you saw the shores of Ireland?" came a voice from behind.

"I've come and gone many a time over these past years, first back home, then to the corridors of Rome and the halls of the King of Spain, but I've never walked the fields of Ireland and seen them free. They've given tokens of help, but never enough. The lords of Ulster are strong, but not that strong. I've prayed hard, and this is the best my prayers have been answered in a long time. How about you?"

"I've served for the armies of the Spanish Crown for many a year. But now I want to pledge my services to the new O'Donnell. My brethren say he'll revive the O'Donnell power of old. He'll need men like me."

"Bless you, son. And may the waves carry us home all the faster."

Seamus and Eunan entered a valley. There was no avoiding it since it was the quickest way back to Fermanagh and the most obvious route the Maguire would use to send men to help. Its sheer sides, rock-strewn river and wooded valley forced any travellers along a narrow path.

"I don't like this," said Seamus. "It's the perfect place for an ambush."

"I'll send more men ahead to scout the route and see if reinforcements are coming from the Maguire."

Seamus scowled. "That makes us weaker in case of attack."

"But they can see if anyone is ahead and warn us. I'm the chieftain, so I'm giving the orders."

Seamus grabbed Eunan by the forearm.

"Do you remember our conversation where you said you'd leave military matters to me?"

"That was then. It's time I took on more responsibility."

Eunan shook Seamus off. Seamus turned a shade of red, dug his heels into the sides of his horse, and rode off to check out the mountains.

The men drove the cattle down the valley until they reached a choke point with the river on one side and a wood on the other. Eunan and what remained of the Galloglass drove the cattle towards the gap. In their way appeared three horsemen, one with a familiar face. Eunan rode up to them.

"Niall Garbh, are you here to offer us help on our way back to Fermanagh?"

"Of a sort," Niall Garbh said. "I'm here to take back what is mine and your actions will decide how many bodies I leave lying here."

"You can't kill me. Red Hugh would immediately seek revenge," said Eunan.

"You overestimate the loyalty of Red Hugh at your peril. What's a few dead Maguires to him for all the O'Donnells he's killed to get himself to power? Now hand over those cattle, and we'll see if I'll let you live."

Eunan went for his axe. A flurry of arrows killed most of the Maguire Galloglass behind him.

"You won't be able to lift that axe above your head before my men shoot you down. Why don't you come with us and we'll see if we can get a nice ransom for you."

Niall Garbh's men surrounded Eunan and took him prisoner. Seamus could only watch from the hills.

Eunan and Seamus rode back into the village, not on speaking terms. His old Galloglass warmly greeted Seamus while the people who fled from the surrounding countryside treated Eunan as a curiosity, as they barely knew him, and that was only by vague reputation.

Seamus dismounted and made straight for his house. Finn was there, with Seamus's wife Dervella, waiting for him as he had been living there minding the house in Seamus's absence.

Finn was keen to impress his master with what he had accomplished in his absence. His master's anger was an opportunity not to be wasted to get one up on his rival.

"Welcome, lord. What tales of glory and adventure do you have upon your return?"

Seamus walked past him and went over and kissed his wife.

"I come back to you with empty pockets and a heart as barren as your womb."

"I, for one, am glad you are back. For as much as you fight the world, you have a warm heart. How is the boy?"

"So weak-willed. Much troubled and a heart that bleeds for any that wish to tweak it. I hope he is the making of us, but fear he will be our downfall."

He took off his soaking blood-stained chain mail and threw it on the ground.

"Excuse me, dear wife. We must momentarily postpone our reunion. I must speak with Finn before I can relax."

Dervella invited him into the house and once there, left the room. Finn sat down, for he feared the news would not be good.

"For all the toil and labour I have been through, I return to my village empty-handed," said Seamus as he poured himself some ale.

"How come, lord?"

"It is a long story, but my temper is short. So I will tell it to the limits of it."

Seamus sat and drank.

"No sooner had we completed our almost unending series of tasks for Red Hugh than the boy, in a fit of stupidity, goes off and visits a priest. That priest poured into that idiot's brain a load of nonsense about being righteous, Saint Colmcille, Red Hugh being the chosen one, etcetera. Guess who takes all of that seriously?

"Then comes pay day. There we are, both standing before Red Hugh with me about to stick my hand out. What happens then? He pledges Red Hugh his axe. Then our money. He gives away one third to Red Hugh's war effort, a cunning name for Red Hugh's pocket, a third to the priest who made mush of his brain, the final third he kept. But how did Red Hugh choose to pay us? In cattle!

"So there we are, the two of us standing in front of only two hundred cattle. That is the first time I could compare our reward against what we had to do to earn it. Needless to say, I was furious. But then you have two hundred cattle with only two of us and twenty raw Maguire Galloglass to herd them through south Tirconnell and most of Fermanagh. Most of which is hostile territory. But as soon as we got across the border, we were hit by a raiding party led by Niall Garbh, of all people. The boy was captured, and all our men were killed. I had to follow them and slip into the enemy camp in the dead of night, to slit the throats of the guards, all to save an ungrateful boy.

"We returned to Hugh Maguire penniless and had to tell him all his men were dead. He told us to ready our men for war was coming, and we could quickly make our fortunes again."

Seamus took a long drink.

"You should have taken me with you," said Finn, an undisguised quiver of anger on his bottom lip. "Why do you favour him over me?"

Seamus threw his cup on the floor.

"I haven't time for your petty jealousies, nor do I owe you an explanation," said Seamus. "What has been happening in the village? How many men have you raised? How prepared are we for war?"

The edge of Finn's lip curled.

"I have accomplished much, unlike the one you favour," said Finn. "There's good soil to feed our rapidly growing community. The stockades are up. We have a few self-sufficient islands in the lake now. We have forty men that we could hire out as Galloglass and would not disgrace us. Plenty of Kern. A half dozen horsemen. Better than when you left."

"Good. Now leave me be, and I will spend some time resting with my wife. You are in charge until I am rested. Watch Eunan. Make sure he does nothing stupid. A fine warrior he may be, but he is way too easily led."

Finn tutted, rose and walked towards the door.

"Just as you like them."

Several days passed until Seamus rested enough to come out and join the villagers again. Eunan had shown his younger age and restless spirit and was already back in training and beating some of the older Galloglass. However, Finn had received word of some ideas he was trying to spread and went straight to Seamus, who was indulging in some carpentry and expanding his house. He was not pleased to see Finn.

"Why do you deem it fit to disturb me when I am here with my wife?"

"Eunan is trying to recruit some of the Galloglass into joining the Knights of Saint Colmcille. I would never do that to you."

Seamus flung down his tools and marched into the house, and grabbed his battle axe. He stormed over to the training field. Eunan stood telling stories of their adventures in Tirconnell and how he would form a band of holy Galloglass to fight the English in the impending war. Seamus came up from behind him and shoved him into the mud. He turned to the Galloglass, who formed a circle around them.

"I don't suppose he told you the part where he gave away most of what we earned, for your welfare, to Red Hugh and a bunch of priests! Then he got robbed of the rest!"

He turned to Eunan, crawling on the ground.

"How can you call yourself a Galloglass? In your first battle with the English, you would try to convert them, turn your back, and then they would slice you in two! We're not going on a crusade! We're trying to survive! No sooner have you made an ally in this world, he stabs you in the back and steals all your cattle. This is not a world for priests and trying to be holy! This is a cruel and vicious world to be carved out by the axe. The axe of proper Galloglass! I put my life on the line to get robbed by him and bandits. Don't let him lead you astray. He is young and foolish, and his way leads to certain death!"

Eunan had got back up by now and charged at Seamus. Seamus stepped aside, dodged him, and then tripped him up. Eunan fell face-down in the mud.

"Stay down!" said Seamus.

This time, Eunan did not get up. Seamus turned to the onlookers.

"I will return in the afternoon to train. Continue as before, but without him as your instructor."

Seamus stood over Eunan.

"Clean yourself up and come to my house. We must sort this out now before it goes any further." With that, Seamus stomped towards his house.

Eunan picked himself up from the mud. Only the mud shielded the red hue of humiliation from his fellow Galloglass, except they had all turned their backs on him and got on with their training. Eunan did not know which was worse, being humiliated or being ignored. He picked up his axe and walked back to his house. The sucker marks left by the leeches itched. He would soon need another session.

Eunan knocked on Seamus's door.

"Come!"

Seamus sat eating, casually dressed in a tunic, with his wife in attendance. Eunan had never seen this domestic side of Seamus before, sitting contented at home. Eunan thought him not capable of showing any affection or sweetness, but there it was before him.

"Sit!" Seamus thrust forward a stool with the sole of his foot.

Eunan sat.

"Eat!" Seamus thrust forward a bowl his wife had filled.

Eunan ate.

"Listen!" Seamus wiped his face and threw the napkin on the table.

Eunan listened.

"We must put what happened behind us and ensure it doesn't happen again."

"What exactly?"

"All of it. From all our escapades to what happened. All of it."

"What do you propose we do?"

"I take care of all negotiations. If you pull anything like you did with Red Hugh again, I'll rip out your tongue with a pair of red-hot tongs."

"I will do with my money what I want! I am the Maguire here!" Eunan said.

Seamus took a breath.

"I like you, but you have a limited amount of use to me, especially after what you did recently. Don't test those limits. I'll be fine without you."

"So, where do we go from here?"

"You are going to the bed chamber. We need to maximise our exposure to the Maguire. I have sent a message to him to find you a suitable wife from noble Maguire blood. You will be married as soon as we can arrange it."

Eunan leapt from his chair.

"What if I object? What if I don't like her? You are not my father!"

"The less said about that, the better. If it makes you feel any better, you can say it is repayment for all the monies you lost us in Tirconnell. Don't worry. You won't miss out on anything. You'll probably be away fighting most of the time, and there are plenty of prostitutes near any battlefield."

Seamus's wife slammed something hard in the other room.

"Sorry! He's young! I'm trying to sell him a good marriage!" Seamus shouted towards her.

"Anyway, we'll leave for Enniskillen as soon as something is arranged. You should get back to training. The war should start any day soon."

Eunan stood defiantly before Seamus.

"You haven't gone yet. Have you something to say?" said Seamus.

"I am the Maguire here, and I say when I get married!"

"I'm the leader of the Galloglass here, and you'll do as you're told. If it were up to you, we'd all be in poverty, on our knees praying for salvation, waiting to be cut down by the English so we could all float off to heaven. My way gives us a fighting chance. You must do your best for your people and what is best is to make an advantageous marriage. I'm only asking you to marry someone, not love them. There is a great difference."

Crashing was again heard from the other room.

"Those last sentences have nothing to do with you!" Seamus projected towards the other room.

Eunan glared at Seamus.

"Now do your duty, and I'll be at training within the hour."

Eunan did not move.

"Go, go," and Seamus swished him away.

Eunan walked out.

Several days later, a messenger returned. Hugh Maguire thought the marriage idea was a good one and would arrange it as soon as he found someone suitable. Eunan, Seamus and their men were ordered to come to Enniskillen castle with all haste.

Twenty of their best men accompanied them. Finn stayed behind. Seamus and Eunan were brought straight to Hugh Maguire.

"Welcome, gentlemen," said Hugh, who looked in a bit of a fluster. "I have good and bad news, both of which cannot wait. I have a perfect match for young Eunan to marry. Róisín O'Doherty O'Donnell, a distant cousin of Red Hugh. She is supposed to be a looker, but if that does not prove true, the marriage will benefit the Maguire family and their alliance with the O'Donnells nonetheless. Upon your acceptance, we will proceed as other matters are pressing."

Eunan thought of Father Michael and the leeches.

"Very well," he whispered.

"What?"

"He accepts!" cried Seamus. "Now let us arrange it!"

"Now for the bad news—"

"Is it war?"

"Not quite," said the Maguire. "Captain Willis has arrived in Fermanagh with three hundred men."

"Where is he?"

"Down south."

"I'll bet Connor Roe Maguire has taken him in."

"Aye. Captain Willis works his way towards Enniskillen."

"Why is he here?"

"They say he wants to become the sheriff of Fermanagh. We agreed to a sheriff with the Lord Deputy, but our money and cattle have always been enough up to this point to defer it. My agents tell me Willis is here of his own accord."

"We must stop him!" said Eunan.

"That is why I called for you two. I heard so many good things about your exploits in Tirconnell."

"Are we going to strike a bargain?" said Seamus, not letting the opportunity slip.

"I think we may strike the ultimate bargain. The freedom of Fermanagh!"

Seamus scowled as Eunan's eyes lit up.

"When do we leave?" said Eunan.

"First, to seal the marriage, my artist needs to make a quick painting of you to send northwards while you are still pretty. You may leave upon its completion."

"If we are staying briefly, please, would you direct me to the nearest priest?"

"Marriage isn't going to be that bad!" said Seamus.

It was Eunan's turn to scowl.

"There are many monasteries on the islands of Lower Lough Erne that may suit your needs. Take a guide and tell them what you are looking for. But let my artist do his work first, and you can find a priest while the paint dries." Hugh turned to Seamus. "Please choose the men you wish to take besides your own. You may face opposition if Willis has teamed up with Connor Roe."

Eunan and Seamus bowed and bade Hugh Maguire farewell.

After being perched on the side of a chair like an agitated ape posing for his picture, Eunan was soon on the lakes looking for his perfect sanctuary. He landed on a large island covered in trees. He climbed the hill to the centre of the island to a small church and several huts. A priest came out and met him. The priest could supply him with leeches and prayers to help heal him of the bad blood, just as the guide had told him. Eunan emerged several hours later, spiritually refreshed but drained of blood. His guide rowed him back to Enniskillen as he lay back wrapped in a blanket, recovering.

# CHAPTER THIRTY

# A LETTER ACROSS THE OCEAN

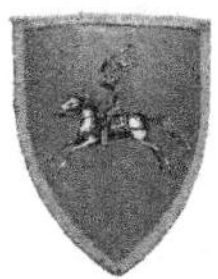

Eunan and Seamus were soon back on their horses and riding towards south Fermanagh. Connor Roe Maguire had indeed given Captain Willis sanctuary, but had not overtly come out and supported him. Captain Willis began raiding the farms and villages of south Fermanagh on the eastern side of the lake, so Eunan's lands had not yet come under threat. Eunan's mind was aflame with thoughts of the captain burning down his village and killing his family. He rode his horse hard, for the desire for revenge consumed him. In the meantime, Hugh Maguire sent word to his allies that Captain Willis was attacking him.

Captain Willis's force of three hundred men was too large and too well-armed for Eunan and Seamus to take on directly. However, instead of waiting for reinforcements, Seamus countered Captain Willis's cattle raids by harassing him and stealing the cattle back, albeit diverting them back to Eunan's lands to make up for the cattle stolen from them. Seamus soon ran out of men, for they were sent to bring the cattle back to Seamus's village, and the southern Maguire chieftains grew very disgruntled at how Seamus was running the campaign.

Soon Captain Willis had them on the run towards Enniskillen. Eunan and Seamus received reinforcements from the Maguire but could not slow Captain Willis's advance. The best they could do was to divert it away from their lands.

However, Hugh Maguire had received reinforcements from his northern allies. Cormac MacBaron, brother of Hugh O'Neill, had arrived with one hundred foot soldiers and twenty horsemen. The foot soldiers had been trained in modern warfare and were armed with pikes and shot. In previous years, Hugh O'Neill had been allowed English trainers as part of his role as Marshall of Ulster to aid his battle against Turlough O'Neill. Hugh O'Neill was granted a certain allowance of men to have trained in modern warfare and he had trained up to that allowance and then let the men go and taken on more raw recruits to train up to the quota, let them go and so on and so forth. Donnell and Donough O'Hagan, Hugh O'Neill's foster brothers, also arrived with one hundred and twenty shot. Alexander MacDonnell Óg MacSweeney, sent by Red Hugh, came with one hundred Galloglass. These reinforcements considerably increased the fighting capacity of Hugh Maguire. Hugh himself took to the field. He advanced, and after a couple of skirmishes, had Captain Willis on the run. Hugh Maguire and his men soon had Captain Willis trapped in a church in the middle of Fermanagh.

Hugh O'Neill's men were apprehensive about the repercussions of assaulting a church containing an English sheriff and sent word back to Dungannon, the capital of Tyrone. In the meantime, Hugh Maguire settled in for a siege.

Eunan sat in the camp and scratched the dark rings the leeches had left behind. Seamus sat down beside him, and Eunan expressed his displeasure.

"If you weren't so greedy, we could have beaten Captain Willis like we did the last time."

"If looking after you and your adopted clan is greedy, then I am guilty," said Seamus. "He had too many men. Look at how many it took to overpower him now. Save your energy, for the arrival of Captain Willis is just a prelude to what is coming. Anyway, we need to secure our pay. No better way for the Maguire to get out of paying his debts than to get all the people to whom he owes money to die for his cause in a war. Not greed, clever." Seamus tapped on the side of his head to reinforce that he had a big brain.

Eunan tutted.

Messengers arrived at the camp and were directed straight to Hugh Maguire's tent. Hugh emerged, holding a piece of paper, and looked very disappointed. He called for Eunan.

"You know him from Tirconnell. Go deliver this to Captain Willis and bring us back his response."

Eunan bowed and fled the tent. He almost soiled himself. Eunan regained his composure, walked through the Maguire lines towards the church and held his hands up. He was armed only with the envelope Hugh Maguire had given him.

"I come in peace!" he shouted, and he edged his way across no man's land.

A musket shot rang out. Eunan half ducked, not knowing from where it came.

"Stop right there!" came a shout from the church. "I won't fire a warning shot next time!"

"I come in peace! I have a message from Hugh Maguire!"

"Shout the message from there! I'm sure it's not worth risking your life for!"

"I have a letter in my hand. A letter from Cormac MacBaron, brother of Hugh O'Neill!"

"What does it say?"

"I don't know."

"Open it and read it!"

"I can't read!" Eunan lied.

"Give it back to Cormac MacBaron then!"

"I promised to give it to you!"

There was silence from the church.

"Bring it here, then. Slowly!"

Eunan staggered towards the church with his hands in the air. He stood and waited until three muskets pointed at him.

"Throw it on the step and leave!"

"I have to wait for a response."

The door of the church opened slightly, and the point of a sword crept out, stabbed the corner of the letter, and dragged it back in. Sweat poured down Eunan's back while he waited.

"Is this letter true?" said the voice.

"Cormac MacBaron uses the name of Hugh O'Neill and Hugh O'Neill always keeps his word."

"Who will escort us out of the county and guarantee our safe passage?"

Eunan almost choked. This was the plan to give the murderer of his family safe passage out of the county when they had him trapped. Eunan looked back at the besiegers and the scowls on their faces. The Maguire was there rolling his hands to get him to hurry.

"Cormac MacBaron has been sent especially by Hugh O'Neill to ensure that you get to Monaghan safely."

"What possessions can we take?"

Eunan did not know the answer and looked at the distant hand gestures of the Maguire.

"You must leave all your weapons and anything you acquired in Fermanagh."

"What if we refuse and shoot you dead here?"

"You'd all be dead within the hour."

The door slammed shut. A few sweat-soaked minutes that felt like a lifetime passed for Eunan. The door squeaked open again.

"We begrudgingly accept. What happens next?"

Eunan waved his arms, and Cormac MacBaron and his men marched up to the church and formed a circle around the door. Captain Willis and his men crept out, not knowing if they were stepping into their deaths. When they realised they would not be hacked to death, they threw their weapons in a pile in front of Cormac MacBaron. They were escorted away. The men of Fermanagh cheered.

Donnacha O'Cassidy Maguire had by this time arrived with news from Enniskillen. A downcast Hugh Maguire dispatched Donnacha again. Hugh ordered the army to leave for Enniskillen castle.

Seamus slapped Eunan on the back. "You did good out there today."

But Eunan could not accept the compliment. He went somewhere private to throw up.

When Eunan and Seamus arrived, a shroud of secrecy surrounded the castle. Hugh Maguire was expecting some distinguished guests. Donnell and Donough O'Hagan were in the fields surrounding the town, training the Maguire men in the arts of modern warfare and how to use pikes and muskets. Hugh informed Eunan that his bride was on her way from Inishowen and could not wait to meet him. Eunan was very much in two minds and retreated to the castle chapel for some contemplation. Finn had arrived with twenty reinforcements from the village, Galloglass whom they had trained from scratch. He went straight to Seamus.

"What is the news from south Fermanagh?" Seamus said.

"Captain Willis has retired in good order to the Pale. Connor Roe Maguire is preparing for war, and I think he's going to side with the English."

"Think?! He is the Crown choice to be the Maguire, and I think they will inaugurate him soon. But on a brighter note, Eunan's bride should arrive shortly. Hopefully, she will be vivacious enough to keep him distracted from his previous stupidity and keep him fighting."

"How long do we need to keep Eunan around for?" said Finn.

"What do you think I am? Some kind of monster? He will be a great warrior one day, and with the right guidance, who knows what he could become?"

"I know what kind of man you are. You never did this for me, despite everything."

"Only you could get away with such cheek. But I have my limits." Seamus felt the shaft of his axe.

Finn got up and left, while the going was still good.

Horns blew from the top of the castle tower.

"Whoever is coming must be here," said Seamus to himself, picking up his things and heading to the main building.

Seamus and Eunan went to the main hall along with the most senior commanders of the Maguire army and Cormac MacBaron, who had returned, Donnell and Donough O'Hagan and Alexander MacDonnell Óg MacSweeney. A wall of MacSweeney Galloglass marched into the hall to give way to Red Hugh and Ineen Dubh. Following behind him was Hugh O'Neill.

"There must be something big about to start now," whispered Seamus in Eunan's ear. "Bet this is the start of the war!"

"Clear the room, except for the commanders and the specially chosen MacCabe Galloglass!" shouted Donnacha O'Cassidy Maguire.

There were several nervous gulps around the room. Such a room clearance when surrounded by hand-picked guards would generally be a cue for murder. However, on this occasion, several members of the northern Catholic clergy walked in.

"Lords of the north, today we sign another plea to King Philip of Spain!"

Everyone cheered.

"To summarise, before we all sign, we are asking the King of Spain to send an army of no less than eight thousand men, but preferably ten thousand, to land here in the north."

There was another loud cheer.

"Then, with his help, we will throw out the English!"

There was an immense roar of approval.

"We have also asked for his ongoing protection and that we would swear loyalty to him."

The cheers were more muted.

"Ladies and gentlemen, that is what we agreed," said Hugh Maguire.

"Indeed, it is," said Hugh O'Neill. "We are too weak to beat the English by ourselves. We need weapons, training, and experienced soldiers used to fighting pitched battles to beat them. We must be united and stop all this infighting!" He raised his goblet. "To the northern lords!"

"The northern lords!" came the response as mugs met goblets and alcohol spilled over the sides and fell on the ground.

"It is time to sign!" said Hugh Maguire.

Everyone roared again.

Hugh Maguire handed the quill to Hugh O'Neill, as the senior lord of the alliance. Hugh O'Neill scribbled his signature and symbolically gave the quill to Red Hugh. He scratched his name, held the quill aloft, and handed it to Hugh Maguire to sign. He signed and rolled up the scroll. Hugh Maguire gave the letter to the bishop who made haste to a waiting boat on the river which would lead to the sea, whereupon a ship would bring him to Spain.

Hugh Maguire shouted over the cheering crowd. "The northern alliance is now sealed!"

A boisterous night of alcohol ensued where new friendships were forged and old grievances were temporarily forgotten.

The next day Red Hugh left after inspecting the Galloglass he left behind. Hugh O'Neill stayed slightly longer, leaving behind experienced military men; both Irishmen who had served in continental armies, and Spanish survivors from the Great Armada.

He hugged Hugh Maguire before he left.

"No matter how it appears from the outside, I still support you. I'm not strong enough yet to take on the English."

"Thank you, father-in-law. I put my trust in you."

"And put your faith in the King of Spain. His last ship may have sunk and taken Archbishop O'Healy to the bottom of the sea, but we'll keep trying and will succeed."

"I only wish my father was here to see the day we are finally free!"

"And that day will come soon. Goodbye!"

## CHAPTER THIRTY-ONE

# REALISING ONE'S PLACE

Amongst the confusion that surrounded the gates of Enniskillen Castle that morning, a carriage with a modest retinue of horsemen was seen rolling in from the north. Finn cursed as Seamus assigned him to watch out for Eunan's new bride. Out through the gates rolled various major and minor lords of the north, merry on the copious amounts of alcohol drunk and the hope generated by the mass signature of the letter to the Spanish King. Finn walked through the ranks of Galloglass. His head hung low and his heart seethed with the poison of jealousy.

"I served him faithfully for years, gave him my everything, but as soon as Eunan came along, he gave everything to him. We both bear the same curse, yet Eunan is propelled in the world, and I am left to suffer."

He looked around and all he saw was the privileged Galloglass. He thought about how Seamus had always stopped him from joining them. He saw no bride and had no wish to suffer Seamus's wrath by returning empty-handed. But his enthusiasm was drained, and he wandered off to be alone by the road and found himself a rock to sit upon so he could nurse his misery.

"Curse you, Eunan Maguire, and all your privileges. Curse Seamus MacSheehy and Desmond MacCabe for elevating you so."

"Curse Desmond MacCabe? Now there's a name I haven't heard in a while. I'm always up for a bit of cursing Desmond MacCabe, but pray tell, why do you wish to do so?"

Finn looked up to find himself in the shadow of a red-haired giant of a Galloglass that dwarfed his six-foot axe. Finn gulped and hoped that whatever answer he gave would not be the last thing he ever said as the Galloglass's henchmen surrounded him.

"His former servant is going to be married in the castle today. It is Seamus's attempt to join the Maguire nobility." Finn gulped, closed his eyes, and hoped that the blocking of the sun was not an axe being raised above his head.

"What is that to you that would inspire such vitriol?" said the giant.

Finn opened his eyes once more and gained a little confidence, for if the giant was still questioning him the more chance there was he would survive.

"We both suffer the same curse, but Seamus favours him over me and refuses to make me a Galloglass. He would have never done this for me."

The giant laughed. "So you want to be a Galloglass?" The giant turned to his men. "Throw him an axe and let us see what he can do." It was the men's turn to laugh. They stepped back and threw an axe in front of Finn.

"Well, then?" said the giant. "Pick it up. This is your chance to prove yourself worthy of being a Galloglass. Swing the axe and give me the best you've got."

Finn stood up slowly and thought this was it. If he was ever to be a Galloglass, he could at least go out fighting. He picked up the axe but then had second thoughts.

"If it helps, you pretend I am Eunan Maguire. Your other alternative is to stand there and I will slay myself a servant of Desmond MacCabe, wipe my blade, and then think nothing of it."

Finn summoned up all his rage and swung at the effigy of Eunan Maguire. The giant easily side-stepped him but allowed Finn to make another pass. They clashed axe shafts, and Finn exchanged a couple of blows before succumbing to the butt of an axe in the calf. He lay on the ground, waiting to die. He watched the arc of the axe swing down while his mind replayed the arc of his life. So apt that the Galloglass blade which had eluded him all his life would end his. But an axe did not come, an index finger did.

"You are mine now. You belong to Aonghas O'Braoin," said the giant. "If you follow me and do as I say, we'll be rid of Desmond, Eunan, and Seamus MacSheehy. I am the only one who will make you a Galloglass, but I demand your full loyalty. Give me your pledge or meet the blade of my axe. It is your choice. What will it be?"

Finn did not have to pause. "What is your bidding, lord?"

That evening, Hugh Maguire held a wedding feast for Eunan. Eunan and Seamus sat at the top table for the first time, alongside Alexander MacDonnell Óg MacSweeney, one of the leaders of the MacSweeney Galloglass septs, and the bride's father and brothers, who had been finally found and brought to the castle by Finn. They ate, drank and made merry while they waited for the bride. Donnacha whispered in Hugh Maguire's ear. Hugh stood up and banged his knife on his mug.

"Lords, ladies, and those of you of ill repute!"

The Maguire men roared their approval.

"It gives me great pleasure to strengthen further the ties to that great clan and our friends and allies, the O'Donnells."

"To the O'Donnells!" Seamus saluted.

"The O'Donnells!" the Maguire men chorused back.

"Now let me not make the groom wait any longer! He has to consummate the marriage before he leaves for war!"

"Hurray!"

"Now, Eunan, let me introduce your bride, Róisín!"

Her father jumped to his feet. "No, no, no. We agreed they shall only meet at their wedding. These were my terms. Let me just say that my daughter has seen the groom and deemed him acceptable and she shall be married with the full rights and obligations of a Brehon Law wedding. What say you to this, Eunan Maguire? Is this acceptable to you?"

All eyes were now fixated on Eunan, and he wilted beneath them. From a well of silence, Seamus leapt to his feet.

"Well, it wouldn't be a wedding day without a surprise, would it?" Seamus raised his mug. "To the bride and groom!" The room rose to salute the bride and groom, but Eunan did not rise to protest the hijacking of his choice. He rose to greet his friend Desmond, who had come to his wedding.

The pre-wedding party quickly broke down into drunkenness and song. Seamus went over to drape his arms across the shoulders of the O'Donnells and O'Dohertys and sing songs of war and ancient heroes. Desmond took the opportunity while he was gone to saddle up beside Eunan, who had remained in his seat, a little dazed, as he let his circumstances settle in his mind. Desmond slapped him on the knee.

"You have come far since we last spoke." Desmond's smile flickered in the erratic light from the fire torches. Each flicker revealed a different emotion. By the time Eunan came to reply, he had settled on concern.

"Are you coming to warn me?" said Eunan.

"I would be a negligent guardian if I did not. See who benefits from your wedding and what do those benefits accumulate for you. Ask yourself why Seamus MacSheehy favours you so highly and wishes to elevate you to such a position. What is in it for him and when will he be done with you? It is easy to see the daggers in his eyes that Seamus's lackey has for you. There is something there that you don't know but must find out."

Eunan hung his head.

"Why must you spread such melancholy the night before my wedding? Can you just be pleased for me?"

Desmond projected his stern finger.

"Don't be foolish, boy, and think this is a real wedding. She does not love you, she does not know you. She may have seen you in the distance and agreed you were a tolerable match for her political wedding. She is a good girl doing her duty for her clan, and you are a good boy doing your duty for his." Desmond sat back. "I am proud of you, boy, but fear you are being used. The politics of the Maguire grow ever darker and my spies tell me that the agents of Connor Roe are turning Donnacha's head. I only hope that Seamus MacSheehy has your best interests at heart, but I just can't see it."

Eunan sighed. "I've had enough of warnings and depressing talk this evening. Can we not sit as friends and drink and reminisce about past times?"

Desmond shook his head and tutted. "You haven't listened to a word I said. Tomorrow is the signature of an alliance with the obligation on you to look after the O'Dohertys' daughter and leave her with child. I cannot stay. It is rumoured that Aonghas O'Braoin is here intending to cause mischief and I have little protection from him. I must leave while the drink distracts him. Heed my words and if you need help, come find me on the islands. There will always be a bed for you in my home."

Eunan grabbed at him to force him to stay, but he had already disappeared into the crowd.

# CHAPTER THIRTY-TWO

# THE WHIRLWIND

Eunan barely slept that night. It was hard for him to work out whether the alcohol of the evening before had eased or enhanced his whirlwind of emotions as life, love, and family and his place within them whizzed through his mind in a jumbled mess. At no point did he feel at ease with himself, and when he finally peeled himself off his bed, his body was ridged with tension.

A knock came upon the door of the room that Hugh Maguire had lent him in Enniskillen castle, especially for his wedding.

A merry Seamus stood at the door in a white shirt with a mug of ale in each hand.

"Happy wedding day!"

Eunan slumped his shoulders and turned into his room. His wedding clothes had been neatly draped over the back of a chair. Eunan walked straight past them and flopped on the bed. Seamus handed him an ale.

"Drink that. Let me help you prepare." Seamus picked up individual items of clothes and supervised as Eunan put them on.

"I am so glad you saw it as your duty to the Maguire clan to marry this woman. As long as she is with child after tonight, your duty will more or less be over. We can drop her off at the village and then come back to Enniskillen and join in the preparations for the war."

Eunan grunted.

"What if I don't want to do that?"

Seamus continued his tucking and straightening for subduing Eunan's protests was taken as a given.

"Which part?"

"Drop her off."

"What? Are you going to make her a horse boy and get her to carry your axes? Don't be so silly. You've just got pre-wedding nerves. We will get the ladies to give you a potion to ensure you are extra virile tonight."

Seamus stepped back.

"There. You look like a lord on his way to the Irish Council. That lady won't believe her luck in getting to marry you."

Eunan fiddled with his clothes and scratched his leech scabs.

"Enough! Don't do that! You'll undo all my good work!" Seamus straightened everything again. "Now try not to fidget until after you are married. Once you have done that and she is with child, then and only then can you do what you like."

"May I not live my own life?" Eunan's pleading eyes were wasted on Seamus.

"You have so much to learn about being a chieftain," said Seamus.

Eunan hesitated and sized up Seamus's mood. He was hungover yet jovial, as good a time as any to seek receptive ears.

"Desmond came to me last night."

"Oh yeah?" Seamus's ears had proved receptive.

"He warned me that an old Galloglass called Aonghas O'Braoin was here to cause trouble and that he was trying to turn the head of Donnacha."

Seamus took a turn for the stern.

"You leave all that to me. Make sure everything in your trousers is in good working order for tonight and don't drink too much."

Eunan sighed. Perhaps that reception was the best he could have hoped for.

A knock came upon the door, and it was time for Eunan to be married. He climbed the stairs feeling hot and drowsy. He groped at the wall. Seamus reached from behind and took his rib cage in his hands and propelled him upward.

"It'll all be over soon," said Seamus.

"If that was meant to be reassuring, it sure didn't feel like it," said Eunan.

Seamus brought Eunan to the main hall where a guard of honour of Galloglass led the way to a small number of dignitaries from both the Maguire and O'Donnell clans alongside the bride's O'Doherty family. Edmund Magauran stood at the end of the guard of honour, for he had agreed to officiate the ceremony to impress the O'Dohertys and O'Donnells as to Eunan's status.

Eunan stood before the archbishop and waited. His brow sweated and his stomach quivered, but his nervous smile convinced no one. Eunan continually glanced at the door and only ceased upon receipt of an elbow in the ribs from Seamus. The bride arrived a couple of minutes later, escorted by her father. She was an opulent vision in white. She stood before Eunan and took his hand at the invitation of the bishop. Eunan stared at her veiled face and tried to pick out her eyes from beneath the mesh. She smiled and looked at the floor. At that moment, Eunan could see a bit of him in her, just wanting to be loved but held back by something she could not control. From that moment, she was beautiful to him. He listened to the bishop, but stared at Róisín. It was like an outside voice said 'I do', but it was him. He could tell by the way Róisín looked at him. The white veil revealed her face. Big brown eyes and a face of a pleasant pale complexion and curtains of long brown hair. He kissed Róisín, his stomach twisted some more, and everyone cheered.

Once the ceremony had ended, the rest of the invited guests were invited into the great hall for the wedding feast. The great, good, and Galloglass all filed into the hall and began another boisterous feast. The Maguire rose to his feet and gave a rousing speech showering Eunan with such lavish praise that you could have sworn, had he not been sitting in front of you, that he was long dead and buried in the fading dyes of the tapestries that adorned the walls. The O'Dohertys and O'Donnells cheered heartily, for they did not know beforehand that they had entered into so prestigious a marriage, but such sentiments were not reflected in the benches of the Maguires.

Seamus was working the room with a mug of ale in hand, and once he had finished with the O'Donnells and O'Dohertys, he found himself among the benches of the MacCabes. A foot protruded out and blocked his way.

"That boy is not of noble blood. He is the ex-secretary of the disgraced ex-leader of the MacCabes. Who made him the pawn in such a prodigious alliance?"

Seamus looked at the foot and traced it up the leg and large muscular body to the grinning face of Aonghus O'Braoin.

"Well, they couldn't use you, for it would have been too horrific for her to look at your ugly mug and then to face the disappointment of having you strip off and be faced with your tiny ginger cock on her wedding night."

The grin slid into anger, and the knuckles turned white on the contemplation of violence. Another Galloglass constable saw what was unravelling and jumped between Seamus and Aonghas. Cúmhaí of the fiery temperament saw the chance to impress his master and save his honour.

"This is Maguire business," he said to Seamus, "and none of yours, you mercenary whore". He leapt from his seat and attempted to thrust his forehead into Seamus's face. If there was one area of combat Seamus was a master of, it was seeing when a man was off balance. As Cúmhaí rose, he met the full force of the back of Seamus's hand and was sent reeling back into his comrades' dining table, throwing food and ale all over the floor and walls.

The Maguire erupted at the intrusion into his party. "What goes on there? Who is disturbing the Maguire's peace?"

The constable held back Aonghas, and Cúmhaí rolled around the floor in a daze. Seamus stepped into the breach.

"Sorry, lord, for the disturbance. This young Galloglass here," and he pointed to Cúmhaí on the ground, "he got a bit jealous of the happiness of the bride and groom, was overwhelmed by my good looks and wished to give me a peck on the cheek. I had to tell him that even though he could recite a couple of lines of a love poem he got from a bard; the only kiss he was getting was from the back of my hand until he learned the rest of it." The whole hall laughed.

"Well, try to control yourselves, lover boys, and if you can't, take it outside," said the Maguire.

Seamus smirked and walked off. Aonghas gave him a gentle shoulder as he passed by.

"This isn't over," he whispered into Seamus's ear.

"It had better be for your sake, if I could down your man that easily." Seamus went over to Eunan and Aonghas picked up Cúmhaí and they were escorted out.

The whirlwind of a day continued for Eunan, and he soon found himself a little drunk beside the marital bed. Róisín was dressed head to toe in a grey nightgown. She was on her knees, but to Eunan's disappointment, knelt beside the marital bed, saying a prayer for help and guidance on her wedding night. She got up and lay on her back on the bed. She pulled her nightgown over her waist, enough so that Eunan could gain access.

"You can get on now!" she said.

Eunan went red, hoping his face was hidden in the dim candlelight.

"Er, right."

He lay beside her and wondered what would happen now. He leaned over to give her a kiss but saw she was as tense as a plank with her eyes firmly shut. Eunan remembered what Seamus had told him to do that morning. Eunan shook his head when he remembered his wife's prayers and dismissed Seamus's advice as only fit for prostitutes. He remembered back to what the Enniskillen boys had told him. He spat on his hand, shoved it down his pants, and rubbed it until he was ready. He perched on the end of the bed and looked at the outline of Róisín's body underneath the nightgown. Róisín opened her eyes when she felt the bed move, but no weight on top of her.

"What are you waiting for?" she said.

"Do we not have a little kiss and I tell you how beautiful you are like the lines of a bard's song and then—"

Róisín scowled. "I need to tell my father that I consummated the wedding, am potentially with child, I am happy and well looked after and he can leave with peace of mind. If quoting a bard's song gets you there, then by all means go ahead. But I am lying here waiting." She pulled the bottom of her nightgown over her head to show her impatience.

Eunan blushed, and his hand shook with nerves. He imagined the eyes of the Maguire court upon him. His bad blood boiled in his arms. Is this how the bad blood spread? From what his mother used to shout at him, it seemed the most likely explanation.

"What are you waiting for?" said Róisín. "Do I have to fetch your uncle to show you what to do?"

Eunan blushed again. "Of course I know what to do. I've been with plenty of girls in my village. I was just trying to make it special for you. And he's not my uncle."

"The only way you can make it special is to get it over with."

Eunan got on and, with some guidance from Róisín's hand, stuck it in. Róisín turned her head and prayed some more. Eunan found that off-putting but carried on, as he considered it to be his husbandly duty. He continued until he was done. He pulled out and kissed Róisín on the cheek. After which she got up, cleaned herself, and got into bed.

"Goodnight, husband." She rolled over and went to sleep.

Eunan sat at the end of the bed. Was that it? Was his wedding night over? Was she with child? Nothing would be answered that evening as Róisín was already asleep. Eunan lay down beside her.

The next day came too soon, for Seamus was banging his fist on the door.

"Get up, lover boy! It's time to go!"

The aggression of the knocks made Eunan think there was something wrong, like the English had invaded or they were under siege. He dressed quickly and ran down the stairs and out into the courtyard.

Outside, the Maguire nobility were readying their horses, and inside the castle, the O'Donnell and O'Neill men were lined up, waiting.

Seamus went over and slapped him on the back.

"Now that you have emptied your sack into her holiness, we can get back to business."

Eunan blushed and brushed his hand away.

"Don't be so tetchy! You've only known her for less than a day," said Seamus. "You've got to get used to the banter of fighting men. They need it to get rid of the images of slicing through other men's heads, which has the irritating habit of haunting them. Come on, let's do some deeds. You can pretend they were glorious and boast to her about them when you see her again in the village."

Eunan stood back and his face creased as Seamus's words sunk in.

"Village? Am I not coming straight back here to see her, then?"

Seamus shook his head.

"No, it is far too dangerous for her here. If the English return, the first place they are heading is Enniskillen."

"What about her family?"

"They have their own lives to lead, their own battles to fight."

"Who will bring her to the village? Can I not do it? I am her husband!"

Finn came along with five of their Galloglass.

"Finn is going to take her," said Seamus. "He has to go back anyway to raise more men."

Eunan fought back the tears, for he knew they would only bring ridicule.

"Take good care of her, Finn," said Eunan, threatening him with his index finger in as much as his embarrassment would allow. "If you don't, you'll have me to answer to!"

Finn smirked.

"I will take as good care of her as if she was my own wife."

"Don't make her your wife!" Eunan yelped.

Finn glanced at Seamus, who ignored him.

Hugh Maguire came out and walked up to Eunan, slapping him on the back.

"That was a great thing you did for the clan yesterday." The glint in his eye told of mischief when he asked: "I'm sure everything went well to consummate the marriage so we can send the O'Dohertys home happy?"

The Maguire slapped him on the back again upon receipt of Eunan's blush and nod. "Good man, well done. Now come on! Let's go steal some cattle!" he said, walking off.

"Why is everyone congratulating me as if I did them a huge favour?" Eunan asked Seamus.

"They know you feel a great sense of duty and responsibility." Seamus did little to hide his smirk.

"I do, but it is still confusing!"

Seamus laughed. "Get on your horse. It's time to go."

"Can I not say goodbye to Róisín?"

"No time. She will be all the more delighted to see you when she hears you were so important you had to leave straight away."

"But...where are we going?"

"Connacht."

# CHAPTER THIRTY-THREE

# FOR THE CAUSE

The Governor of Connacht, Sir Richard Bingham, had aggressively driven out the local Irish chieftains from his province and stolen their wealth. Many of the chieftains and their men had joined Hugh Maguire and made Fermanagh their new home. Partly in response to this, and also to undermine the Maguire, the governor was a frequent raider into Fermanagh. This had been a source of much agitation to Hugh Maguire, especially since the Irish Council ignored his many protests. Once he received the blessing of Hugh O'Neill and secretly allowed the use of the men he had left behind in Fermanagh, Hugh Maguire set about getting revenge.

He assembled his forces, and a raid comprising one thousand one hundred men went into Sligo. They made their way to Ballymote Castle, for their scouts had informed them the main English troops in the region were there. The Maguire moved with such swiftness and stealth, he caught the English totally by surprise. Hugh Maguire ordered the burning of the town and the blockade of the English garrison in the castle. Hugh Maguire then divided his forces. Half the army continued the siege and half, including Seamus and Eunan, continued the raid.

They marauded around Sligo, looking for things to steal or destroy. The Maguires burned seven towns and took as many cattle as they could find. They retreated to Ballymote as soon as they encountered any serious resistance. Hugh Maguire considered the raid a success, so they abandoned the siege and returned to Enniskillen.

Hugh Maguire was so overjoyed with the success of his last raid that another one swiftly followed. This time, he targeted the county of Roscommon and would penetrate deeper into Connacht if the opportunity arose. Hugh Maguire assembled his men. Eunan and Seamus were part of the raiding party again. Eunan rode with Archbishop Edmund Magauran, acting as his bodyguard, while Seamus was in charge of a section of Galloglass.

Hugh Maguire probed into Roscommon and did not experience serious resistance. However, Sir Richard Bingham soon heard of the new raid and swiftly moved his forces to counter.

Hugh Maguire's men concentrated around Tulsk and soon clashed with the English scouts. Bingham moved up his soldiers, but a thick fog smothered the battlefield, which prevented both sides from properly engaging. However, when the mist cleared, Hugh Maguire realised he was heavily outnumbered. A couple of covering volleys from the O'Donnell musketeers and Hugh Maguire sounded the retreat.

However, the fog cut off Eunan's group of horsemen. When the fog lifted, they found themselves in front of a section of English shot.

"Retreat!" shouted Eunan, and he dug his heels into the sides of his horse.

But before they could turn, the English dispatched a volley. Eunan could only look on as the bullets lodged in Edmund Magauran's chest and he fell to the ground.

"No!" Eunan cried and dismounted from his horse and ran for his friend.

The English grappled for their powder and bullets. Eunan grabbed the dying body of Edmund and slung him over the back of his horse. Eunan just had time to mount himself and dig his heels in before he was driven off the battlefield by another volley of shot.

Eunan rode to Hugh Maguire, and by the time he got there, Edmund was dead. With a heavy heart, Hugh Maguire ordered his men back to Fermanagh.

Once back in Enniskillen, Archbishop Magauran was laid out in the castle chapel, and Eunan cried bitter tears for his dead friend and mentor. Hugh Maguire retired to his room, for he had to write to Red Hugh and Hugh O'Neill and tell them that their principal contact with both the King of Spain and the Pope was dead. Hugh Maguire held a funeral mass for the bishop of Armagh in the chapel in Enniskillen castle.

Eunan held his head in his hands. He had met death before but she had been kind enough only to take away people who had been cruel to Eunan, but now death had struck down a friend and mentor. He suffered mourning for the first time without the conflicted and confused emotions, and it hurt. His thoughts now turned to his wife for there had been a whirl of activity with the death of the archbishop and now his head was free for more personal matters. He sent a messenger to the village and three days later Finn arrived at Enniskillen castle and was directed to Eunan, who sat in the courtyard waiting for him. Finn saw his down-turned face and suggested they should go somewhere quiet and Eunan got suspicious.

"What happened to you? Where did you get those scars?" Eunan said.

Finn turned pale and felt the bruises on his face.

"When did you return to the castle from the raids?" Finn said, hoping to divert Eunan's anger away from him.

"A day or so ago. Why?"

Finn shifted from foot to foot.

"You didn't hear what happened?"

Eunan leaned forward, for he felt Finn was not being straight with him.

"Obviously not!"

"She is gone," said Finn as he looked at the ground. "I was bringing her back to the village as instructed and agents of Connor Roe Maguire set upon us. Our men and I fought our way out, but your wife, unfortunately, was captured."

Eunan's fingernail cracked upon clawing at Finn's chain mail.

"What do you mean she was captured? You were supposed to defend her with your life! Yet you come brazenly back with barely a scratch on you! You're lucky I'm not Seamus, but maybe I should ask him what I should do!"

"We were ambushed in a forest, lord. We got split up into groups! I tried to fight my way back, but there were too many of them! We hadn't a chance!"

Eunan threw him aside.

"Go! Get out of my sight before I change my mind. You are lucky we need all the men we can get to fight the upcoming war or else you would be going straight back to Connor Roe Maguire to retrieve her."

"Thank you for your mercy and wisdom, lord. I would gladly lead any mission to get her back if Hugh Maguire would allow us."

"I will speak to Hugh Maguire once I figure out what to say to him. The embarrassment of an alliance so long in the forging broken so quick." The white of Eunan's knuckles bled around his fist. "Do not stray far, for you owe your lord. If I call and you don't respond, I will hunt you down and cut you in two."

"Yes, lord!" Finn bowed and ran away.

Eunan fled to his room, for he needed to take his frustration out on something. After some venting he now had to clean up the remains of several of the Maguire's cushions he had taken his axe to and he prayed they were not valuable. Eunan's scars from his leeching itched as if they were the compounding punishment for all his failures. He had to save Róisín, or he was no man, husband, or servant of the Maguire. The castle was busy organising another celebratory feast for the recent raids since a suitable amount of time had elapsed since the archbishop's death, so Eunan slipped away. He went to the river moorings and paid a ferryman to bring him to his island. His scars burned as his bad blood bubbled beneath his skin. His eyes welled with tears, and he stared at the shore to not show the ferryman he was weak, even though the ferryman did not know who he was. Even at times of such despair, pride boiled in his veins. The ferryman reached the shore and Eunan jumped out and threw him his coin. Eunan went ashore, and the priests recognised him in the dying light of the day. They knew why he was here. Eunan lay on the table. He prayed, and the priests prayed. The physician priest applied the leeches and Eunan felt the bad blood drain from his body along with his memories of everyone he had disappointed.

Eunan had been to confession on the islands and prayed with the priests for a resolution to his problems. He resolved to free Róisín himself without telling the Maguire, for he wished to avoid a major diplomatic incident if he could help it. Eunan recruited ten of his village Galloglass into his newly formed Knights of Colmcille and told them they had a mission in south Fermanagh that he could only reveal to them once they were there. He swore them all to secrecy about the knights and their mission.

Eunan yearned to break free of Seamus's grip as he considered himself to be a chieftain in his own right now, and that Seamus was holding him back. Eunan thought that once the war came, Seamus would be distracted by greed or reassigned to lead Galloglass somewhere else, hopefully far away from Fermanagh. However, Eunan's idea had not gone down well with all the village Galloglass. Some had humoured him so as not to incur his wrath. But they went behind his back to Seamus to prevent the mission. Upon hearing the rumours, Seamus went to confront Eunan, where he was camped outside Enniskillen Castle.

He brought Finn with him, for he was unsure of how he would be received. He arrived where Eunan sat and stood over him. Eunan continued to sharpen his axe.

"Good afternoon, Eunan. You might hurt yourself if you make the blade too sharp," said Seamus with a smirk.

Eunan just looked at him and kept sharpening.

"You're not taking the loss of your wife, who you only knew for one day, too well, are you?"

Eunan gave Seamus a pithy look.

"I'm going to rescue her and my men are going to help me!" The Galloglass looked resolute. Seamus recognised them from the village and knew their ring-leader was Sean O'Reilly, a refugee from Cavan and a good fighter and organiser of men. He would have to persuade him if he were to win the men back.

Seamus turned to the men and shook his finger.

"You men remember who's in charge! You'll regret any disloyalty to me!"

The men shifted uncomfortably in their seats. Seamus turned to Eunan.

"Why didn't you come to me with this? Why did I have to hear it from Finn?" Seamus looked insulted that Eunan did not trust him. Seeing only the top of Eunan's head, he returned to disgust. "There'll be no incursions into Connor Roe Maguire's territory without the explicit permission of Hugh Maguire. He doesn't want to start a war without good cause!"

Eunan's anger was inflamed and he spoke through gritted teeth.

"Is kidnapping the wife of a Maguire chieftain not a good enough cause?"

Seamus threw his hands in the air.

"You knew her for less than twenty-four hours! I'm sure you had tussles in the hay for longer than you knew her. I could get the marriage annulled for you if it wasn't consummated."

Eunan was silent and looked away. Seamus whistled.

"I never knew you had it in you! The prostitutes of Donegal town would love you if you weren't so busy praying. How about lying? I can still get it annulled if you say it wasn't consummated."

Eunan looked away, his anger having dissipated a little.

"And dishonour the woman I married before God?"

Seamus threw his arms up and looked to the sky.

"If I knew it was going to cause this much trouble, I would never have arranged this! Anyway, she is probably dead now. How long will you leave it until you consider her dead?"

"I'll never consider her dead until I see her body with my own eyes," said Eunan.

"You're going to see enough death in the coming times. Forget your 'wife', pick up your axe and prepare to defend Fermanagh. If you're lucky, we can pay a visit to Connor Roe Maguire, and you can greet him with your axe."

Seamus went to walk away.

"What about the Maguire's alliance?" said Eunan to his back.

"We'll have to bide our time until we tell him or hope something comes up."

"That's it?" said Eunan.

"That's it." He walked a few steps further and turned.

"Are you coming?" he said to Eunan.

"I'm good here."

Seamus turned his attention to the Knights of Colmcille.

"And the rest of you?"

The ten Galloglass remained seated, and Seamus walked over and stood before them. He twisted his axe shaft and pointed the blade at them.

"I trained you. You are my Galloglass. You either come, or I split your heads open here and now!"

Nobody moved.

"Is not one of you going to challenge me? Have I trained you that badly that you're all cowards?"

Eunan put his hand out to reach for his axe shaft. Seamus wagged his finger.

"I have been good to you, Eunan. Don't make me think they were moments of weakness I have to make amends for!"

The Galloglass looked at Eunan and saw he would not back down.

"I will follow you, lord," said Sean O'Reilly. He turned to Eunan. "Sorry, but what Seamus says makes sense and you would be wise to listen." He picked up his weapon and stood behind Seamus.

"Any more to chase this fool's errand?" said Seamus, pointing at Eunan.

One by one, the men stood behind Seamus until Eunan sat alone.

"Well, are you coming? We've got a war to fight!" said Seamus, again offering a way back for Eunan.

"I'll rescue her myself."

"Let me explain your options to you. You can come with us now, and we'll forget all about this. We'll even try to rescue her when we raid south Fermanagh. Or else you can try to rescue her yourself. If you do, you won't get past the gate as nobody starts a war without the permission of the Maguire. As a Maguire chieftain, you should know that. You'll have thrown all your good work away for an arranged marriage that lasted a day. What'll it be?"

Eunan did not move.

"Don't be a fool all your life!"

Eunan stood up, picked up his axes and his belongings and walked towards Seamus, and then past him towards the castle. Seamus came up from behind and ruffled his hair.

"Good man! I knew you'd see sense in the end. They all said you were a thick-headed, obstinate brute, but I defended you!" Seamus smiled, but it was not the friendly smile of old.

"I'm sure you did."

In the meantime, Hugh O'Neill did not waste the distraction Hugh Maguire's raids had provided him. Phelim MacTurlough O'Neill, the main ally of Sir Henry Bagenal and the Crown north of Lough Neagh, was brutally murdered by the O'Hagans, the foster brothers of O'Neill. O'Neill's men also attacked lesser clans in the region and forced them to submit. This led to the wavering lords of northeast Ulster allying themselves with Hugh O'Neill. However, the Irish Council was now alarmed and summoned Hugh O'Neill.

Hugh O'Neill appeared before the Irish Council to answer a litany of allegations. These ranged from not being able to control or being in league with Hugh Maguire, the murder of Phelim MacTurlough O'Neill, being in league with the Spanish Crown, plotting a rebellion against the Crown, and any other complaints his enemies could throw at him. All parties spent the primary fighting season of 1593 sending endless letters between Maguire, O'Neill and the Irish Council.

The allegations against Hugh O'Neill lacked sufficient evidence for a weak Irish Council to act. The fear of Hugh O'Neill striking out towards the Pale was enough for sufficient councillors to decline to prosecute.

Hugh Maguire returned from another unsuccessful negotiation with the Irish Council emboldened, for he saw they were weak. With Hugh O'Neill's and the dissatisfied MacMahons' encouragement, he secretly drew up plans to raid Monaghan. He called his chieftains and allies together and outlined his plan. Eunan was ecstatic. The opportunity to rescue, or at worse avenge, his wife had come sooner than expected.

## CHAPTER THIRTY-FOUR

# THE DEEDS OF THE MALCONTENT

The next morning, amidst the chirping of the morning birdsong and licked by the fog from the lake, Finn brought out for training the reconstituted village Galloglass. The emotions swirled in Finn's head and would not settle. At least he still had Seamus's protection. His nerves were on edge as he looked over his shoulder. He could feel an unsettling presence coming into his orbit. He turned to appease whatever was coming.

"Good morning, lord. Are you here to inspect the men? Are we going on another raid?"

Eunan stood motionless, his face a contortion of pain and despair.

"Indeed, we are. That's why I'm here."

Finn hid his shaking hand behind his thigh. Eunan would not remove his eyes from him. Finn had to break the silence.

"Excellent, lord. I have been recruiting horse boys, so we have a full complement of men." There was no reaction from Eunan, so Finn kept talking. "Do you wish to see the Galloglass fight? You can fight one of them yourself if you wish?"

Finn almost begged Eunan to take up his offer of a fight, for at least it would distract him, if only momentarily. But Eunan was having none of it.

"Now is not the time. I wish to speak with you in private."

"If you wish, lord." Finn turned to the Galloglass and instructed them to keep training. Eunan pointed to behind the tents in the campsite and invited Finn to walk in front of him. Finn took every step with the dread of receiving a knife in the back. Seamus had seen Eunan approaching Finn and had kept out of sight. He crept up and sat behind another tent but within earshot. Eunan loomed over Finn with only the burning desire for revenge in his eyes.

"Tell me exactly what happened when my wife got kidnapped. Every detail is important, for our next raid is into Monaghan, passing through the territory of Connor Roe Maguire."

Finn gulped. "I'm sure revenge boils in your blood, lord."

"It does. But see this as your opportunity to atone for your mistakes."

Finn winced at the comment, but nodded his head all the same.

"As I told you before, we were in a forest strung out over a narrow path—"

"Which forest?"

"A common one, above the upper lough on the way to the village. If we were to go there on this raid, we would need to leave the raiding party temporarily."

"That can be arranged. Continue with your story."

"There was a man who lay injured beside the road. We went to help him. Then we were descended upon."

"Who were they? Bandits?"

"No, we could have fought off bandits. They must have been Galloglass. I'm sure they were a raiding party sent by Connor Roe."

"Which way did they escape?"

"They chased me away, so I do not know."

Eunan's nostrils flared.

"What kind of Galloglass are you? Prepare the men! The raid starts tomorrow! They must be ready to break off and search for Róisín!"

Seamus came out from behind the tent and shook his head.

"That wouldn't be wise. I'll go with you instead."

Eunan's resolve stiffened with Seamus's resistance.

"It would make more sense for the whole unit to break off. We have to assume we'll meet some resistance," said Eunan.

"They would notice too easily," said Seamus, "and we would undo all the good work we've done previously. Trust me, the two of us will be more than adequate."

Eunan drew the front of his shirt into a fistful of fabric.

"How will we know where to start our search?"

Seamus tried to reassure him with a smile.

"Then make that three of us. Finn will show us where."

Finn grimaced but knew he could not refuse, for it was not a request. Eunan gripped Finn's shoulder and marched him back to the training ground. He was not going to let Finn out of his sight.

The next day the Maguires, disaffected O'Rourkes, O'Reillys and others joined the MacSweeney Galloglass and O'Hagan brothers and assembled outside of Enniskillen. The malcontent MacMahons would join them as they entered south Fermanagh. There were more than a thousand men in the raid, with three hundred more MacMahons ready to join them.

They made their way quickly through Fermanagh, but such a large force could only evade Connor Roe Maguire's scouts for so long. They combined with the MacMahons in south-central Fermanagh. Eunan and Seamus took this opportunity to break off, and Finn led them to where he was ambushed. It was a couple of hours' ride from where the main raiding party was.

They entered the forest on the road to their village. Finn took them to the spot where he said the ambush had taken place, but there was precious little evidence left.

Eunan searched with swollen eyes the undergrowth and pathways for clues that his wife was still alive. Seamus looked at Finn and shook his head in disgust.

"So it either never happened here, or we have some very tidy bandits." Finn looked away and tried to ignore him.

They looked a little further, then Eunan threw down the stick he was using to search the bushes.

"How would you tell one piece of thievery from another without specific evidence?"

Seamus suspected something was up, but he did not have any evidence to tell what.

"It's time to go," said Seamus. "We cannot be absent for too long, or we'll lose track of the raid. Someone will miss us."

Eunan's trashing of the bushes became more violent when Seamus restricted his time.

"Come on, Eunan, it's time to go!"

Eunan stood up.

"I want to follow the route they would have followed if they were taking her to Castle Skea."

"We don't have time!"

But Eunan stood firm. "If we ride quickly, we can make the time!"

Seamus could see there would be no persuading Eunan.

"So be it, but we must leave now."

The three men jumped on their horses and rode as if Róisín's life depended on it. They skirted around the upper lake and kept an eye out for evidence of Róisín, the location of the raiding parties, and Connor Roe's spies.

After riding for several hours, Eunan suddenly veered off the path and rode down to the edge of a gully. He leapt off his horse and walked to the verge. A piece of cloth fluttered in the wind, snagged on a thorn bush. He rolled it on his fingertips and sniffed it. A tear rolled down his cheek. Seamus grew concerned and got off his horse. He walked over to Eunan and looked over the edge. On the rocks below was a woman's body, broken and covered in blood, her limbs a tangled mess. Beside her was the carriage Róisín had left Enniskillen in. Seamus wanted to throttle Finn. He had not decided if he would defend him if Eunan turned upon him. However, Eunan knelt on one knee for a few minutes and quietly said, “Come on, let’s go.”

Seamus placed his hand on Eunan’s shoulder. “Aren’t you going to bury her?”

“There’s no time,” said Eunan. “I could climb down and drag her up and give her a decent burial, but in the meantime, the raid goes through Connor Roe Maguire’s land, and my chance for revenge evaporates.”

“Very sensible,” said Seamus.

Eunan bent down and made a little cross of twigs and twine and stuck it in the ground.

“Thank you,” said Eunan to the sky as he got off his knees, his prayers finished.

Finn brought the horses. Eunan turned and took a throwing axe from his belt. He walked up to Finn and thrust the blade into the lower hairs of his beard. A red stream of blood dripped onto Finn’s shirt.

“My wife is dead. I didn’t know her long, but it makes no difference. If I find you had anything to do with it, you’ll be dead too!”

“Hey! No fighting! You don’t have any evidence that Finn had anything to do with it!” said Seamus, moving to get between the two of them. Eunan blocked Seamus’s access to Finn and continued to press the blade to Finn’s throat.

“It doesn’t quite add up, does it? No sign of any struggle where you said it would be, and then she was thrown down a ravine when it would have been easier to hold her for ransom!”

“Please! I tried my best to defend her!”

“Maybe she tried to escape and rather than be recaptured threw herself down the ravine," said Seamus. "You don’t know what happened.”

“Stay near me, Finn, for if I see you are trying to escape, you may just find an axe in the back of your head!” Eunan threw Finn to the ground.

“Mark my words,” he said as he pushed the shaft of his axe back into his belt. “If I find you had anything to do with this, you are a dead man.” Seamus went over and slapped Finn over the back of the head and pointed to his horse.

They mounted up together and rode for Connor Roe Maguire's lands in south Fermanagh.

They soon found the raiding party, for it had progressed little further as small groups of MacMahons joined in fits and starts. Seamus and Eunan found their Galloglass and joined the march through south Fermanagh. They went past Connor Roe Maguire's lands, much to Eunan's disappointment, to maintain the element of surprise. The raiders spilled over the border and spoiled all the English tenanted farms they came across, destroying crops and stealing cattle. Then they went for Monaghan town and the English garrison there. The English occupied the walled abbey in the town and had a good complement of men. Hugh Maguire assaulted the abbey but could not overcome the volleys of shot and fortifications. Seamus and Eunan led some assaults and lost ten men to the English volleys. This was a significant loss for them to bear, so they joined in the retreat. After the unsuccessful assault, Hugh Maguire blockaded the garrison, burned the town, and raided the surrounding lands. The raiding parties reached as far as Louth when the Maguire sounded the retreat.

Hugh Maguire retired again to Enniskillen while distributing the spoils of the raid. Much went to the MacMahons, partly to compensate them for their loss of lands and partly to ensure their future loyalty. On the retreat home, there was no major raid on Connor Roe Maguire's lands, although minor spoiling occurred. Eunan was most disappointed by the whole raid. He lost ten men, found his wife had been killed in suspicious circumstances, and was not allowed to take his revenge against Connor Roe Maguire. He sat alone outside his tent in the fields outside Enniskillen. He drew pictures in the mud, his stick getting caught in the stones and grass just as his mind could not free itself of melancholy. His dead wife dredged up the past and the death of his parents and his village and he sat and wondered why he had been spared to walk the earth. His mind turned to the Maguire and how he would have to be told how he failed him. Seamus came and sat beside him and placed his hand gently on his shoulder.

"It has been a difficult number of weeks for you, and I don't mean to make it any harder," said Seamus.

Eunan raised his head, for gone was the usual derogatory attempt at wit that Seamus would normally greet him with, replaced by a seriousness bordering on kindness.

"To what do I owe this visit?" Eunan said.

"We sit outside the Maguire's castle, yet we have not been straight with him and told him about your wife and his alliance."

Eunan placed his head in his hands.

"It may not have looked like it, but I was sitting here enjoying my last hours as a Maguire chieftain."

Seamus patted him on the shoulder.

"You may need to come to Tirconnell with me, for it is probably easier to avoid your new relatives than to avoid the Maguire in his own lands."

"Now is not the time for wit," said Eunan, not lifting his head.

"Who said I was trying to be funny?" Seamus looked at Eunan but saw only the top of his head. But he had to say what he came for because he knew time was limited.

"I will help you find who did this to your wife," said Seamus.

That raised Eunan's head.

"For what price? With you, there is always a price."

Seamus stroked his beard in his search for wisdom or excuses.

"I wish you could have known me in my youth. We probably would have been friends, we would be so alike. But a cynical old man sits beside you who seeks to draw advantage in every quest he undertakes, to extract something that will propel himself to a better place. But you are correct, I do have a price and one that I cannot explain but if you knew you would appreciate it. We are no nearer to solving what happened to your wife, and I fear Finn would be blamed.

We could see him hang on the castle gates to appease the O'Dohertys and the O'Donnells."

Eunan gave a vengeful grin. "Chances are, he'd deserve it."

"If you delay telling the Maguire, I will confront Finn and get the truth from him. However, if he knows nothing, I'll find the truth wherever it may lie and we'll both tell the Maguire. If you let me deal with Finn, I'll shoulder half the blame in front of the Maguire."

Eunan stared at Seamus. "How do I know you will do all this and not stab me in the back?"

Seamus's face hardened. "You have my word as a Galloglass. Ask any man who knows me of old. I am good for it."

Eunan stared at the ground to make room for himself to think. He wracked his brain to figure out what advice Desmond would give him in this situation. He rose with a jerk.

"I will go see the Maguire to ask his permission to return to the village. But I will not lie to him. All I can promise is that I will not tell him what he does not seek."

Seamus's nerves jangled, but he realised that was all he would get out of the emotional sanctimonious boy.

"I shall wait here to find out my fate."

The morning passed and slipped into the afternoon, and still Seamus waited. Finally, Eunan emerged. He was alone.

Seamus smirked at the look of defeat on Eunan's face. But which of Eunan's ever changing emotions had been defeated?

"Will I need some ointment for my neck to deal with the rope burns so I slip into the afterlife a little easier?"

Eunan's shoulders slumped.

"We return to the village. I must speak to a priest for a sin has been committed. The Maguire knows all he asked for, but the death of my wife is still a buried secret."

Seamus breathed out in relief. It was the boy's piousness that lay defeated in an open grave.

The roads were busier than before as people moved to areas where they felt safer. All over the north acts of assassination, intimidation and spoiling took place as the lords of the north consolidated their positions and suppressed any deemed threats in their clans, which led to the larger volumes on the roads. Upon reaching the village, Seamus set about recruiting some replacements for the men they had just lost. He had ordered Finn and some of his men to retrieve Róisín's body and bring it back to the village. Eunan went into mourning and took out a boat, rowing on the lake to search for a suitable burial ground for her. When he spotted something appropriate, he rowed towards the selected island, moored his boat, and went ashore. It was deserted and covered in woods. Its diminutive size did not reduce its immense beauty, and a small tree-covered hill on top of the island was what Eunan sought. He went back to his boat and got a shovel, and dug Róisín's grave.

When he rowed back across the lake, Seamus was waiting for him on the shoreline. Seamus directed him back to his house, where on the table lay Róisín's body, all wrapped in cloth. No one was allowed to unwrap the body. The priest came and gave mass. Eunan and his men carried the body on their shoulders down to the boat on the shore. They carefully placed the body inside. Eunan climbed in by himself and rowed away. He returned the next day.

# CHAPTER THIRTY-FIVE

# A DATE WITH DESTINY

Hugh Maguire held a secret meeting with Hugh O'Neill straight after the Monaghan raid. As a result of this, Hugh O'Neill again petitioned Lord Deputy Fitzwilliam for a pardon for Hugh Maguire and the minor lords of the region because the attacks were in reaction to the provocations of the English provincial governors. However, a response was not forthcoming. Hugh O'Neill advised Hugh Maguire to prepare for war.

When Dublin finally responded, it was to declare Hugh Maguire a traitor. Sir Henry Bagenal was given the commission on the 11th of September 1593 to raise an army and to move against the Maguires. Sir Henry raised a substantial force of over a thousand men, mainly Irish soldiers, both from the Pale and from those already under his service. He also had several English officers to lead the Irishmen and also a small core of English soldiers. The Irish Council gave Hugh O'Neill the commission of assisting Bagenal, and Hugh promised twelve hundred men.

When Bagenal assembled his forces, he moved first against the MacMahons of Monaghan, who had supported the last Maguire raid. After spoiling their lands, he moved into south Fermanagh. He spared Connor Roe and his supporters because of Connor Roe's ongoing loyalty to the Crown. Sir Henry marched across south Fermanagh, taking the route north of Upper Lough Erne, thus sparing Eunan's village.

Meanwhile, Enniskillen castle was alive with messengers coming to and from Fermanagh and the north. Seamus readied himself for battle while Eunan sat by the fire in their camp outside Enniskillen, for Hugh Maguire had recently recalled them.

"War is upon us! The English are coming!" cried a messenger as he ran through the camp.

Eunan picked up his throwing axes and sharpened them.

"I hope they do you some good on the battlefield with all those muskets and pikes around," said Seamus. "You're young and can adapt. Why don't you take up a modern weapon, or even better, become a commander like me?"

Eunan's head tumbled with anger, resentment, guilt, mourning, and visions of his bad blood. But anger usually won through, as it was his simplest and rawest emotion.

"It was always my destiny to become an axeman, ever since my mother told me I had Viking blood seeping through my body."

Seamus shook his head and laughed.

"One of your litany of problems is that you listened to that mother of yours. All she ever did was mess with your head!"

Eunan sneered.

"Demean another woman in my life, why don't you!? Who are you to berate me so? My father?"

Seamus laughed again.

"You'd have been much better off if I was. You cannot be this sensitive and go into battle wielding an axe. If you don't think yourself to death, you'll continue to be scarred for the rest of your life."

"I already am scarred for life." Eunan scratched his leech scabs. "At least if I died a good death for a worthy cause, I may get some redemption."

"All the more pity that nobody will notice your redemption, except maybe for you. It may give you some solace just before you die."

"All you do is sneer and put me down," said Eunan.

"I'm trying to teach you. Where's the glory in having a stump of an arm and living on charity for however long your neighbours can recall whatever battle you were in? And it's no good losing a limb in a battle you lost or ran away from. Scant charity you'll get then."

"We're going to win this war, and I will seek revenge for my wife."

"I'm tired of arguing with you. Just stick near me, boy, so I can keep you alive until you get some sense."

A messenger approached.

"All men of rank are to be addressed by the Maguire in the castle. Come quick!"

They were directed to the great hall once they arrived at the castle. The hall was packed, standing room only, and Seamus and Eunan slipped in at the back. Hugh Maguire stood on the raised platform beside the seat of the Maguire. He paced up and down, waiting for everyone to arrive. Donnacha quietened the murmurs so Hugh could speak.

"Noblemen of the Maguire clan, I have grave news to bring you. The war has started. The English have crossed the south Fermanagh border with a large army and are headed straight for Enniskillen. It is up to every one of you to defend Fermanagh to the last. I have sent messengers to our northern allies, and we will need to hold off the English until they arrive. What I do not doubt is our ultimate victory! Once the lords of the north are united, no one can defeat them!"

The Maguire men cheered. The MacCabe Galloglass cleared the room and Seamus and Eunan went to prepare to move south and stop Bagenal from attacking Enniskillen.

Eunan and Seamus arrived at the camp at Liscoole the next day and immediately assisted in the construction of earthworks. In the meantime, Hugh O'Neill set off from Tyrone with his forces to join Bagenal. His first act was to spoil the lands of Connor Roe and steal the majority of his cattle. He met up with Bagenal on the north side of the River Erne. Hugh only brought six hundred men and two hundred horse, much to Sir Henry's consternation. They planned the campaign but could agree on little as old rivalries bubbled over. In bygone years, Hugh O'Neill had attempted to ally the Bagenals to himself through marriage, and when this was refused, had eloped with Bagenal's sister. As if relations could sink any lower, the two had been deadly rivals for the dominance of Ulster, only united now as they were seemingly both agents of the Crown in their appointed roles there. After much argument, Sir Henry attempted to force a crossing at Liscoole ford over the River Erne.

Hugh Maguire had been well supported by his O'Donnell allies. Besides the MacSweeney Galloglass, they had supplied him with several units of shot, which while they may not have been the most accurate, still made enough noise to put off a hesitant enemy. The Maguires dug a trench and constructed some earthworks and covered the crossing with their shot. Sir Henry abandoned attempting to cross after he made a few half-hearted efforts. He considered his next move. He estimated he would not make progress via frontal assault without having to overcome some serious resistance.

Sir Henry then went to O'Neill, and their discussions about what to do next quickly descended into an argument. Bagenal wanted to assault the ford and encircle it, but O'Neill refused to divide their forces. They eventually agreed to outflank Maguire and go around Lower Lough Erne and cross at the Belleek ford. They decamped on the 7th of October.

Hugh Maguire's spies and secret communications with Hugh O'Neill informed him that Bagenal was going to cross the river at Belleek. Hugh rushed his old-style Galloglass and Kern northwards.

Seamus and Eunan were glad to be on the move. Eunan was impatient for his first taste of a proper battle, but Seamus was happy to wait. They marched for a day and found themselves on the south side of the River Erne digging earthworks. Eunan threw himself into it, leading his men in felling trees and carving spikes. They created their fortifications in a bend on the river that jutted into the Belleek ford.

The Maguires received further reinforcements from the O'Donnell under the leadership of Niall Garbh O'Donnell in the form of sixty horsemen, sixty swordsmen, and one hundred Galloglass. The O'Donnell positioned the rest of his forces in southern Tirconnell, poised if needed.

Seamus took Eunan aside when he saw Niall Garbh O'Donnell arrive.

"Why would the O'Donnell send him to any battle if he didn't want him to come back dead? I think we're digging our own graves here!"

"How can you say such a thing? The Maguire is defending the homeland! He would never do such a thing!"

"Oh yeah? Where's all the shot? There's only a few of them in the trench. Where are all the pikemen? Where are all the Maguire men apart from us lot from south Fermanagh? It's all old-school Galloglass, Redshanks and men they don't want to make it off the battlefield!"

Eunan looked around, and his heart sank.

"Don't despair," said Seamus. "Just make sure you have somewhere to run."

"Galloglass don't turn their backs. You taught me that!"

"As soon as the English touch the south side of the river, this army will break. Galloglass need to live to fight another day. Whatever song your soul becomes part of, you will soon be forgotten if you die in this battle. The dead of this day are expendable!"

"I, for one, will make a stand."

"If you die here today, the village dies with you. You'll not avenge Róisín."

Eunan scowled at the mention of her and returned to his men and continued to toil on the earthworks. Seamus surveyed the locality, mainly for escape routes.

Bagenal made camp a mile north of the ford. Hugh O'Neill arrived shortly after and set up another camp nearby. Bagenal sent a messenger to O'Neill to come to his camp to discuss battle plans. Pessimism followed O'Neill to the meeting.

"They look well dug in on the other side. We'll lose many a good man if we try a direct assault."

Bagenal scowled at such negativity. He called for his subordinates. Two English officers entered the tent and saluted.

"Hugh, this is Captain Lee and Captain Dowdall who have the honour of leading the infantry on this expedition. The time for dithering and delay is over. They will lead the frontal assault today. Please, Captain Dowdall, tell us your plan."

Captain Dowdall leaned over a hastily drawn map of the Irish defences around the ford.

"The ford is deep but perfectly crossable. It depends on what missiles the rebels fire at us."

"I hear they have muskets," said O'Neill.

"I hear they are cowards and run at the first sign of trouble," said Bagenal.

"May I continue, sirs?" said Captain Dowdall.

Bagenal nodded.

"We must advance along a narrow front, the same width as the ford and force our way over. As I said earlier, our men would initially be vulnerable to missiles as they cross the river, but there is an advantage in the terrain for us that the rebels may not have spotted."

"Which is?" asked Bagenal.

"We can concentrate our musket fire from both sides at the section of their defences directly opposite us and pin them down, limiting the number of missiles that can fire at us. The line should break if we get enough men across the river as quickly as possible."

Bagenal turned to O'Neill and smirked.

"Do you have any objections to this plan?"

"We could incur a lot of casualties if it goes wrong. I don't want O'Neill men leading the charge."

Bagenal waved away his objections.

"Duly noted in our victory dispatch to the Queen. Are you going to do anything for this battle?"

"Let me supply the cavalry."

"And may they do their duty to Crown and country."

Hugh O'Neill went back to his camp and sent half his men home.

# CHAPTER THIRTY-SIX

# BATTLE OF BELLEEK

A breeze blew through a chilly morning, and the sheets of rain eventually stopped, which allowed the few Irish musket men some respite to dry off their weapons. Eunan and Seamus took their positions behind the earthworks, opposite the ford. Beside them were the Galloglass and swordsmen of Niall Garbh O'Donnell.

"I hope that fucker brought our cattle!" said Seamus.

"Shut up! You'll get us killed!" said Eunan.

Seamus's silence was only temporary.

"Look at the weapons they have. Even I think they belong in a curiosity collection, and I'm old," said Seamus.

"As long as they fight, we have the advantage," said Eunan as he patted an enormous wooden spike protruding out of the ground.

"I've been to many battles, boy. The Irish hate fighting out in the open. They can't wait to fuck off. They like jumping out from behind trees. This army is made to break. Those spikes will only get in your way when you are 'retreating'."

"Don't be so cynical. We're going to stand, fight, and win."

Seamus sighed.

"You're not some ancient warrior-hero your mammy told you about, who'd pull his axe out of his arse, kill everyone and then all the priests and girls would love him."

Eunan glared at Seamus.

"All right, sorry. Stories you overheard other mammies telling their boys."

Eunan lifted his axe and pointed the blade at Seamus.

"Be careful with that. Don't hurt yourself before the big battle starts."

Captains Dowdall and Lee drew up their men on the other side of the River Erne from Belleek Castle. The pikemen drew up in their squares and readied themselves for battle. The English musket men cleaned their weapons and split into two groups. One group positioned themselves opposite the spur of land, where the Irish had their earthworks with Belleek Castle to their left. The other group went around the spur and hid in the woods on the other side. Once the musket men were in position, Captain Dowdall drew up his men to cross the ford.

Hugh Maguire surveyed the battlefield from the rear. O'Donnell shot, Galloglass and Redshanks massed behind the earthworks, with most of the Maguires spread out on the wings. Sean Óg Maguire was beside him to receive instructions, for he was the commander of the earthworks.

"Have you received word from Hugh O'Neill?" asked Sean Óg.

"His parting words to me were 'live to fight another day'. Adhere to that, please."

"As few Maguires will fall today as possible."

Sean Óg bowed and rode off to take up his battle position.

Captain Dowdall signalled the advance. The musket men on both sides of the spur volleyed into the Irish earthworks. The Irish returned fire. But their inferior weapons meant any effective volley disintegrated at one hundred yards. The superior weapons of the English, however, meant that their volleys laid down effective covering fire. The earthworks provided some protection for the Irish defenders, but hiding behind the earthworks meant they could not lay down missile fire over the ford. The Irish shot had lost the first stage of the battle.

Captain Dowdall's men marched forward in good order with only the odd musket ball or arrow whizzing over their heads. They entered the water. The river was swift and deep, but thankfully narrow at the chosen point of crossing. The men were soon up to their armpits in water and held their weapons over their heads. Their musket men did them a good service, and the Irish could not provide a meaningful missile deterrent. Captain Dowdall's men marched up the south bank of the River Erne but were completely soaked. They drew up their formation again, lowered their pikes and marched towards the Irish defences. Captain Lee's men then entered the ford. O'Neill's cavalry followed Captain Lee's men. The few Irish musket men let off a volley, but it had little effect on the oncoming English pikemen. First, Lee's men and then O'Neill's cavalry climbed the bank. Dowdall's column almost reached the Irish line, and the Irish line broke. As the Irish retreated, the English musket men fired volleys into their flanks, which created chaos.

Eunan braced for the impending assault, hiding beneath the earthworks to avoid the musket shot. Musket balls fizzed off the top of the wooden walls. Seamus looked over the wall and turned to him.

"I have no ambition to die for the Maguire, especially not today. I'll be back!"

"Where are you going?" said Eunan, but Seamus was already gone.

The English volleys crashed into the Irish lines with ever increasing frequency. Eunan looked through the cracks in the wooden wall and saw the English soldiers wading through the river, almost unopposed. Eunan looked for the commander, Sean Óg, but could not see him anywhere. He wondered if the plan was to spring up as soon as the English set foot on this side of the river. However, once the English soldiers drew up formation, the cavalry came up behind them. Then Niall Garbh O'Donnell's men fled. Once they left, the rest of the line broke. Eunan pulled out his axe.

"Let's get these bastards!" he shouted raising his head, but even his own men started to run.

The front of the English column crashed into the earthworks, crushing the wooden wall. Eunan swung his axe, but it made little impression on a wall of pikes. A hand landed on his shoulder and dragged him away. The Irish soldiers were caught in the funnel that was the spur of the land in the river. They fled, ran into each other and all coherence was lost. The only resistance that temporarily halted the English was the earthworks.

Hugh Maguire sat on his horse and watched the battle predictably unfold. He turned to his commanders.

"Have we lost many today?"

"Redshanks and Galloglass from the O'Donnell coin."

"At least some of their debts died on the field. They can be grateful to me for that. Don't engage the O'Neill cavalry. Rally the men, and we'll reassemble at the rendezvous point."

With that, Hugh Maguire turned and left with the noble horsemen of his clan.

The English pikemen marched onwards, but there was little to engage with, as the Irish were far more mobile than them and were already leaving the field. The second English column of Captain Lee with Bagenal at the head advanced towards the retreating Irish.

Eunan was on the run, with Seamus leading the way.

"Follow me! We must go past Belleek Castle so we can escape into Fermanagh. The English won't follow us there."

Eunan looked behind him and saw the second column crossing the river with the general at its head.

"No! I must show some fight!"

Seamus reached out, but Eunan broke free of his grip and Seamus lost sight of him in the mass of retreating bodies. Eunan pushed his way past his fleeing comrades and towards the English general. He came upon the pursuing English soldiers, and with several blows of his axe, downed two of them. The English general was coming within range. Another English soldier lurched at him, and then another. Eunan reached for a throwing axe. His battle-axe thrust down the pike, trapping it to the ground, and the throwing axe plunged into the side of the man's head. The next soldier received the spike of the battle-axe in his cheek. Eunan pulled the axe out. The commander was in throwing range. He threw his axe as hard as he could and ran.

Sir Henry Bagenal followed his troops forward. He trusted his captains and would have typically left them to conduct the forward operations of the battle, but he did not trust O'Neill. The English soldiers marched forward, and the Irish fled before them, just as he had predicted.

O'Neill came across the river and rode up beside him.

"Leave this to me!" said O'Neill as he rode off with his men after the Irish.

A musket backfired near Bagenal, and there was a loud bang which caused his horse to rear. An axe came flying towards him, but Bagenal changed position due to the horse rearing. He felt the thud of an axe hit his leg. He took out his pistol and fired it towards the retreating Irish. One of his men came up to him.

"Are you all right, sir? That looks like a nasty scrape. Do you want to see a physician?"

Bagenal surveyed the battlefield.

"The day is won. They can do without me to finish them. Lead the way, soldier!"

Eunan saw the axe fly, but not land. Too many English. Even he did not want to die on a day that would bring no glory. He ran towards Belleek Castle as Seamus had instructed. Most of the Maguire men also ran in that direction. O'Neill's cavalry did not appear to follow them. They chased to the west, where the Redshanks and Niall Garbh O'Donnell had fled.

Most of the Maguire men retreated south and reassembled in such good order, it was like it was planned. Seamus looked for his men. Eunan looked for a way to escape, for his leech scabs burned. Seamus found most of his men with only two missing. All in all, Hugh Maguire lost around three hundred soldiers; including those missing, around a third of his force. Most of these were Redshanks, or Galloglass, sent by the O'Donnell, who performed poorly in battle and bore most of the brunt of the O'Neill cavalry. Niall Garbh O'Donnell had disappeared, along with most of the men sent by O'Donnell. They were believed to have retreated northwards.

Bagenal now sat in western Fermanagh, victorious. He sent messengers to Sir Richard Bingham, Governor of Connacht, proposing to invade Tirconnell and decisively defeat the retreating Scottish mercenaries. O'Neill and his men left for Tyrone, as O'Neill had sustained a minor injury. Red Hugh rallied his forces in south Tirconnell to counter Bagenal. The messenger returned with a message from Bingham, who refused to cooperate with an invasion of

Tirconnell. Bagenal now found himself isolated between the armies of Hugh Maguire and Red Hugh.

He had defeated the Irish and still held the field. Bagenal decided this was enough to paint as a victory in his reports to the Crown. He set off back to Monaghan via Enniskillen. As he marched, any resistance melted away before him. This reinforced his belief the Irish were well beaten.

Bagenal again stopped outside Enniskillen, which again was well defended. He decided not to attack. It was coming on to winter, and the Irish conscripts who made up a large percentage of the army wished to get back to their farms and save what remained of their harvests. No point in being out campaigning while the family starved at home.

Bagenal stopped off at Liscoole, where Hugh Maguire had previously prevented him from crossing the River Erne. He stopped long enough to damage the fort, just in case he had to come back and assault Enniskillen.

Hugh Maguire followed Bagenal at a safe distance down Fermanagh.

Bagenal went to Lisnaskea to the newly appointed sheriff of Fermanagh, Connor Roe Maguire. He left Captain Dowdall and three hundred men in Castle Skea to assist the new sheriff in administering the county.

# CHAPTER THIRTY-SEVEN

# CONSULTING THE WATERS OF TRUTH

Hugh Maguire marched down to Enniskillen with his newly reformed army. The residents came out and greeted him like a liberator. It did not feel like a defeat to anyone as they still had what they had before the English army marauded through their lands, but now the English were gone. Their lands were spoilt, but Hugh Maguire had had the foresight to send most of his cattle to Tyrone for safekeeping. But Hugh realised that this was only the beginning. He split his men in two and sent half to harass Connor Roe Maguire and Captain Dowdall, while half stayed to repair some of the damage done to the town and surrounding villages.

Eunan visited the priests and physicians on the islands for some leeching before he presented himself as fit for duty. Seamus and Eunan were assigned to start a resistance against Connor Roe Maguire in south Fermanagh, so they returned to their village.

They found Captain Dowdall and his men had burnt their former village to the ground. They entered the destroyed perimeter walls to discover the burnt-out huts and boats, but there were no bodies.

"If there are no bodies," said Seamus, "they should all have escaped to the islands. We need to get some boats and search for them."

Seamus divided the men. Some searched for their families in the ruins, and some searched for boats. The destruction tore at Eunan's heart, and raw recent traumas were again exposed. Tears streamed down his cheeks as he berated himself for abandoning his villagers for the reward of fickle glory. His leech scabs burned, and he itched uncontrollably. Seamus saw his distress and came and put a hand upon his shoulder, but only anger poured forth.

"This is what you get for supporting the Maguire," said Seamus. "My wife was here, but I'm sure she escaped to the islands if there were no bodies. We can avenge ourselves, but I fear the traditional O'Keenan Maguire lands will offer no sanctuary in the times to come. We may have to live on the islands or go west if we are to know peace."

Eunan fought back the tears, as he did not wish to look weak in front of his mentor.

"I fear peace will never shine upon us again. Bagenal pushes from the east and Bingham from the south and west. I have faith in the Maguire and God, but my heart shrivels with the more people I lose. My father was the chieftain, and all the villagers died. I was the chieftain and abandoned them on a folly, and now they are all gone."

A voice came from the distance.

"We have boats!"

Seamus took Eunan by the arm, considering his current sensitivities.

"Come. Let us search for our people before we fall into a pit of despair. We must not let down those who are still living."

Eunan followed him to the boats, which had their bows pulled up on the shore.

"There are some bodies further down the lake shore," said one of the men who fetched the boats. "I didn't recognise any of them, and God only knows where they came from, floating on the lake like that."

Eunan sat and thought.

"Let's go to the most obvious places they could hide first, and then look at the bodies later." He turned to Seamus. "Let's split up, as we'll cover the area quicker."

Seamus got in the other boat and sailed towards the islands on the right, while Eunan sailed towards the left. Seamus stood at the top of the boat and called for his wife. When there was no immediate response, he called for other prominent people from the village. He saw movement ahead and urgently ordered his men to press on. As he neared the islands, people came out of hiding, and when they recognised Seamus, they waved at him and invited him to land. Seamus jumped into the water when they neared shore and dragged the boat to its moorings. He was soon back in the warm embrace of his wife.

"Where were you?" she said.

"Fighting the wrong set of English. What happened?"

"Oh, we saw them coming from far away. It was Connor Roe Maguire's men, led by the English, that did this."

"Did anyone die?"

"No, we saw the bodies floating across the lake from another village and we all fled to the islands as planned. They burned the village to the ground and stole all the cattle. We heard them say that the warriors in the village supported Hugh Maguire instead of Connor Roe and that they should all be strung up."

"How many people are on this island?"

"Twenty."

"You'll never survive here. We need to go to the mainland."

"They have packs of soldiers all over the countryside, burning out and evicting the supporters of Hugh Maguire."

"Then we must leave and head north so that the Maguire can protect us properly." Seamus turned to the gathering crowd. "Take your things. We are leaving for Enniskillen tonight."

Everyone murmured and debated the announcement.

"We have plenty of boats to bring you onshore. Once you are there, my warriors and I will escort you to Enniskillen. You will be a lot safer there than here!"

Seamus organised the boats to ferry the island dwellers to the shore. All in all, about a hundred cold and hungry villagers stood and waited for hope, with only the clothes on their backs. Eunan also returned, but he only had a handful of stragglers with him.

Seamus gathered everyone into the smouldering central square.

"Everyone, gather your belongings, and we'll set out for Enniskillen. My men will arrange carts and transport. We will ensure you make it to Enniskillen securely. You will be safe there."

"What if we get ambushed?" said one frightened villager. "The woods and countryside are full of bandits and English. I don't want to die in a ditch!"

"If you stay here, the best you can hope for is to live on an island, hope the war ends quickly and hope the Maguire wins it."

"But what if he doesn't?" said another. "What sanctuary then? Where are all the MacMahons now? Hiding out in the north somewhere? A skivvy for an English lord when they once owned the land? What choice are you offering us? Become a permanent refugee or take our chances on our own land?"

"We will protect you," said Seamus.

"When? You're never here. We're not your people. You're a MacSheehy. At least Eunan is vaguely a Maguire. But all his people are dead. You're never here, always off somewhere else fighting for the Maguire. I, for one, am going to go live on the Islands. Who is with me?"

After some initial reluctance, the villagers split in two. The original Mac-Sheehy Galloglass and their families stuck with Seamus, and everyone else went with the man who wished to remain and hide on the islands. Eunan stood in the middle.

"Well? What about you?" asked Seamus.

"It is my destiny to fight for the Maguire," said Eunan. His head hung low as he trudged over to stand behind Seamus.

The two sides looked at each other, but no one moved towards the other. The half that was staying went back to the boats and returned to the islands. Seamus ordered his men to find carts, horses, and any other type of transport that would help them on their way. It took several hours to find a couple of carts, such was the thoroughness of the destruction of the marauding soldiers of Connor Roe. The Galloglass and their families gathered what few belongings they had left and set off with most of the villagers walking behind the carts.

Crowds of people swarmed the roads, moving west to avoid the impending war. Seamus and Eunan picked up many stragglers along the way, as there were few soldiers offering protection.

Eunan hung his head as he wondered whether he was a chieftain anymore. He had abandoned his homeland, half his adopted clan, and was now a refugee relying on the kindness of the Maguire to feed his people. Were they his people at all, or were they the families of Seamus's Galloglass, using his position to further themselves with the Maguire? He did not know anymore, but his leech scabs itched.

They passed through a forest, and Seamus squeezed the column together so no one got isolated. Darkness descended.

"We only have a couple of miles to go before there is a clearing, and we can rest for the night," said Seamus.

They huddled together and waddled towards the promised clearing. A hiss of arrows came from behind them.

"Take them onwards. I'll take care of this," said Eunan to Seamus.

Eunan reared his horse and positioned himself at the rear with five Galloglass. Arrows whistled above their heads. Eunan stood still to create some distance between himself and the villagers.

"Do you want to know what happened?"

Eunan heard a voice, but he did not know if it was real or in his head. He saw movement in the trees. He jumped off his horse.

"Guard her with your life!" he shouted at the Galloglass, and Eunan ran into the woods. Two of the Galloglass ran behind him.

Darkness surrounded him. An arrow whistled past his head.

"Do you want to know what happened?"

Eunan whirled around in a frenzy, trying to locate the voice.

"Yes, I bloody do! Stand still long enough so I can kill you!"

A body moved. Eunan ran after it. He saw another body move to his right. It was close. He grabbed a throwing axe to be rewarded with the crunch of bone, swiftly followed by the squelch of brains. Eunan ran to retrieve his axe. He heard a yelp of pain. A moment later he ran into one of his Galloglass wrapped around a spear. Guts spilled out on the ground. The man groaned wretchedly. Eunan beheaded him to help him pass.

"Do you want to know what happened?"

Another body appeared. Eunan threw his axe. His axe-throwing skills had improved immensely, but his luck had not. He retrieved his axe from the head of his other Galloglass.

"Do you want to know what happened?"

"No! Tell me!" Eunan screamed into the trees.

Eunan turned to see an arrow pointing at his face.

"Move if you want to live!"

Seamus worried when Eunan did not return. He rode forward to make sure the road ahead was free of bandits or Connor Roe's men. Once he was reasonably reassured, he turned back to his ever-growing column of refugees.

"Finn, come with me."

Finn gulped at the sternness of Seamus's face but obeyed nonetheless.

They rode for a little while until they came to a stream in a clearing in the woods. Seamus dismounted, tied his horse so she could drink in the stream, and paced over to beneath the shadow of Finn's horse.

"Dismount your horse and let her drink," said Seamus. "You and I need to have words."

Finn broke out in a cold sweat.

"Have you brought me here to kill me?"

Seamus's cold eyes set in a fixed gaze. "That very much depends on you. Throughout the time I have taken you under my wing, you have tested me. Now I need the truth. Get down and tell me what happened to Eunan's wife."

A second man came up from behind. They marched Eunan through the dark of the forest.

"If you're going to kill me," said Eunan, "you should at least show your face and look me in the eye before you do it. That's the way a soldier would do it. The other way is cowardly. Are you a deserter?"

"Be quiet and watch your step. We're nearly there."

Eunan half turned his head to gain a sight of his captors.

"I have two Galloglass waiting for me. They'll come looking for me. Release me now and run away and live!"

"They're dead. No one is coming to save you!"

They reached a clearing in the wood, and the captor forced Eunan to sit. The man with the arrow wore a hood, and the other stood behind him.

"Throw your axes over there!" ordered the man. "Now get up!"

They led Eunan at arrow point to the lip of the ravine at the bottom of which once lay the body of Róisín. Eunan felt a surge of adrenaline through his body. His bad blood tingled as if this was to be the climax of his life. This is what he deserved. Everyone he ever cared about was dead because of him. He deserved to die on the rocks with Róisín. The bad blood would smash on the rock face, seep into the ground, and descend to hell where it belonged. Eunan walked out to the edge of the cliff. He shut his eyes and looked to the heavens.

A warm hand was placed gently on his shoulder and pulled him back from the ravine.

"What are you doing, lord? Do you want to know what happened?"

The voice was vaguely familiar. It should not have come, for surely he was not dead yet. Eunan stepped back and opened his eyes.

"Sean O'Reilly!? I thought you were dead?"

His captors took off their masks. They were the Galloglass Seamus had trained, who he tried to recruit for the Knights of Saint Colmcille.

"What are you doing here?"

Finn kept Seamus firmly in his sights as he carefully dismounted and ensured his weapons were in easy reach.

"If you go for your weapons," said Seamus, "I will view that as an admission of your guilt. If you attack me, all of my obligations to my brother will end and his ghost will protect you no more. Be a man and face me and tell the truth."

But Finn was no man and quivered in front of Seamus.

"Are you here to belittle me as you have done all my life? Eunan and I are the same, yet you always favour him over me. Why was he given a princess and me a broom to muck out the horses?"

Seamus heaved his chest up and let out a tremendous sigh.

"I am tired of your constant whining, tired of your constant failure, tired of having to evoke distant happy memories of my brother and wring any positive emotions from that to forgive your latest evil deed. Tired of warning you that this is your last chance, tired of your petty jealousy. You looked guilty, but I persuaded Eunan that you were not and that I would take care of it. Yet here you are, reaching for your weapons when you are cornered rather than expressing your guilt. What is it to be? Can you be honest with me for all those years I put up with you, or are you going to fight your way out?"

Finn hesitated. He saw the determined look on Seamus's face. He was cornered. He went for his axe.

Sean O'Reilly smiled at Eunan, which reassured him enough for him not to consider himself a prisoner anymore. Sean invited Eunan to sit before he began his story.

"After we sided with you, Seamus viewed us as being untrustworthy. So he gave us a test. Five of us were chosen, with five of Seamus's men to escort Róisín to the village. As we rode down, we'd hear whispers of what the other Galloglass and Finn were talking about. They laughed and joked about how Seamus wanted to get you married to distract you from making your own way.

"We were on our way to the village, but before we reached the top of Upper Lough Erne, we diverted towards Castle Skea. We were uneasy about it, but Finn assured us it was all part of our planned route to throw off anyone who may have followed us, and because of the numerous bandits on the road, this route was safer. Our weapons were at the ready. We came to this forest and this very clearing. We slowed down and found ourselves surrounded by Galloglass from Enniskillen. It was Aonghas O'Braoin and his men. We always thought they were in league with Connor Roe, but here was our proof. There were too many for us to fight. Finn ordered us to down our weapons. Aonghas walked up to Finn and asked, 'Where is she?' There was no animosity between them except for a little subservience on Finn's behalf.

"There was only one woman with us. Finn pointed towards the carriage and stood back. Aonghas climbed into the carriage. He tried to grab Róisín, but she kicked out at him and drove him out. Aonghas wiped his bloody mouth and spat on the ground. He climbed in, determined to wrench her out."

"What did you do?" Eunan said.

"We were surrounded by Aonghas's men and could do little about it. Anyway, Aonghas grabbed at Róisín and got her by the ankle. He pulled her until she was almost out the door. With one last gasp, she kicked him in the face. He reeled back and grabbed his face, his hands covered in blood streaming from his nose. We picked up our swords and axes and fought. Aonghas climbed into the carriage again, and in her panic, Róisín tried to scramble out the other door. She must not have realised how close the carriage was to the edge. We heard a scream as she fell to the rocks below. We fought with Aonghas's men. We fought with Finn's men, and we lost half our number. But the three of us fought our way out and into the forest. We have lived as bandits ever since. We didn't know who to trust until we saw you."

Eunan jerked his head to the side, sniffed, and looked at the sky to hide his tears.

"That indeed is a sad, sad tale. But why would Finn wish to give Róisín to Aonghas O'Braoin?"

"I can only but suppose, but if she were a prisoner of Connor Roe, it would embarrass the Maguire to have his new alliance ruined and disgrace Seamus and yourself."

"But Finn and Seamus are tied at the hip! I have often wondered why Seamus puts up with him, but surely Seamus would not allow Finn to give up Róisín? And why would he give them to Connor Roe?"

"Seamus is the most devious fox I have ever met," said Sean. "If he pays you attention, he has a reason for it that will benefit himself. Maybe he sees Connor Roe as the ultimate winner and wishes to switch sides before the spoils are split?"

Eunan wiped the tears from his face and composed himself.

"Let us get our revenge and go to Enniskillen and confront Seamus and Finn. Are you with me?"

Sean O'Reilly and his companions cheered and gathered their belongings. They set out on foot towards Enniskillen as the Galloglass, who was minding Eunan's horse, had already left to catch up with Seamus.

Seamus and Finn clashed axes, but it was not long before Seamus's skills with the axe staff had consigned Finn's axe to the bushes. Seamus let rip an almighty punch and Finn reeled back, holding his nose. He grabbed Finn by the throat and thrust his face into the stream. Finn's blood and air bubbles from his lungs mixed in the gently gushing waters, breaching the peace of the tranquil woods. Seamus wrenched Finn's head out of the water and held his ear to his mouth.

"Now is a good time for the truth before I soil this beautiful stream too much with your dirty blood."

Finn gasped for air. "I should have married the princess. I am the older."

"Not ready to talk yet? We can fix that." Seamus plunged Finn's head back into the waters of the stream. A splurge of bubbles broke on the surface of the water, and the curses within were condemned to be silent forever. Seamus pulled Finn's head out of the water when the ferocity of the air bubbles had subsided.

"Want to talk yet?"

Finn coughed and sputtered. "You should have made me a Galloglass long ago."

Seamus shook Finn's head. "I can do this all day, but I fear you can't. Nobody would miss you if I accidentally killed you." He ducked Finn's head into the water again. Finn banged his free hand on the ground. Seamus dragged him up once more and threw him aside.

"I'm glad you tired of being drowned, for I'm tired also," said Seamus. "Now I suggest you talk now, for if I duck you again you are not coming back up."

Finn rolled around on the ground coughing and spluttering and threw up some of the water he swallowed. He turned to Seamus and looked like a demented creature of fairy folklore with a large goblet of spittle hanging from his mouth.

"I found someone who would make me a Galloglass and give me the respect I deserve."

Seamus smirked. "Who is this master of reading character, pray tell?"

"Aonghas O'Braoin."

Seamus laughed. "For as much as your treachery pains me, you deserve each other. I trust you brought Róisín to him, and he would have brought her to Connor Roe?"

Finn nodded. "So what is to be done with me?"

Seamus reached for his axe and pointed it at Finn. "Now I disown you for being a traitor to me. Whatever obligations I owed to my brother have been fulfilled. Go now, for if I ever lay eyes on you again, I'll consider you to be my enemy."

Finn took his horse and scurried off into the woods before Seamus could change his mind.

# CHAPTER THIRTY-EIGHT

# PROFESSIONS IN THE MUD

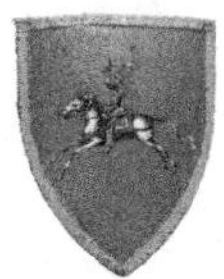

Eunan made his way north with his two Galloglass. They acquired some horses and scoured the countryside, but could not find Seamus and Finn. Word reached them that Hugh Maguire was in mid-Fermanagh with the bulk of his forces, and Eunan changed direction.

Upon his arrival, Eunan was directed straight to Hugh Maguire's tent. Hugh was surprisingly upbeat and greeted him warmly.

"My lord," said Eunan as he bent his knee.

The Maguire smiled.

"Get up, my faithful brother in arms and friend. We may have tasted defeat, but it is not the end."

"You still have faith, lord?"

The Maguire burned with the passion of a zealot. "I almost fell into the hands of the English, mistaking some of them for my own. But fate rescued me, and will rescue the Maguires and the lords of the north."

Eunan paused for considering the ebullient mood he found his master in, now would be a good time to raise the subject of his wife. If anything, he would introduce the subject slowly.

"We are truly blessed by your survival. How would you have me do your bidding?"

"Where is Seamus? Did he survive the war down south?"

The emotions flowed through Eunan's face as the mention of Seamus made him reconsider coming clean with the Maguire. He needed to fully resolve her death before he could make his approach. His thoughts turned to Seamus once more.

"He's like a cockroach. You can never assume he is dead unless you see his body and that his chest no longer expands. I went south with him to witness the destruction meted out by the English. But he returned north separately with his men, as I had other business to attend to. I assumed he came to you, but obviously not from your question."

"I have not seen Seamus since both of you went south. The English this time are well led. Captain Dowdall is a crafty and resourceful beast. He ambushed our ships on the river and then acquired some of his own. He wreaks havoc in what was once our safe lands and controls the river and upper lake. I need you to go to Enniskillen. The castle must not fall, or he will also threaten the lower lake. I will follow you there, but I must secure our forts on the lower lake first, and then see what our northern allies wish to do. If Seamus is not already in Enniskillen, I will divert him there."

"Yes, lord. I look forward to meeting you soon in Enniskillen."

They held each other by the forearms and then embraced. Eunan departed with his Galloglass.

Finn rode as hard as he could, his tears forcing themselves past his eyelids, resisting the force of the bracing wind. Fate had been cruel to him, Seamus a tormentor, Eunan the thief who stole what was rightfully his. But a fissure had opened up through Fermanagh and whoever was brave enough to cross that fissure would end up in the land where opportunity lay. He evaded most patrols of English soldiers and their Irish lackeys from the Pale and the south.

He only had to produce the emblem given to him by Aonghas O'Braoin when he approached the perimeters of Castle Skea.

Aonghas sat beside a fire in a camp outside the castle, warming himself as he waited with his men for instructions for the new campaign. Finn leapt off his horse and ran towards him. Aonghas calmed his anxious men, but gripped the hilt of his dagger as he waited to see what Finn would do. Finn threw his axe in front of Aonghas and lay prostrate on the muddy ground.

"My lord, I am ready to commit my axe to you and become your Galloglass. Tell me, what is your bidding?"

Aonghas sat down and smiled, and his men relaxed and took their hands off their weapons.

"What is my greatest spy doing here? If you want my bidding, you were already doing it by spying on Seamus MacSheehy."

"On pain of death, I, along with the plot to kidnap the whore from the north, was discovered." Finn remained prostrate and spoke into the mud, for he did not want his new master to see his failure. He was lucky, for in his anger, Aonghas considered crushing Finn's hand with his foot, but he needed more information first.

"Was this recently discovered?" he said.

"I came straight to you."

Aonghas paused to think. "That is something, at least. Does the Maguire know?"

"Seamus has set out for Enniskillen but is encumbered with refugees."

An evil grin manifested itself on Aonghas's face. "So the Maguire does not suspect I am a traitor?"

"Only Seamus knows the truth," said Finn.

Aonghas leapt from his seat. "Clean yourself up and eat. I shall return shortly to discuss what is to be done with you."

Finn had barely washed and eaten before Aonghas strode back.

"Prepare to leave, men. Victory is almost upon us." He turned to Finn, where he sat. "Upon the death of Seamus, I will make you the last MacSheehy Galloglass. Do not dishonour the name."

Seamus sighed. He had been left with the families of his Galloglass and many others who had sought his protection on the road north. He had been reduced to cart pace as the perils had multiplied with every morsel of news by Maguire warriors from the east passing him on the road. He sent two of his men to scout his eastern and southern flanks, for if there were danger approaching, at least he would be forewarned. Not even a day passed before the scout from the east returned.

"We are being followed, Seamus," he said without dismounting.

Seamus looked to the east but could only make out a blur of forest and field. "Are you sure?"

"I tracked them for a while to make sure, but I cannot tell if they are friend or foe. They are gaining on us rapidly."

"Go track their movements. I will be waiting to receive them at the next opportunity."

Seamus stood alone in the forest clearing, holding his axe with both his hands, dangling at his midriff. The column of refugees, including his own wife and the families of his Galloglass, had been ordered to proceed to Enniskillen and wait for him there before continuing their journey northwards.

Aonghas O'Braoin and his men pulled up their horses when they entered the clearing and dismounted. Aonghas walked forward to confront Seamus with his men lagging behind to back him up.

"Who are you, MacSheehy, a foreigner in our lands to block our peaceful passage to Enniskillen?" said Aonghas.

Seamus spat on the ground.

"I believe you have an ex-apprentice of mine in your ranks. Does he have the courage to show his face?"

Finn stepped forward. He could not look Seamus in the face.

"I can show myself."

"Is here to be your grave? Is your first combat for your new master to be where your old one disposes of you with a swift blow to the head? Was all the anguish and treachery worth it just for that?"

Finn grimaced and raised his axe, but Aonghas stepped forward, for he could see through Seamus's game.

"Surrender now to the Maguire's Galloglass and let us bring you to him to face his wrath for getting the princess of the O'Dohertys killed and placing his alliance with the O'Donnell in jeopardy."

Seamus laughed. "Get yourself a scapegoat and kill one of your rivals at the same time? Good thinking, but too obvious. Eunan left long before me and by the time you reach Enniskillen, it is you that will be hanged as traitors."

It was Aonghas's turn to laugh.

"The Maguire is not in Enniskillen and if Eunan was going to tell the Maguire, he would have told him by now and he would also have been banished in disgrace." Aonghas looked back at his men, and they were ready to attack. "However, there are more men in my ranks that have it in for you. I suggest they resolve their grievances with you through trial by combat. Do you still have enough Galloglass honour in your blood to accept?"

"Bring them on." Seamus readied his axe.

Aonghas grinned and signalled to Cúmhaí Devine, the tormentor of Desmond, to come forward. Cúmhaí raised his axe and charged.

Enniskillen and the surrounding countryside made preparations for war. The peasants gathered what food was available in January and filled the stores of the castle and town. Those that could not find accommodation behind the protective walls got in their boats and made their way to the islands of Lower Lough Erne.

Eunan entered the castle and immediately made himself and his men available to Dáithí MacCabe, the commander in charge of the defence. Dáithí MacCabe put them to work, expanding the moat and digging earthworks both on the approaches to the castle on the mainland and on the main island. It was hard, intensive work, especially for men exhausted after war and travel. But Eunan treated it as penance for his sins, for the bad blood coursing through his veins, for bringing death and misfortune wherever he went. His sins were many, and the moat much wider than when initially a righteous man had taken his shovel to it. Daylight faded, and Eunan and his men went to the castle to eat, rest, and warm themselves by the fire.

The castle was full of refugees from all over Fermanagh. Soldiers, women, children, priests. They rationed the remains of their food, for the harvest had been taken up but distributed to various storehouses around the county, mainly concentrated on the islands of Lower Lough Erne, where most of the population had fled. Eunan was grateful for what food he could get.

After devouring the food, he left his men, for he desired his own company to take a few moments to rest and contemplate. But there were few places to be alone in a crowded castle. He sat beside a different fire with different company.

"You look troubled, son," said a voice.

"Aren't we all? War has come to Fermanagh, and I fear worse is to come. I fear the destruction of our county and the end of the Maguires," said Eunan, not looking to see who was speaking.

"With the Lord God's help, the Maguires will endure. Maybe not as you know them now, but the Maguires will endure. God is our only true master."

Eunan looked to his right, and an old priest sat beside him. He could not see the priest's face for he wore a hood. Shadows danced on the priest's robes in time with the flames of the fire. Eunan bent forward.

"Is the destruction of the Maguires punishment for our sins?"

"Do you think the heathen English with their made-up God sin any less than you?"

"All I know is destruction is coming my way, for my sins, for the blood that flows through my veins. Conceived in sin, and bringer of misfortune and death for all those unlucky enough to share their lives with me. The Sodom and Gomorrah of my heart will fall, and all those around me will turn to bitter salt."

"We can all be redeemed through the Lord. Every warrior here, be they of any experience, has killed someone. If you have killed an English blasphemer or one of their lackeys, you have done it to preserve Ireland and the church. It may be a sin, but a sin committed for the right reasons, and the Lord will forgive you. Trouble yourself not, for you will need all your courage in the heat of the battle. You must strike the blow without thinking or remorse, or else the Lord and the Maguire will lose one of their best warriors."

"You don't understand."

"I never do, but think about it, and you will find solace."

Eunan sat in silence. But his peace was soon shattered.

"The English are coming! The English are coming!"

Cúmhaí charged across the clearing and swung his axe toward Seamus's head. Seamus easily parried him, for even though the man's bulk made him strong, it slowed him down and made him easy to read. Seamus knew this fight had to be quick, for Aonghas had signalled to his men to form a circle around him and if it were not, he would be surrounded. Cúmhaí swung for him again, this time aiming for the ribs. Seamus blocked this once more and kicked Cúmhaí in the back of the standing knee.

"Come on, Cúmhaí, finish him," said Aonghas. "Don't have us come to rescue you."

This spurred Cúmhaí on, and he renewed his attacks. Seamus parried all of his blows despite the force of them wearing him down. But every time Cúmhaí charged to attack, Seamus would concentrate on kicking at his right knee and, most times, he would connect. Cúmhaí attacked again, but Seamus could feel there was less power than before, and it was now his turn to take the offensive. He cast his axe straight down towards Cúmhaí's head and Cúmhaí easily parried by holding his axe shaft above his head. Seamus kicked out and felt Cúmhaí's solid right shin in front of him. Seamus glided the shaft of his axe down the solid parry of Cúmhaí's and smashed the butt on Cúmhaí's knee. Cúmhaí's howls were short-lived. Once he was down, Seamus caved his head in with his axe blade. Aonghas froze, for he did not expect his man to go down so quickly.

"Now!"

Seamus's men shot arrows from the surrounding tree branches and took out two of Aonghas's men with arrows to the head.

"Down!" cried Aonghas, and his men scrambled to gain cover in the surrounding trees. In the ensuing chaos, Seamus and his men took to their horses and rode for Enniskillen.

A commotion came from the gates that attracted everyone's attention. One last set of warriors entered the castle as the gates shut behind them. Seamus was at their head.

"Who is the commander here?" he said to the guards at the door. They pointed towards the castle tower and Dáithí MacCabe came out and declared it was him.

"The band of warriors behind me are English traitors," said Seamus. "Do not let them in."

Dáithí looked over Seamus's shoulder to the guards on the tower. "Who approaches us?"

"It is Aonghas O'Braoin and his men," said the guard. "They wish to come in as the English are behind them. They pledge their loyalty to the Maguire."

"Of course," said Seamus. "What else would you expect a spy to say? If you let them in, they will open the gates for the enemy."

Dáithí pondered a moment.

"Let them in. I have not heard of him being a traitor before. They are still MacCabe Galloglass, and we need all the men we can get."

"You fool!" said Seamus.

Dáithí thrust his index finger towards Seamus's face. "Any more of that insolence and I will hang you from the walls. Now find yourself a position on the ramparts to defend."

Seamus stood firm, but Dáithí's men put their hands on their weapons. Seamus reconsidered. "Yes, commander, my men will take a section of the wall."

Aonghas O'Braoin's men came through the gate and received a warning that any violence involving Seamus would result in them all being hung. O'Braoin and his men were assigned an opposite wall to defend, well away from Seamus. Eunan winced at the sight of Seamus walking across the courtyard even though he had not seen him, and automatically went for his axe, but the priest grabbed his arm.

"Do you know this man?" said the priest.

Eunan regained his composure. He was confused but did not want to give away his true feelings about Seamus.

"Of course. He's my mentor, my guide. He's like a father to me."

"He's a very dangerous man," whispered the priest, who placed his hand reassuringly on Eunan's extended arm. "If you are who I think you are, I know of your bad blood."

"What!?!" Eunan wrenched his arm back.

"Come with me!"

Dáithí MacCabe climbed to the top of the tower, for he feared the English were closing in. He ordered his archers on the ramparts to shoot fire arrows into the night sky to locate the English army, but they could do little to penetrate the darkness. Anxious that they would soon be surrounded, Dáithí MacCabe called an experienced scout into the empty main hall.

"Take this letter and guard it with your life. Bring it to the Maguire on Devenish Island. Tell him the English are approaching. We will hold them for as long as possible, but he must come with the entire Maguire army and save us."

Connor O'Cassidy took the letter and bowed. He knew the woods of north Fermanagh like the back of his hand.

"Upon my life, I will return with the Maguire and save my brethren."

"Go swiftly. There is a small boat waiting for you by the river gate. Make haste, for we eagerly await your return."

Connor O'Cassidy bowed again and was gone.

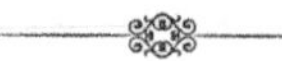

The priest and Eunan searched the castle and its buildings for somewhere quiet to talk, but the castle was crowded and chaotic, and the priest trusted no one. After dawn, when the English army had not appeared, and the residents went to sleep, Eunan and the priest found a secluded spot in an undercroft behind some barrels and a cart.

"Tell me about your youth, son," said the priest, putting his hand on Eunan's shoulder.

Eunan sat and bowed his head. The priest sat beside him.

"It was hard. My parents hated me. They beat me all the time and confined me to the outhouse. They said I had bad blood. Something inside me made me evil. I asked priests before to help me, but they couldn't." Eunan showed the priest the leech scabs on his arms. "I just want to be normal. Why can't I just be like any other young chieftain? Why do I have to feel like this all the time?"

"Why do you think your parents hated you?" said the priest. He thought he knew who Eunan was, but had to probe a little more to make sure. If he was not considerate, he feared Eunan might erupt.

"My mother was not shy about telling me. She was a cripple. She had a child who died in childbirth when I was young. Something went wrong. She couldn't walk after it and always blamed me. My mother said I was like a Viking who clawed at her womb when she gave birth to me and ripped all the goodness out for I did not want to leave and face the earth. She said I cursed her womb, so it lay fallow, and no other child could lie in there and live. My mother said my curse was so strong that she was crippled when she tried to have another child."

"Why didn't you try to run away? A strong young lad like yourself could have joined the Galloglass at a much earlier age?"

"My father made me stay, and then the guilt spawned by my mother compelled me to look after her. Then, I was not there when she needed me the most."

"How did she die?"

"She was thrown down a well by the English when they raided our village."

The colour drained from the priest's face.

"Rest your axe on the ground, son, and brace yourself. I have a story to tell you that may give you some peace. My name is Father Patrick. I am old now, but in my younger years, I used to roam around Fermanagh as a priest, saying mass and doing priestly duties for some of the more remote villages. One such village I used to tend to was that of the O'Keenan Maguires. I used to speak to the chieftain there, Cathal O'Keenan Maguire, who I believe is your father. I used to visit him and take his confession and also the confessions of the villagers, who I believe are now dead. I know that what I have pieced together may violate the confessional, but if I tell you, their souls and yours will rest a little easier, no matter where they are."

# CHAPTER THIRTY-NINE

# BAD BLOOD

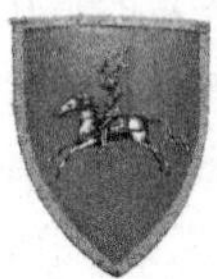

Eunan braced himself, for he thought he would hear as near to the truth as he ever would know. The priest blessed himself, looked to the heavens and asked for forgiveness. Eunan was confused as for what, and of whom, he was asking forgiveness. But he did not pursue it, for he felt the answer would be in the story. Father Patrick took a drink and began his tale.

"War came to the peaceful climes of Fermanagh as the MacMahons fled west to escape from the invading forces of the Crown. The Maguires of Lisnaskea were under pressure, so Cúchonnacht Maguire, the Prince of Fermanagh, sent his mercenary Galloglass into the county to protect his lands. One such battle of Galloglass arrived in the village of Cathal O'Keenan Maguire, and as chief of the village, he was expected to make them feel welcome and supply them with 'coign and livery' for as long as they remained there. Cathal thought he had to show that he shared the burden, so he invited one such Galloglass into his home.

"The Galloglass was as unwelcome a guest as a leech upon a cow's udder. This monster took every morsel of food, every drink of ale, every piece of cheese, drop of milk, every coin from the market. Time wore on, and war did not come. But famine did. No matter what the villagers could produce, the Galloglass took it. Cathal appealed first to the deaf ears of the Galloglass constable and then to the

Maguire, but they told him his sept had to do their duty to protect the county of the Maguire. So the Galloglass stayed.

"Winter came and campaigning season was a long way off. Cathal and his fellow villagers had to resort to hunting rabbits to feed everyone. Every evening, the men of the village would go off to hunt and leave most of the Galloglass behind, for they wanted to stay and drink. One evening Fiona, Cathal's wife, brought the Galloglass some ale, purchased with the last of their money. The Galloglass ordered his knave Finn to play his pipes, and the Galloglass began to drink and dance. Fiona looked worried, but encouraged her husband to leave. Cathal looked back, and his wife meekly smiled back at him. He closed the door.

"He was gone for several hours. It was quite a successful evening, and he caught three rabbits which would make a decent meal for himself and his wife if the Galloglass had drunk himself to sleep. The knave may be awake, but he would have to wait until morning to complain if he did not want to be subjected to his master's wrath if he woke him up.

"As Cathal approached the house, he noticed something odd. There was a small fire outside and silence inside. At this hour, the Galloglass would normally still be awake and making merry, and his poor wife would either be hiding or attempting to repair the destruction left in his wake. But there was silence. He opened the door. The house was a wreck. The stools were upturned, the kitchenware all over the floor, and the fire smouldered, neglected. The Galloglass lay slumped in a drunken heap beside the fire. He grunted and snored like the greedy devil he was. Cathal despised the Galloglass. It was the only time he thought that life might be better going over to the English than living under the oppression of this beast.

"Finn appeared, grinning as per usual. Cathal often imagined drowning this devil child in the lake if he was not otherwise thinking of more painful and imaginative ways of killing him. How could the Maguire put him through this? Cathal looked to the left, and the knave scurried behind his master. There was a heap of cloth on the floor. Fiona had never left the house like this. Where was she? He saw a foot poking out from beneath the cloth.

“Cathal ran over. The cloths were drenched in blood, and he could see the pale skin of a protruding arm and the top of Fiona’s head. Cathal gently unwrapped the cloths, taking particular care around the bloodstains. He picked up her battered body, and she groaned. Cathal pulled together the remains of her tattered clothes to cover up her private parts. She was bruised and battered on what parts of her body he could see through the blood. Cathal held her tightly in his arms and wept. She groaned in response, for everything hurt. The knave saw his chance and dashed to the door.

“‘You little beast!’ cried Cathal, reaching for his hunting knife. He cornered the boy before he could make it to the door. ‘I’m going to gut you like a rabbit for what you did!’

“‘Master, master!’ cried the boy, but the beast snored on.

“‘Come here, boy! You’re not going to get away!’ screamed Cathal, and he lunged at him.

“Cathal missed. The boy took his water bottle off his belt and threw it at the head of his master. His aim was true. His master awoke with a grunt and a string of curses. He was a red-haired giant, a foot taller than Cathal, and a veteran of many battles. He saw Cathal, knife drawn, and reached for his sword. His fingers met with thin air. He roared at his knave, who saw his chance and ran out the door. The Galloglass arose and searched for his weapons. Fiona groaned in the background. Cathal realised he was dead either way, for the knave would get help or the Galloglass would slice him in two and then watch his wife die as he stripped them bare of their last belongings. He was the representative of the Maguire. How could he die, murdered in this pit, by this beast, standing over the body of his raped wife?

“Cathal charged forward and swung at the Galloglass. He missed. The Galloglass punched him in the side of the head and Cathal fell into the fire. Cathal howled as he beat the flames from his sleeve. The Galloglass continued to look for his weapon. Cathal could hear a commotion outside. He could only assume that the knave had gone to fetch help. He could die at the hands of this beast or fight back and throw himself at the feet of the Maguire. Cathal lunged towards the Galloglass, who easily evaded him. The Galloglass found his sword underneath some assorted debris on the floor. He unsheathed it and advanced towards Cathal. Cathal swung his blade, but he had nowhere near the reach of the Galloglass. The Galloglass edged Cathal into a corner and raised his sword above his head to slice Cathal in two. Cathal raised his arm to protect his head.

"'Lord, save me!'

"'No lord will save you now!' bellowed the Galloglass, and the sword was extended fully behind his back and started its descent.

"Cathal's life dangled beneath the point of the sword. He heard a groan and saw his wife move. She scrambled amongst the debris on the floor to find something to save her husband. She raised herself to her knees with the last of her energy.

"Fuck you, beast!"

She plunged the Galloglass's own dagger through his calf until the tip showed through his shin. The Galloglass cried in agony and collapsed onto one knee. He dropped the sword. Cathal saw his chance. He ran and leapt upon the Galloglass and plunged his dagger into the Galloglass's heart. The Galloglass fell back but was not dead. He writhed around on the floor and grabbed Fiona's leg as she tried to crawl away. Fiona screamed. Cathal picked up the sword.

"'May this be the end of you, devil!' he cried. The Galloglass raised his head, and Cathal lopped it straight off.

"The front door came crashing down. Finn and the constable of the Galloglass came rushing in to see the Galloglass's head hit the floor. Finn raised his javelin to avenge his master, but it was knocked out of the way before it could connect.

"'No,' said the constable. 'I've got a better way. Take him.'

"Several other Galloglass entered the house and picked Cathal up by the arms and dragged him out. By now, everyone had heard the commotion. They came out of their houses to see Cathal being dragged through the streets. The Galloglass threw Cathal to the ground in the centre of the village. The fire torches of his neighbours and the Galloglass surrounded him. The constable stood beside the kneeling Cathal and put his sword to Cathal's throat. The constable was Seamus.

"'Your chieftain killed one of my men,' he said. 'Therefore, he must pay. However, he is the man in the village who represents our paymaster, the Maguire. Therefore, the village must pay. Along with the coin and keep owed to us for defending you from the English, the MacMahons and whatever cattle raiders may come along, we want twenty cattle in compensation for the death of my man.'

"'We don't have twenty cattle to spare!' cried a lone voice from the crowd.

"Cathal O'Keenan Maguire, the representative of the Maguire, will ensure we receive them, or we will take it out on the village. What this man didn't realise was that he killed my brother. Not my brother in arms, but my flesh and blood brother. Therefore, I will live with him instead, and he will supply me with the coign and livery owed to my brother, as well as the coign and livery due to a Galloglass constable!'

"Cathal almost fainted onto the tip of the sword.

"So Seamus moved into Cathal's house. Cathal became no better than an indentured servant to the whims of the constable. He became hated by the other villagers because the other Galloglass became more vicious in extracting their coign and livery from them to avenge their fallen comrade.

"As time passed, it became apparent that Fiona was with child, and from her reaction, it was probably not her husband's. Seamus showed his paternal feelings with the tip of his sword. He ensured Cathal fetch and carry for his wife while he shared his rations with her to protect the child. The villagers did not see what went on in the house and became jealous, for they saw his wife with child and how she prospered more than them.

"Suspicion grew about the relationship between the three when Seamus beat Cathal black and blue. Cathal would only leave the house covered in a cloak to hide his bruises. But rumours quickly spread that he had fed his wife the wrong type of herbs and left her very ill. She would have lost the child if Seamus had not caught him in time.

"Nine months elapsed, and the child was born and was fit and healthy despite of Cathal's efforts. Only Seamus wished to remember the birth of the child, but nobody celebrated, not even him. Still, Seamus cared enough to ensure that the child was nurtured and did not die after childbirth.

"At last, war came to the country, and the Galloglass were called upon to fight. Even though war could mean famine, death and destruction, the villagers were inwardly delighted, for it meant that the Galloglass would be leaving. However, Seamus delayed their departure until he knew the baby would survive.

"Seamus packed his things and stood before a silent Fiona, Cathal and Eunan, the baby.

"'I will return. I expect to see that baby alive and well and if I do not, I will slice the both of you in two.'

"Cathal did not react. He had become accustomed to ignoring threats and avoiding punishment over the past couple of years. Seamus instructed his knave to pick up his bags.

"'Remember my words,' and with that, he was gone.

"Fiona turned to her husband and cried on his shoulder. That evening, they stared at the crib of the child of the dead Galloglass. They looked at each other and discussed how they could raise such a child. Surely a boy born of such circumstances could only bring bad luck to them and the village. They remembered an old Irish folk tale of fairies taking away children and bringing them to a better place, swapping them for a fairy child instead. The fairy child surely could be no worse than the Galloglass child. Or even better, no child at all. They decided it was worth the risk.

"They took the baby from the crib and wrapped him warmly, for they did not want the child to die before the fairies took him. Cathal left the house first and signalled for his wife to follow when he knew it was safe. They set out for the woods beside the lake, thinking the moonlight reflecting on the water would attract the fairies. They followed the winding path until they found an old tree, shaped a little like a cradle. Fiona placed the child there and wept. The baby joined in with his mother. Cathal and Fiona turned to leave.

"'Sorry, no changeling for you!'

"Before them stood Seamus and his men, the knave grinning from behind him. He must have tipped them off.

"'Fiona, pick up the baby and bring him back to the village. Men, grab him!' The Galloglass took hold of Cathal.

"Cathal was dragged in front of a circle of his neighbours yet again. The tip of Seamus's sword touched his forehead while he knelt before the villagers.

"'Not only has this wretch killed one of my men, but he also tried to kill his own baby!' roared Seamus.

"The crowd made its anger known.

"'Should I kill this man, who has the protection of the Maguire and risk the wrath of the county coming down upon us all? Or should I show mercy?'

"The crowd was silent.

"'Since you cannot decide, I declare myself the protector of the child! Once the war is over, I will return for him. If I return and the child is dead, my Galloglass will level the village, no matter the wrath of the Maguire. And if this man and his wife have looked after the child and he is fit and well, I will absolve you all, he included, of your debt. So decide what you wish to do. Do you wish this man to declare the child as naturally his, or for me to exact revenge for his heinous crimes?'

"The crowd was again silent, but not for long. Cries of 'save the child!' soon rang out around the circle.

"'I take it you have made your decision. Cathal O'Keenan Maguire, do you swear this child is your flesh and blood and you will look after him always, and upon my return, he will be fit and healthy?'

"Cathal looked to his wife, who nodded back to him.

"'I will take the child as my son.'

"'And?'

"'And look after it if it were my own. Until he comes of age.'

"'Then get off your knees, feed and put the child to bed, and let us never speak of this again.'

"Cathal got up and went to his wife and put his arm around her shoulders. They walked to their house. The crowd dispersed.

"Later, Seamus knocked on Cathal's door.

"'I meant what I said.' With that, Seamus turned and departed for the war."

# CHAPTER FORTY

# SINKING IN

Father Patrick took another drink. Eunan's shoulders slumped as he stared into the fire. Father Patrick dared not go on until he could assess Eunan's state of mind. He looked to the heavens once more for inspiration.

"Is your story finished?" said Eunan finally.

"Sadly not. We must bring it up to the present day." Father Patrick paused once more for water.

"The story then moves to the time of your youth, and when I first became aware of you and your story.

"Seamus and his band of renegade Galloglass had hidden out in the woods. They had been in the pay of the MacMahons but had abandoned them when the money ran out. Seamus said he had planted a seed in Fermanagh, and that it should be ripe for the picking now. He promised them riches as long as his special child was still alive. Seamus sent some of his men to the village as traders with the last of his cattle to seek Cathal O'Keenan Maguire and to see what had happened to his child. One of the men was Finn, because he would recognise Cathal O'Keenan Maguire, but Cathal would not recognise him since Finn was no longer a boy. When they arrived in the village, they saw no child, only you.

"Seamus was ecstatic. But Finn was consumed with a jealous rage. He sent a message to the English sheriff in Monaghan to tell him that the cattle raiders who had ransacked Monaghan were from the village of Cathal O'Keenan Maguire. The English sheriff sent his captain to retrieve his goods. The captain, a Captain Willis so I am told, killed Cathal O'Keenan Maguire for resisting him and then searched the village to retrieve the supposed stolen cattle and also for valuables to compensate them for the inconvenience. They heard that Maguire warriors were on their way, so they fled. They killed your uncle and anyone else they could find.

"Seamus and his men had been hiding in the woods, watching all of this happen. Seamus ordered his men to attack the English and rescue you. However, the anger in Finn could not be contained, and Seamus's men were starving and could not be controlled. They ransacked the village and stole what they could. Finn found your mother on the floor of your house, as she had fallen out of her chair. He dragged her to the well and cast her down in revenge for his master's murder. Then they followed you until you reached the woods, where they ambushed you."

"How do you know all this?" asked Eunan.

"I was their priest."

The English had been busy while Eunan searched for a quiet spot to hear the tale. They had dug trenches and laid siege to the town. The English cannonballs began striking the walls just as the priest finished telling his story. Eunan sat in silence, clutching one of his throwing axes to his chest, contemplating the priest's story. He finally spoke.

"Why are you telling me this, priest, when my heart is so low, and my axe is a tool of my rage?"

"I thought you needed to know."

"So who is Finn? Is he the horse boy of the Galloglass that raped my mother?"

"Thou should not kill in anger," pleaded the priest.

"Answer me straight, priest. Is he the horse boy, the knave?"

The priest clasped his hands in prayer. "If I tell you, you will promise not to kill me?"

Eunan gave him an icy stare but reluctantly agreed.

"That he is. But he is much more than that!"

"What else is he?"

The priest bowed his head and prayed for the strength to be honest and face Eunan.

"Your father, your real father, was a disgrace to his family, the Galloglass, and all he served with. But he was the only family Seamus had, so he made excuses for him and defended him. You were not the first bastard he fathered by forcing himself on his hostess, but Finn is the only one I know by name."

Eunan took a step back and went completely white. "I have a brother?"

"You do, but he is like charcoal in that he absorbed every undesirable trait of his father. At first Seamus indulged him, but with every evil deed he committed, Seamus doubted himself. When Finn killed your mother, Seamus did not punish him. Rather, he reiterated his promise never to let him become a Galloglass and left it at that."

Eunan froze as all the different elements of the story whirled around his brain and he tried to make sense of them. He could not reconcile what Finn had done, who he was, and why Seamus indulged and enabled him. But anger was the spark, and he sprang back to life. He stood up and grasped the shaft of his axe.

"Is that it? Seamus should have strung him up for the cowardice of killing a cripple. But you are a priest. How did you let this happen? Surely you should have stopped this?"

"How? I am but one old man against twenty and one Galloglass. I can only tell them of their sins and hope to steer them towards the virtuous path."

Eunan swept his arms in the air as if possessed, grasping for words or a way out of this tangled mess. His tongue returned.

"Excommunicate them, curse them, banish them, I don't know! What would God have you do? How could you let this happen to me? How could God have let this happen to me? I am a good man, yet bad blood burns through my insides. How could you let this happen!?" Eunan gripped the axe handle with both hands.

The priest got up and backed away.

"Now look here, Eunan, I was only trying to help-."

"Help! How much worse could you have made this?"

"We both may die when the English attack. You wouldn't want the blood of a dead priest on your soul when you try to get into heaven, would you?"

"Some priest you are! God would be grateful if I got rid of you!"

Eunan had him cornered against the wall. Dust fell from the ceiling as the English cannonballs pounded.

"Answer me one thing, and remember, you are a priest. How do you know so much about my mother's death? Where were you at the time?"

"I know I'm a weak man. I should have done better and stood up to Seamus, but I was afraid. He would not care about a priest's blood on his conscience, but I know you are better than him."

The priest fell to his knees.

"Please have mercy on me! I am weak! I failed you. I failed your mother. I failed your village. But I can pray for them. I can! I can pray that their souls get to heaven!"

"Don't be a coward all your life! Tell me the truth. Where were you when my mother died?"

"I was there! I was there! Forgive me! I pleaded with Finn to have mercy, but he would not listen, and I was powerless to do anything! Have mercy on me!" The priest wept and clawed at the bottom of Eunan's chain mail shirt.

The bad blood seared in his veins.

"It's God that deals in mercy. I deal in death!"

Eunan lifted his axe to sweep the priest's head clean off. He closed his eyes to pray for the departing soul. But to his surprise, came a vision of his mother. She could walk, and she smiled sweetly at him as she had never smiled at him before. There were no comments, no judgement – just a sweet smile.

"Please!" the priest croaked, and the image was gone.

Eunan swung his axe. But it was not like any axe swing he had experienced before. He swung, and an English cannonball disintegrated the wall and flying stone and fragments knocked him off his feet, and he fell and bashed his head on the ground.

Some hours later, Connor O'Cassidy rowed silently along the river under a dark and cloudy night sky. It would be several hours before he reached Devenish Island but he had to row with the greatest of stealth, such was the importance of his mission. However, the clouds abandoned him and the moon betrayed him. He found himself alone on the moon-illuminated waves of the River Erne. He heard shouts. He rowed faster. The noise of men grew louder. The moon hid the shame of its betrayal behind a cloud. Connor O'Cassidy heard the cacophony of oars lapping up the water coming towards him. Once more, he could barely see into the night. He must dispose of the letter quickly. He put his hand in his shirt to retrieve it. A boat crashed into him and knocked him off his seat. He tried to pull himself up, only to find a dagger in front of his face. A heavy object to the back of his head knocked him out.

Eunan woke with water spilling on his face. He spat out the water, liquefied dust, and fragments of rock that had gathered in his mouth and sat up to brush himself down.

"Are you all right?" said a voice.

"The priest, the priest!" Eunan clawed through the rubble. "There was a priest here, too. I don't see any blood. Is he buried under the rubble?"

"There was nobody in this room but you," said the man. "Maybe you were about to die, and a priest came before you got to heaven to take you back? You are here now, and we need all the soldiers we can get to fight off the English assault. Clean yourself up and get out on the ramparts. Come on, we need everyone fit to fight!"

Eunan stood up and made sure he was all right. He could feel blood on his face, but he could stand. He splashed some water from the bucket on his face and ran out to fight.

A bucket of water ensured that Connor O'Cassidy had a rude awakening. Sneering faces, bad breath, and broken teeth surrounded him.

"I am so glad you are awake now," came a distant, educated voice. "Thanks for the letter, by the way."

The faces moved to either side, and Connor saw an English officer sitting behind a small field operations table. Connor's mouth fell open.

"Sweet Jesus."

Captain Dowdall had the letter to the Maguire in his hand.

"I don't want to execute you for being a rebel, but you need to prove to me your loyalty to Queen and country."

Connor scowled. "Kill me now! I'll never talk!"

"Please! Don't be so dramatic. How about if you help us take the castle? We'll make you a knight of the realm and grant you some of this land you seem to love so much?"

"Kill me now! I'll never turn on the Maguire! Never!"

"I'm a great believer in redemption and by the time my boys finish with you, you'll love the Queen, gladly become a knight and relish in delivering Enniskillen castle to us. Gentlemen, roast his feet on the fire and do whatever it takes for him to be pliant and co-operative. There's no rush. I'll be in my tent when you are ready."

The sneers, bad breath, and broken teeth overwhelmed Connor O'Cassidy Maguire.

# CHAPTER FORTY-ONE

# THE TOWER

The bombardment of the castle continued for eight days. Every soldier was needed to man the ramparts, and every corner of the castle was taken by either civilians seeking shelter or wounded soldiers seeking solace. The castle was small, and Eunan soon saw the priest, but the priest saw him first and ran and hid or loitered near the wall Seamus guarded. Eunan saw Finn on the ramparts, and the way Finn looked at him told him that Finn knew he knew. He stood with Aonghas O'Braoin's men on his section of the wall and looked impossible to prise away. The priest must have escaped and warned both Finn and Seamus that Eunan knew. Eunan saw Seamus, but Seamus was far too involved in the defence of the castle to have time for Eunan's issues. The defenders were a rapidly diminishing force as the English bombarded the castle from both the main island and across the River Erne. The cannons battered the walls, it seemed, without pause. Musket fire swept the ramparts. Surely it was only a matter of time until the castle fell.

On the ninth day at dawn, a shout came from the top of the tower.

"Ships are coming! Ships are coming from the south!"

Eunan was in the main building and scrambled up the stairs to the roof to see for himself. To the south were three large riverboats.

"Who are they?" he asked the watchman.

"They are the ships of the Lisnaskea Maguires."

"Are they here to relieve us?"

"I don't know. Wait!"

Aonghas had the perfect view of the river from the south. He grinned and slapped Finn on the back.

"Those fools must be delirious from lack of food if they think Connor Roe is here to save them. This is the time for you to earn yourself the title of Galloglass. Stay here on the ramparts and make sure Eunan and Seamus can see you. If I can make sure Connor Roe can penetrate the castle before they can get to you, then only their blood will be spilt and you will have truly earned the title of Galloglass. I have every faith in you, boy."

Aonghas placed his hand on Finn's shoulder and looked him in the eye. Finn went pale and shrank before him.

"I'll put that down to starvation," said Aonghas as he pinched Finn's cheek. "Do your job and you'll have everything you wished for and more."

Aonghas grinned as he released Finn's face and half his men peeled off to follow him and half stayed with Finn.

"Ships to the north!" cried the north-facing watchman.

"Whose side are they on? Are they the Maguire ships from the lakes?" said Dáithí MacCabe.

"They certainly bear the same design," said the watchman.

Hope rose within the castle. However, Eunan observed the musketeers and artillery of the besieging army on the surrounding lands ready themselves. He went to speak to Dáithí MacCabe, who stood on the northern ramparts near Seamus.

"What are the ships going to do?" said Eunan. "Are they going to land above the English, and we sally forth and join them?"

Dáithí stared out over the river and drummed his fingers on the top of the wall. "It's too early to say."

The ships drew ever nearer. More and more of the defenders lined the walls facing the River Erne to look out and see what they would do. The English guns remained silent. Eunan looked south, for those boats were closing faster.

"Come on, Connor Roe Maguire, come through for your clan," said Eunan through gritted teeth as the ships came within five hundred yards. "I'll forgive you for everything if you don't let us down now."

The castle had no cannon, for only the Spanish survivors of the Great Armada knew how to use them, and no northern lord had any. What few muskets they had were all with Hugh Maguire and the main army. So the defenders could only wait.

Four hundred yards, three hundred yards...

"Do we fire on them?" shouted Eunan at the castle commander, who had joined them on the roof.

"No! They may be friendly. Wait until they make their declaration!"

Two hundred yards...

On the largest of the boats approaching from the north, Captain Dowdall readied his men for the assault. Connor O'Cassidy was reduced to using crutches, for both feet were heavily bandaged to help them heal from the burns. He had taken much persuasion, but that was of little solace to him now. He dared not look at the castle, but set his gaze on the empty shore on the opposite side of the river. Captain Dowdall approached him.

"It's a beautiful countryside, isn't it? You can have your pick if the walls prove as vulnerable, where we are going, as you claim they are. Or else you will be the entertainment for the men back in the camp tonight as they contemplate their defeat."

"I am true to my word, Captain," Connor said.

"I hope, for your sake, you are. Or at least truer to me than you were to your former comrades."

However, Seamus was not so naive as his fellow defenders. He had been in many a siege and a long day would pass before you could play a trick he had not seen. He grabbed one of the MacCabes, who he knew was a longstanding guard at the castle.

"Where's the secret door to the river?"

The guard looked nonplussed.

"The door or my axe," said Seamus as he pointed his axe at the man's head.

The man shuddered and pointed. "This way."

The men in the castle watched as the boats to the south lifted massive wall-scaling ladders from their decks.

"It's the English! It's the English! Fire on the boats, fire on the..."

The besieging English land army opened with a volley of fire from their cannons, and the musketeers tried to pick off individual men from the ramparts. The boats from the north raised ladders from their decks. A volley of musket fire came from the ships as they closed to a hundred yards. Men fell from the wall and the tower to their deaths in the river. The boats crashed their sides into the walls of the castle. The men threw up hooks that settled and bit into the inner face of the ramparts. They rested their ladders on the top of the walls and came pouring in. Captain Dowdall's ship moored beside a weakened, undefended wall. He looked back at Connor and grinned.

"Arise, Sir Connor O'Cassidy!" he saluted, and he joined his men in scaling the walls.

Connor O'Cassidy could only stare down over the side and into the river on the other side of the boat. He saw his gaunt white face and the ghosts of the comrades he had condemned to die that day and he threw up all that his empty stomach would allow.

Seamus and his men rushed to the door under the wall beside the tower that bordered the river. The door was undefended, and he could hear the pounding of axes from the other side.

"We must fill up this doorway or we're all dead men," said Seamus. "Get every brick and boulder you can and build a wall."

"I wouldn't bother with all that," came a voice from behind. "You're a dead man anyway, Seamus MacSheehy."

Seamus turned to see Aonghas O'Braoin and his men standing behind him with their axes at the ready. Seamus was outnumbered two to one.

"If you bury us here, you also bury yourselves and the Maguire," said Seamus. "Are you sure you want to do that?"

Aonghas grinned.

"You and the Maguire can rot here for all I care, for I'll be dining at the table with the victors. Cut them to pieces men, and leave Seamus to me!"

Seamus readied his axe as the door to the river shook under an avalanche of axe blows from the other side.

Eunan stood on the ramparts with Dáithí and several Galloglass as a myriad of ladders thudded against the castle walls. He ran to push the top of the nearest ladder back to where it came from, but it was already weighed down by assaulters climbing its rungs. Eunan prepared to swing his axe, but a voice came from what seemed like the distance.

"Abandon the walls!"

Eunan looked around to see if the voice carried authority but saw the English soldiers had already swarmed the wall and cast aside what token resistance had been offered. His escape was cut off. He had no wish to die alone on the wall, so he threw himself down to the courtyard and landed with great strain on his ankles, but he was still alive. He joined the stream of defenders running towards the tower.

Seamus parried the blows from Aonghas, but Aonghas's men descended like wolves on the rest of Seamus's companions. One by one, they fell as they were surrounded and showered with blows from front, sides, and rear. Seamus was forced closer and closer to the door to the river, but the besiegers could not batter it down. Seamus edged away from the door so his back was against the wall.

"You need to decide, Aonghas. What is it to be? You won't take me before help arrives and you die, or you can open the door for your master? What is it to be?"

Aonghas sneered. "You are too arrogant to see you die either way. Cover me, men."

Aonghas ran to the door to unlock it. Seamus scythed the air with his axe to create space as Aonghas's men lunged at him. The door opened and the English soldiers piled in. Amongst the chaos, Seamus gripped a rope from the ramparts above. He wished for luck as to what contents it would bring. Luck came down as a shower of brown liquid of a hellish odour intended for the aggressors outside the castle walls but fell just as comfortably on the usurpers within. Seamus ducked and dodged his way past Aonghas's men and ran for the door of the tower.

Eunan found himself on the stairs behind the entrance door. He was the last man, and he watched as the horde of attackers swarmed over the walls and the gate.

"Close the door! Close the door!" came a voice from upstairs. "Our men are all inside."

Eunan placed his shoulder behind the door and pushed. An axe from the outside slammed into the rapidly closing gap.

"Eunan! It's me! Let bygones be bygones and let me in. You need all the men you can get."

Eunan looked around the door to see the pleading face of Aonghas O'Braoin.

"Let us die together as heroes of the Maguire," said Eunan. He nodded, and Aonghas grinned as he and three of his men ran in. Eunan closed the door and placed the huge wooden beam in its brackets.

"No one will get past that," he said to Aonghas.

Aonghas smiled back at him. "Why don't you leave the door to us? I see Finn is upstairs. Why don't you rest a moment and see how your friend is?"

All Eunan heard was the name 'Finn' He ran up the stairs, axe at the ready.

## CHAPTER FORTY-TWO

# THE LAST STAND

Seamus stood on top of the tower with Dáithí MacCabe, surveying the assault on the castle. The boats had all landed now and English soldiers and their allies swarmed through the gates. There was no sign of any relief army coming to save them.

"I'm not as familiar with the castle as you," said Seamus. "Is there an escape tunnel in the basement?"

Dáithí turned to him. All hope had drained from his face.

"Alas, one of the downsides of building a castle on an island is that you can't tunnel beneath the river."

Seamus slammed his fist on the castle wall.

"Any secret door or other means of escape?"

"The English used the secret door to gain entrance to the castle," said Dáithí.

"So what is the Maguire supposed to do if he is besieged here, besides surrender?"

"Die in glory and have a tapestry made of it." Dáithí stared out onto the river.

"Well, nobody is going to make a tapestry of me," said Seamus. "Can we jump into the river?"

Dáithí smiled and shook his head. "You'd have to jump out far enough to avoid the rocks below and hope you find somewhere deep enough to absorb your fall. If you jumped in armour, you're a dead man. Then you'd have to avoid all the English river boats. You'd be better off dying in the castle with your axe in your hand."

Seamus stood up straight and readied his axe.

"Then I had better prepare myself for my glorious but anonymous death."

Eunan stood in the doorway of the Maguire's great hall. Its greatness had been removed for safekeeping to Devenish Island, where the Maguire hid while his castle fell. Within the bare walls of the hall now stripped of its tapestries, anger had similarly stripped Eunan of all sense and he prowled the hall amongst the wounded defenders looking for Finn.

"There are no traitors here, only the soon to be dead," said one man who leaned up from his resting place, curious to find out what had possessed Eunan.

"Where is Finn?" hissed Eunan as he looked around the room. "I was told he was here."

"I am behind you, brother, walking in your shadow as always," said Finn.

Eunan turned and saw Finn standing in the doorway, dagger in hand. Eunan hunched over his axe, ready to pounce.

"You've been a coward all your life, too afraid to reveal yourself to me," said Eunan. "What was wrong? Too ashamed of your father?"

Finn grinned.

"I lived under your shadow and Seamus's thumb for far too long. Seamus showed all his devotion to you and saved all his scorn for me. As he tried to advance you in the Maguire clan, I was reduced to being your horse boy. But I got some revenge when I attacked you as a boy in Enniskillen, when I killed your mother for her part in killing our father, when I murdered your wife when she should have been mine, as I am the elder son. But now I shall have my revenge as I have taken up with Aonghas O'Braoin and he will open the door below to the

English and they will slaughter you all and I will be granted your family's lands. I may even make a shrine at the well where I drowned your mother."

The tears blinded Eunan as he put his head down and charged.

Seamus descended the stairs slowly and deliberately. With each solemn step he went over every fight where he considered himself in a tight spot and went over what he did to get out of it. He considered this the tightest spot of all. He saw the back of Finn standing in the doorway of the great hall with his dagger in his hand. Seamus winced, for he could not summon up the courage to strike him down where he stood even though it would be some redemption for all the evil he let Finn get away with in his time on earth. He saw Eunan charge towards Finn, and he knew who he hoped the victor would be. But then he heard the voice of Aonghas in the stairwell and rushed down the stairs towards it.

Aonghas lifted the heavy beam of wood off the brackets of the door and cast it aside.

"Come in, my comrades," he cried out to those on the other side of the door. "Be careful for the first Galloglass you will meet in the stairwell are your friends who let you in."

The English soldiers first thrust their swords through the gap and, not meeting any resistance, put their heads around the door. Aonghas looked up the stairwell to see Seamus grimace at the top of it. He gave his broadest victory grin and ascended the stairs at the head of his men and the English soldiers.

No soldierly swing of the axe for Eunan. His anger would only be satisfied by pummelling Finn to death with his bare fists. He charged at Finn and tackled him to the ground. They wrestled momentarily until Eunan punched Finn clean in the cheek with an unrestricted blow. The knife flew from Finn's hand but he punched Eunan in the ribs, causing him to wince and weaken his grip. Finn threw Eunan off and ran for the door. Eunan reached for his belt and threw one of his trusty throwing axes at Finn's head. But the trust was misplaced, and the axe ricocheted off the wall and fell harmlessly into the corridor.

Seamus braced himself for his last stand at the top of the stairs. A few men had joined him, mainly the wounded who could stand, and those that had risen with difficulty from the floor of the once great hall and supported themselves on the stairwell walls. Aonghas and his men rapidly ascended the stairs, followed by a porcupine of swords, axes, and the odd unloaded gun belonging to his English allies. A throwing axe fell at Seamus's feet. He picked it up and looked at the blade, and then at Aonghas.

"Aonghas O'Braoin," Seamus said. "You have no honour and are no Galloglass. Therefore, I deny you the honourable death of a Galloglass."

Aonghas sneered and laughed. Seamus aimed the axe straight at him, and the axe lodged itself in Aonghas's forehead. He fell back to be trampled underfoot by the soldiers climbing the stairs.

Seamus placed his hands on the shoulders of two of the injured men who stood at the top of the stairs with only swords to defend themselves.

"For those wounded men who are about to die, I salute you. But I for one, am going to escape, for there is no glory if there is no one to tell your story."

He turned to leave but collided with Finn trying to make his escape. Finn fell to the ground and edged away. Seamus reached down and grabbed him.

"You said I would never make you a Galloglass, but I make you one now. You can replace Aonghas O'Braoin. Now go to your men and lead them."

Seamus pushed Finn down the stairs and into the bristles of the human porcupine. Most were now soldiers who knew nothing of Aonghas's treachery.

"Take that, you rebel scum!" came the cry.

Finn was sliced up and then trampled to the ground as the soldiers advanced up the stairs to take the rest of the castle.

Eunan emerged from the no-longer-so-great hall wild-eyed, like a bundle of nascent energy hell-bent on completing his revenge. He searched frantically for Finn, but he was gone. He saw the wounded soldiers and the thirst for revenge in his eye subsided and he dutifully picked up an axe and went to join the men blocking the stairwell. Seamus had moved out of sight and into the stairwell that led to the roof. He saw Eunan was about to be consumed by duty and the English blades.

"DO YOU WANT TO KNOW WHAT HAPPENED TO YOUR FUCKING MOTHER?"

The fury was back, and Eunan turned and pursued Seamus up the stairwell.

He reached the roof in time to see Seamus on the other side by the river, stripping off his chain mail. Eunan paused, for he was confused. He expected Seamus to be waiting for him, axe in hand, ready to fight, but not this.

"Take off your armour and anything heavy," said Seamus. "Our only way out is via the river."

Eunan froze to process what he was witnessing. Seamus extended his arms to reason with Eunan.

"You only have a few seconds to decide. We can stand here and argue about the past or jump and hopefully live. Which is it to be?"

Eunan stood swaying backwards and forwards. Before him stood the man who let his mother die. The commander in the field is always responsible for the actions of his men. If Seamus had not killed his mother with his own hand, he had facilitated Finn to do it and let the deed go unpunished.

Seamus saw the anger boil in Eunan's eyes.

"Can we not resolve this later? Now is the chance for us to live. I would rather die at the hands of my enemies than the axe blade of my relative."

The recognition that he was a relative of Seamus's only stirred the ire in Eunan.

"The vengeance of my parents comes before any petty fight over who controls a field of cows."

"This is going nowhere," said Seamus. "So, which parents are these? The ones who got herbs to kill you before you were born and tried to leave you in the woods to get eaten by wild dogs? What would be a suitable vengeance for them?"

"Feeding you to the fishes!" Eunan raised his axe and charged at Seamus. Seamus parried the blow with relative ease.

"Why would I want to kill my brother's child when I have spent so much of my time and energy keeping you alive? Are you not a chieftain? Have you not come from nothing to being a friend of the O'Donnells and possibly the next Maguire, and now you want to kill me for two people who resented and hated you?"

Eunan turned and charged, and Seamus parried again.

"You're far too angry to fight. I could easily kill you, but I don't want to. Let us try to escape!"

Eunan plunged his axe downwards, but Seamus blocked it.

"You killed my mother. You threw her down a well! How could you be so heartless?"

Seamus threw him back.

"Finn killed her, and now Finn is dead. I may have indulged him in the past but these repentant hands pushed him to his death. But if you heard the story correctly from that cowardly priest, how can you be such a sentimental fool for someone who tried to kill you as a baby? I'm the only reason she brought you up. When your father died, who was going to become chieftain? You? You're a bastard. Who was going to cry from the roofs that you're a bastard? Your mother. Then you would never become a chieftain."

Eunan stood back and shook with anger.

"I never wanted my mother to die! I never wanted to become chieftain!"

"Then you are a fool!"

Seamus swung his axe at Eunan and forced him on the defensive.

"Why do I have to waste my time on you? The castle is about to fall. If I have to kill you to survive, I will!"

Seamus swung his axe and drew blood as he shaved Eunan's cheek.

"Give up while you still live!"

"Not while you breathe!" Eunan swung his axe and grazed Seamus's arm.

"Be careful, Eunan. You may be blood—"

"Bad blood!"

"But you are not a chieftain anymore."

"I am still the O'Keenan Maguire!"

"A chieftain with no lands and no people."

Eunan landed a blow. Seamus stood back and felt the breach through his shirt. He sucked the blood off his fingers.

The commotion downstairs was getting louder. He knew he did not have long.

"This is your last chance. Do you want to live or die?"

Eunan charged at him again, and Seamus parried the blow.

"I'll take that as die!"

Seamus swung his axe down on Eunan, which he blocked. Seamus forced his axe downwards, and Eunan's energy slowly crumbled. They were locked together, axe to axe, with their faces almost pressed one against the other. Seamus could feel Eunan weakening.

"You were always like a son to me!" With that, Seamus gave a last heave to force Eunan's axe shaft down. Seamus thrust his forehead over the axe shafts and crashed it down into Eunan's face. His nose disintegrated into a mass of blood and bone. Seamus could feel Eunan's axe fall, and butted him again, as hard as he could on the forehead. Eunan collapsed, out cold.

"Sorry!"

Seamus heard the sound of fighting getting nearer. He lifted Eunan up and stripped him of his chain mail. Then he picked up the unconscious body and walked to the ramparts. Once he had a clear shot, he lifted Eunan's body as high as he could and cast him towards the river. Eunan crashed into the water near one of the assault boats. The boats were attracted to the splash, so Seamus knew he would have to wait before he dived himself.

Seamus collapsed, for his energy was spent. The sound of footsteps on the stairs made him reach for his axe. He stood up.

"For my brother, father, forefathers, and all MacSheehy Galloglass. May the last of you not die this day."

The men reached the top of the stairs and stopped. They halted at the sight of Seamus, the last defender at the last point of sanctuary in the castle. The men all looked like beasts with their frenzied eyes, blood-spattered shirts and weapons that celebrated the crushing of the castle defences by dripping blood onto the hands of their masters.

"Well, come on then!" shouted Seamus.

A masked figure forced his way to the front and stood, axe ready.

"Hello, Seamus!" came a familiar voice from beneath the mask.

"Let it be quick," said Seamus to himself, and he raised his axe to go down fighting.

# About Author

If you enjoyed this book please would you leave a review on the retailer where you bought it.

Join C R Dempsey's mailing list for monthly updates, offers and insights.

*QR code for the C R Dempsey newsletter mailing list.*

C R Dempsey is the author of 'Bad Blood', 'Uprising', Traitor Maguire', and 'Breach of the peace', four historical fiction books set in Elizabethan Ireland. He has plans for many more, and he needs to find the time to write them. History has always been his fascination, and historical fiction was an obvious outlet for his accumulated knowledge. C R spends lots of time working on his books, mainly in the twilight hours of the morning. C R wishes he spent more time writing and less time jumping down the rabbit hole of excessive research.

C R Dempsey lives in London with his wife and cat. He was born in Dublin but has lived most of his adult life in London.

C R can be found at:

https://www.crdempseybooks.com/,

https://www.facebook.com/crdempsey,

https://www.instagram.com/crdempsey/,
Twitter: @dempsey_cr

# ACKNOWLEDGMENTS

Thank you to all my family and friends and all of those who helped to create this book.

Special thanks to Mena (endless patience and support), Eoin (advice and inspiration)

Thank you also for the professional support of:

Book cover: Dominic Forbes

Editing: Josie Humber, Robin Seavill

Both these individuals can be found on www.Reedsey.com

# BAD BLOOD TIMELINE

While 'Bad Blood' is a fictional novel it is based around historical events. Below is a summary of the main historical events in Ireland over the time period covered in Bad Blood. It is compiled from several sources and some of the exact timing of events are unknown. Therefore, some events are not dated and are placed where they logically or probably appear in the timeline.

1569

The Queen's county of Fermanagh formed

1570

Enterprise of Ulster. This was an attempt by the crown to counter resistance in Ulster by granting land to English entrepreneurs and settlers.

1584

East Breifne (County Cavan) indentured (traditional home of the O'Reilly clan).

October – three lieutenants were created for Ulster: Sir Henry Bagenal (Tyrone), Hugh O'Neill (Fermanagh), and Turlough O'Neil (Coleraine)

Sir John Perrot made Lord Deputy of Ireland

1585

Oriel (County Monaghan) shired.

May - Connor Roe Maguire knighted

Composition of Connacht. This was a form of surrender and regrant where the Gaelic lords of Connacht agreed to set tax payments to the crown in exchange for hereditary English titles.

Summer - the parliament of 1585 gave Hugh O'Neill title of Earl of Tyrone

Mac Shanes gathering power. Hugh O'Neill took control of central Tyrone which was indentured from Turlough O'Neill for seven years.

Turlough O'Neill retained overlordship of Maguire and MacCann

Harsh winter. Many cattle died. This made baring the soldiers all the harder.

Hugh O'Neill bargains down the number of troops in Ulster to 550

Maguire, O'Donnell and O'Cahan eject troops

Composition of Connacht collapses

1586

Maguire surrenders to the crown and pays 500 cows - 200 stolen by Lord Deputy John Perrott

O'Donnell agrees to high rent of 700 cattle (plus 700 cattle fine) to be free of troops

1587

Red Hugh O'Donnell engaged to Rosie O'Neill, Hugh O'Neill's daughter

Hugh O'Neill secures Tyrone

O'Neill settlement - Maguire remains under Turlough

Sir Ross MacMahon (subservient to Hugh O'Neill) accepted surrender and regrant without O'Neill's permission, so does Sir Oghy O'Hanlon. They are invaded by Sir Henry Bagenal and forced to take a sheriff.

September - Hugh Roe O'Donnell imprisoned in Dublin castle. Tirconnell breaks down into several warring factions

Hugh Maguire joined up with Art O'Neill (Turlough O Neill's son) to attack Scots invading County Down. Maguire then turned on O'Neill on their way back towards Fermanagh

1588

January - MacMahon back in control of Hugh O'Neill. Maguire under pressure from MacMahon and Donnell O'Donnell

April - Hugh O'Neill defeated by Turlough and Hugh O'Gallagher (leading an O'Donnell faction) at Carricklea

April - Maguire lost to Hugh O'Neill and then regained by Turlough O'Neill

Sir John Perrot removed as Lord Deputy of Ireland to be replaced by William FitzWilliam

July/August - Spanish Armada off the coast of Ireland

Maguire in league with the O'Rourkes and Burkes to retrieve and hide Spanish survivors from the Armada

Hugh O'Neill massacres Spanish prisoners at Inishowen

October - Turlough O'Neill hires English mercenaries. Captain Mostian's company reasserted Turlough O'Neill's control over Maguire

Late 1588 early 1589 - Maguire goes back to Hugh O'Neill

1589

Hugh Maguire Inaugurated by Donnell O'Donnell in Sciath Garbha and receives military aid from him

Turlough O'Neill enters an alliance with the MacShanes

Red Hugh O'Donnell kidnapped

Sir Ross MacMahon dies - the succession of the MacMahons begins. Brian MacHugh Og MacMahon made himself chieftain. Lord Deputy Fitzwilliam and Hugh O'Neill tried to impose Hugh Roe MacMahon but were defeated by Brian Og. Brian Og potentially bribed Fitzwilliam. Hugh Roe MacMahon imprisoned, put on trial and executed.

1590

Spring – West Breifne (county Leitrim) led by Sir Brian O'Rourke invaded

Hugh Gavelach MacShane captured by the Maguires and ransomed to Hugh O'Neill and then executed. Hugh O'Neill held under house arrest for most of 1590 and put on trial for the murder

3rd September - Donnell O'Donnell defeated and killed by Ineen Dubh at Doire Leathan. Tirconnell falls into chaos

Sir Henry Bagenal made chief commissioner for Ulster and Marshall of the Irish army

September - Captain Willis arrives in Tirconnell

1591

Minor wars of succession continue for both the O'Neills and O'Donnells

February – Brian O'Rourke arrived in Scotland

April - Brian O'Rourke handed over to the English by the Scottish King

October - Brian O'Rourke hung as a traitor in London

1592

January - Red Hugh O'Donnell escaped from Dublin prison

February – Red Hugh O'Donnell drives Captain Humphrey Willis out of Donegal

April - Inauguration of Red Hugh O'Donnell in Kilmacrenan. Hugh McManus O'Donnell stands aside

May/June - Red Hugh O'Donnell attacks Turlough O'Neill

June - Red Hugh O'Donnell supports Lower MacWilliam Burkes revolt in Mayo

July - Red Hugh O'Donnell submits to Lord Deputy in Dublin, brought by Hugh O'Neill

August - Red Hugh O'Donnell takes care of his rivals - ambushed Hugh McHugh Dubh's men in Belleek castle and executed 16 gentlemen - Niall Garbh also surrendered (then married off to Red Hugh's sister Nuala), Sean Og O'Doherty captured at a parley and thrown in prison until he surrendered, got rid of the bandits in central Tirconnell mountains

December – the Bishops plot. Edmund Magauran sent to King of Spain - returns with the promise of Spanish troops

1593

January - Red Hugh O'Donnell attacks Turlough Luineach O'Neill in support of Hugh O'Neill. The O'Donnells burn Strabane and make an agreement with Turlough O'Neill who retires

Spring - Captain Humphrey Willis appointed as sheriff of Fermanagh in spring. Captain Willis has command of 100 men and tried to turn disaffected Maguires against Hugh Maguire

April - Hugh Maguire besieges sheriff and party in a church. Hugh O'Neill intervened on behalf of the sheriff and saves him.

8th May emissaries sent to Spain to seek help

May – Maguires raid Sligo

June - the marriage of Red Hugh O'Donnell and Rosie O'Neill

June/July- large cattle raid into Connaught which reaches Tulsk

11 Sept - Bagenal starts campaign in Fermanagh

24 Sept - reaches Enniskillen but does not have the equipment to lay siege

October - Hugh O'Neill raids Connor Roe Maguire

10 October - Battle of Erne ford / Belleek

1594

Jan 24 - Feb 02 - siege of Enniskillen

# CLANS AND MILITARY FORMATIONS

## Clan structure

Irish clan structure came from ancient times. Clans were kinship groups that would have various septs beneath them. Therefore, there were usually various family branches, each with different strengths of claim to be the clan leader. The clan leader is usually referred to as being 'the' and then the clan name (e.g. 'the Maguire'). Within this system, you could have septs with a different surname that would still be part of the clan (e.g. Keenan Maguire).

They used a tanistry system to elect their leader, so to be elected leader, you had to galvanise support amongst the men eligible to vote. This inadvertently created several different power bases, and therefore rivals, within the clan. After being elected, and during the normal course of events, it was usual for the clan leader to demand the eldest male children of his rivals to be handed over for lengths of time as guarantees of loyalty.

These clans usually had subservient clans, outside their internal sept structure, that paid tribute to them. The example in the story is that the Maguires switch between paying tribute to whoever was the dominant O'Neill and paid tribute to the O'Donnells for a period.

Gallic military formations

At the time of the outbreak of the Nine Years War, except for the O'Neills, the fighting formations of the Irish were at best outdated, but in truth obsolete. The main European fighting formations were pikemen and shot. The main Irish battle tactics were the ambush, to which their soldiers were suited. They were not capable of facing the English in a pitched battle. Hence the urgency of O'Neill and other leaders to train their men in the use of firearms, import weapons from the continent and Scotland, and get as many Spanish trainers as they could.

Below are the main troop types of the Irish clans at the time of the outbreak of the Nine Years War:

Galloglass – mercenary soldiers usually Scottish or from Scottish descent. These were heavily armed mercenaries who used long axes with curved blades. The main Irish houses usually had clans of Galloglass that worked for them permanently. A Galloglass leader was called a constable, a formation of Galloglass a battle and a Galloglass usually had the support of a horseboy or Kern and this was referred to as a spar. Galloglass got paid around three cattle per quarter.

'Cogin and livery' (referred to in the book as 'coin and keep' for simplicity sake) – the clan leader would hire Galloglass, and to share the burden of paying for them, he would assign them to different areas. The population assigned would be responsible for the payment and upkeep of the Galloglass for a time period at the discretion of the clan leader.

Redshanks are 'new Scots' or Scottish mercenaries hired directly from Scotland, usually on a seasonal basis. They were called Redshanks because they went barelegged. They were usually armed with swords and bows. They normally got paid the same as Galloglass, around three cows per quarter.

Kern – traditional Irish light infantry. They were usually not armoured and supplied their own weapons. The weapon of choice was the dart. They also used javelins, swords and bows. Their main uses were to support the heavier armed Galloglass, capture and herd cattle away from enemy territory, and against the English, they were used for lighting attacks and harassment. They usually got paid around one cow per quarter.

Horseboys – Galloglass usually had horse boys to support them. When they fought, they normally functioned as light infantry armed with javelins.

Horsemen – these were usually the nobility of the clan. They rode without stirrups, which potentially made them unstable when facing heavier English cavalry, and were usually armed with javelins.

Shot – these were armed with muskets. The Irish lords tried to retrain their Galloglass and other experienced soldiers to become either shot or pike as fast as circumstances would allow. The amount of shot the Irish armies could field would depend on the clan. The O'Neill formations were mainly armed with shot while the smaller clans were not.

Pike – there is little evidence that the pike was widely available to the Irish rebels. These formations also did not suit the Irish style of ambush warfare. Again, mainly the larger clans such as the O'Neills would have had the most pikemen.

The Irish formations were supported by experienced Irish mercenaries who had fought mainly with the Spanish army in the Dutch Revolt. These men would have been skilled in modern European warfare and made a vital backbone to the Irish military formations.

## English military formations

The English forces in Ireland usually came from four sources: Irish conscripts (mainly from the Pale), Irish allies, raw recruits from England and veterans who had served in France, the Scottish borders or the Netherlands. There was much changing of sides between the Irish on both sides.

Shot – the English were mainly armed with calivers but also had a small number of muskets. The men armed with calivers, the lighter of the two guns, were mainly used for skirmishing. The muskets were used to support the pike as the muskets were heavier and less manoeuvrable.

Pike – Pikemen were the core of the army. They had a ten to fifteen-foot spear, a helmet and breastplate armour and were mainly used for defence. They could also make a very effective charge.

Horsemen – these were comprised mainly of Irish cavalry. They were more heavily armoured than the Irish cavalry and were armed with a lance, sword and occasionally a pistol. They were the most feared element of the English armies. They were mainly used for skirmishing.

English system of government in Ireland

Lord Deputy – the representative if the Queen and the head of the Irish executive under English rule

Irish Council – the executive branch of English rule in Ireland

Lord President (Governors) were the English military leaders for the various provinces of Ireland with wide-ranging powers.

London Privy Council – the body of advisors to the Queen

# GLOSSARY OF TERMS

Brehon law – ancient legal system of Ireland

Composition - a formal arrangement for the payment of taxation for a particular geographical area to pay taxation to the crown. These arrangements normally meant the formal abandonment of tanistry and the adoption of hereditary English titles and the passing of land to your direct relatives.

Crannog – usually an ancient partially or entirely artificial island in a lake or estuary. They were normally repurposed as forts or storehouses

Lordship – the territory ruled by a Galic lord

Sept – a branch of an Irish family

Surrender and regrant – the surrender of a Galic lordship and the regrant of the land with English hereditary titles, the abandonment of tanistry

Tanistry - was the Irish system of passing on titles and land. Candidates were elected by all the males of the clan. The candidates were usually from a specific branch (sept) of the family who could trace their ancestry back to a particularly notable figure in their family history.

The Pale - the strip of land on the eastern coast of Ireland that comprised the most Anglicised part of the country. This area would have covered Dublin and the coastal parts of Louth, Meath and North Wicklow.

# FURTHER READING

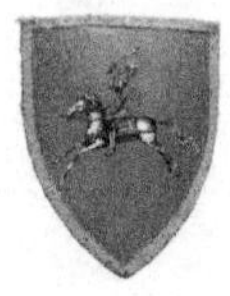

There are a number of excellent books available that I used for research that are history books rather than works of historical fiction. They are listed below, and if you enjoyed the subject matter of this book, you should thoroughly enjoy these. There are other books available on the subject matter that I have not read. I am sure some of these books are excellent too, but unfortunately, there comes a stage where I have to stop doing research and actually write the book!


Tyrone's Rebellion - Hiram Morgan

The Nine Years War 1593 -1603 - James O'Neill

Red Hugh O'Donnell and the Nine Years War - Darren McGettigan

Galloglass 1250 - 1600 - Galic Mercenary Warrior - Fergus Cannan

The Irish Wars 1485 - 1603 - Ian Heath

Elizabeth's Irish wars - Cyril Falls

# ALSO BY

To read more books in the *Exiles* series click on the covers or the links to be brought to your favourite online ebook store.

★ ★ ★ ★ ★ *"Fully action-packed, this pulls you further into Eunan and Seamus' story; making you question who to support the whole way through," – Reedsy Discovery*

Printed in Great Britain
by Amazon

17389111R00214